THE SKIN PALACE

Jack O'Connell

THE SKIN PALACE

NO EXIT PRESS

This edition published in the UK 2001 by

No Exit Press, 18 Coleswood Road,

Harpenden, Herts, AL5 1EQ

www.noexit.co.uk

A CIP catalogue record for this book is available from the British Library.

ISBN 1-901982-29-7 The Skin Palace

2 4 6 8 10 9 7 5 3 1

Printed by Omnia, Glasgow.

For
Nance & Claire & James

r≪l on≪

I was certainly a well-trained dancer. I'm a good actress.
I have depth. I have feeling. But they don't care.
All they want is the image.
—Rita Hayworth, 1973

ESTABLISHING SHOT

The Ballard Theatre. Night.

Enter the boy. Fifteen years old. He is an immigrant. He has been in the city for only a week. At times, he has difficulty breathing. He is dressed formally, in a dark, old-fashioned suit that is wet from the storm outside. He has only a tentative grasp of the native language. This does not matter, as the film he has come to see is a silent feature—the original Phantom of the Opera, *starring Lon Chaney, Sr.*

Enter the young woman. Twenty-two years old. She stands in the entrance to the theatre and removes her yellow rain slicker. She shakes her head, pushes her matted hair back from her face. She moves down the center aisle and takes a seat several rows in front of the boy.

They are the only individuals in the theatre. This may be due to the storm outside. Or possibly the fact that few people have an interest in seeing a silent movie in this day and age.

Several minutes pass. The silence of the theatre is broken occasionally by the wheezing of the boy's lungs as they strive for a full, deep breath.

Then, finally, the curtains roll back and the wonderful sputter-sound of the projector issues and a beam of blue-

white light shoots out above their heads and falls flat against the screen.

The boy and the young woman each watch the film in different ways, with different expectations and objectives.

The boy wishes to break every image down into its smallest components. He wants to analyze technique, to understand the mechanics of this display.

The young woman wants the entire experience of the film, the total package, the overall sensation of another world that she's been allowed to spy on for the price of her ticket.

This is impossible, as the young woman cannot stop thinking about last Tuesday, when her mother was diagnosed with a terminal illness. The fishhooks in Lon Chaney's mouth cannot compete with the image of the doctor's office, the whiteness of the doctor's coat, the vague, grey hue of the X-ray sheets suspended against an illuminated background.

And within minutes the young woman is crying again, as quietly as she can manage, slouched down in the Ballard's velvet seat, turned sideways, her knees brought up close to her chest.

The boy is more confused than annoyed. His vision is torn over and over between the actions on the screen and the silhouette of the young woman ten feet in front of him, the crown of her head just visible over her seat, her sobbing the new sound track for the movie, giving the film a meaning it previously didn't have.

The boy would like to approach the young woman, ask her if she needs any assistance, if he can call someone for her, if there's anything at all he could do. But he stays in his seat, as fascinated as he is sympathetic.

He's never known a film to affect someone else this profoundly.

three years later

I

A woman's face appears on the screen. The face is as large as a house, as big as any three-decker in the city. Because of this enlargement, each wrinkle and fold in the skin becomes a dry riverbed, a crevice of incalculable depth. The woman's eyes are red and sunken, as if she's spent a lifetime weeping. After a time, her mouth opens and she looks out over the gravel parking lot and says, in the most wounded voice imaginable,

On October first, my daughter, Jennifer Ellis, disappeared while walking home from the Ste. Jeanne d'Arc elementary school on Duffault Avenue. Jennifer is ten years old. She is four and a half feet tall. She was dressed in her school uniform, a green plaid jumper and a white blouse. I implore you, if you have any information at all about what happened to my baby, please call the number on this screen. Please help me find my daughter. I beg you.

"God," Perry says, "I wish they'd stop showing that clip. It's on TV every night. I hear her voice on the radio driving to work every morning."

Sylvia takes a sip of wine and says, "Do you think they'll find her?"

"They've got to find her," Perry says. He takes a breath, uncomfortable with the conversation, looks across the parking lot and asks, "You think the line'll be bad at the snack bar?"

"No drive-in food," Sylvia says. "We'll both regret it in the morning."

Perry smiles, nods his agreement, lets his head fall back against the seat.

Sylvia would love to shoot his face this way. To frame it in exactly this light, exactly this expression. But she's learned. It makes Perry tense when she takes the camera out at moments like this. He smiles, but you'd have to hear the tone of his voice when he says, "Is it necessary to record everything?"

The answer is no, of course not. Most of life is more or less insignificant. But Sylvia's argument, her defense, would be that what she does with the camera has nothing to do with recording. Her intention isn't to nail down the image for some kind of documentation. She's not all that interested in that kind of history. She doesn't see things that way. And she'd have thought Perry would know that by now.

Anyway, Sylvia doesn't want an argument tonight. So she leaves the camera in the trunk of the car. But it's loaded with a fresh roll of Fuji. Just in case.

Perry had called her from the office around three. She was in the cellar, developing yesterday's shots from the Canal Zone. She was working on a print of Mojo Bettman, the guy without the legs who sits on his skateboard selling newspapers and magazines all day. Perry must have let the phone ring twenty times. Sylvia ran up the three flights of stairs and grabbed the receiver, pulling a little for air. Perry said, "The Cansino. Eight o'clock. Big News."

And then he hung up. He hates the phone. And he knew if he stayed on Sylvia would press for details.

She's not sure why he feels the need to be so dramatic. They've both been waiting for the big news for months. Perry's been aching for it. And Sylvia has been fearful of it. She doesn't like acknowledging that. It makes her feel vindictive and kind of spoiled, maybe mean-spirited. This news is what Perry wants. This is why he puts in all the hours. After she hung the receiver back into the cradle on the wall, Sylvia stood there for a second and tried to picture Perry as he heard the words. She's sure it was Ratzinger that took him to lunch. Probably at the top of the bank building, that restaurant that used to revolve. The firm has an open account there. Perry says Ratzinger eats there every day of the week.

She pictured them both holding club sandwiches in their hands, little leaves of purplish lettuce hanging over the corners of the toasted bread. Ratzinger dabbing mayonnaise off his lips with the rose-colored napkin. She pictured Perry nodding, that sort of slight, humble tilt of the head, as Ratzinger listed all the things they liked—the studiousness, the ease with the clients, the ability to work on the team.

She could see Perry clenching down on his back teeth, curling up his toes inside his wing tips, waiting for the moment when Ratzinger actually said the word, let it fall from his lips as the waiter cleared the coffee cups: *Partnership*.

They're in the backseat of the Buick and they've got the top rolled down. It's the same car Perry was driving on the day they met—a maroon '65 Skylark that guzzles gas. Last year they dropped a wad getting the floorboards replaced. Now, with Perry's big news, Sylvia is sure it's only a matter of time before he starts pushing for a Saab or a Volvo. For all she knows, Ratzinger may have already made the suggestion.

"This is the part I love," Perry says. So far there are about a dozen parts he loves.

"We're going down in the elevator," he says, "and Ratzinger waits for this guy to get out at the garage level, okay? And then he turns to me and he does this clap on the back, and the whole time there's no eye contact, you know. He's got his eyes on the floor numbers. And we get to the street level and before the doors open he says, 'and by the way, there'll be a little something extra come Fridays from now on.' "

He bites in on his bottom lip and slaps the driver's seat.

"A raise," Sylvia says.

He's nodding at the words. "This is the way these guys work, you know. He never mentions a figure, okay? Just *a little something extra,* you know. Make me guess. Make me wait for Friday so I can see the numbers."

"You deserve every dime," she says.

The Cansino Drive-in is one of the last of its kind in the country. In high school, Sylvia came here a handful of times with a packed carload of forgotten friends. It's gotten a lot seedier since then. The Buick is parked in the very last row of the lot where asphalt gives way to a scrubby dirt patch that dissolves into full-blown forest. The parking lot is half-filled with teenagers. Lots of pickup trucks with fat tires and skinny girls with blonde hair down to their behinds. The kids all sit in the truck beds around coolers of beer. They smoke cigarettes and make constant trips to the snack bar.

The movie's sound track is beamed at them over the radio. Those beautiful, ribbed-silver window speakers are long gone, but the white mounting posts they hung from still stand, circles of weed springing up through the posts' tear-shaped concrete foundations.

They're half-watching something called *The Initiation of Alice.* It's a pretty standard soft-core exploitation job by Meyer Dodgson. Lots of female nudity and beach locations, but nothing too explicit. Upon the screen, a topless coed is admiring her own reflection in an ornate, full-length mirror.

"I spoke with Candice, who got the same pitch," Perry

says, "only from Ford. I knew Candice would be the other one they tapped."

"I remember. You said Candice."

"We both figure they'll run us around the track for a year, maybe a little less. Then they'll give us the title."

"Partner."

"Big day, Sylvia. I want to remember this day."

"You'll need some new suits."

He sits back, lets his shoulders slump a little.

"I want to buy you something, Sylvia."

"Okay, next movie's on you."

His voice goes lower and he reaches over and takes her hand.

"I'm serious. Something nice."

"A movie would be nice. I don't need—"

He waves away the thought. "I know you don't *need,*" he stretches out the word. "This isn't about need. Isn't there something you want?"

She shakes her head, passes him the wine bottle and picks a licorice twist out of its bag.

"C'mon, I want to mark this occasion. If you don't help me out I'll pick out something on my own."

"Perry—"

"Some awful piece of jewelry you'll keep in the box in the dresser . . ."

She nods and squints at him and bites the end off the twist. He's referring to this enormous silver bracelet he gave her last Christmas, which makes her arm look like it just came out of a cast. But she knows the thing cost a fortune and feels guilty every time she opens her drawer to take out a sweater.

She says, "I thought we were going to start saving."

"We are, believe me. Second check starts the down-payment fund."

Perry's all hot for buying a house this year, but Sylvia loves where they live now.

"C'mon, give me some idea. I'll go out blind and buy earrings. It'll be scary. Don't make me do it."

He can still make her laugh. And he usually gets his way when he's being funny.

"Okay, there is something . . ."

He's thrilled. He does a drumroll on his knees with his fingers and says, "Bingo."

"I was down in the Zone last week . . ."

Already, she's said the wrong thing. Perry hates the Canal Zone.

"Yes," he says, dragging out the *s,* trying to prepare himself for anything.

"There was this ad. On a bulletin board in the Rib Room—"

"God," he says, forcing a smile, trying to make his distaste into a weary joke. "I hate it that you eat down there. I just don't think it's healthy."

She cocks her head to the side, purses the lips a little.

"Sorry," he says, annoyed with himself for jarring the mood. "Go ahead. An ad."

"It was a good price. I checked the catalogs. And they said it was in mint condition."

"A good price on . . ."

She takes a breath and lets it out, "An Aquinas."

"An Aquinas," he repeats.

She nods, not sure whether to get defensive or laugh at herself, like it's the same old Sylvia and some things never change.

He says, "Another camera?"

"It's an Aquinas, Perry—"

"What does that make? Four, right? Four cameras?"

"Four?"

"Yeah, four. The Canon, the Yashica, and the Polaroid."

She stares at him, her mouth crooked like he's been sarcastic, but still inside the margin of funny. A beat goes by and his expression remains unchanged and she realizes he's being serious.

"The Polaroid? C'mon, Perry, that's like a twenty-dollar camera. I just use it for proofs. I just use it for taking note of something I'll want to do later."

"A Polaroid isn't a camera? A Polaroid suddenly doesn't count as a camera?"

"Okay, forget it," she says, looking up at the screen as the young woman in front of the mirror starts to rub sunscreen into her shoulder. "It was your idea. You brought up buying something."

He reaches across for her hand again.

"I meant, like, diamond stud earrings or something, I meant—"

She squeezes the hand and lets it go.

"Diamond stud earrings, Perry? When would I wear diamond studs? They'd clash with the decor down at Snapshot Shack."

Perry has begun to hate Sylvia's job. She works in one of those tiny film booths you see at the edge of every mall parking lot in America. To a degree, she understands his feelings. Those little huts are about five feet square. Barely enough room inside for you to turn around. She thinks just the sight of them gives a lot of people a kind of unconscious jolt of claustrophobia. And the particular booth Sylvia works in is even worse. It was built as an enormous scale replica of an old Brownie camera. But she likes the job. Right now, it's exactly what she wants to do. Maybe it's this visible lack of ambition, this absence of a career that bothers Perry. Maybe he can't envision turning to Ratzinger over lunch and saying, "Sylvia? She sells film from inside of a big camera . . ."

"There'll be all kinds of places to wear them," he says. "Believe me."

"Look, I said forget it."

His eyes narrow a little. He shifts over to sit next to her. He doesn't want the night to go bad.

"Okay," he says, smiling, being indulgent. "Tell me about the . . ."

"Aquinas," she says.

"Doesn't sound Japanese," he says, putting on a shocked expression.

"It's made in Italy," she says.

"Good camera?"

"It's about the best you can get."

He says, "Why go for a used one? Isn't it like a used car? Like you're buying someone else's problem?"

She smiles at him. He's trying. He has to force the interest in cameras. She knows that he'd rather be talking about house hunting. Or maybe even wedding plans.

"You want to guess what a new Aquinas would cost?"

"Not a clue."

She takes a deep breath. "Try over ten grand."

This genuinely shocks him.

"You're kidding."

She shakes her head *no*.

He leans forward and says, "The house I grew up in? Okay? My parents bought it for around ten grand."

"Yeah," she says, "but the Aquinas doesn't get water in the basement."

"How much are they asking for this used one?"

She smiles and shakes her head *no* again, but says, "The ad said fifteen hundred."

He stares at her and starts a slow nod and at the same time tries to hold off from smiling. He can't manage it and the smile breaks and he turns his attention up to the screen as Alice starts a long jog down a supposedly deserted beach.

Then he looks back and says, "All right, let's get it."

She starts to fight him. "Perry . . . ," she says with this small pseudo-whine to her voice that she can't stand.

He holds up a hand and says, "Listen, Sylvia, I want to get you something. I honestly do. And this is what you want."

She shrugs. "I'd have to check it out. I mean, I'd have to check the age and the condition. See what's included. Lenses. A case."

"You check it out. If it looks good, if it's what you want, write the check."

She stares at the side of his face, more excited than embarrassed.

"Really? I should really get it?"

She thinks she sounds like a teenager. Like her mother said she could use the car on Saturday night. But Perry seems suddenly delighted with himself. He turns to her, leans in and puts his arm around her.

"If it looks good," he repeats, "buy it."

"You're sure?"

He brings his mouth down to the side of her neck, kisses there a few times. Then he moves up to her ear and whispers, "I still want to get you the diamond studs."

In five minutes Sylvia's jeans are off and Perry's pants are down around his ankles and she's straddling him, riding him, her knees indenting the Buick's backseat as Perry watches the exploits of the surf-bimbette flashed up on the Cansino's huge and dingy screen.

And as Perry's breath starts to catch and Sylvia feels the muscles in his thighs buck and tense and release and tense again and he starts to make that suppressed-whine sound through his nose, she's thinking of the Aquinas. She's thinking of the first time she'll hold it up to her eye and pull something into focus.

She's thinking of the rush that will come when she presses down on the shutter release and opens the lens and imprints some flawless instant, some slice of life. Some instinctively chosen and absolutely perfect image.

She's wondering what it will be.

Z

Until recently the Hotel St. Vitus served as a convent for a
sect of Eastern European nuns known as the Sisters of Perpetual Torment & Agony, a cloistered Order always ru-
mored to be on the precipice of papal destruction due to
heretical word and deed. The nuns' catechistic practice
somehow managed to splice their traditional Catholicism
with a vague line of occultist teachings. No one in
Bangkok Park knows exactly what the Sisters dabbled in,
but there was loose talk of midnight rites during the
equinox, a kind of earth-mother, druidic gloss layered over
their prayers and chanting.

For their part, the Sisters almost seemed to encourage
the dark rumors, never venturing out of the convent but for
the weekly shopping trip to the all-night Spanish market.
Even then they'd remain encased in a cloud of silence,
their bodies wrapped head to toe in black wool habits, their
faces obscured by hanging black-lace veils. They seemed
to purchase bulk quantities of blood sausage, sweet red
wine, and candles.

In public, Bishop Flaherty tolerated the Order with pleas
for an understanding of the deeply spiritual quest the
women had devoted their lives to, but during private
lunches with his banker pals in the chancery dining room,
Flaherty called them *spooky old hags,* and *voodoo fanatics.*
And alone in his room, after his nightly prayers, the bishop
looked out his window toward Bangkok Park and genuinely wondered if *the witches* had it in for him.

Officially, the Quinsigamond Police Department does

not know what happened to the Sisters. The nuns no longer occupy their old convent. A week after their disappearance, the chancery released a statement that the entire flock had returned to Eastern Europe where their services were desperately needed. The statement made no mention of the rumor that the walls of the abandoned convent's chapel had been found covered with a mixture of human and animal blood. One of the Canal Zone's more hysterical newsrags offered speculation that all the sisters had been massacred and the FBI was blanketing the entire event. Another weekly announced there was no mass murder, but rather the nuns had splintered from the Church and become some kind of pagan-feminist terrorists, vanished into an undisclosed mountain region of South America for training and recruitment. The *Spy* never bothered to cover the story beyond the box ad in the real estate classifieds announcing that the diocese of Quinsigamond was offering the convent for sale at a very reasonable price.

Hermann Kinsky picked up the building for a song and rechristened it the Hotel St. Vitus. He's held the deed to the property for close to a year now but has yet to check in his first guest. This may have something to do with both the location—on Belvedere Street at the western end of Bangkok Park—and the fact that Hermann nevèr bothered to renovate the place. The St. Vitus is still outfitted as a dark, icon-choked convent, full of stark wooden corridors hung with pictures of obscure and grotesquely martyred saints, small, mattressless cots in cell-like rooms, and a kitchen whose only concession to this century's progress is running water.

But Hermann doesn't care if he's failing as a hotelier. He needs a profession for the tax forms and *innkeeper* is as good as any. And he's immune to the spartan, gloomy ambience of the St. Vitus, the haunted, Gothic flavor that emanates from every crevice of the rambling building. It reminds him of his hometown of Maisel in Old Bohemia, the thousand-year-old city of golems and alchemists from which he fled three years ago with his only son, Jakob, his nephew, Felix, and his oldest friend and most trusted business aide, Gustav Weltsch.

In the old country, it had been a given that Hermann could rise only so high, that his will and his intelligence, his savvy and his tenacity would always be undercut by his ghetto birth and the mind-numbing, sloughing grip of decades of Communist puppet-regimes. But here in America, here in the new world, possibilities were endless. You practically had to shun them as they pounded on your door, day and night, saying, *here's a new idea, here's a fresh venture, here's another chance for improvement, investment, progress, success.*

Back in Maisel, Hermann had labored by day as the owner of Kinsky Neckware, a small, open-air haberdashery booth in Old Loew Square, but it was his night work in the back alleys of the grey marketplace that earned his exit fee—the cash he had to pay to a whiny subminister of Emigration—to bring himself and his three charges to Quinsigamond. He sold contraband gasoline, cigarettes, racks of horse meat. He ran dice and lottery games. He advanced an always growing book of illegal loans, broke a record number of recalcitrant kneecaps. And ultimately, in a manner that became his trademark and gave an additional, darker meaning to the phrase *face the music,* Hermann garrotted an army of desperate but doomed men with *Schonborn* piano wire. *I only use Schonborn,* he would tell his gasping victim, *it never breaks.*

His wife had died giving birth to Jakob, and his greatest regret is that she was never able to see the bounty of all those long, often bloody post-midnight hours skulking around Kaprova Boulevard in fingerless gloves. There are still late nights when the boys and Weltsch are asleep and he sits at his desk, a former altar, in what was once the St. Vitus chapel, a room of poor lighting with an enormous stained-glass window that depicts a weeping woman being crucified upside down, and Hermann Kinsky allows himself to take out his paper-thin wallet and withdraw a fading photograph of his only love and whisper, *Julia, I did it all for you.*

Hermann has no use for the irony that the quality he most loved in his late wife is the very one that disturbs him when he sees it in his son. That dreaminess, that vague, lost, otherwordly sense of *absence,* as if the boy were living on some different plane of existence, as if Jakob believed that by not acknowledging the ugly facts of this life, he could avoid them. It came from the mother. She could keep that same look in her eyes, that glazed, unfocused sheen. In fact, they looked very much alike, both with the thin, almost brittle physique, the small bones and dewy eyes and thin lips, the ears that wing out. Both with the spots on the lung and all the breathing problems. Nothing like Hermann or his nephew Felix with their stocky frames and barrel chests.

Julia loved the movies, just like the boy, just as passionately, as if the picture shows were some kind of religion, were something to be taken seriously. It was the only way she would consent to date Hermann when they first met. *For a night in Cinema Kierling,* she would sometimes tease, *I would walk on the arm of the village idiot.*

And if it was Julia's genes that planted the seed of this movie-love in the son, it was that fishwife, the fifteen-year-old governess Hermann hired out of the Schiller ghetto, that ultimately poisoned little Jakob. Bringing that girl into the household was the mistake of a lifetime. She dragged Jakob to the cinema each day, even when he got older and should have been in school. Felix was immune to the nanny's influence from the start, born without any interest in artifice. But Jakob was lost from the moment he entered the Kierling. And now Hermann curses the day some foolish genius invented this thing called film.

Because it's one thing for a woman to waste her time with such trifles and another altogether for a young man. And it's a prescription for disaster when that young man is heir to the fastest growing crime dynasty in town. Hermann has tried every trick he can think of to get the boy more interested in the business. He's taken the harsh and angry road. He's taken the understanding and patient road. He's yelled, wheedled, begged, threatened. He's even tried bribery, buying the son his own movie camera, a 16mm Seitz, stolen contraband negotiated out of the trunk of a nervous cabdriver. *Remember,* the hackman said at the close of the barter, *tell him it belonged to Uher himself, his first camera.*

Hermann asked Weltsch to speak to the boy, thinking maybe it's a problem of blood, being too close, the father too large a role model for the son to comprehend. Weltsch—with his CPA and recent law degree, his absolutely dispassionate, almost mathematical sense of logic, numbers as a personal dogma—came back shaking his head, unable to penetrate the fantastic cloud perpetually swimming around Jakob's skull. *He insisted on speaking of a film noir, whatever this is,* Weltsch said, his voice as halting as if he'd discovered a new tax code he couldn't decipher, so befuddled that Hermann found the day's deposits miscalculated when he reviewed them that evening.

So odd that Felix, the nephew, the brother's boy, nineteen and just a year older than Jakob, should have all the attributes that the son lacks. Felix has the head for numbers, the instinct to note the viable venture from the probable loser, the anger that could allow him to put a gun to an enemy's temple, pull the trigger and then go to dinner without another thought. And most important, Felix *wants.* He wants to be Prince. He wants to emulate his Uncle Hermann in every way. He desires Jakob's birthright the way his lungs desired air on the day of his birth—an unusually large baby, the midwife said for years that he screamed loud enough to wake all the dead in Strasnice Road Cemetery. Felix wants the number two spot at the table so badly that, unfortunately, Hermann can see he's come to resent his once-loved cousin. If Weltsch can't understand Jakob's dreamy, antibusiness ways, Felix despises them.

But there is hope, there is one deal on the horizon that could bind Jakob into the Family, and make an honorable percentage in the process. First, however, a bit of unpleasant discipline must be dispensed. *These nickel-and-dime Asians,* Hermann thinks, *why do I even bother?*

Jakob Kinsky thinks of his bedroom on the top floor of the Hotel St. Vitus as the smallest studio in cinematic history. But that's all right. He's still a one-man operation and so far the bedroom fits all his needs. A year ago, upon moving in, he decided that since this tiny cell was where he'd be spending the majority of his time, it should reflect his aesthetic principles. So he's made everything stark black and white and shadowy. His bed is a metal-frame cot that looks like it was scavenged from Spooner Correctional. The lighting is supplied by a bare bulb hanging from a short length of electrical cord. His clothing—three black suits and three white cotton shirts—hangs from a gunmetal coatrack in the corner.

It isn't that Jakob sees his room as a blatant rejection of Papa's bid to make good in the New World. It's simply that Jakob has a theory that by living day and night in this bleak and boxy terrain, he can't help but completely realize the imagistic imagination that he's been striving for since the day his nanny, Felice Fabri, brought him to the Kierling Theatre back in Maisel and together they watched a non-subtitled screening of *Beware, My Lovely.*

He was just six years old. And he knew, upon emerging back into the blinding, headache-inducing sunlight of Loew Square, that he had to make films. Over the years and countless trips to the Kierling that followed, he knew that he had to make strange, haunting, black-and-white crime films. That he had to become the *noir-est* of all noir directors. That, in fact, he had to move beyond the confines of simply directing and become a true auteur—conceiving, writing, casting, editing, virtually willing his total vision into celluloid being.

That first screening was a dozen years ago and Jakob's pursuit of his dream has never flagged. The bedroom, the studio, the original home office of his imagined company—*Amerikan Pictures*—is a shrine to his persistence in the face of paternal incredulity. The walls are completely papered with old movie posters—*The Blue Dahlia. Shadow of a Doubt. So Dark the Night.* The cot is covered with dog-eared copies of dozens of screenplays—*Thieves' Highway. The Tattooed Stranger. Sudden Fear.* The floor looks like some demented architect's model for a black, plastic city with towers of videotapes stacked and tottering everywhere—*The Big Combo. Call Northside 777. Cult of the Cobra.*

The only other things in the room are a black-and-white TV hooked to a VCR and currently playing *This Gun for Hire* with the volume off, a Hubbard 2000 vaporizer, a wrought-iron bookcase filled with cinematography texts, a portable, manual Clark Nova typewriter, and Jakob's prize possession, the thing he sleeps with, his most cherished appendage, a Seitz 16 mm movie camera.

Jakob knows the Seitz was intended as a bribe from Papa. But it's his ticket to attaining his dream and though he sometimes feels a bit guilty about the implications of accepting such a present, there's no way he can part with it now. Not when he's this close to a start date for filming on his first feature, on the work that will announce his arrival into the world of film, a masterpiece he's titled *Little Girl Lost.*

He's been writing *Little Girl Lost* since the Family arrived in Quinsigamond. He thinks he needs one more polish on the screenplay before he's ready to turn the Seitz loose on the world. He writes every chance he gets, staying up all night in the tiny studio, clicking out rewrite after rewrite on the Clark Nova, scribbling notes and cost sheets and location possibilities in his spiral notebooks. But even with all the hours he's put in he can't believe his script is close to completion.

He picks it up now, this revision on yellow paper, holds it gingerly in his hand, stares at the title page:

16 mm: B & W "Lumiere Flat"
Revision 9
An Amerikan Pictures/H.A.G. release
Maisel/Quinsigamond

Little Girl Lost
a screenplay by

Jakob Kinsky

dedicated to the memory of Felice Fabri
lover of film

"the image must be pure to the point of horror"

He turns the page to the first scene and reads once again

FADE IN

TIGHT SHOT - THE DOOMED MAN

FILLS SCREEN. CAMERA studies his panicked, sweat-drenched face, partly obscured in shadow. His eyes are blinking and darting from left to right and back again. His Adam's apple heaves as he gasps for breath. Camera pulls back to

MEDIUM SHOT - EXT. TRAIN STATION - NIGHT - RAIN

The Doomed Man is attempting to hide himself behind a large steel girder. He presses his back against the beam, steals furtive, rapid glances in either direction down the train yard. The collar of his coat is turned up against the wind and driving rain. In the distance, a chorus of barking dogs can be heard, the sound, once detected, getting progressively closer.

CLOSE UP - EYES OF THE DOOMED MAN, RAPIDLY BLINKING

MEDIUM SHOT - FREIGHT CAR ACROSS THE YARD FROM THE DOOMED MAN

The Doomed Man makes an awkward, tripping dash across the open yard, planting feet in deep, muddy puddles, finally reaching and boarding the ancient, rusted, wheelless freight car. He sits inside on the floor, huddles into himself, cups hands and blows on them, stares up, terrified, at the smashed-out windows of the train. Finally, he pulls from inside his coat a crumpled page of newsprint.

POV/THE DOOMED MAN

Camera tracks in on the newspaper. The headline reads:
BODY OF MISSING GIRL DISCOVERED
Divers recover remains of Felice Fontaine
Accompanying photo shows sweet-faced, ten-year-old child.

TIGHT SHOT - FACE OF DOOMED MAN

as he reacts to newspaper. Face dissolves in weeping horror. He crumples newspaper in hands, brings it to face as if a handkerchief, and begins to cry into it.

A throat clears behind Jakob. He jumps, pulls the script into his chest. His cousin Felix is standing in the doorway wearing an annoyed grin.

Felix shakes his head and says, "We're ready to start the meeting."

Hermann Kinsky is seated at the head of the altar. Weltsch has left this month's ledger before him but Kinsky hasn't bothered to open it. Hermann doesn't need a balance sheet to tell him when he's been betrayed. He feels the Judas in his stomach, senses the transgression the old way, in the blood and the spleen.

Felix sits next to him on his left and Uncle Hermann knows his nephew is anxious to tell of this week's exploits by the resident Kinsky muscle, a growing gang that's come to be known as The Grey Roaches. Hermann doesn't know why Felix has settled on this appellation, but there's something about it he likes. He's upset, however, by the fact that the Roaches take their marching orders from Felix rather than Jakob. It's a bad sign to hang out to the neighborhood, a gesture that could easily be misinterpreted. And for this reason he refuses to pay too much attention to gang business. He lets Weltsch keep track of the pack's extortion accounts and pharmaceutical dealings.

Jakob sits to his father's right, dressed, as always, in his black bar mitzvah suit, though he's outgrown it by a size or two. Look at the boy. It's as if he's uncomfortable with his own presence. As if each moment of his short life has been lived on the trap of a gallows. Why can't he have some of his cousin's confidence and bravado? How did two boys, raised together since Felix was orphaned in the July Sweep, end up so different? *Kinsky blood running through both sets of veins,* Hermann thinks, looking at his son's profile, *but they're night and day.*

What Hermann doesn't realize is that through the open chapel door, Jakob can see across the hall into his bedroom and makeshift studio where he's left the TV on, playing a tape of *This Gun for Hire.* The volume is turned off and as Alan Ladd mouths dialogue, Jakob can hear each line in his head.

Jakob would love to be Alan Ladd, or rather, Ladd's character on the screen: Raven, the heartless, hired killer, the contract assassin who walks through a beautifully moody, 1942 black-and-white world in his trench coat, possessed by his legion of inner demons. When Laird Cregar asks Raven how it feels to kill someone, Jakob mouths the response, "It feels fine."

Weltsch enters the chapel with Johnny Yew, one of Hermann's new mid-level managers based down in Little Asia. Johnny runs the sex co-op on Alton Road that the Kinsky's picked up in a very hostile takeover last May. Hermann brought in a Bulgarian contractor for the move and disappeared Yun-fat, the cooperative's founder and Johnny's former boss. Normally, that kind of brassy nerve would have triggered some all-out reprisal, but since Doc Cheng was eliminated last year, Little Asia has been up for a lot of quick grabs.

Weltsch sits down next to Felix without a word and Johnny Yew slides in next to Jakob, saying, "Good to see you, Mr. K," across the table to Hermann.

"It is good to see you, Johnny," Hermann says in a low and unusually warm voice, so friendly-sounding that Jakob looks away from the distant television screen for a second to study his father's face.

"Gustav tells me you have something important to discuss," Yew says, both nervous and excited. He's dressed in a double-breasted shark-skin suit that looks a little like the one Felix is wearing.

Hermann gives a slow nod.

"I've asked you down today, Johnny, to discuss your future with the company."

Jakob hears Yew swallow, feels his legs shift under the table.

"We're extremely pleased with the job you've been doing for us down at the co-op. You've settled in nicely."

Johnny's head bobs. "It's a wonderful position, Mr. Kinsky. I've worked hard and—"

Hermann waves a hand.

"We know you have, Johnny. Gustav and I never anticipated such returns. To be honest with you, there were doubts at the start."

"Yes, sir. Doubts."

"Huge doubts," Felix pipes up and his uncle puts a hand on the nephew's shoulder.

"You have to understand, Johnny, Little Asia is not our home base. We didn't know quite what to expect from the locals. Yun-fat was a popular man."

"Popular, yes, sir."

"We envisioned some degree of backlash. Resentment against a foreign investor."

"You cleaned the place up, Mr. K. It was a mess under Yun-fat. Merchants always fighting. A poor selection of goods. The quality of service shot up immediately."

Hermann smiled. "You're being too modest, Johnny," he says. "We couldn't have done it without you. You're only as good as your people on the front line. You'll need to remember that."

"I will, Mr. K. I'll remember."

"Because when we send you out on the road, you can't be calling back home every few minutes. You'll have to develop some personnel skills. You'll have to learn how to pick the cream of the crop."

Johnny sits up in his chair. He looks from Weltsch to Felix, wonders if this is some kind of confusing joke.

"On the road?" he finally says.

Hermann pushes up from his seat, walks to Yew's back, puts both hands on the manager's shoulder and says, "Tell him, Gustav."

In a bland and quiet voice, Weltsch says, "The co-op has proved so successful that we've decided to back a franchise. Ultimately we'd like to go national if arrangements can be made with the Families. For now we will initiate a pilot program. Keep things in the northeastern China-towns. You move in for the entire length of the start-up and training programs. I estimate a three-month stay in each town."

"You'll need your own bankroll," Hermann says from behind. "We've already begun to contact the appropriate people about lines of credit. But you'll have to seek out the workforce and the merchants. I'd be happier if they didn't speak English. At least at the beginning."

Johnny Yew can't believe his ears. He made the jump to Kinsky only six months ago and now he's about to become a trusted lieutenant. He's about to become wealthy. He's about to become a man of influence and respect and im-portance in the scheme of this Family. Johnny Yew, who escaped Hong Kong and a street hustler's short life by sell-ing his sister to a freighter captain, who spent his first years in Quinsigamond washing dishes and gutting fish around the clock for any noodle house that would have him, who doesn't even have his first gang tattoo yet, *this* Johnny Yew is about to become the chief sales rep for the Kinsky Fam-ily. He'd like to dive into the Benchley tonight, find what's left of Yun-fat's body, pull it to the surface just to spit in the skeleton's face and say, *Fuck you and your tribal preaching. I'm not your shop clerk anymore, asshole.*

"All our projections say we can't miss," Hermann says. "The sexual appetite is something you can bank on. You'll want to monitor which booths become our top grossers,

see if this differs from city to city or if there's a standard
we can rely on."

"We should be tracking the demographics from the
start," Weltsch adds.

"What's to track?" Felix says, staring at Johnny. "Every
hard-up chink in the country. There's your customer base."

"Felix!" Hermann barks and glares at the young man.
"Forgive my nephew, Johnny. He has a weakness for crude
humor that I can't seem to curb. I don't have to tell you that
we harbor no exclusionary policies in this family. The co-
ops will be open to all peoples."

"Everyone's money is green," Johnny says.

Hermann nods. "You are a real find, Johnny Yew."

He reaches into his pocket and slaps a wad of crisp new
cash in front of Johnny.

"You go out and celebrate tonight, young man. You are
on your way, as the saying goes."

Hermann's hand slides back into his suitcoat pocket.

"I know of the perfect club," Hermann says. "You must
take your young woman. Do you like music?"

Johnny just stares down at the money. The top bill features a picture of Grover Cleveland. Across the table, Felix
stares up at the ceiling and laughs.

"Mr. Kinsky . . ." Johnny begins and immediately goes
silent, unable to harness words powerful enough to express
the enormity of his gratitude.

Herman pulls out a length of Schonborn wire, twines it
in equal lengths around both of his meaty hands.

"Piano music, Johnny?" he asks. "Do your people like
the piano music?"

"How can I thank—" Johnny starts, shaking his head at
the immensity of his good fortune, beginning to turn
around and smile on his benefactor.

It's a single, fluid move, one honed into a reflex in the
alleys off Kaprova back in Maisel. Nothing harsh or jerking, a simple arc over the Asian's head and then the retrac-

tion backwards. The wire has already bitten its groove into Yew's neck before Johnny realizes he's choking.

"You steal from me," Hermann explodes now. "You pathetic yellow cur."

The piano wire passes in all the way to the trachea as Johnny's eyes do the patented bulge and his hands flail upward furiously but ineffectually.

"You steal from Kinsky," Hermann screams, his body an unmoving block of stone, the fat hands doing all the work, keeping the wire taut and ever-closing.

Blood is oozing down Johnny's chest, soaking the tailored shirt under his jacket. The body begins to jerk in its seat as if the impetus toward death were electricity. Felix stares at the scene, tries not to blink, studies his uncle's form, concentrates on the victim's tortured upheaval.

Jakob stares out the door and across the hall where Veronica Lake is doing a combination magic act and song and dance routine.

But the sound track to Veronica's performance is the horrible noise seeping from somewhere in Johnny Yew's face, a muted scream grafted onto a nauseating gurgle, all accented by the furious scuffling of his loafers off the floor and the chair legs.

And then, finally, it is over.

Hermann unwraps the wire from his left hand, takes hold of Yew's bristly buzz-cut and pulls Johnny's head back, which opens the running gash fully from ear to ear. The smell of blood gulfs around the table and no one speaks.

Hermann leans forward until he's inches above Johnny's slack face. Then he spits into the left eye and Felix hears him mutter, "Never steal from Hermann Kinsky."

Hermann turns and walks to the far side of the room until he's standing before the stained-glass window, bathed in the transformed light of the moon. Weltsch and Felix nod to each other, get up simultaneously, take hold of the body, and begin to carry it from the room as if they were

disapassionate medics who have seen too much of an endless war.

The silence in the chapel is awful.

Until Hermann turns away from the window and stares
at the quivering back of his only son and whispers, "You
see how easy it can be, Jakob?"

3

They get home, both a little drunk, Perry worse than
Sylvia, though he drove. They try to be quiet helping each
other up the back stairs to the apartment, hoping they don't
wake Mrs. Acker, the landlady, or trip over one of her cats.
It's not that Mrs. A would get angry. She'd just start in
again, asking Perry about the legal ramifications of her re-
fusal to return the grocery cart she appropriated from
Blossfeldt Discount Mart. *But they've got so many carts,*
she always ends up yelling with her hands at the sides of
her head.

There are mornings Sylvia see Mrs. Acker from the living room window, coming back from the grocery store or
Levi Park, and the landlady could be mistaken for some
homeless streetperson. But Perry got talking to her one
night and found Mrs. A has six figures planted in mutual
funds that she tracks on a daily basis. She's really a sweetheart and she's been kind to them, but Sylvia doesn't want
to talk with Mrs. Acker right now because Perry's hands
are everywhere. The back stairway has always had this effect on him, even when he hasn't had a drink. When they
first moved into the apartment, they could barely get in the
door with their clothes on.

Sylvia remembers the first month they lived together, coming in from the movies, groping each other with more force and speed at each landing, and finally making love with her back pressed up against the door to their third-floor apartment, the bedroom six yards away, one of the calicos mewing around Perry's ankles.

Now he just grabs her behind and tickles her and slides his hands inside the waist of her jeans. It's more playful than passionate and that's okay. She jiggles the key inside the old lock and Perry leans against her, rests his head against her back.

"The Counselor's a lightweight," she says, opening the door.

"The Counselor is getting old," he says, following her in and locking up behind them.

Sylvia turns on the kitchen light and shrugs out of her blazer. Perry pulls off his tie and unfastens the top button of his shirt, looks at the stack of catalogs on the counter and asks, "Anything come in the mail?"

"Junk," she says, going to the refrigerator for some ice water. They're both going to want aspirin before bed, so she pours a full glass. She closes the door and turns around, leans against it and looks at him as he browses the new offerings from the book club. His eyes look heavy.

"You done good, partner," she says.

He looks up from the mail, still hunched over the counter, leaning on his elbows.

"Partner in the corporate sense or the romantic one?"

"Both," she says, extending the water to him. Then she adds, "Which one buys me the camera?"

He laughs, thinks and says, "The lover buys you the camera." He comes upright and puts his hands on the small of his back and arches backward. Sylvia actually hears a cracking sound.

"But the attorney pays for it," he says.

*   *   *

In ten minutes, Perry falls into one of his heavy-breathing wine-comas. Sylvia knows that when she makes the bed in the morning he'll have drooled on the pillowcase.

The wine seems to be having the opposite effect on her lately. They've started buying it by the caseload, direct delivery by an import company out of Boston. Perry's delighted and kind of proud of the enormous discount they're getting. But having that much wine in the house all the time encourages you to kill a bottle with every dinner. For a while there they were crazy for these heavy reds and then, somehow, Sylvia got the idea that red wine can lead to edginess and paranoia. She dipped into a couple of reference books to back herself up, but couldn't find this theory confirmed in print. Once it was in her head, though, it was as good as true, so their next purchase was twelve bottles of a four-year-old French Chardonnay. She fell in love and Perry called the importer and loaded in three more cases.

They've made this small makeshift storage rack down in the cellar, around the corner from where Sylvia has set up the darkroom. With two of her favorite pastimes situated there, the basement has become a dank retreat for her. She's drawn to it more and more often. She's not content on the couch in the living room anymore, labeling Polaroids while Perry dozes on the couch with the television tuned to a sports network. She finds herself thinking *Why am I listening to the sound of kickboxing from Reno, Nevada, when I could be playing with the enlarger, sipping a glass of '88 white burgundy.*

She doesn't want to give the impression of dissatisfaction. Perry has pulled her life together for her. They've known each other almost three years now, lived together for over a year, and before Perry there was no direction. After her mother died, Sylvia quit her job at the front desk of the Baron. She'd had one night too many of taking smut from the mouths of fifty-year-old bellhops. She moved into her mother's apartment, closed the drapes and became a kind of secular nun in the religion of grief and confusion.

Her father had died when her mother was seven months pregnant with Sylvia. Ma had never had a lot of money, but what she left behind was burned through by the end of that year. Because she couldn't bring herself to move any belongings out of her old apartment, Sylvia paid rent and utilities on both places. From June through Christmas, she stayed on Ma's couch, like she was in grammar school again and had come down with the flu and was watching old *I Love Lucy* reruns on the TV and Ma would be bringing in a tray of toast and tea before the next commercial.

She read a couple of the paperbacks she'd found jammed in the drum table by the front window, big fat novels that usually chronicled some family of immigrants who toughed it out through unbearable hardships to make good in America. But mostly she watched dozens of old forties movies on some all-night cable channel. After a while they all seemed to star Rita Hayworth.

While she was growing up, Sylvia and her mother shared a consuming passion for movies. It never felt as if her mother had actively instilled this love in any way. It was more like she'd passed on a rare gene, that Sylvia picked up the obsession in utero, came into the world already addicted to film. When she recalls the nights of her childhood, she thinks of sitting in her mother's lap, in an overstuffed easy chair, both of them staring at the blue-white beam from the RCA watching *Tales of Manhattan* or *You'll Never Get Rich*. As she entered adolescense, Sylvia's devotion increased like a religious vocation or an eating disorder. And her mother encouraged the calling. They went to every new release that opened, then came home and pushed the TV into the bedroom and fell asleep watching the classics.

So it shouldn't surprise anyone that when her mother died Sylvia's life boiled down to watching old films and sleeping. She slept about fourteen hours a day. Always in her clothes. And always on the couch.

Twice a week, she'd force herself outside for food and supplies. She'd walk down to the corner at two in the morning and buy everything at the all-night convenience store. She didn't care that she was paying double the price for things she could have gotten six hours later at the supermarket. She considered the cost part of the deal, the charge for the privilege of shopping while everyone else was alseep.

When Perry first heard the story of her life as a hermit, his immediate response was, "Didn't anyone come looking for you? No friends? No relatives?"

He had a hard time believing that the answer was simply "No." Sylvia knew nothing about her father's family or even if there was one. Her mother had one older brother who'd died in the Korean War. Sylvia had gone to college out in the western part of the state and hadn't kept in touch with any childhood friends she might have had.

She remembers Perry shaking his head as she told him this. His reaction got her slightly angry. She said, "These are the facts. I'm not making this up. People have lives like this."

The day after Christmas, as she sat on the couch and opened the checkbook to pay some bills, she realized she had no money. She closed the checkbook and stood up, and pushed it in under one of the sofa cushions. Then she put on Ma's winter coat and went outside and started to walk. She wasn't used to the sun and with the glare off the snow, she was half-blind for the first block. The freezing air was kind of painful going into her lungs and yet she didn't want to go back inside. She wanted just to keep moving, to keep her legs in motion. She didn't care about direction or destination. She just wanted to be walking and breathing. She didn't want to think beyond those two actions.

About three miles from Ma's apartment was a small

shopping plaza, an old fifties kind of thing, a strip of a dozen linked stores all housed in a large one-story rectangle of a structure with a flat roof and dingy metal canopy that hung out over the sidewalk. There was a five-and-ten and a drug store, a liquor store, a soft-serve ice cream shop, and a shoe repair place. More than half the shops were empty and the plate glass windows were whited out with what looked like soap. Sylvia stood and stared at the soaped windows and wondered why they did that. Didn't that just call attention to the demise of the business and contribute to the seedy feeling of the place in general? It drove her kind of crazy that she couldn't come up with a single decent reason for whitewashing the window of an empty storefront.

She crossed the street to the plaza and noticed, at one end of the parking lot, what looked like an enormous old camera. It took a second to realize it was a drive-through photo shop. The Snapshot Shack, one of those boxy huts where you pull up to a little window and drop your film for developing and the clerk always tries to push new film on you. In this particular store, the drive-up window looked like an enormous round lens, which was okay, even kind of cute. The problem was that they'd painted the place this awful shade of brown, like an old camera, but at this scale—five feet high and wide—the brown was drab and sort of depressing.

To this day, Sylvia has no idea why she walked over to the shack. But as she approached the window, she saw the hand-lettered cardboard sign taped to the glass that read

HELP WANTED
No Experience Necessary

and when the obese woman inside slid open the window and asked if she'd come about the job, Sylvia shook her head yes and took the clipboard and questionnaire.

Then the fat woman slid the window closed again and Sylvia stood out in the cold with this horribly dull pencil filling in her name and age and work experience and her breath kept forming a cloud in front of her eyes. She had to knock on the window when she was done and the woman acted annoyed as she took the clipboard back inside. The clerk was reading a supermarket tabloid and Sylvia had always remembered one headline: Screen Siren Denies Porno Past.

The fat lady started to read the application and stopped halfway through. She looked out at Sylvia like she'd been insulted and said, "This says you went to college," all accusatory, like she was some suspicious prosecutor and had uncovered hidden evidence. Her tone was confusing and Sylvia just shrugged at her.

The lady moved up closer to the window until her head was framed between inside and outside. "It says you got a degree in fine arts."

Sylvia nodded.

The lady turned her head from side to side like she was looking at these invisible assistants crammed somewhere inside the shack.

"What the hell do you want this job for?" she snapped.

Sylvia said the first thing that came to mind, which happened to be the truth: "I'm very interested in photography."

About a month later, at the beginning of February, Sylvia was getting ready to shut the Shack down because of an approaching blizzard. Perry pulled up in the Buick just as she was hanging the Closed sign. He dropped off a roll of 24-exposure Kodak 200 Gold and they got talking. He was just finishing at the public defender's office at the time, just making the move to Walpole & Lewis. He sat with the car idling for fifteen or twenty minutes as the snowfall started to pick up. Before he drove off, Sylvia agreed to meet him the next night for spaghetti at Fiorello's down on San Remo Ave.

That's when everything changed. That's when Sylvia re-entered the world and real life regained its status as slightly more relevant than Rita Hayworth dancing her heart out through the musical number "You Excite Me."

As she gets undressed, Sylvia stares at Perry, all hunched up in the bed. And she tries to imagine what her life would be like right now if he hadn't driven up to the Snapshot Shack that day.

4

Sylvia wants to be clear about her feelings for the Canal Zone. She's not an insider. She's never lived there. She knows that half those people would just as soon spit on her as give her the time of day. She's fairly sure that most of the poetry readings are really just clashes in the latest fashion war, that the bulk of talent that hangs out on Rimbaud is in the areas of posturing and attitude. And she can't say Perry is totally wrong when he points out that the lines between the Zone and Bangkok Park are blurring more each year.

She's never pretended to be some cutting-edge bohemian. It's not like she wants to carve some place for herself down in the clubs, to integrate herself with the Black Hole group or Mona Jackson's clique. It's just not like that. She's older than most of these people. She never got kicked out of any of the great schools. She's never dyed her hair to some attention-grabbing shade. She's not great with obscenity. She doesn't even own a whole lot of leather.

It's just that, compared with the rest of the city, in the

Zone it's all right to want to spend your days scouting images, looking for that one sweet shot. In the Zone, her job at the Snapshot Shack is like a hip career and, given the choice, she'd rather someone view her eight hours inside an enormous camera as some kind of oblique statement rather than a sign of laziness or retarded ambition.

And maybe she is too concerned with what other people think of her, but if they're going to start dwelling on her faults, this would be pretty low on her list. The thing is, the Canal Zone can also be a lot of fun. It's never stagnant. People are outside all the time, middle of the night, middle of the winter, they're standing in small packs, imported cigarette smoke engulfing their heads, their eyes jumpy from lack of sleep. She can usually find a way to ignore the trendiness and the retro-snobbery. She tried to tell Perry that she gets what she wants out of the Zone. Dozens of weird little one-room ethnic restaurants open and close every month. Every corner has some old bibliophile hold-out ranting against the big chain stores and offering you some coverless Verlaine paperback for a dime, a buck for volume *J* of the eleventh-edition Britannica. There's some kind of bizarre parade every other day and it's always a challenge to decipher the theme. The handbills posted on the telephone poles and stop signs are invariably mondo tracts, little Cliff's Notes to the Kabbala, even when they're just advertising a new band or a common boycott or a special at the Afghani deli. It's like a funny, ongoing flea market, she tells Perry. It's like a little front against boredom. What's so bad about that?

Jack Derry's Camera Exchange is supposed to be down on Waldstein. That's near the border of Bangkok Park and if Perry knew she was that close to the war zone, he'd have a fit. The city has pretty much given up on the Park. Everyone accepts now that you'll never really know what goes on in Bangkok. The *Spy* has begun to act like the place just didn't exist, as if they'd already filled some quota for murder and drug and gang stories, as if the nightly body count in the Park no longer qualified as news.

Sylvia had one experience, a long time ago, in Bangkok Park. It's the kind of story that will always lose something in the telling because it had more to do with her interior reaction than with the landscape. For that reason, she's never told Perry about that day. It's like trying to put words to someone's first look at one of Kettelhut's Cambodian photographs. No matter how perfect the phraseology, it's destined to fall short of what really took place in the viewer's heart and brain. She doesn't mean to be melodramatic, but she was only nine years old at the time and things can hit you as a child, things can take hold of you.

She can't remember what year it was, but there was a gasoline shortage, a crisis—that was the word they used—and her mother was driving a Ford station wagon that was on its last legs. It was the beginning of summer and Ma had lost her job. The wagon's transmission was going and they didn't have the money to get it fixed and they didn't have the money to buy a new car and every time Ma got in behind the wheel and turned the key it was like the woman willed the Ford to work. Like strength was coming out of her body and passing into the engine of this dying car.

So it was nighttime and they were coming back from a drive they'd taken to see about a job at a resort in New Hampshire. Only the job had turned out to be a chambermaid position at a back-road motor court and the manager had been this greasy little pig of a guy and they wasted the whole day and all this gas. And by the time they got back to the city, Sylvia could just tell her mother was really beat and down. Ma didn't want to talk or sing or play and Sylvia climbed into the rear of the wagon and was lying on her stomach looking at the highway slide away behind them when the wagon started to make this god-awful noise, this horrible grinding metal noise. And she heard Ma

say *no,* not yelling but in a voice that said she was on the
threshold of crying. Then Ma pounded the dashboard.
Sylvia had never seen her mother hit anything in her life
and no one said a word as Ma steered the car down the first
expressway exit they came to.

Only it turned out to be the exit into Bangkok Park. And
the next thing either one of them knows, they're barely
rolling their Country Squire station wagon down the east
end of Goulden Avenue. And the noise they're making is
calling attention to them. Every hooker and pimp and
dealer is squinting to see what kind of monster has invaded
their sleazy quiet. And Sylvia just lay there in the back of
the wagon, staring out at all the neon and all these strange
faces, these exaggerated circus faces.

And at some point, Ma turned a corner. And the car
seized up for a minute. Or maybe it was just Sylvia's imagination. But in that instant, she looked out at this woman,
this prostitute, this girl who was probably younger than
Sylvia is now. And they stared at each other. They each
took it all in under the spot from the corner street lamp.
The hooker had red permed hair. And this strange peach-
colored knit dress. And a purple ring around her left eye. A
big, ugly, black-and-blue welt orbiting the whole of her
eye and seeming to make the eyeball itself bulge slightly.

Then Sylvia and the hooker were separated. And Ma
forced the Ford out of Bangkok and into what's now called
the Canal Zone. The wagon died maybe four blocks from
Sylvia's vision. They left it there, unlocked, and took one
of the last buses home. And Mother wept on the bus. She
never made a sound and Sylvia saw her trying to bite on
her lips to stop, but the tears slid down her face anyway.
She never wiped them away and her daughter didn't move
to touch her.

When they got home, neither of them turned on a light.
Sylvia got undressed and climbed into bed and Ma walked
over to her and just touched her forehead and said *I*

promise it will be all right. Sylvia didn't know what the woman was talking about and was close to terrified, probably because it was the first time she'd seen Ma lose her grip. It was also the last time. Years later, Sylvia remembered thinking about that night and realized they must have been in real trouble moneywise. But right now, she doesn't think money had much to do with her mother's promise.

About a week later Ma found a job in a bakery. Sylvia doesn't know what happened to the Country Squire. But the vision of that prostitute—the red hair and the purple eye and an instantaneous look that said she lived someplace past desperation—it held onto Sylvia like a religious apparition. She can see the hooker now. She can call her up. The hooker is a personal icon. A definition of knowledge that Sylvia doesn't want to have. The sight of her face was like a hammer to the head. A terrible epiphany that said *there are worlds you can't even imagine yet* and *things can always get worse.*

Sylvia has driven through Bangkok a couple times in the past few years. Always during the day and never stopping. It's still an unsettling experience. It should be a photographer's paradise. There was a rumor in the Zone about some midwesterner just out of design school who got a grant to go in there with his Minolta. Something about doing a big coffee table book on graffiti. The rumor said, of course, the guy never came out, that a week after he disappeared a roll of film got mailed to the *Spy.* And when they processed it they had thirty-six shots of a torture ballet: The photographer stripped naked. The photographer hanging a foot off the ground, handcuffed to water pipes in an empty factory loft. The photographer toasted like a marshmallow, jet-flamed with a welder's acetylene torch.

Sylvia pulls her notepad from her jacket pocket and checks the address. She moves down the street trying to position herself but none of the storefronts show numbers.

She walks past two hookers in front of Poligny Discount Liquors and one of them quotes her a price in this throaty singsong whisper. She moves by Jeannie B's Imposter Club, Buquet's Grille, and Krause & Company, all of them seeming to be in a kind of middle state between operational and out-of-business. The storefronts all date from around the 1930s and their names are uniformly announced above display windows in half-lit, cursive neon, mainly green and rosy-pink. A hand-lettered sign in Buquet's reads *Back at 2:30*. Whatever products Krause & Company traffic in will be a mystery forever—the front window is empty and covered with two ragged pieces of white, bandage-like tape formed into an X as if the proprietors secured the store for a hurricane and then left forever.

She turns a corner and is shaken to see the huge and frozen face of Jenny Ellis, the missing girl, staring down at her from a billboard atop some generic mill. It's a close-up, Jenny's grinning, unaware face caught in surprise, the eyes wide and blue, the thin blonde hair parted in the middle and hanging down close to the shoulders. The billboard reads

Have You Seen This Child?
Jenny Ellis was last seen on October 1
leaving the schoolyard of Ste. Jeanne d'Arc Elementary School
She was wearing a green plaid jumper with white blouse
She is 10 years old, 4 ft. 6 in. tall, 65 lbs.
blonde hair, blue eyes, slight overbite
If you have any information concerning the whereabouts of
Jenny Ellis please
call 1-800-FIND-JEN
Reward Offered

Sylvia would like to avoid looking at it, but her eyes are inevitably drawn upward each time she passes one of these signs and she can't help staring into this little girl's face, backed by the hyper-clear autumn sky, the child's eyes looking down on the city, displaying the innocence of her years.

So far, at least according to the local press, there isn't a single indication of what happened to Jenny Ellis. It's as if she walked a block away from her grade school and then was assumed bodily into the clouds.

Sylvia breaks eye contact, moves on, speeding up her pace, and at the end of the block, sharing a dividing wall with Brody's Adult Books, she finds Jack Derry's. In the window are cardboard displays for cameras that Kodak stopped making when she was a kid. The people in the ads are dressed in wildly outdated swimsuits and there's a caption that reads *Save that vacation forever!* The door of the place is covered with metal bars, but a plastic *Open* sign is hanging from the doorknob.

She steps inside and her first impression is that Perry was right. She's made a mistake coming down here. The place is a disaster. The walls are fitted with a cheesy old rumpus-room kind of paneling, only it hasn't been cut right and different sections fail to cover the gouged plaster walls underneath. The floor is covered with a scarlet shag carpet that looks like it's never been vacuumed. Heads of stubbed-out cigarettes and faded candy wrappers are everywhere. There's a drop ceiling that's missing half a dozen tiles and the ones that remain are either mismatched or display huge brown water stains. The plywood counter looks like it could tumble with a touch and behind it there's a wall of metal shelving loaded to bursting with a ridiculous assortment of camera equipment. Nothing is even close to being organized. Boxes of film are everywhere. Camera parts and lenses, straps and cases are piled on the shelves and on the floor behind the counter. And there's a blanket of heavy dust coating it all. The place has a stale, smoky odor. The lighting is yellow and dim.

"We're closed," comes a yell from a back room.

"The door was open," Sylvia calls back.

There's no response and she starts to think about leaving when the burlap curtain covering the back doorway is pulled open and a tall, emaciated man steps forward with his huge hands covering his eyes, his fingers and thumbs massaging the sides of his temple.

Finally, he removes his hand and stares at her, takes a labored breath and says, "Forgot to lock the door," nodding his head too fast.

It's hard to hang an age on him. He looks haggard, but somehow still kind of soft. His skin seems doughy and too white. He's bald but for a crown of still-red hair that's cut close to his scalp. He's over six feet, but he's got rounded, bony shoulders. He's wearing a summer jersey covered by an argyle wool sweater-vest, both tucked inside the waist of army green fatigue pants. Sylvia can't stop herself from leaning forward a little and she sees he's got on leather sandals and black stretch socks.

She wants to run. She wants to go home and wait for Perry and say, "You were right. We'll go with the jewelry."

The guy behind the counter looks her up and down and then plunges both his thumbs inside his waistband like some demented geek of a cowboy. He says, "We're not interested in any damaged equipment. And we pay in merchandise credit. No cash."

"But—" she begins, and he cuts her off with an annoyed shake of his head.

"Look, we won't have an argument here. No exceptions. Store credit. No cash. That's all I can do."

Now she's more annoyed than unnerved and she squints up at him and gives a mildly disgusted exhale. When he shuts up she says, "I'm not selling anything. I'm here to buy."

His tones changes immediately. He brings a palm up to

his mouth, goes from gunslinger dork to embarrassed schoolmarm.

"Oh God, I'm sorry. It's just, we get so many desperation sales. You know. They just dump the camera on the counter and plead with you. 'Whatever it's worth,' you know. 'Name the price.' "

"Like I said. I'm here to buy."

"Of course. Whatever you'd like." He kind of steps sideways and his arm swings out from his body in a clumsy attempt to present the mishmash behind him.

"We're not really set up for browsing," he says. "Is there something specific you had in mind?"

She stares at him for a few seconds to show she's not going to be placated so easily. Then she pulls out her notepad and reads, "One nineteen seventy Aquinas 500 C/M medium format SLR. Fine condition. With original carrying case, instruction booklet, and Polaroid magazine attachment."

She looks up from the notepad and stares at him.

He waits a second as if he thinks she's going to continue and when she doesn't his head bobs down and his eyes bug out and he says, as if mildly shocked, "Oh, the Aquinas."

"Yeah," Sylvia says, "the Aquinas. There was an ad on the bulletin board at the Rib Room. Is it still available?"

He seems to get nervous and looks past her at the door. She turns around and looks, but the door is still shut. No one's come in. She looks back at him and gives a shrug and says, "Did someone buy it already? Am I too late?"

The hand comes up to the mouth again and this time the eyes close for a good ten seconds. When they open, he shakes his head *no*, but appears a little off-balance. He holds up his index finger to indicate she should wait a minute, turns on his heel and disappears through the curtain into the back storeroom. She hears noises, sounds like cardboard boxes being shuffled around. Then there's the sound of glass breaking, followed by the clerk giving out a high-pitched, "Shit."

Finally he comes back to the counter holding a boxy beige leather case against his chest, kind of cradling it like an oversized kitten. He puts it down on the counter gingerly, wipes dust off the top of the case with a studied sweep of his hand. Then he takes a step backward, puts a fist on his waist and starts to massage the back of his neck with his other hand.

She stares at him. She wants to get across that she's not crazy about his act. That his weirdness is not endearing here. It's not good for business.

"This is it?" she says.

"That's it," he says. "Go ahead, take a look." But he doesn't sound like he means it.

Sylvia steps up to the counter, takes the case in her hands, looks it over. She presses in the silver metal clips on the sides and opens the top of the case back on its hinges. Instinctively, she puts her face close down and takes a deep sniff, takes in the aroma of old, long-stored leather, a fragrance she always names *age*. And she's surprised and suddenly thrilled by the wonderful, slightly sour, acidy bouquet of old film or wax, a closed-up smell, something you'd expect to come from a wooden cabinet in the dining room of an ancient and forgotten Victorian. She brings her head up and looks to see the clerk staring at her as if he were being forced to watch an autopsy, something terribly unsettling, some sight the squeamish should avoid.

She ignores him and takes out the main body of the camera. It weighs a ton. It has that solid, fixable quality of density, something that will never blow away. It's beautiful.

Sorry Perry, Sylvia thinks, *I'm in love.*

She's only held an Aquinas in her hands once before. Perry and she were spending a long weekend driving around the Berkshires. It was a sleepy Saturday afternoon near the end of fall. It was cold and they were walking the main street of a storybook town, this too-immaculate postcard street, where all the storefronts are weathered shingle cottages that house antique shops and gift boutiques that sell gorgeous quilts and handmade sweaters that cost a week's pay. Perry went to browse in the window of a real estate office and Sylvia wandered into a homey little camera shop and got to talking with this old bearded man in a navy cardigan. He had one Aquinas in his display case and he was just thrilled for the chance to take it out and put it in her palm and give her the spiel, the showcase pitch that might nail down a single ten grand sale. Perry came into the store halfway through the lens-grinding section, just after the mini-lecture on the life of Pasqual Aquinas.

Perry head-motioned her outside and she had to hand back the camera and interrupt the sermon. That was over a year ago and she still feels guilty about leaving the way she did.

The pitch whet her appetite, though, and she started to do a little reading up on the Aquinas, started to tell herself that if she ever hit the lottery she knew what her first purchase would be. The camera is a five-inch-square black box trimmed in silver with a fat two inches of lens protruding off the front and a winding crank jutting out of its right-hand side. Placed on its film-magazine back, with the lens pointing upward, it resembles a kind of sleek and threatening jack-in-the-box.

She pops open the viewing hood, stabilizes the camera body against her chest and brings her head to hover above the hood. She looks through and focuses on the clerk. The light in the store is lousy but as she brings his image into clarity it's clear he's still hesitant, kind of upset. He's staring at her, staring into the lens. And he looks like he's watching a car accident beginning to happen.

Sylvia looks up from the hood and raises her eyebrows, hoping maybe the guy will feel self-conscious and give her some explanation for his wariness. But he just says, "Have you ever owned an Aquinas before?"

She shakes her head *no* instead of answering. She wants to keep the pressure on. She wants to find out what the problem is here.

He's really squirming now. He looks down at his sandals and mumbles, "You don't often find them used. I mean, you know, secondhand. They don't come on the market too often."

"I know," Sylvia says. "The ad really surprised me. You must hate to part with it."

He bites in on his bottom lip. "Oh, no," he says, as if she's confused him. "No, it's not like that. It's not my camera. It's not a shop camera. I'm selling this for someone else. It's a consignment sale. A commission . . . I mean, this is a . . ." then he just drifts off with a sigh and a shake of the head.

"Person must really need the cash," Sylvia says, trying to sound sympathetic.

"Well, no," he says, blurting it out, like he can't decide whether to explain or not. "That's the thing. That's the tragedy, really. It's just awful."

"It's awful," she repeats, trying to keep him going.

"It's just one of those horrible ironies. You know, like that pitcher, that baseball pitcher who lost the arm to cancer. You know, *that* arm. The pitching arm."

"Horrible," she says, frowning, shaking her head along with him.

"It's one of those stories you hear and you just think, you think to yourself, you know, nature can just be absolutely cruel. Deliberately cruel."

She doesn't know what to do but nod.

"I don't know him well," he says and gestures to the camera.

"Something happened to the owner?" she says, looking at the camera, not making eye contact.

"He had a fairly well-established little business. Did the

weddings. Graduation shots. And he freelanced on and off. Talented eyes. Until they went . . ."

There's a long, dry pause while both of them take a breath and in that moment the shop seems to darken a little, as if the bulbs in the hanging light fixture were losing power gradually. Finally, Sylvia puts her hand on top of the camera and say, "What was his name?"

The man pulls his head into his neck; a six foot, badly dressed turtle. She's confused him.

"The man who owned this camera," Sylvia says. "Would I know his name?"

"I doubt that," he says and then his tongue darts out of his mouth and moistens his lips.

"Well, what was it?" she says, trying not to sound too persistent.

He gives up a practiced smile. "I really can't give out that information."

Sylvia thinks about this. "Well, can you tell me, you know, I'm just kind of curious here, what was the story with his eyes? What exactly went wrong with the eyes?"

"That," he says, "I wouldn't know."

"Did he go blind?" she asks. "Did he lose the sight altogether?"

"I just don't have the details," he says.

"But if this guy's been around for twenty-five years—"

But he cuts her off and says, "You know, I really have to start locking this place up."

"It's three o'clock in the afternoon."

"Our fall hours."

"Fall hours?" she repeats.

"I'll tell you what," he says. "Do you have a driver's license on you? Some identification?"

She nods.

"All right, I'll tell you what. Let me just copy down your name and address and you can take the camera home and try it out. See how you like it."

She puts her hands in her jacket pockets. "You're going to let me take this camera home? An Aquinas?"

He nods and smiles. "With this big a purchase," he says, "you should know what you're getting into."

Sylvia shakes her head, digs out her license. "When do you need to know if I'm buying?"

"You try it out," he says, taking the license and looking around for a piece of scrap paper. "Shoot a roll. See how it feels. If you still want it in a week or so, we can do all the paperwork then."

"Don't you want a deposit, at least?" she asks.

"I know where you live," he says, crouches down to the floor and starts rooting through a pile of used cardboard boxes. "And you don't look like the transient type."

He finds a box he likes, brings it up on the counter, packs the Aquinas and the accessories into the leather case, then loads the case into the carton.

He lifts the carton over the counter and places it in her arms.

"This is really trusting of you," Sylvia says.

He comes around the corner and takes her arm, starts to lead her to the door.

"Store policy," he says. "That's how we've stayed in business for so long."

He pulls open the door, pokes his head out a bit and looks into the street.

"I'll be back in a few days," she says. "I'll be trying it out tomorrow at the latest."

He doesn't seem to hear her, just keeps nodding, his eyes darting from Sylvia's face out to the sidewalk.

"I'm sure you'll find it does everything you've heard," he says.

She steps outside and says, "Thanks for your help."

But he's already bolted the door. She's not sure what the hell has just happened. But suddenly it occurs to her that she's standing on the edge of Bangkok Park with a fifteen-hundred-dollar camera in her arms. She starts to hurry down Waldstein. At the corner, as she begins to cross Goulden, she looks back to Jack Derry's in time to see the lights go out.

5

The Cadillac is a 1966 Fleetwood Seventy-five sedan, a huge, black, box of a car with seating for nine and a V-8 under the hood that on a good day could launch you to Mars. This particular model has a few customized features installed by a manic-depressive mechanic named Jimmy Clifton. There's a thirty-gallon gas tank, bulletproof glass and four Sturmgewehr MP44 submachine guns mounted in the trunk. The Caddy is registered to Castle K Enterprises, a privately held corporation whose entire board of directors is currently seated inside the vehicle. So, pragmatic as always, Gustav Weltsch, the treasurer and comptroller of Castle K, decides to use the drive time for their annual meeting.

Felix, though secretary of the company, resents his chronic dual status as wheelman. He loves the car, but he'd rather be enjoying it from the backseat, like his cousin Jakob, an individual upon whom status and comfort are utterly wasted. Felix glances in the rearview, tilts the mirror until he can see Jakob, the eternal putz, a schlemiel who never grew out of his schoolboy imaginings, who thinks all of life is story-time. Jakob doesn't even hear Weltsch droning on about the size of the loss Castle K will have to eat due to that firebombing over on Diskant Way. Look at the little weasel, turned sideways in the seat, away from the old man, his back to the old man for Christ sake, staring out the window at the lights of the Canal Zone, every now and then bringing his hands up near his face, thumbs out at right angles pointing to each other, fingers pressed together and straight up in the air. What is that crap? *Poor Uncle Hermann,* Felix thinks, *it must be so humiliating.*

Jakob is scouting locations, looking into the mouth of every alley they roll past and making judgments about the light and the shadows. When the Caddy drives by a pack of teen hookers on the corner of Edeson, he tries to capture each face, see if there might be some raw talent he could build on, a pair of eyes that would be loved by the camera, a pair of legs that would look captivating in flight, some composite quality that could be made to look six or eight years younger.

There are times when he's made uncomfortable by this chronic reflexive impulse, this need to objectify, to mutate real life, as it's happening around him, into manipulated images on a finite screen. *It's anti-life,* he admits, in his most honest moments, *it's cannibalism.* But it's also a compulsion. So he lets himself wonder what the small-boned redhead might look like in black and white.

He thinks suddenly about the article in this morning's paper, the update on the search for the missing child, Jenny Ellis. He remembers something Felice Fabri once said to him back in Maisel, as they exited the Kierling Theatre: *Nothing is safe in this life, Jako, and sometimes people disappear.*

And now he's lost his appetite for scouting locations and actresses. And Gustav Weltsch's babble is giving him another headache. So he closes his eyes and thinks back to the old country and his days with Felice.

The Kierling was on Havetta Boulevard in Old Loew Square, just three blocks away from Papa's haberdashery. It was an old building, originally used for live performances, particularly those of the touring Yiddish troupes that passed through Maisel seasonally. It was purchased the year before Jakob's birth by an insomnia-plagued Zionist named Yitzhak Levi-Zangwill who converted it to the city's first all-night cinema. And though the Kierling was forever in a state of evolving disrepair, its original, homey beauty managed to shine through its ramshackle facade. It could only seat a little over two hundred people and its offerings usually consisted of scratchy prints of decades-old, B-budget, American crime dramas. But there were always homemade dumplings and cinnamon *kava* for sale in the lobby and if a splice broke before the movie ended, Yitzhak gave a full refund and a promise of a double feature the next week. This invoked a loyal camaraderie among the regulars, among whom no one was a more faithful visitor to the Kierling than Felice Fabri.

Felice began taking Jakob to the movies when he turned six. She'd rush through the cleaning and the laundry, then run the length of Jesenska Way with the boy in tow, just in time for the afternoon matinee. Cousin Felix balked at the Kierling from the start and Felice began to leave him with the neighborhood women so that she and Jajob didn't miss a screening of *The Reckless Moment* or *A Double Life.* Then after the show, as the credits rolled, she'd reverse her sprint, falling into the kitchen in time to make supper for Hermann. At the evening meal she'd always cringe with the fear that Papa Kinsky had discovered how she and the boy were spending their days. But the patriarch simply grunted for more boiled ham and stewed fruit, his mind a thousand miles away from the comings and goings of the servant girl.

Years passed in this manner and the Kierling Theatre became Jakob's sole reference point, his school and his playground. And something more. As Felice often whispered to him during the coming attractions, *Remember, little Jako, this is our church.*

If the Kierling was a holy building, Jakob wondered if this meant the people he watched on the screen—bodies blown up beyond life-size, faces spread out as big as the houses on Diamant Road—were prophets. Or maybe angels. Non-human beings full of arcane wisdom whose job was to lead him toward salvation. Their strange names seemed like something out of a foreign and sacred book— *Alan Ladd, Gloria Grahame, Dan Duryea, Coleen Gray, Neville Brand, Audrey Totter, Farley Granger, Valentina Cortesa, Ray Teal.* His young brain tried to memorize the lessons of their black-and-white movements, draw conclusions from the turmoil of their tormented, shadowy lives. In the end, all his trips to the Kierling became stations in one long pilgrimage. And if a decade of chewing prune jelly drops for lunch didn't help his general health and constitution, by the time he entered adolescence, Jakob Kinsky had an aesthetic sense that went beyond convictions about art and beauty. He had an elaborate cosmology regarding how the universe is put together. And how it comes apart.

Which was shaken to the point of rupture during one cold autumn weekend. Jakob had just turned fifteen years old. And while cousin Felix was already starting to extort from his first merchants and assemble a loose gang of boy-thieves to do his bidding, Jakob was still worshipping at the patched white altar of the Kierling, taking his first steps into the priesthood of the film-religion by buying a small notebook that he could hide under his mattress and fill with his virginal attempts at a screenplay.

Felice at this time was more edgy and distracted than ever. Jakob couldn't understand her skittishness. It couldn't be the increase in the street beatings, as those were directed mainly at the Hasidim. And they'd stopped worrying about Papa's wrath years ago when they both came to realize that nothing happened in Old Loew Square without Hermann Kinsky's knowledge and consent and as long as supper was ready when he came through the door each night, they could spend their days in Moravia for all he cared.

Then came the moment that Jakob now thinks of as the fall from grace. He had stayed up late into the night, scribbling in his notebook, writing down dreamlike images of a doomed man in a crumbling city. He fell into nightmare still gripping his pencil and woke in the morning to find the apartment empty, Papa and Felix already out on the prowl for fresh veins of blood and money. When he failed to smell coffee or the harsh smoke of her cigarettes, Jakob knew Felice had not arrived. He found a note slipped under the door—

Kiss Me Deadly
this afternoon at the Kierling.
Meet me in Dvetsil Park.

Felice was waiting for him on one of the benches by the Pietà where the university students came to neck. She'd already purchased their two tickets. As they made their way to their favorite seats in the rear of the Kierling, Jakob saw Yitzhak Levi-Zangwill wink at the governess in a manner that brought on chills.

An hour into the film, as Jakob stared up, fascinated by the strangeness of this story, as he tried to pull apart how the *look* of the picture was achieved, he heard Felice shift in her seat. A moment later, he felt her hand in his lap. Confused, he offered her his popcorn. She took the box of buttered kernels and put it on the floor, then slid her arm around his shoulder, pulled his body toward her and began to kiss and suck at his neck.

Jakob's first instinct was to flee the Kierling, but he stopped himself and as a warmth spread through his legs and stomach, he gave in to a flood of jumbled but intense sensation, pulses shooting through his system that lacked any precedent. Without being fully aware of his actions, he pulled Felice Fabri—his lifelong nanny, a woman twice his age, his mentor, his counselor, his only benign, working definition of *human* into his lap and he began to kiss and fondle and grope her with no regard to the pockets of watchers lodged just a few rows away.

It was the first time in a decade he missed the end of a Kierling feature.

"We're almost there," Hermann Kinsky interrupts. "Jump ahead to new business, Gustav."

Gustav Weltsch hates altering the orderly flow of his thoughts. He finds it a waste. Hermann lets the numbers and projections bounce off him. Kinsky decides on a new venture based entirely on the sensation in his stomach. And it makes Gustav feel as if he's present at these summits merely as decoration, an icon, the brainy, bean-counting analyst that a man of Hermann Kinsky's growing reputation should have at his side. If only Hermann would *listen* once in a while. They could have goosed their gross take twenty percent over the past eighteen months. Gustav has tried to tell the man that the future lies in soybean-based fast foods and genetic manipulation. Weltsch has the statistical models and theorems to back it up. It's plain as day. But Kinsky is lodged in dying notions of real estate and banking and the vice markets. The world is ready to leave Hermann behind. He bases his moves on superstition, revenge, and instinct. And the fact is that Hermann's intuition fails him on occasion. Those film booths he picked up from Yun-fat are bleeding him day and night. They don't even generate enough dollar volume to serve as minor laundries for semi-sour cash. You can't even dismiss them as trophy boutiques, like the nightclub or the gambling lodge or Der Geheime Garten. There's no sex or flash to these Snapshot Shacks. It's like owning a garbage dump. Vulgar. Common. Better to drop the match tonight than waste another month on these embarrassments.

Gustav knows, though his boss will never admit it, that Kinsky held onto the Shacks for Jakob, thinking something vague like: *They're shaped like cameras, the boy likes the cameras, the boy will like this business.* No spreadsheet in the world can argue with motivations like that. It's the apples and the oranges. So, once again, Gustav nods and moves on to new business."

"We will be meeting with the proprietor himself, a Mr. Hugo Schick. Research says he's a grand egotist, Hermann. If you find yourself wanting the deal, you may have to tolerate a good amount of preening."

"I've dealt with narcissists before," Hermann laughs and Weltsch thinks, *every morning, my friend, in the shaving mirror.*

"Schick is a nationalized citizen out of Austria. There was a good deal of family money in the early part of the century, but it's been bled away over generations. They seemed to have a knack for backing the losers in all the major conflicts."

"Nazi bastard," Felix pipes in, imitating a favorite, tough-guy comedian.

"Jump ahead," Hermann snaps. "How is the operation structured?"

Felix swings the Caddy onto Brodine and just misses a collision with an oncoming Harley. No one comments. He rights the car and Gustav continues.

"Schick arrived here in Quinsigamond almost twenty years ago," Weltsch says. "He had a good deal of money with him, though no one knows where it came from. Essentially, he's an enormously talented con man. When he took title to the Herzog Theatre it was in total disrepair, on the verge of being condemned by the city. We know he's burned through a half-dozen investors in his attempt at restoration. Some old Windsor Hills money. Some shadow banks with cash to hide."

"He makes the movies himself?" Hermann asks.

"He has what he calls a family of players, a cast and crew that he uses from film to film. He has two studios above the theatre itself. He makes and edits the films, then tries to run his own distribution. A suicidal plan, but he insists. What is the saying, too many irons in the fire? That will be one of the first things we will want to change, Hermann."

"You're getting ahead of yourself, Gustav. How do you see the specifics of the deal?"

"Schick is starving for revenue. Some of my sources say he could be on the street in a matter of months. He's had to halt the finishing touches on the theatre. He's attempting to wrap up what he thinks of as his masterpiece. A film he's been trying to make for the past seven years. This is a crucial moment for him."

"Every moment is crucial, Gustav."

"If you choose to go forward, we advance the money immediately. Reasonable terms. We let things appear to be within the parameters of normalcy. We suggest the building and the stock as collateral. If my data remains relevant, he should begin to default in eight weeks. You would own the property and the businesses by the first of the year."

Hermann reaches over the seat, squeezes Weltsch's shoulder. "Fine work, my friend. You pick the restaurant tonight."

Behind the wheel, Felix rolls his eyes, knowing they'll be dining on roast tongue in juniper sauce at Boz Lustig's ratty Jidelna.

"Here's what I wish to do," Kinsky says. "We listen to the man. Let him present his case. Whether I've decided yes or no, I will play undecided. No commitment one way or another. We say we call tomorrow. We will call the day after tomorrow. Gustav, you are the voice of reason. You are anxious to leave this sinful place," Hermann pauses to chuckle at himself, "Felix, you are the threat. You are interested, but only on your terms. You leer. You come to the edge of insulting, yes? If there is a woman present, you give her a bit of uncalled-for attention."

Felix smiles, pleased with his lot, wholly confident of his ability to deliver.

"And son," turning finally to Jakob, "if things progress as I suspect they will, you are to be our inside man. This is a fine opportunity for you, Jakob. This is the one we have been waiting for, no," squeezing the boy's thin arm through his top coat. "This is perfect for us. Perfect for you, Jakob. You know this business from birth. Your mother would be so happy tonight."

Jakob stares straight ahead into the rear of Felix's neck and makes himself nod as the car pulls to a stop in front of Herzog's Erotic Palace. All noise ceases and everyone stares out and up at the building. It's as if, in driving a few miles west from their home, they've been transported to some kind of haunting and ethereal landscape where the senses are made doubtful by ridiculous amounts of colored light, strange angles, a hint of engulfing fog.

"I've seen it," Hermann whispers, "during the day, but it never looked this, this—"

"Beautiful," Jakob finishes for him.

The doors of the Caddy are pulled open by steroid-enhanced men all dressed in identical uniforms—black spandex jackets with a breast-pocket logo that tries to replicate the splendor of the theatre in a line drawing.

The foursome reassembles on the sidewalk, Felix forgetting to tip the valet, who drives away too fast in the Fleetwood. But nobody notices. They all have their heads tilted back, their eyes furiously trying to take in the architectural dream rising up before them. Suddenly, their stark bachelor quarters back on Belvedere seems unsuitable and, in Hermann's case, degrading. He leans to the side and begins to whisper into Weltsch's ear.

Jakob doesn't notice the transaction. He's too busy playing Moses, looking out on the expanse of an ever prophesied Promised Land and hearing a voice in his head, the voice of the woman who sometimes comes in his dreams. Maybe Felice Fabri. Maybe his long-dead mother. It's a voice of revelation, a voice of piercing truth and instant epiphany. It's a sound that's coasting through his nervous system at a greater and greater speed, making his body vibrate, making his heart take on a rhythm it's never known before. It's a noise that says, *This is it, Jakob. The time has come.*

Herzog's Erotic Palace is a textbook example of form following function, if the text's author was a visionary egomaniac living on hallucinogens and gothic novels. It's theatrical to the point of self-parody, but it never quite crosses that line. It's too impressive, and in some ways foreboding, to mock its own harsh angles. The theatre is five stories high, divided into three platform levels, an eccentric, dramatic mix of French château and Bohemian *Sondergotik* styles which somehow yields a baroque and, at the same time, fortress-like aura to the structure. The granite walls are covered with intricate etchings that depict the likeness of forgotten actors all the way up to the slightly smaller second level that features a series of vaulting archways and rounded, turret-like corners that rise into spires. The crown of the building is an extra-wide steeple rimmed by an open-air balcony.

But what the eye is immediately drawn to is the marquee, the lone signifier that this is, in fact, a movie theatre and not the headquarters of some occult inquisitor or hemophiliac prince. Out of place with the severity of the rest of the building, this winged canopy hangs out as far as the curb and runs close to a hundred feet down the length of Watson Street. Its neon garishness suggests a kind of cheap humor at the heart of the structure's stone earnestness. And the green neon that spells out *HERZOG'S EROTIC PALACE* in an elaborate, cursive script looks like a monumental practical joke that the structure itself doesn't yet know about.

They sit in the darkness, in the front row of the theatre proper. There's a faint undercurrent of music that only Jakob recognizes as a wildly overblown rendition of "Some Enchanted Evening." Slowly the immense and heavy-looking maroon curtains begin to pull back. The procedure takes quite a while and when they're finally fully receded, the clan stares up at the enormity of a stark white screen, the largest movie screen any of them have laid eyes on. The screen is illuminated by a single narrow white spotlight that impacts at a low, center point and spreads onto the lip of the stage. The overwhelming whiteness, and maybe his proximity to it, gives Felix a slightly queasy feeling.

They begin to hear a distant sound, a clicking, like tap shoes walking across a concrete floor. The noise increases and Jakob knows it's being enhanced by a fairly sophisticated sound system.

Finally, a figure emerges onto the stage and walks in an odd, kicking march-step out into the path of the white spotlight. It's a tall, bulky, bald man, dressed in a tuxedo. The man's head is massive and the skull gleams under the spot. The man turns right and then left, though there's no one else in the theatre beyond the four guests in the front row. The man brings a hand to his forehead as if to salute, but instead only shields his eyes and looks down on his audience, to whom he now gives an elaborate, lengthy bow.

"The Esteemed Family Kinsky," he says. "It is my great honor to entertain you tonight. I am," a pause, "Hugo Schick."

Jakob feels there should be applause. The moment calls

out for it. The entrance was built for applause. But instead, cousin Felix calls out, "We're not here to be entertained."

Gustav Weltsch grinds his teeth, but Hermann says nothing, just stares up at this ego-fat lamb begging for slaughter. Hugo Schick is thrown off, but only for a moment. His recovery is admirable and telling. He begins to nod and moves forward to the lip of the stage.

"Of course, you are right," he says. "I was merely attempting to give you a sense of the majesty of our surroundings. I have forgotten your interest lies elsewhere."

"It's a magnificent theatre," the voice unexpected and totally out of character.

Felix turns to look at Jakob, to see if the kid has lost his mind. He waits for Hermann's elbow to crash into the son's ribs and is shocked to see another, entirely different reaction. Hermann Kinsky is beaming at Jakob. Nodding, smiling. He claps the boy on the back and says, "You are right, my son. You are absolutely right. Magnificent is the word. Forgive our rudeness, Mr. Schick. We were, perhaps, overcome by the grandeur."

Even Weltsch looks confused. This is not a good turn of events. When Hermann decides on a course of action, even if it's the choice of a restaurant or a newspaper, he never wavers. When the event is a crucial business meeting, he becomes resolve incarnate. What the hell is going on here?

Hugo Schick claps his hands together, forgets his improvised "let's-get-down-to-numbers" tack, and falls back to the "impress-the-peasant-wise-guys" routine he's worked out all week.

"There are bigger theatres," Schick says in a grand opera voice. "*The Congress* in Chicago. *The Valencia* in Queens. Surely, *The Million Dollar* in LosAngeles—"

"*The Paramount* in Oakland."

"Excuse me," Schick says.

"The Paramount," Jakob says. "It originally had three thousand, four hundred and seventy-six seats."

The expression on Schick's face grows more smug than distracted.

"How delightful," he says. "We seem to have an expert on out hands."

"The boy likes the movie shows," Hermann says.

"How wonderful for the boy," Schick says.

Hermann nods and stares at Jakob, then he rises out of his seat and walks to the stage and grasps the brass railing, his head now level with Hugo's shoes. He looks straight up to the domed ceiling, stares at a mural, a reproduction of *Saturn Devouring his Children.*

Hermann lowers his voice and says, "How much money do you need, Mr. Schick?"

Felix and Weltsch stare at each other, horrified.

Hugo is taken off-guard. He'd been told Kinsky would make him grovel. Now he's not sure what to do. Figures are running through his head, inflating themselves as they go.

"I'm really not . . ." Schick begins. "I wasn't prepared, that is, there are many, you see," he takes a breath, begins again. "There is the restoration itself. And then the production expenses. The distribution costs. I don't know where to—"

Hermann cuts him off.

"This is my attorney," thumbing over his shoulder in Weltsch's direction. "He'll draw up the terms of our agreement tonight and have the paperwork on your desk in the morning. You will determine how much of an infusion is required and we will fill in the blanks when we sign the contracts. This is acceptable?"

Hugo doesn't know what to do beyond tug at the collar of his shirt.

"Mr. Kinsky," he finally says, "don't you even want a tour of the building?"

"That won't be necessary," Hermann says. "I'm sure you are a very busy man."

"But, Mr. Kinsky, we haven't even discussed—"

Hermann waves away the objection.

"We are *both* very busy men, yes? You will find my terms the most reasonable in Bangkok, Mr. Schick. You will profit and I will profit. The technicalities are all very standard and, I assure you, exremely boring for men of vision like ourselves."

"But, Mr. Kinsky—"

Hermann brings an index finger to his lips to indicate the need for quiet, then he says, "There is, however, one unusual condition to my approval of our venture."

"Condition," Schick says.

Kinsky's finger floats out into the air and becomes a beckoning tool, calling Hugo forward. Schick squats down and duck-walks a few steps to the edge of the stage, turns his ear toward Hermann.

"It's my son," Hermann says, "my boy, Jakob. He's a brilliant young man. Very creative."

"Creative," Hugo whispers and the sound carries around the theatre.

"You would find him extremely helpful in your line of work," Hermann says.

"I'm afraid I don't—"

"Men like you and I, Mr. Schick, we need all the help we can get, yes? Our burdens are very great."

"You want me to hire—"

"I believe the phrase is *assistant director,* yes?"

"Mr. Kinsky," Hugo says, "I already have—"

"You look at your staff tonight," Hermann says. "You see if you have need for this assistant director. My attorney will come by in the morning. You tell him your decision then."

And then Hermann does the signature belittlement. Before Hugo Schick can respond, before he can speak or even change his posture, Hermann Kinsky pats him on the head like a dog, like a Viennese mongrel he stumbled upon in the park. Kinsky turns and moves for the center aisle, snapping for his people to follow him at once. Weltsch and Felix bound from their seats and parade to the exit behind their leader.

But Jakob lingers for a moment, staring at the theatre, pivoting his head in a slow pan, trying to take as much in as the darkness will permit.

He comes to Hugo Schick, still squatting, watching the hulking shadow of Papa exit the theatre. At the back of the hall, the doors swing open and closed.

Hugo looks down at the boy, takes a breath and says, "It will be a pleasure working with you, son."

Δ

There are probably things Sylvia hates worse in this life, but right now, standing at Perry's side like this well-groomed, brain-addled, pseudo-spouse, listening to Ratzinger hold court with his circle of pre-partner associates, she can't think of one. Every time this guy makes another denigrating joke about his wife, she digs her nails deeper into the palm of Perry's left hand. There's a sycophant tax guy named Gordon-something who's choking himself on forced laughter, spilling shrimp cocktail sauce on his designer tie. Sylvia's feet are killing her and the room is too hot. She wants to be home. She wants to be down in the cellar. Down in the darkroom with the Aquinas on the worktable, going over the instruction book step-by-step, removing and installing the lens. Maybe even hooking up a flash and shooting some of those Polaroids.

Right about now, channel 6 is starting their weeklong

Peter Lorre film festival. They're going to begin with *Mad Love* and close out with *The Patsy*. They're going to run all the Warner Brothers dramas from the forties. There will be a roundtable discussion of *The Lost One*, a trivia quiz on *The Maltese Falcon*, and the first uncut, local screening of *Pionier in Inoplastaldt* with the corrected subtitles. She just wants to be back home waiting for the Sydney Green-street collaborations, checking the schedule for *Passage to Marseille*, now and then looking at the picture on the tube through the Aquinas.

And she wants to be wearing her sweats and her sneakers. She wants to have her hair pulled back and her face washed. It's not like she's reactionary when it comes to dressing up. She's got on the black velvet dress and the pearls Perry gave her at Christmas a year ago. She knows he likes her like this and she'd be lying if she said she didn't get a kick out of his reaction as he came out of the bathroom with a towel wrapped around his waist and saw her in front of the bureau mirror and said, "God. Just gorgeous."

But it's so close and humid in here. She wants to grabs one of the waiters and tell him there's a sweet tip if he can locate the air-conditioning and lower the temp a little.

The killer is that on the drive downtown, Perry started in on how they've got to get used to all these receptions and fund-raisers and open-house deals the firm throws. That there are only going to be more in the future and once he makes partner his presence is always going to be required. Sylvia said, "Fine, but why does that mean my presence is required? I don't work for these guys. I don't even have a law degree."

He said, "Because it looks better. It looks good. For you to be there with me." And she gave a little laugh she couldn't help and then regretted it right away. He's still pumped up about the partnership offer and Sylvia honestly doesn't want to ruin it for him.

He said, "You don't think so, fine. But it still works this way. It sends a message to the old boys. The guys above Ratzinger. It says I'm stable. It says I've got plans and direction. Focus. And, I'm sorry, I don't want you to take this any way but as a compliment, but it says I've got taste. That if this looker came with me there must be something."

She stared at him as they pulled into the underground garage. She stared until he said, "What?" in this kind of great, flinching whine.

"Looker," she said.

"Jesus, Sylvia."

"Looker?" she couldn't get over the word. "Did you, like, age a generation in the shower?"

"Sylvia, c'mon—"

But Sylvia couldn't stop. "Looker? Is this part of the deal now? We have to change the way we speak? Should we practice tonight? *Perry, could you have the darkie bring your cupcake a martini . . . "*

So she stepped over the line at the end there. He was self-conscious and hurt and she had to calm him down in the garage before they went up to the reception.

Walpole & Lewis has rented out the main gallery of the art museum. If she'd listened more closely Sylvia would know all the details, but she was thinking about the camera while they were getting ready to go. She was thinking about just getting home and playing with it, taking it apart and getting used to the feel.

Perry mentioned something about a new client, some political action group that's really up and coming and got "a pool of money and a national network." Sylvia doesn't know what their grudge is, but they've just tossed a wad to W & L as a retainer and she knows Perry said something about "they really want us to put our best teeth in the mayor's ass."

The fact is, Sylvia's just not a political creature and

never will be. There's no juice in it for her. No charge. And for her to make a connection with something, to give it her time and her thought, there has to be some natural gravitation, an ongoing connection where she's dwelling on it in her sleep, where she's thinking about it in line at the supermarket or while she's getting her hair cut.

On Sylvia's thirteenth birthday, at about six o'clock at night, her mother put the supper dishes in the sink to soak. Then Ma brought this small cake out of the refrigerator, this chocolate cake with butter cream frosting. And after Sylvia blew out her candles, Ma put a small box in front of her, about the size of a doughnut box, maybe a little smaller, and wrapped in pink and white paper with a bow saved from some other holiday. Sylvia sat there a minute to let the excitement build, to consciously savor the feeling and let it expand just a little. She carefully unwrapped the box and handed the paper back to her mother and watched as Ma smiled and sort of absentmindedly refolded the paper on the kitchen table. Then Sylvia looked down to see a bright yellow display case and the red letters on the top that said *Kodak*. It was a hinged box and she lifted the top back and there, sitting in these black, mock-crushed velvet inserts, was a flashcube, a black plastic cartridge of film, a detachable black plastic wrist strap, and her first camera, a classic Instamatic, all grey and silver and this round bug-eye lens in the front.

She pulled the camera from its resting place in the box. And she was honestly speechless. She stared up at her mother and, she still has no idea why, she started to cry. The tears just helplessly came down her face. And the horrible thing was that Ma immediately misinterpreted the reaction. She thought Sylvia was crushed by what must have been the inappropriateness of the gift. Ma got terribly upset and started repeating, "But you asked for one, last summer, you asked for one."

And it was probably ten minutes before Sylvia could

convince her mother that she was crying from the excitement, from the thrill, that she didn't know why she was crying but that she loved the camera, that it was, in fact, exactly what she'd wanted. Ma huddled with her and they read the instructions and loaded the film and tried to memorize the *Tips For Better Pictures* booklet. And then Ma agreed to pose in every room of the dingy little apartment up on Harper Ave. And Sylvia used up the flashcube that had come with the set, then turned on all the table lamps, hoping it would make things bright enough.

It didn't. The next day her mother brought the film to the drugstore and Sylvia waited out a god-awfully long week until the photos came back. Only four shots were printable. But that was enough. The pictures were wonderful. There was her mother, in full color, captured forever inside a three-inch-square frame of glossy paper, posed, laughing, embarrassed but pliable: At the kitchen table where they ate together every night. Tilted back in the paisley rocker in the living room. Perched on the edge of a too-small twin bed with her hands folded in her lap. Close up and in profile before the refrigerator, looking like a practice mug shot.

Ma hated them all, good-naturedly threatened to tear up the prints and negatives. Sylvia laughed off her complaints and was oblivious to the eight blackened squares on the negative strips—the shots that hadn't come out. She was infected. She was converted. Very simply, she knew, without doubt or hesitation, with a surety that usually visits the religious or the lovesick, she knew what she wanted to do with her time. She wanted to take pictures. She wanted to bring this miraculous black box up to her eye as often as possible and press that silver rectangular button, and expose her visions to film, enshrine them, verify them, make them into something lasting.

Sylvia had fantasized about going to some hip art school, someplace like RISD or the Kertész Center in

Boston. But there was just no money, so she took out loans and went to a state college and studied fine arts with a concentration in cinema. Now, those four years are like a blurry filmstrip for her. Isolated images that refuse to flow together. She got pretty good grades and worked in the dining commons. She wrote papers and took exams and for one semester she shot pictures for the school paper. In her sophomore year, she slept through a standard bout of mononucleosis. In her junior year, she slept with her *Cronenberg: Fear, Fluids, & the Body* professor. The word *slept* is a misnomer. The guy seduced her in the projection booth of the campus cinema while screening a double feature of *Rabid* and *The Parasite Murders*.

Basically, Sylvia bided time, lived like a phantom, made few friends, and spent virtually all of her free hours either watching movies or shooting film in the little nearby farming towns, then developing prints in the school darkrooms.

That's what she remembers about the years she came of age—focusing a lens at a rusted tractor, a grade school playground, a row of icicles under a railroad bridge. And hours alone in narrow, windowless, closetlike rooms, breathing chemical-thick air and straining her eyes in deep red light.

They're standing in a circle next to the bar which has been set up in a small room off the main gallery. Actually, it's not a room at all, but, as the plaque on one of the walls points out, it's a

Chapter House
French, 1160–1175
Painstakingly reconstructed and
originally part of the Benedictine
Priory of St. John, at Le Bas Nueil,
a hamlet north of Poitiers in
West Central France.

It's a stark, low, dome-ceilinged, chapel-like cove of a room that makes Sylvia feel they should all be praying instead of making insipid small talk. And though she doesn't like how severe and cold the surroundings are, she can't take her eyes off the sculpture in the corner. She leans away from Perry and squints at the info-plaque next to the artwork.

Virgin & Child
French, Late 14th century
Limestone
By arranging the Virgin with her weight resting on one foot, the sculptor gives the figure a gently swaying motion. The serenity of the Virgin's face conveys the awe and majesty that early Gothic artists sought in their images of divine personages. Combined with this ideal quality is a certain amount of naturalism which points forward to the realism of the late Gothic style. The realism is further evident in the child with his grinning, mischievous expression and peasantlike features.

She reaches up to touch the Virgin's face, feels how cold the stone is. And she hears, "Sylvia and I were just discussing this last night, right dear?"

It's Perry's voice and Sylvia tunes in to see the whole circle suddenly focusing on her. And she has no idea what they've been talking about.

"That's right," she manages.

Last night. Last night I was riding Perry in the last row of the Cansino Drive-In. And there's a part of her that wants to blurt this out.

"Well, I have to say, this surprises me."

It's Ratzinger, the closest thing Perry has to a boss and a guy who will spend his life anguishing over the fact that his father's bloodline will always keep him from being pure WASP. Ratzinger's closing in on his fifties, but tries to dress himself ten years younger. Perry's told Sylvia all about the twenty-year-old the man keeps in a high-rise condo down by the reservoir, a quick fifteen miles from the Windsor Hills wife and therapy-addicted son, Sylvia thinks Ratzinger colors his hair.

She tries to fake understanding. "Surprises you?" she says, smiling.

He gestures to her with his champagne flute. "Yes. You being a photographer and all. And by now I think all of us have been beaten into accepting photography as a legitimate art form."

Perry gives her hand a *please don't* squeeze.

Sylvia can't help it. "I'm not a photographer," she says.

"But I thought—" he begins.

And Sylvia opens her mouth to cut him off with something about his need to understand what a beating is, but Candice, a blonde from Perry's department, gets there first and says, "C'mon, Earl, please, just admit that it isn't an aesthetic argument. This is power politics at its most anal. You'll push the mayor and Welby will push back and you'll measure each other's column inches in the *Spy*."

Ratzinger turns full attention to Candice, surprised but clearly impressed by the show of what he calls *office balls*.

"Did you see the Mapplethorpe exhibit when it passed through town, Candice? Did you come down here and take a look?"

But Candice stays loose and friendly. "I did, Earl. But my judgments about the exhibit have nothing to do with what's really going on here. The old boys—"

"Watch it," Ratzinger says, smiling through a squint.

"The senior partners," Candice continues, shaking her head slightly, "couldn't care less about obscenity or the First Amendment or the moral disintegration of America. You know this better than I do. Every one of us here knows this. The senior partners' big hope is that they can cash a new check before their pacemakers shut down. FUD's money is as green as anyone else's. That's the issue. That's why we've got a fat new cow to milk."

"Candice," Gordon scolds, but Ratzinger is amused and nodding like he agrees with the woman's pronouncement.

"Well let's try it this way," he says. "Let's say you're one of the old boys. You haven't had a thing to do with the real work in ten years. Your big job is P.R. and an eye on the bottom line every month. You're a figurehead who's steered Walpole & Lewis through enough miles to think you deserve all your last years at the widest part of the trough. Okay, Candy? Can you hold that picture? Now, your favorite congressman calls up one day and says he can put something sweet in your lap. Something that will really send you out in style. Okay? So you go up to the top of the bank building and you eat some red meat with the congressman's new friends. And after the chocolate mousse is resting in your belly, the FUD boys offer to write a check. Pay to the order of W & L. Ready for deposit in the corporate account. And that check is going to change all the numbers next quarter. It's going to trickle down to the maintenance crew, for Christ sake. And all you've got to do is slap your best people on their team and say a few *Amens* for the cause. What decision does Candice make? I want to hear."

They've both kept the argument civil. They've both showed how smooth they can play conflict without rolling over. They've sounded intelligent and savvy at the same time. Informed but colloquial and always sure of themselves. Sylvia wonders how people end up this way.

"What do I do?" Candice says. "I endorse the check and say *Praise the Lord* to the comptroller. Every one of us would do what the old boys did. That wasn't my point, Earl, and you know it. I'm saying let's admit we're hypocrites—"

"Pragmatists," Perry says and Sylvia sees Ratzinger nod to him.

"Whatever," Candice says, now looking at Perry. "We've cashed their check. So we're in bed with the Families United for Decency. But that doesn't mean we're married to them. Does it, Earl?"

She scores with a not-so-subtle shot about the mistress. Sylvia would call it suicide, but Candice is a smart woman and she must know Ratzinger gets off on the clash, gets some juice from a little rough sparring.

Ratzinger raises his champagne toward Candice, lowers his voice and says, "A First Amendment fetish." He gives a put-on, too-loud sigh and adds, "I guess some of us will never get over our years at Berkeley."

Sylvia would give a night in the darkroom to hear Candice's comeback, but the gallery fills with that awful microphone whine and everyone turns to see this crew-cut, squinty-eyed guy in a tux craning his neck and looking impatient behind a heavy wooden lectern. He's positioned in front of a massive medieval tapestry that hangs from an upper balcony. The tapestry depicts what might be a Grail scene, some crude-looking knights and horses about to enter a dense forest.

"Ladies and Gentlemen," the guy says, "If I might have your attention."

The crowd converges and forms into a loose semicircle and gradually voices start to lower.

"As some of you know, my name is Raymond Todd and I am a broadcast journalist at Quinsigamond Radio WQSG."

"Jesus," Sylvia says into Perry's ear, "I thought the voice was familiar."

"He's just doing the intro," Perry whispers.

Todd waits for everyone's full attention, gives an annoyed glance to a waiter still taking a drink order, then begins. "It is my great honor tonight to have been asked down to the museum to introduce you to some new friends of ours. Some very brave, very hard-working people who have decided to lend a hand in the struggle of a lifetime. Now it may be apparent to you that Raymond Todd is in an extraordinarily fine mood this evening. And it may occur to you that this is not the demeanor you've come to expect from Raymond Todd. My friends, I will not argue with you. I yield to your incisive judgment. I agree with the verdict. Because, my friends, Raymond Todd has been waging a very lonely crusade that began to appear less and less winnable with each passing dark day."

He does his trademark pause, goes into the rubbing of the sore neck and the slow, daunted shaking of the head without ever breaking eye contact.

"I, like you, have watched this, my native land, my native city, the place of my birth on this planet, plummeting downward, racing brakeless toward the bowels of damnation. You know, people, you don't have to be some historian, some insulated, book-touting academic, to know that at some point in the past few decades, every value and moral and treasured teaching that our chosen nation has embraced has been uprooted and cast to the ground, trampled under the feet of everything from progress to good intentions. You've heard me speak before. I'm not going to run down the whole litany for you."

"Wanna bet," Sylvia whispers, but Ratzinger hears her and gives a patronizing smile.

"Simply put, we have lost track of what is important. We have, through ignorance or willful pride, turned our backs on the only things that should matter during our time on this earth. Now I'm as guilty as the next man of losing heart, people. You've all heard it. You've heard me throwing in the towel, ready to forsake the good fight. Seems I'd forgotten one small truth that should have lit the way."

And he closes his eyes and delivers the patented slap on the lectern that echoes through the gallery and causes at least one gin and tonic to crash to the marble floor.

Then Todd opens his eyes, points a finger into the thick

of the crowd, lets a greasy smile spread across his lips and intones, *"The wheels of God grind slowly, but they grind surely."*

A pocket of listeners down near the front breaks into applause. When they die down, Todd takes a good breath and speeds up, loudens up, gets wildly dramatic. "The wheels are in motion, my friends. That's why we're all here tonight. We're here to turn the key together. We're here to watch the mighty wheels of judgment begin their trip through the city of *Quinsigamond.*"

He spread out the last word with this weird, pseudo-Southern drawl and widens each syllable. There's a wave of murmuring throughout the hall but Sylvia can't tell whether people are spurred on by this misplaced evangelical sermon or just plain confused. Todd claps his hands together and raises his arms over his head like some uncoordinated boxer. Sylvia looks around to see if anyone else is finding this pretty bizarre entertainment for a museum reception sponsored by a WASP law firm.

"Without any further delay," Todd bellows, "I give you the national coordinating director of Families United for Decency, Reverend Garland Boetell."

The gallery floods with applause and whistles and hidden speakers somewhere play "The Battle Hymn of the Republic." Sylvia changes her position to get a look at Reverend Boetell as he walks in under an exhibit banner that reads *Goya: Moralist Amid Chaos.* He's a little battleship of a character, a short, pink bull, all permanently rouged cheeks and a spray-cemented cover of silky, golden-white hair. He's got on a navy blue double-breasted suit that clamps in his girth and he takes the lectern holding a leathery, bendable Bible that he uses to wave to the crowd. On his heels is a small, reed-thin Hispanic kid of about eighteen years, dressed in a plain white robe and hemp belt, leather sandals on his feet, stooped forward and looking extremely uncomfortable.

The applause seems excessive, verging on the raspy kind of hum you'd get at a small rock concert. Perry leans into Ratzinger and whispers something in his ear. Ratzinger continues clapping his hands together, but turns his head and whispers back and they both give guilty smiles.

Sylvia puts her hand on Perry's back and he looks at her and shakes his head, rolls his eyes and says, "The crowd up front, they're all shills. The radio guy, Todd, he brought them with him."

Sylvia nods, but somehow this information isn't as funny to her. She wants to ask Perry when they can leave, but Reverend Boetell raises his hands up like an Olympic high-diver and the crowd starts to quiet down.

"My good people," the Reverend says. "My good northern neighbors. What a genuine thrill it is to be here with you tonight in the splendid museum here. What a wonderful honor to be asked to break bread with my new friends."

"Amen," someone down front barks out.

"Amen is right. And bless his holy name. I *am* the Reverend Garland Boetell. And I know you are *all* familiar with my trusted assistant Fernando, saved as a child from the horrors of São Paulo on our very first Brazilian mission. Praise the Almighty."

Boetell pulls the young man in the robe forward, this walking prop of redemption, and pats his shoulder as more whistles and cheering erupt. It's like a high-fever dream— the staid Quinsigamond art museum transformed before everyone's eyes into a tent revival. Sylvia looks around at the tapestries and the Rodin sculpture, a little fearful they're suddenly going to transform themselves into something else. Hay bales. Burning crosses.

"Now I want to start off by thanking the esteemed legal firm of Walpole & Lewis for throwing this beautiful reception and helping us inaugurate the campaign they are *going* to remember. Praise Jesus, they will not forget this night, my friends. Years from now, when our coming battles are righteous memories, when you sit with your children and try to tell them how the ways of justice and virtue finally triumphed in our land, you *will* begin with this very night. You *will* recall these moments in this great hall, as the start of the new crusade."

The gallery explodes with *Amens* and Sylvia suddenly starts to feel hot and squeamish. She looks around, trying to see if anyone else knows what the hell this man is talking about.

"It is no secret, ladies and gentlemen, that there is blight on this country. That our very nation, *selected* by the Lord above himself, has fallen under the wheels of a most heinous corruption. We have lost the way. We have lost our vision. We have sacrificed our *divine* birthright, people, handed it over like change at the tollbooth. When Mr. Todd speaks to you of pessimism, I know from whence he comes. I know how sick and lost a soul can feel when it looks out upon this sprawling land, this once pure paradise, this once chosen Judeo-Christian Eden, and sees how terribly far we have fallen. I, too, lived through that very dark, very long night of the soul's despair. I, too, my people, have felt the fires of the evil victor's breath on my weakened shoulders."

A big, sudden yell now, "I have seen *doom* on America's horizon and I have shuddered in the abandonment of the *e-tern-al* savior."

The crowd is silent, transfixed. Boetell's got it. He makes Raymond Todd look like an amateur. The Reverend cannot be ignored.

The voice backing down now. "Some say, my friends, I will have to pay for my lapse in faith. Like Moses himself, my people, I will have to own up to my failing on that horrible night. I can't escape my actions any more than any of you can. But I woke from my nightmare with a vision. A vision the good Lord has asked me to pass on to you. There is a time for every purpose, my friends. There is a time to eat and a time to refrain from eating. There is a time for sorrow and a time for joy. And make no mistake about this, ladies and gentlemen, at your very peril, make no mistake," the voice building again, "there is a time for peace. And there is *absolutely* a time for war. And this hour, this very moment is the moment we declare the war. We delcare war on the forces of darkness that have taken our land."

His last words are half-drowned by the crowd as if someone was working a neon applause sign. Sylvia touches Perry's arm. He turns to her and shakes his head, leans his mouth to her ear and says, "Is this bizarre or what?"

"We've got to get out of here," she says, but he motions toward Ratzinger and gives a guilty shrug.

Boetell calms the faithful, takes in some air and begins again. "Now I don't need to stand here tonight and tell you who the enemy is. You people know who the enemy is. You have eyes. You can see its presence in every city in this country. But there is surely strength in numbers, friends. And one look into the bosom of this crowd tonight and my heart just surges. Because I know with support like this, we will triumph. You are a prayed-up people. You know the path. You *are* willing to make the sacrifices. You simply need direction."

A pause and then a big smile.

"And friends, that is where *I* come in."

The shills go crazy. Sylvia closes her eyes and runs a hand over her forehead. She tries to remember if she's got any Tylenol left in her purse.

"Now back where I come from, Families United for Decency has been growing by leaps and bounds for over a year now. We've had our share of skirmishes already. And you people can learn by our mistakes. Our funding has been growing steadily and of late we've managed to bring on board what you might call some heavy hitters from the corporate sector. We've now got close to a dozen Crusade Buses out on the road at all times. One dozen, my friends. We are *out on the road.* Now our coordinating committee has determined that we need a high-exposure skirmish. We need to get our story out on those airwaves. We need to dispense the truth to the good people of this nation, to tell the story in big, colorful pictures. And friends,"

Another perfectly timed pause, another broad smile.

"*That* is where *you* come in. We have done just a slew of field studies. We have gone from Atlantic to Pacific. From the Canadian border down to the Gulf of Mexico. But it wasn't until I received those heartbreaking letters from your own Mr. Raymond Todd that I knew, that I positively *believed,* that we had our theatre, that we had our perfect battleground, that we had been *given* the site where the real war begins. And my friends, that site is the sad and fallen city of," a pause, "Quinsigamond itself."

It's the big finale. The gallery fills up with all kinds of excited noise and it can't be coming from Todd's shills. The real guests, the people Walpole & Lewis invited, they must be caught up in it. And Sylvia has no idea what the Reverend is talking about.

"And so, let the war begin," he bellows and Ray Todd jumps up to the lectern and the two men start to embrace as a rain of red, white and blue balloons is released from some netting up near the ceiling and the speakers start to play some kind of generic march music.

Sylvia starts to get small, stabbing pains in her abdomen, as if the music had triggered them. She grabs Perry's arm at the elbow and pulls him back to her and says, "Please, let's leave. Now."

He gives her a strange look, comes to her ear and says, "Are you okay? You look really pale."

"I'm not feeling well," she says.

He gives a concerned-looking nod and says, "Okay, let's get you home."

He claps a hand on Ratzinger's back and tries to tell him they're leaving but the room is so loud he has to shout to make himself understood. Ratzinger steps over to Sylvia and says, "Sorry you're feeling ill," and she nods and closes her eyes, thinking she's about to faint. Her knees buckle, but Perry moves fast and catches her and she leans against him as they move for an exit.

"You going to be sick?" he asks, a little panicky as they move out into a hallway.

"Just get me home," she says, suddenly short of breath.

He steers them toward the garage exit.

"It's probably the champagne," he says. "You didn't eat any dinner, did you?"

She doesn't want to talk. She just wants to be home. Out of these clothes. Away from this noise and the balloons and the awful music. Away from the sound of Reverend Boetell's voice. Her head is throbbing and all she can hear is this drawl of an echo saying, *That* is where *you* come in."

7

Sylvia changes out of her dress as she watches Perry hang up his rented tux. He's fastidious, making sure the creases of the pants' legs are lined up, untucking the flaps of the jacket pockets. He talks over his shoulder as he brushes down the lapels with these snapping, karate-like moves of his hand, as if he was attacking something unseen, some microscopic parasite that lived on the surface of the dinner jacket.

"I'm saying you don't take care of yourself. I'm concerned about your health."

Sylvia digs a pair of her mother's old slippers out from under the bed and says, "Perry, you're concerned about my health? Then please, don't ever take me to another one of these hell-nights, okay? Please?"

"So the Reverend was a little over the top—"

"Over the top? Perry, we just spent three hours in the goddamn Twilight Zone. What the hell was that all about?"

"Sylvia," he says in this weary adult tone, as if having to explain this to her is an enormous sap on his energy. "It was a reception for a big new client. That's all it was. Yes, these people are a bit zealous. Agreed. And yes, maybe the museum was a poor choice for a meeting place. But you know, I didn't see anyone else reacting quite so strongly."

"Your friend Candice didn't seem too happy with the Reverend and his gang."

"Candice was playing the politicized animal. Candice wants to position herself as the conscience of the firm. She's expected to spout the opposition view. The big thing about Candice is she knows she can get away with it. She knows Ratzinger gets a little buzz from their skirmishes. It adds to his day. She can't lose. But I don't think there's much behind it. Candice is great at polemic. She should write speeches for a living."

She sits down on the edge of the bed, pulls a sweatshirt out from underneath the pillow.

"Let me get this straight. Nothing that guy said tonight bothered you? Nothing at all?"

He zips the tux inside the plastic carrying bag, hangs it on the back of the closet door and says, "You know, in the long run it's going to be cheaper for me to buy one of these."

And it's a second before Sylvia realizes he means a

tuxedo. That he should buy a tuxedo. That he expects to be going to enough black-tie affairs that it would be cost-effective to make the purchase.

"Perry," she says.

He comes over and sits down next to her.

"Syl," he says, "I don't take it that seriously. Political crap like that just bounces right off me. Goes right over my head. It's just crap. It's like it doesn't have any meaning. It's like he's using words I don't understand. So let him. Doesn't affect me. You should do what I do."

"Which is?"

He smiled, shifts his position, puts his hands on her shoulders and starts to massage her. "Which is ignore it. Just tune it out. Let the guy babble. I'm standing there tonight thinking how much of the raise I'm going to take home, you know? I'm thinking interest rates and how much we can afford to put down on a house. Speaking of which—"

She cuts him off by rolling her head back on top of his hands and moaning. "Oh no, Perry, c'mon."

He gets defensive immediately. "What? I didn't say a word here."

"I'm just tired and you know I'm not feeling well."

"Sylvia, I didn't say a word. What did I say?"

"It's just late for this discussion—"

"What discussion?"

"What discussion? The 'it's time to plunge ourselves into debt and leave this great apartment' discussion. Please. C'mon. I'm really not feeling well."

He gets up and goes to his bureau, takes off his watch and ring. His voice goes edgy and tight. "Yeah, well maybe if you'd gotten home in time to have a little dinner, the champagne wouldn't have hit you quite so hard."

She honestly doesn't want this to escalate into a fight. She lies back on the bed and looks up at the cracks in the corner of the ceiling. "I'm sorry. You're right. I lost track of time. I got caught up with the camera and everything. I didn't realize how late it had gotten."

But they're already over the line and Perry doesn't want an apology. "It's okay," he says with that sarcastic edge. "I guess eating dinner together these days is just a little too bourgeois for you, right?"

She lets it go for about five seconds and then says, as evenly as she can, "What's that supposed to mean, Perry?"

He turns around, leans his behind against the bureau. "It means," he says, the words singsong and drawn out, "How come you're so concerned about debt when it comes to buying us a home, but not when it comes to buying another goddamn camera."

She stands up. "I thought the goddamn camera was supposed to be a gift."

"And I thought we were supposed to be having dinner together at five-thirty. That's what families *do,* you know Sylvia. They eat together. They talk to each other."

"Thanks for the tip. Did Reverend Boetell tell you that?"

She walks out of the bedroom into the kitchen, goes to the fridge and pours herself a glass of Pinot Grigio. He stands in the doorway fuming and says, "I thought you were sick."

She says, "I am," and goes out the back door and down to the basement.

The darkroom is at the rear of the cellar. Sylvia moves past the two huge, ancient furnaces and opens a padlock on this rickety chicken-wire door, steps into a little compartment room filled with all the forgotten junk that a hundred years' worth of owners and tenants have left behind. She pulls on a string and lights the room with a bare forty-watt bulb. She looks down on steamer trunks filled with heavy, rusted old tools, defunct magazines, rough pieces of scrap wood. In one corner sits an antique child's bicycle without any wheels. In another there's a silver industrial hair dryer, this big helmet-like unit mounted on a heavy pole. It looks like a prop from some campy old science fiction movie— a brain scrambler or a time machine. She's always wanted to bring the thing upstairs, clean it up, maybe turn it into a lamp or something. And she realizes now that the reason she never has is because Perry would hate it, would say something like, *You're kidding, right, this old piece of junk*...

There's a small door next to the hair dryer. She keeps it secured with her combination lock from high school. Inside used to be a small closet of some kind, sort of a storage bin, just 5 x 7, but nice and dry. Last year Sylvia asked Mrs. Acker if she could make it into a darkroom and Mrs. A was all excited by the idea. Sylvia spent two weekends cleaning the place out, then nailed some brackets to the plywood walls and hung some shelves. She managed to wedge in two small tables for counter space and ran an extension cord off the light fixture in the outer room. For water she hooked a garden hose up to the spigot near the furnaces.

She bought all her equipment secondhand, got some good deals by watching the classified ads in the *Spy*. She picked up a nice Durst enlarger at a yard sale over on Mann and got all her pans and tongs, her safelight and a good LePrince timer from a woman who was moving to Europe—Germany, she thinks—and just said, "Make me an offer." Mrs. Acker donated a padded step stool that Sylvia uses as a chair.

There are no windows in the darkroom. She keeps her mother's pocket radio on one of the shelves and there are nights when she finishes up her work and tunes in some no-talk jazz station, something from down the Zone with a lot of P.H. Cunningham rotation or maybe some Imogen Wedgewood. And she just sits there in the absolute darkness, can't see her wineglass in front of her, and she kind of just perches on Mrs. Acker's stool with the stuffing pushing through the red plastic covering, just swirling the wine around in her mouth, just feeling the soft roll of the horns on the radio, smelling the chemicals drying on the prints that she's clothespinned to a wire strung between walls. She just sits there for maybe ten or fifteen minutes, feeling not exactly happy, more like contented and secure and relaxed, the muscles of her neck and shoulders finally getting loose.

She's locked the Aquinas in the darkroom. She keeps all her cameras down here, though Perry says they'd be safer up in the apartment. She's not so sure about that. And she likes seeing them all together on a worktable. It's like pretending she has a studio or something. She remembers back in high school, the first time she saw Antonioni's *Blow Up* on TV late one night. David Hemmings as the perfect mod fashion photographer, living in London, driving around in a Rolls convertible. He had that big, funky studio that he lived and worked in. He'd set models up under the lights, those ninety-pound girls dressed in those horrible, glittery smocks. And when everything was set, the man just turned into this whirlwind, just fired off shot after shot and you could hear that great shutter-click sound over and over. He had something like half a dozen cameras spread out on the floor and hanging around his neck and he'd be jumping from one to another, you know, grab a Nikon and click off ten shots, then pick up a Minolta and click off a dozen more, all the time yelling at the girls, the models, wooing them one second and insulting them the next. Sylvia thought Hemming's character was a jerk, but she never got over all the cameras.

She turns on the safelight, pulls the stool up to the table, sits down and opens the Aquinas case. She takes out the camera and puts it on the table. She picks it up, plants her elbows on the table and brings her eye to the viewer. She's still got the lens cap on and the dark-slide in. She just wants to feel the thing. She just wants to get used to the weight and the design.

It's a fairly heavy piece of equipment. Probably around four pounds. Once Sylvia met a wedding photographer who said he'd only work with an Aquinas. He said, "You use the Aquinas, you look at the prints, you can count the circles of lace on the bride's gown." The downside was he had to go to a chiropracter once a month from lugging the thing around. "But it's worth it," he swore. "That's the price you pay."

She pulls out the instruction booklet, adjusts the safelight and opens to the parts illustration. There are two mechanical drawings of the camera, one illustrating from a front perspective and one from the rear. They're line drawings, really detailed with the camera taken apart so that every component is visible. There are lines extending from each piece to a number. Below the drawings is an index showing the official name of each numbered piece. There are forty-three separate pieces to know about, things like *depth of field preview buttons* and *winding crank bayonet* and *exposure value indicator.*

She turns from the booklet to the camera itself. She takes off the magazine, the smaller box on the back of the camera that holds the film. She looks at the status indicator, sees the tiny red letters that read LOADED.

She opens the magazine. There's a roll of half-exposed film inside—old Lumière stock, a pricey import they don't make anymore. She puts the magazine down and picks up her wineglass, stares at the camera for a minute and tries to think. Is it possible that someone, no, not just someone, a professional, would offer their camera up for sale and not realize they'd left half a dozen pictures inside?

She takes another sip of wine. She reaches up to the shelf and turns on the radio at a low volume. The darkroom fills up with a too-sad piano-and-sax piece. And the next thing she knows, she grabbing the film tank and loading the Lumière.

She moves quickly, trying to keep her mind off what she's doing beyond the basic step-by-step process of development. She knows she's got no business, no right, to print up these shots. They don't belong to her. It's an accident that they're in her possession. And processing them is an invasion. But she can't stop herself. Clearly, the owner has forgotten about the photos. It's possible the film is blank, just some kind of mistake that happened in the midst of the photographer's upheaval.

In an hour she's got a dried strip of negatives suspended between plastic tongs and held up to the safelight. There are seven squares filled with images. The rest of the strip is black. She gets a pair of scissors from the worktable and cuts away the useless end of the strip.

Then she goes to work at the enlarger. She doesn't have the patience to print a test strip. She simply throws a single-weight 8 x 10 sheet under the easel and instinctively exposes it. She doesn't bother with the timer. She just hits the switch and stares at the reversed image and when it feels right she shuts the enlarger off and carries the sheet to the pans.

She watches the image start to form under the bath of developer. She takes her tongs and moves the paper around a bit underneath the fluid. Gradually, definition seeps through, shades of black and white arrange themselves, but she still can't make out the specific image. It's a dark shot, very shadowy. She looks at her watch. She leans her head down closer to the pan. She jostles the print a bit with the tongs, impatient. She tries to concentrate on the music, checks the watch again, then removes the print and slides it down into the stop bath. There's no use straining her eyes. She's going to need full light to make sense of the image.

She moves the print to the fixer, agitates it, then for the

next fifteen minutes she paces around the darkroom with the Aquinas in her arms, stopping every now and then to bring it to her eye, look through the lens into the red-darkness of the room.

When the radio finishes playing a scratchy rendition of Disderi's "Sucker for a Good Joke," Sylvia goes back to the print, removes it from the pan, grabs a squeegee and runs off all the excess liquid, then pins the print to the drying line. She goes back to the enlarger and starts the whole process again on the next shot.

In all, she comes up with seven photos. When the last print is dripping on the line, she secures everything, turns off the safelight and flips on the fluorescent desk lamp on the worktable. She bends its gooseneck up like a spotlight, shines it at the line of drying prints.

First she stands back at the opposite end of the darkroom and looks at the whole line. Her first impression is that these photos form a series, that these shots are intended to be looked at together, to be displayed in unison, a family of similar visions, variations on a single strain.

There's a woman. Shot from seven different angles and ranging from a maximum distance of, she'd guess, maybe twenty, twenty-five feet, down to a slightly overhead, rear field shot, all silhouette, looking down over the left shoulder, shadow everywhere. The only unifying factor in all seven photographs is that in every single shot the woman's face is somehow obscured, either cloaked in shadow or turned away from the camera. The woman is draped in a kind of flowing cape or shawl, some sort of serape-style throw. The shawl covers the woman's right shoulder, but then trails off the left, as if it had fallen away, and in the closer shots, in a soft, almost misty focus, her left breast is exposed and an infant is seen suckling.

And given this subject matter, maybe it's the setting that

makes the shot so intriguing and disturbing. The woman is perched on what looks like a chunk of stone, possibly marble, in the center of an eerie and cavernous hall of some sort. It's strewn with rock and rubble, a museum to decay. Some sort of lighting, sun or maybe full moon, makes it through the unseen ceiling and juts down on the woman in well-defined rays, like a storybook depiction of heaven or the voice of God. But the interior of this hall looks bombed out, ripped apart and forgotten. There's almost a postwar feel to the room, like those stark shots of Berlin and Dresden after the bombing, maybe a bit gentler than that, more like an old church or monastery that's been abandoned for generations and has started to fall back into the earth. What can be seen of the ground looks like a bed of dark stones and cinder. An occasional larger boulder and pieces of what appear to be scrap wood can be made out in the longer shots. The walls of the hall seem distant and huge. Cathedral walls. And in the longest shot of all Sylvia can make out what looks like the beginnings of a stairway in the far left-hand corner.

But clearly it isn't this hall or cathedral or museum that the photographer wants us to concentrate on. The setting is intense and completely effective. But it's subliminal, it's background, like a sound track used to evoke or underscore a mood. The photographer's subject is the Madonna and child. The photographer's whole world is the woman and the infant.

Sylvia is tempted to go farther for some reason. To focus in, hard and adamant. She's tempted to say the photographer's *only* concern is the woman and the child. Is the skin of the woman and the child. The woman's bare shoulder, her flowing hair and exposed, succulent neck. Her nursing breast. And the baby's bare skull, closed eyes and extended tiny hand.

In front of Sylvia are seven photographs, suspended by spring clothespins from an arcing silver wire. She's spent the last dozen years of her life—since her mother gave her that first Instamatic—attempting, almost obsessively, to make her images do this.

She's never succeeded. She's taken shots that please her. And though she'd never said this to anyone, Perry included, she's taken half a dozen that might possibly step beyond the competent and into that vague and personal definition of feeling and judgment called *Art*.

Possibly.

But she's never come close to this. And until these photos, she's never known exactly what she's been looking for. Sylvia has spent over a decade trying to learn, spent countless hours in libraries looking over fat volumes of all the masters since Niepce and Daguerre invented the camera. She's read technical manuals and dense texts full of theory. Then she's always gone out into the world with her equipment and tried to apply what she's learned. But she came to feel that no matter how much she learned, making image into art would always be a hit-or-miss proposition. At least for her. Technically, barring accidents, she can always nail down the image. She can reproduce anything on film. But technical consistency is never going to be enough. And after a time it can become even depressing.

Mastering the technical never showed Sylvia how to take shots like the ones hanging in front of her. And after she'd nailed the technical she didn't know where else to go. The past few years have brought that kind of funk where she's started to think you're either born with that *other* kind of knowledge or you're not. You either know how to make shots like these seven before her. Or you don't.

And when that thought proved too depressing, she decided that maybe it isn't the photographer at all. That maybe it's always just the coincidence of image and time and lighting and motion and a hundred other things coming together at exactly the right moment. And it's luck that determines who's in the right place at the right time. Holding a camera.

So, she's operated on a shaky faith, assumed that if she spent enough hours walking around with a loaded camera, waiting, prepared, maybe sooner or later she'd be on the scene when all the elements came together. She'd be the one to lock them up in the frozen instant. She'd be the receptacle for the image, the conductor between the image and every pair of eyes that it might ever grace.

Whoever this photographer is, he found his moment here. He stood focused at the correct place and instant. He opened his shutter seven times, let in the light, introduced the image to the film, to the play of chemicals.

Sylvia gets an almost tactile sense while looking at the shots. She can almost feel how smooth and cool the woman's shoulder is. She can almost feel the grit of ash and stone under the woman's feet. She can practically flinch at the shower of dust, barely visible in the cones of light rays, falling on the head of the infant.

She spends another two hours in the darkroom. She gets out her magnifying glass and peers over every inch of each photo. She rearranges the order in which they hang on the dry line. She sits on the step stool and attempts to imitate the woman's posture, the arch of her back, the tilt of her shoulder and head. At one point she even takes off her sweatshirt, drapes it over her right shoulder and back, and cradles a jug of stop bath to her chest.

That's when it occurs to her. Sitting there half-naked at three A.M., shivering with the touch of a cold glass bottle. She'll go see the photographer. She'll go back to Jack Derry's and explain what she's found. She'll get the photographer's address. She'll go to his home. She'll present the seven photos.

And she'll ask him what it was like.

X

Mr. Quevedo is used to spending large amounts of time in silence. But the silence of the Hotel St. Vitus is unlike any other he has ever known. There's a deeper meaning to this kind of quiet, a sense of something lurking in the absence of noise.

Still, anything to please a customer. So he sits in the dimness of the top floor chapel-cum-office, a room made even more dim by his advancing cataracts, until Hermann Kinsky enters carrying a serving tray filled with a teapot, cups, saucers, milk, sugar, a plate of Oreos and a bulging envelope. Kinsky places the tray on the altar and sits down next to Quevedo.

"The housekeeper's day off," he says. "I hope you'll forgive the tea. I'm not very talented in the domestic arts."

"I'm sure everything is just fine," Quevedo says, though he's neither hungry nor thirsty.

"There was a type of cookie," Hermann says, "in the old country. During Hanukkah, the women of the hills would bring them to my orphanage. A very thin crust. It was said they were made with a touch of arsenic, but I never knew any of the children to die. I cannot find them here."

Quevedo nods his sympathies. "I have the same problem. So many things from my youth, I can no longer locate."

He looks to the tray, but Kinsky makes no move to pour the tea.

"This surprises me," Hermann says. "I would have

thought a man in your position could manage to locate anything he desired."

Quevedo holds his palms out. "You tell me, my friend. Where am I to get the banana water? The *dulce de leche?* Where do I go for a true dish of Bikaner stew? We gain by coming here, but we lose also. You would agree?"

"Perhaps," Kinsky says, a smile spreading, enjoying his contrariness, "some things are best left behind."

"Change," Quevedo says, "can be as kind as it is cruel."

"Is this an Argentine saying?"

"I think," Quevedo says, "it is a universal truth."

Hermann shakes his head. "No such thing."

Quevedo shrugs, nods, smiles.

"I'm moving to a new home," Kinsky blurts, the sudden volume of his voice making his guest flinch.

"So soon?"

"We've outgrown the house. It served us well for a time."

Quevedo motions loosely to the icons and crucifixes hanging around the room. "If you need help disposing—"

"Rest assured, my friend, when the time of the move comes, you will be called."

"Anything I can do to help."

"Yes, yes," Hermann says, getting up and moving to the window, his back now to Quevedo. "And would you be able to help me today, Luis?"

Quevedo knew this was coming, but he still dreads it. There's no reasoning with a man like Hermann. Customers of this nature should be avoided, no matter how profitable. In the end, the aggravation can be deadly.

"As I tried to tell you on the phone, Hermann," Quevedo says patiently, "these types of transactions take time. There is progress. We are still working."

"It has been months, my friend," *my friend* not at all what he means.

"To be a successful collector requires a great deal of en-

durance. An ability to wait for the right moment. To sometimes wait years. You know, Hermann, in trying to hurry
your acquisition, you may well have brought this delay on
yourself."

Kinsky's anger is starting to simmer, but he can only afford to give the dealer so much guff. Judgment is everything.

"Your friend's sudden departure had nothing to do with
me."

Quevedo can barely absorb this kind of insult to his intelligence. But he sucks it up for the promise of a record-
breaking commission.

"As you say. We were dealing with an unstable man.
I've known Jack for some time. I've expected this type of
vanishing act. It is not the surprise to me that it is to others."

"Exactly," Hermann says. "He was nothing to me but a
tenant. I never even visited the property. All the collections
were handled by my nephew and his people."

Quevedo almost chokes on the phrase *his people*. He
finds the gangboys—the Grey Roaches—to be "people" in
only the most generous sense of the word. He's all too familiar with their monthly visits and he promises himself
that if this deal becoems a reality, an exemption from the
standard protection fee will be part of the closing costs.
Quevedo will hand nothing over until he's assured he'll
never have to look at Felix's brutal face again.

"Tell me, Hermann, can I control mental illness? Please,
tell me, how am I to knit a man's mind back to normal?
Jack was diagnosed with the schizophrenia long ago. He
spent years at the Glaspoint Clinic in Algeria. He's been an
outpatient at Toth Care Facility since he arrived in the city.
Treated by Dr. Raglan himself. The medication fails from
time to time."

"This is an answer to me?" Kinsky says quietly. *"The*

medication fails from time to time. This should satisfy me?"

Quevedo's been in the business long enough to know that he can't win. He's here to be chastised and prodded. The sooner he concedes to that, the sooner he can leave and get back to work.

"You've been exceedingly tolerant, Hermann," he says. "Your waiting will be rewarded, I assure you. I have things in motion as we sit here. The machine is turned on, so to speak. I am expecting results any day now."

Kinsky's eyes turn not-so-subtly to the envelope on the tea tray.

"Is there a money problem, Luis? Do we need to purchase additional grease for the wheels of your machine?"

"Grease is good," Quevedo says. "More grease is always a good thing."

Kinsky nods and pushes the envelope just a few inches toward his guest. Normally, Quevedo would ignore the envelope until he was leaving, but he knows Kinsky wants him to take it right now, to put it in his pocket and acknowledge the gesture and its attached obligations. Quevedo lifts the envelope off the tray and actually makes a strained face to mime the heaviness of the package. Another customer might take this as a sign of parody and disrespect. Hermann Kinsky merely nods his agreement.

"Would you forgive me," Quevedo says, "if I ask a somewhat personal question?"

"I'm sure," Hermann says, "that would depend on the question."

Quevedo runs a hand over his face. Now he'd like a cup of the tea, no matter how bitter.

"I know the mores of my profession," he says. "Better than most. I've been in the field for so long. There are ways that things are done. Established modes of behavior. For the good of all parties involved—the buyer, the seller,

and the broker. Usually, *the less said, the better* is the guid-
ing principle.

"But," Quevedo continues, "I can't help violating the
customs in this instance. It's just so odd, really. So out of
my experience, which, as I say, has been considerable—"

"Please, Luis, just ask your question."

Quevedo pauses, leans back in his chair until he's partially lost among the shadows.

"Everything here," and Hermann can just see the broker
spread his arms, indicating the whole of the chapel, "belonged to the missing nuns?"

"The room is as we found it, yes."

"You brought nothing with you?"

"We fled Maisel in quite a hurry," a stiff, wary tone to
the voice. "And we have never been people to attach a
great sentiment to inanimate clutter."

In the dark, Quevedo snaps his fingers. "Exactly," he
says, "my point."

"I don't follow you."

"You don't fit the profile, Hermann. You don't strike me
as a collector. You don't strike me as an art lover. As someone concerned with the elemental images."

"Perhaps," Kinsky says, a sudden, murky pitch to the
voice, "you believe you know me better than you do, Mr.
Quevedo."

Quevedo realizes that he's misspoken in such a large
way that he's no longer sure of the deal. And when Kinsky
takes a step in his direction, he's not at all convinced he'll
be leaving the St. Vitus in the same manner he came in.

"Perhaps," Kinsky's voice now barely audible, his bulk
slowly moving toward Quevedo, "you do not know me at
all."

"I meant no disrespect," Quevedo says, wetting his lips,
shifting in his seat.

Kinsky comes to a stop behind his guest, the scar tissue
above Hermann's left eye pulsing. He puts a hand on

Quevedo's shoulder, reaches into his suitcoat pocket and pulls out a small crucifix. He brings the cross to Quevedo's neck, runs an edge of it across the Adam's apple until he feels the broker's throat engorge and release. Then he drops the icon into Quevedo's lap and walks back to the stained-glass.

Quevedo picks it up and moves it around in his hands, turns it over several times. It's intricately carved, forged from both wood and metal and he judges it to be Baroque Gothic, dating from the early seventeen hundreds, all horror-show details graphically depicting broken bones, torn flesh, flowing streams of blood.

"Are you a religious man, Luis?" Kinsky asks, his voice fallen back to the conversational, his finger tracing the lead borders of the window.

"I am a student of the Kabala," Quevedo answers, relieved and trying to sound serious.

"The cross you hold," Kinsky says, "is, as you say, an *elemental image* for millions of people all over the world, yes?"

Quevedo stays quiet.

"They worship before it, wear it on their persons. They bow down before it. It is a symbol of their faith. It is a sign of something beyond themselves. Beyond this brutal world. I don't understand people who believe in signs and symbols, Luis. But I would like to. I would give more than you can imagine to feel what they feel."

Quevedo looks down at his hands, tries to estimate the weight of the crucifix.

"I find Quinsigamond," Kinsky says, "much like old Maisel. Both are built on seven hills. Both serve as home for many tribes. People brushing up against each other. Each night exploding with transactions of every variety. Everyone trying to summon up one demon and strike down another.

"I will die a committed atheist, Luis. But I was born a

Jew. I can no longer believe in a God, but I made sure I sent the boys to the Talmud schools. Why do you think that is, Luis?"

Quevedo knows better than to try and answer.

"There is no one left from before. Most of my people perished in Lidice. The rest were taken more recently in the July Sweep. My wife, Julia, she died giving birth to my son, Jakob. Now, there is only myself, and Jakob, and my nephew Felix."

Kinsky moves back to the altar and finally begins to pour tea that, Quevedo knows, neither of them will drink.

"Genocide," Hermann says, "is a stunning concept. We see it over and over again. Never too much time in between. But we cannot seem to get our minds around it."

He strolls back to Quevedo, takes the crucifix from him.

"When my mother was horsewhipped to death on the hottest day of the summer, in a two-day pogrom that still has no name, I lost, forever, my past. When my Julia convulsed giving life to Jakob, I lost my present. And when my son finally turns on me, I will have lost my future. There is no way to harm me. There is nothing that can be taken from me. I live for momentum and acquisition. This is neither good nor bad. It is simply the truth."

Kinsky repockets the cross, stares into Quevedo's creamy eyes.

"When people like yourself, like my son Jakob, when they attempt to tell me that images can change something, can change their minds, perhaps their lives, I think those people are lying to me. But I would give almost anything to be sure."

He takes a deep breath. The sound of his lungs expanding and retracting fills the small space between the two men. Hermann puts his hand gently on Quevedo's throat.

"I have no reason to tell you these things, Mr. Quevedo. You are a broker. A facilitator. You take my money and you do a job for me. I am a man with only a certain amount of patience. I ask you to do what is necessary to obtain what I want. Can you do this, Mr. Quevedo?"

Quevedo swallows, breathes in the stale air of the chapel, and says, "I will get you the pictures, Mr. Kinsky."

7

Sylvia has no idea what time she finally went to bed. Her eyes were bleary by the time she locked up the darkroom and came back upstairs. Perry's gone when she wakes up and there's no note on the kitchen table. She'll have to make some kind of peace tonight, maybe cook him some red meat. Bring home a cop video and some German beer. She should make a list.

But first she'll call in sick to the Snapshot Shack. Cora, the manager from hell who always leaves the booth stinking of cigar, tells her this is her last sick day, one more call and she'll lose the job. Cora's been crazy since she met the new regional director of the Shack, a creepy thug named Felix who dresses like something out of the old *Shaft* movies. Sylvia says she's on penicillin, for God's sake. She's got a temp of a hundred and two. They're putting cold compresses on her forehead. Cora says she's been warned and slams down the phone.

Sylvia debates taking the photos with her as she dresses. She thinks about printing up a second set for safekeeping, but she knows if she goes down in the cellar it'll be afternoon before she gets down to the Canal Zone. She leaves the shots in the darkroom. She takes her Canon and on the bus down to the Zone she loads a fresh roll of film and daydreams titles for the Aquinas series.

Skin & Stone, #s 1 -7.
Last Inhabitants of the Cathedral.
Madonna and Child, Forgotten, Post-Apocalypse.

Everything sounds too gallery-hip to her. It's more likely the series has no name, that if the artist couldn't bring himself to finish the work, he probably didn't even consider titling it. She keeps coming back to the question of what was going through the photographer's mind each time he pressed the shutter button. She's not sure why this is so important to her. It's probably another conceit, another hope for a dream methodology, a system for turning yourself into a real artist, injecting yourself with instinct and vision. What if the photographer could, in fact, tell her exactly what he was thinking when he captured those seven pictures? What if he could convey the exact experience, nail down for her the feel of the moment, the aura that came from his subjects, the surety of his focus and timing and overall judgment? What would it get her? Would she walk away from this stranger any closer to finding and nailing her own moment, to freezing her own seven pieces of vision?

She gets off the bus on West Street, walks around the corner onto Waldstein and down a block to Jack Derry's. She pulls open the door and steps into the shop and stares at a completely empty shell. She moves inside, stands in the center of the room and turns full around. The entire store has been stripped. The piles upon piles of unsorted equipment have vanished. The plywood counter is completely cleared. The antique cash register is missing. Even the curtain that hid the back storeroom is gone.

This is impossible. She was here twenty hours ago. The more she looks around, the more she starts to notice small things. Weird, quirky, little things. The store has been more than stripped. It's been gutted. The face plates are missing from the electrical outlets. A full section of paneling has been torn off a side wall exposing the gouged plaster underneath. And behind the counter what might have been a phone jack has been ripped out, leaving a half-inch of multicolored wires hanging in the air. There isn't a single camera or lens or flash to be found. Not a filter or canister of film. If you didn't look at the sign outside, you'd never know what had once been sold in here.

She walks into the storeroom and it's the same story. There's a wall of metal cabinets, the doors wide open and not a thing inside. The walls of shelving are all completely bare. There isn't a bag of rubbish nor a basket of trash. Not a carton of useless junk left behind for the next tenant to deal with. There's not a scrap of physical evidence that yesterday at this time, this store housed a used-camera business that had been in operation, according to the sign out front, since 1965.

She's still standing in the storeroom in shock, staring at the empty storage shelves, when she hears the voice.

"You're looking for Derry?"

Her heart punches in her chest and she spins around, off-balance, to see a tall, elderly man standing in the front entrance. She takes a breath and a swallow and says," Excuse me?" even though she heard his question.

He steps into the store and says, "Forgive me. I didn't mean to startle you."

He's got some sort of accent that Sylvia can't place and as he steps closer she sees he's carrying one of those retractable white canes and she looks up to his face and sees that his eyes are completely whited out, glazed over with such severe cataracts that the pupils are no longer even visible. The glazing of the eyes gives him the look of a malignant librarian. He's got huge ears. His hair is thin and wispy and white and combed back over the crown of his head, but his eyebrows are as thick as caterpillars. The top half of his face is gaunt, the bottom almost jowly. His skin is the color of faded newspaper.

She comes out of the storeroom as far as the front counter.

"No, that's all right. No problem. I just . . . I was in here yesterday. What happened? Where'd he go?"

The old man sighs and shuffles forward until his right hand touches the countertop. He's dressed in a kind of old-fashioned three-piece suit that's gone seedy and permanently rumpled. But there's something about the way he carries himself. Kind of formal and dignified. Really sort of archaic. Like Sylvia's idea of old-time European. Like the way she'd expect some early-century count or duke to hold himself.

"I was hoping," he says, "you might tell me."

She shrugs and then realizes he probably can't see her and says, "I'm just a customer. Was a customer. I picked up a camera here yesterday. I haven't even paid for it yet. I needed to talk to—"

"Derry," he interrupts.

"Yeah," she says, "Mr. Derry. About the camera. I need to pay him."

"I'm afraid," he says, "I have just the opposite problem. Derry owes me a good deal of money. I was worried something like this might happen."

He tilts his head back until his face is aimed at the ceiling. It makes her uncomfortable and she says, "This is crazy. He can't just pack up and disappear overnight. That doesn't happen."

He brings his head back down. "It appears that is exactly what has happened."

"I can't believe this."

The man folds his hands together and rests them on the counter. "You are not one of Derry's regular customers?" he says.

She looks at his face, then looks past him to the front door and it suddenly strikes her how out of place he appears. The old suit and the formal manner. They're in the Canal Zone, for God's sake.

"Do you work here?" she asks.

He gives a brief smile and shakes his head. "Forgive me, again. Derry's departure is no excuse for my rudeness." He actually bows slightly and says, "I am Luis Quevedo. I am the manager next door. Derry was my neighbor, you see."

"Sylvia Krafft," she says and puts out her hand to shake, but he takes it and brings it up to his lips and kisses it.

She gets a little flustered and amused and blurts out, "Next door?" then immediately regrets it. But Mr. Quevedo just smiles and nods, takes a business card from his pocket and extends it toward her. She looks at it and reads

Brody's Adult Books
purveyors of fine erotica
custom tailored to your individual needs
L. Quevedo, manager

"You manage the place next door?" she says.

"For over twenty years now," he says. "It was the first job I found after I emigrated. It has supported me well all these years."

"I'm sorry," she says. "I didn't mean to sound so surprised. You just don't look . . . I mean, you just didn't seem—"

"Have you ever visited my store?" he asks.

"No," she says, biting off a laugh. "No, I don't believe I've ever visited."

His shoulders sag a bit and he nods and says, "Would you like to visit now?"

"Oh," she says, caught off guard. "Well, I don't think so. Thank you for the offer and all. But I should really get going. I should really—"

"It's very slow in the morning," he says. "I could make us some tea. We could discuss our mutual problem."

"Problem?"

"How to find Derry? You still wish to find Derry, don't you?"

"Yeah," she says. "Yes, but—"

"Please, Sylvia, you have nothing to fear from an old man. You can see that, can't you?"

"It's not that. I—"

"I could tell you some things that might help you locate him. After twenty years, a man comes to know some things about his neighbor."

"What things?" she says.

"Come next door," he says, extending his arm like some elderly groom. "Come now. I will give you a tour of my shop. Aren't you the least bit curious? I find most people are."

"What things do you know about Mr. Derry?" she asks.

"Let us have some tea, Sylvia," he says, gesturing toward the door with his head. "We can relax. I'll tell you everything."

She moves around the counter, all set to walk past him and head home. But she surprises herself by stopping at the door and turning back and saying, "After you."

"Wonderful," he says and gives a snap of his wrist to assemble his cane. She's a little startled by the vigor of his movement. He comes up next to her and again extends his arm and not knowing what else to do, she takes it, as if he were some bizarre and long-lost grandfather, and they step out onto the sidewalk.

"The weather people," Mr. Quevedo says, "they are predicting a particularly cold winter."

They step over to the adjoining storefront and he pulls a set of keys from his suitcoat pocket. Sylvia watches his hands tremble a bit as he tries to fit the correct key into the slot. Like Jack Derry's the front of the building is red brick with two inset plate glass windows on either side of the doorway. There's no neon above the entrance, however, just a handpainted sign, slightly faded, with calligraphied lettering that reads *Brody's Adult Books* on what looks like a steel-plated door. The front windows of the shop have some kind of smoked glaze over them that makes it almost impossible to see inside.

"I hate the winter myself," Mr. Quevedo says, pushing the door open and stepping aside so she can enter. It's dark inside until he throws a wall switch and the room fills with an old-fashioned kind of yellowish glow from stencilled globe lamps mounted high up on the walls.

"May I take your coat?" he asks, but she shakes him off.

"No thanks," she says, folding her arms. "I can only stay a few minutes."

Somewhere in the rear of the store a phone starts to ring.

"That's unusual," he says, seemingly to himself. "Make yourself at home. I'll be back in just a moment." He disappears down a tall aisle of bookcases and after a second the ringing stops.

The shop is nothing like Sylvia would have expected. She's never been in one of these places before, but she's got to imagine Brody's is the exception and not the rule. If it weren't for the sign on the door, she'd mistake it for a cozy, secondhand book den, the kind of place you'd stumble upon in one of those semi-sleepy Berkshire towns. The only thing it shares with Derry's location. She expected a kind of sleazy, shabby dump, sort of a gritty, stale shack with dirty linoleum on the floor and peeling paint and steaming radiators and lines of these hard-up raincoat perverts drooling over crumpled magazines.

Brody's is as neat as some tony doctor's office, but a lot warmer. There are beautiful Persian rugs on the floor and the walls are covered with what look like mahogany bookshelves. There are a few prints hanging on an open wall, all framed in antique gilt. She's struck immediately by the one she recognizes—Jean Fouquet's *Madonna and Child,* a painting that's always bothered her a little, probably due to all those wooden-faced angels surrounding the mother and infant. Today, it's like some eerie warning sign of coincidence.

There are two brocade-covered settees facing each other and separated by a low, wide, heavy-looking coffee table covered with oversized art books. It's only when you start to settle in and look closer that the true nature of the shop becomes recognizable. The porcelain figurines displayed here and there on shelves are locked into various stages of lewd behavior. The leather-bound coffee table books sport titles like *Beyond the Kama Sutra* and *A Manual for Extended Ecstasy.* Even the coat rack in the corner seems to have a slightly phallic design to it.

She starts to walk toward a glass cabinet with a sign above it that reads *First Editions—Please ask the manager for help,* when Mr. Quevedo returns to the front of the store. His white cane is gone and he has no difficulty in making his way to the couch.

"Excuse the interruption," he says and gestures that she should take a seat opposite him. "A customer calling from Brazil with an order."

She sits on the edge of the settee. "You have a customer from Brazil?"

"I have several," he says. "The majority of our business has always been mail order. We send out catalogues quarterly. We tend to service what is called the plush end of the customer base. Cosmopolitan. Educated and urbane. Old family money."

"I had no idea. I mean, this isn't what I expected to find in here."

"You've passed by our store before?"

"A few times," she says. "I'm not from this part of the city."

"You're a native?" he asks and seems surprised.

"Whole life. I went away to college but that's it. You're not from here, are you? I hear an accent."

A teakettle begins to whistle and he smiles, mouths the words *excuse me* and moves again to the back of the store. She hears a moment of muffled clatter like dishes clinking together, then the whistle sound dies away and it's silent in the store and suddenly she starts to think she should get up and leave before the old man comes back.

Instead, she opens one of the art books on the coffee table and finds herself looking at a full-page artist's rendering of some obscure and acrobatic coitus. The style is clear and detailed, close to photo-real. There's a man and woman, fully naked, sprawled on a stark white background and depicted from above. And she can't take her eyes off them until she hears Mr. Quevedo clear his throat and turns to see him standing behind the settee carrying a small silver tray that holds a teapot and two cups.

She closes the book immediately and shifts her position. She's both embarrassed and nervous, as if her mother had caught her disobeying some strict commandment. But then it occurs to her—*the man's blind, right? He can't see what I'm doing, can he?*

Whatever Mr. Quevedo can or cannot see, he makes no mention of the book. He places the tray down on the table and fills her teacup with a steaming, rose-colored liquid.

"I was born," he says, picking up the conversation, "in Buenos Aires. A small suburban district called, if you will believe it, Palermo. But I spent a good deal of my formative years traveling the continent. Actually, I've resided here in Quinsigamond longer than anywhere else. It took me years to find a city that fit my needs. I have no intention of moving again."

Sylvia takes a sip of the tea. It has an overly perfumed smell, but it tastes delicious. "And how did you come to live here?"

"That," he says, "is a long and very tedious story."

He pours himself a cup, sticks his little finger into the tea, waits a beat, then uncaps the pot and pours his cup back inside. He brings his hand up to his mouth and dabs at his lips with the little finger.

She looks away, takes another sip of her tea. She says, "You mentioned that you might know how I could find Mr. Derry."

"Possibly," he says and she can't help but stare at his eyes. They're like those cloudy marbles you used to see in the candy store as a kid. They're like sockets of watery milk. They're off-putting and they almost make her cringe, but she can't stop focusing in on them.

"Is there a reason that Mr. Derry would have stripped the shop and disappeared like this overnight?"

He gives her an indulgent smile.

"The problem, my dear, is that there are many reasons." He pauses, changes the tone of his voice and asks, "You purchased a camera from him recently?"

"A used Aquinas. A real find. It's twenty years old, but it's in great shape. The thing is, Derry told me to take it home and try it out. I haven't paid for it yet."

"Forgive me," he says, pours another cup of tea and goes through the same routine with his little finger. This time, however, he leaves the tea in his cup. "Most people would not deem this a problem. I think most people would consider this a great stroke of fortune."

"You're saying I should just keep the camera."

He sips at the tea and shrugs. "You came today to pay the man. Your intentions were honorable. You are not the one who disappeared, are you?"

"Well, no," she says, "but—"

He leans forward a bit. "There is another problem?"

"It's not a problem, really, I just wanted . . ."

"You had questions about the camera?"

Sylvia feels like he's pressuring her, leaning in toward her. She feels like she doesn't want to tell him about the photographs. And yet he may know something about how to find Derry. So she says, "There was some film left in the camera. I assume it belonged to the previous owner. I was hoping Mr. Derry could help me return it."

"Return the film?"

"Yeah. Exactly."

"Couldn't the previous owner simply purchase new film? I'm afraid I don't understand."

She can feel the manipulation. The old guy wants the whole story. And it's clear he's not going to come up with any help until he gets some explanation.

She puts down her teacup. "I guess I haven't made myself clear. You see, the film had been exposed. The previous owner had already taken some pictures. I wanted to return the pictures."

He sits back, makes a big effort at crossing his legs, exerts a lot of energy. Then he folds his hands together and rests them on his belly. He stares at her, suddenly no longer grandfatherly but more like some weary grade-school principal who's too long in his job and too far from retirement. Sylvia's uncomfortable with his look and she wants to leave, maybe drive out to the Snapshot Shack and relieve Cora, sit in the booth alone for the rest of the day listening to AM radio and looking over people's vacation pictures.

"You developed the photographs," Mr. Quevedo says quietly.

"I have a darkroom," she says, "In my cellar. I'm a photographer."

He waits for a minute staring at her the whole time, then says, "Would I be familiar with your work?"

Now she's embarrassed.

"It's not like that," she says. "I don't make my living at it. I just take a lot of pictures. I go out and shoot a lot of film."

"A hobby then?"

She hates the word.

"Not, not at all. Not a hobby."

She's fumbling. She can't seem to order her thoughts.

"I'm just starting out," she says. "I've had some problems. Some . . ."

"Complications," he finishes for her.

"There was a family illness. My mother passed away."

He nods, concerned. Patriarchal.

"I'm very sorry," he says.

"I just got off track for a while," she says. "I lost my focus."

More solemn nodding. He pulls at the stiff cuffs of his shirt and they sit in silence. Sylvia tries to concentrate on the tea, looks down and pretends to study the swirling patterns of the carpet.

"These photographs you developed," he says, "the ones from the camera. What did you find?"

Her eyes come up to his face and she says, "They were stunning."

"Nature scenes?" he asks.

"No. Nothing like that. There were seven shots. All of the same subjects. A woman and her child. An infant. Inside an old building of some sort. Incredible use of shadow. The gradations were—"

"Masterful?" he says.

She's getting annoyed with his interruptions.

"The best thing I can say is they were genuine. They hit me like a bullet. They hung on. It's difficult to explain."

"Believe me, Sylvia," he says, "twenty years in this business, you come to understand the importance of the elemental image."

She looks past him at the Fouquet.

"I guess that would be true," she says, then adds, "I like that phrase. Elemental image."

But he's moved on. He's tapping his chin and mouth with his long index finger.

"You know," he says, "the work sounds very much like Propp."

She waits for him to go on and when he doesn't she says, "Excuse me?"

"Oh, don't misunderstand," he says. "I'm saying it's most likely a talented imitator. Perhaps a student studying the technique of the master."

"Propp?"

"You disagree?" he says. "Well, of course, you've seen the work. And your description was very generic. You have to understand my specialty is more literary. And classical rather than contemporary. As you can imagine, I'm not very well versed in photography. Always a step removed, so to speak. A passing familiarity with the basics. When I hear *shadowy Madonna and child*, naturally I think of Propp."

"Naturally," she says.

"Are you one of the fans or one of the detractors?" he asks. "It has been my experience that there is no fence-sitting when it comes to Propp."

She takes a deep breath. If she tries to act like she knows what he's talking about she'll only look more foolish in the end. So she exposes her ignorance, her glaring un-hipness. She asks, "Who is Propp?"

Mr. Quevedo is taken aback. He straightens up and un-crosses his legs, leans forward toward her. He's no longer the school principal, but the understanding priest of Sylvia's childhood dreams.

He clears his throat, lowers his voice and says, "Forgive me again, Sylvia. I've been quite impolite all morning. I forget that simply because someone is legend in the Canal Zone it does not necessarily mean they are a household word beyond our borders. You are not familiar with Terrence Propp?"

"I assume he's a photographer?"

He nods. "I'm really not an authority. I'm an old man

who takes his supper in the cafés. I've heard the stories and rumors for so long now that I assume the rest of the world is just as soaked in the myth."

"The myth?"

"I can give you the names of some who can help you. Very likely, they can look at the photographs and tell you who took them. Propp is their obsession, not mine."

"You're using words like *myth* and *obsession*. I can't believe I haven't heard of this guy."

He shrugs, gives a smile that's not quite sheepish. He blinks a few times and says, "Is is so surprising really? There is no single pool anymore. There hasn't been for some time. Everything has fragmented. Why should culture follow a different road? Propp is a single particle, floating in a narrow vein. Though I warn you, Sylvia, the faithful will tell you otherwise. And quite emphatically."

"It's just a little strange,"she says. "I mean, I go to the galleries regularly. I hang around the art sections at all the bookstores. I would think I would have—"

"I once heard it said that Propp is only stumbled upon by those he wishes to have stumble upon him."

She thinks for a second and says, "I don't follow you."

He waves a hand at her.

"It was said by a fanatic. So much cryptic babble. You know the young ones down here, they think their art is some mystery religion. That's the problem with cultists. They always lose their capacity for humor. Of course I believe in commitment to the work. And yes, Sylvia, there can be fun in the hoax. In gamesmanship. I'm no stranger to the allure. The stunts we used to dream up back at the Tronador. I could go on all day. But there is a difference between walking the dog and being on the wrong end of the leash. Between using the mystery and having it use you."

Sylvia doesn't know what the hell he's talking about.

"Is there any chance," she asks, "you could tell me where I could find Mr. Propp himself?"

He erupts with laughter. His knee hits the coffee table and tea sloshes out of his cup. Then just as quickly he brings himself under control, seemingly embarrassed by the outburst. He closes his eyes and works his mouth to calm himself, then he says, "I don't know what has gotten into me today. I've been terribly rude to a lovely guest. My mother, she would spin in her grave if she could see."

Sylvia sits silently and waits for the explanation and when Quevedo realizes that she's not going to speak, he goes through another small session of throat clearing, then says, "The truth is, Sylvia, there is no chance I could possibly direct you to Terrence Propp."

"Is he dead?" she asks.

"I have no idea."

There's another round of silence until she says, "Maybe I should go," and this prompts the old man to stand up with a little difficulty.

"Please, I realize this is frustrating, but it's simply because you're not familiar with the history. I truly do not know whether Terrence Propp is among the living or the dead. And believe me, no matter what the zealots say to you, they don't know either. Don't be taken in, Sylvia."

He tilts forward a bit, reaches around to his back pants pocket, pulls out a linen handkerchief and begins to mop up the spilt tea.

"Maybe you could give me the name of one of those people," Sylvia says. "Someone who could tell me more about Mr. Propp."

All Mr. Quevedo's attention seems to be taken up with drying the table.

"Are you sure you want to do this, Sylvia?" He sounds distracted, almost cranky. She wants to say *Hey, Mister, you're the one who dragged me into this store and started the conversation.*

"Perhaps," he says, "you should sleep on it. You could call me tomorrow."

She says, "You could be with Mr. Derry tomorrow."

"I'm not going anywhere, my dear. I'm here for the duration."

"How about that name, Mr. Quevedo?"

He stands there, blank faced, seeming to stare at her with those gauzy, creamy eyes. Then he does a little, stiff march to the front door and opens it, indicating that she should go. She follows him to the door, stops in the entryway and says, "Well, anyway, thank you for the tea."

He nods, clicks his heels together and says, "Rory Gaston. You can find him at Der Geheime Garten. A little café just a few blocks from here. Der Garten, to the regulars."

Then he leans forward and plants a dry, withered-feeling kiss on her right cheek, takes her elbow and ushers her out onto the sidewalk. Sylvia turns to thank him, but he's already closed the door.

10

Sylvia looks up and down Waldstein, then walks back down to Jack Derry's and stares in the window. She doesn't know what she expects to see. It's still deserted and there's still no trace that yesterday she stood at the plywood counter, surrounded by hundreds of dusty piles of hocked and traded camera equipment, and talked with Mr. Derry and walked back out again with her dreamed-about Aquinas. There's no sign that the store was ever anything but deserted. That it didn't fall to vacancy ten years ago rather than last night.

She glances to her left and sees a greasy-looking guy in army fatigues leaning against the stop sign and staring at her, making noises with his mouth that she can't hear. As soon as their eyes meet, he starts making these horrible, exaggerated kissing sounds and he jams his hands into his coat pockets and goes into a bizarre Elvis impersonation, swinging his hips in a slow circle as if trying to keep a Hula Hoop aloft.

She turns away from Jack Derry's and starts to head for Voegelin Avenue. A pack of five or six Zone kids run past her in full bohemian colors—leather trench coats, bandanna'd skulls, earrings that hang to the neck. They're all carrying something in their arms and Sylvia can't see what it is until one of them trips and sprawls into the middle of the road and gets to his knees, his chest covered with running, yellow yolk, and he starts yelling, "My fucking eggs." He gets up, starts to wipe at his chest with his hands, gives up the effort as futile and continues on after his friends.

Sylvia comes around the corner of Voegelin and onto Watson and immediately sees where the artists were headed. She's stopped by a huge crowd that's taken over the entire street. Traffic can't pass and a line of cars is starting to form and lean on their horns. The noise of the crowd seems to increase as she starts to wade through it and then there's an awful squeal, that piercing high-pitched whine of feedback that a radio or amplifier will sometimes make. The crowd flinches in unison as the whine dies and then a rolling, familiar voice shouts, "I'm sorry, people. Very sorry. Is it working, Raymond? Can they hear me?"

She's half a block away from the heart of the action but she can see the crowd's center is in front of Herzog's Erotic Palace, known locally as *the Skin Palace,* a baroque and expansive X-rated movie house that's also the oldest theater in Quinsigamond. More an architectural miracle than a building, it's a five-story Moderne temple and just the sight of it makes all the shoebox mall cineplexes even more heinous.

Sylvia squeezes through bodies until she's directly opposite Herzog's. She spots a mailbox and hoists herself up on it in time to see Reverend Garland Boetell being elevated onto the roof of an old white Cadillac that has the words *Chariot of Virtue* emblazoned on its side in glitter paint. Boetell's got a microphone of some kind gripped in both his hands and as he blows across its head, the street fills with the sound of a moist wind. The Chariot of Virtue has been pulled up onto the sidewalk and it's surrounded by what must be the Reverend's inner core, about a dozen men and women led by the Brazilian teen aide-de-camp Fernando, all of them dressed in what look like heavy robes, kind of like monk's robes, with cowl hoods hanging down the back and loose, rope-like belts. This crew is walking in slow circles around the car, carrying placards with messages like *Whores of Babylon, Your Time Has Come* and *Save the Children From This Filth* and *Carnal Sinners Reside Within.*

In front of the entrance to Herzog's is a line of the Palace's resident muscle, beefy steroid cases all decked out in logo'd spandex jackets and cowboy boots. They've formed a well-pumped barricade in front of the door by standing shoulder to shoulder. They've got their folded hands clasped in front of their groins, secret-service style. And they're looking none too happy. It's clear they'd like to put a quick and definitive stop to this spectacle, but they must have orders from the boss to simply hold the front line until the lawyers decide how to play things.

Boetell seems thrilled by the presence of the bouncers. He's a pro at this kind of media event and it's always more effective to rail against human flesh, no matter how restrained, than inanimate brick and mortar.

"Look at them before us," the Reverend bellows into the microphone, "guarding the gates to hell itself. Boys," he addresses the bouncers directly, "when you stand before the Almighty on your personal judgment day and the Lord asks you how you spent your days on the earth, what, in the name of mercy, are you going to tell him? What kind of answer will you give to the face of your one and only savior? Will you say, *Sweet Jesus, I served in the legion of the antichrist?* Will you say, *Dear Lord A'mighty, I ushered the misguided into the cushioned seats of damnation?* Fall on your knees here and now, sinners, and offer up prayer with Reverend Boetell that we might buy back your immortal souls from the demon."

But the bouncers aren't having any of it. They keep their rigid stances behind their bushy mustaches until one guy at the end gives in to the temptation and flashes Boetell a defiant middle finger.

The Reverend wheels to the crowd and barks, "Then we must pray for them, my friends. It is our mission on this rock. Let us now raise our voices so that the strength of the Archangel might descend upon us and we prove worthy to fight the final battle at the time of Millennium. Sing now with me, people. Sing loud and send your voices soaring to heaven that he might bring the rain of fire down upon this bastion of carnal *hideousness*. That he might smite this wicked temple as he did Sodom and Gomorrah."

As if on cue the gang in the robes circling the Caddy breaks into "Nearer My God To Thee." The first few yards of people beyond them join in the singing. But after that the street is clogged with packs of Canalites and furious motorists and they start in with catcalls and heckling. Boetell yells above the voices of his choir, "Your taunting will only make us stronger. You are advised, one and all, that the *decent* people of Quinsigamond are taking back their city. They *will* not tolerate abominations such as this one," a wildly dramatic gesture toward the Skin Palace. "They are linking *arms* with brethren from the East Coast to the West. The day of the Lord is *upon* us, heathens. Get thee behind me. The family of God *will* trample you under its heel."

It's on this last line that the egg throwing starts. Boetell catches one right on the jaw. The splatter covers his whole face, but he looks more thrilled than shocked, as if this were the perfect turn of events, the next exact step in a scripted pageant. He makes a show of mopping his face with the sleeve of his white suitcoat, but it's really just a brush to a single cheek and the bulk of the yolk still shows like a runny scar.

A kid with a mohawk haircut charges the Caddy with a full, open carton of fresh grade-As, hoping to give the Reverend a complete pelting, but one of the singing disciples suddenly drops into a defensive stance, takes his *2 Thessalonians 1:8,9* placard from his shoulder and starts swinging it like a battle-ax. On his third swing he nails mohawk in the stomach and the kid crumbles to the pavement.

The crowd starts to go crazy, pushing and shoving and screaming. The bouncers look at each other, starting to get edgy, unsure of what to do next. Boetell closes his eyes and turns his head to the heavens. He brings the mike to his lips and yells, "Send us help in our hour of need, Sweet Jesus. Send us a phalanx of reinforcements to battle those who would blaspheme the flesh and defile the soul. On your command let an army of righteous warriors join our holy platoon and war on this lascivious enemy of unbridled lust and perversion."

And the Reverend gets his wish. A column of marching women breaks out of an alley next to the Palace and, with an almost military precision, starts to move in the direction of the Chariot of Virtue. The crowd seems so stunned by their appearance that it parts like a biblical sea and the unit raises its clenched fists in an up-and-down power salute and comes to a stop at the hood of the Caddy.

Boetell falls to his knees, careful not to dent the roof, and says, "You have rewarded our faith. You have sent the enemies of our enemies to help us beat the writhing beast into submission. Let us say *Amen.*"

An amen chorus sweeps through the faithful, followed by a lot of Praising the Lord. The new arrivals, however, seem less than enthusiastic about the revival rhetoric. The women are all dressed in black-and-white striped, smock-like tunics and matching pants. They've got large blocklike numbers stenciled in black on their backs. It's like a costume party where everyone decided to show up as old-time prisoners, like inmates in some ancient jailbreak movie. And they've all got silver tape over their mouths. One woman steps up onto the Caddy's bumper, then up to the hood, holds her hands up over her head to get the crowd's attention, waits a beat, then gives a signal to her people and in unison they all make an exaggerated display of ripping the tape from their faces and hurling it to the ground. The leader then jumps up next to Boetell and grabs the microphone from him.

"We are the Women's American Resistance," and she wheels and faces the Palace bouncers, stretches her arm out and points at them and starts to yell, "Murderers, Murderers, Murderers," in the chanting manner of a basketball cheer, but with a lifetime's worth of hate and contempt behind every syllable. Her crew on the street joins in and goes to work unrolling a banner that comes to read *Pornography Is Genocide.*

The crowd seems to split into choruses of both cheers and boos and turns in on itself. Little donnybrooks erupt everywhere. One of the bouncers whispers into the ear of another, then unlocks a door behind him and runs inside. Sylvia hears police sirens in the distance as she watches Boetell trying to take the microphone back from his new partner and a fresh firestorm of eggs starts to rain down on everyone within splattering distance of the Cadillac. To the left, a gridlocked produce trucker is standing red-faced at the rear of his rig handing shallow wooden crates of tomatoes to brother truckers who look drunk with the prospects before them. A guy dressed in milkman's overalls starts speedballing the tomatoes at the Caddy, but his first assault goes wide and hammers one of the bouncers. Palace security now goes into a crouch position and they all take some kind of black leather saps from the backs of their pants and hold them up chest-level, ready to break some bones.

The zebra-women continue flying their *Genocide* flag, but they've all pulled what looks like tubes of mace from somewhere in their costumes. A burly, bald-headed guy in an old-time baseball jacket makes the stupid mistake of choosing this moment to attempt a solo charge to rip down the women's banner and takes a chemical blast to the face. He goes down like a rock, screaming, hands to his eyes.

And that's when the police horses come in like a three-man cavalry, but almost immediately they're engulfed and the surge of the crowd panics the animals and the horses start to rear up. Before Sylvia turns away, she sees a young kid knocked to the ground by a flying hoof and a panicking cop trying to maneuver his reins with one hand and yell into a walkie-talkie with the other.

Within minutes a riot squad arrives and breaks through to the meat of the upheaval. And it's only when Sylvia sees the bobbing rows of their white helmets cutting through the plain of bodies, making a wedge and checking their way toward the Palace, that she thinks to bring her camera up to her eye.

She starts firing immediately, the first shots reflexive and unfocused, and then she gets her bearings and the shock and fear turn into this adrenal blast and she jumps down from the mailbox and starts moving like this ghost, this bodiless form injected into the melee not just to record, not only to freeze and seal these horrible moments, but to do something else with them. To make them into something more.

She takes steps, locks in place, pivots side to side, scans

the mob and instantly picks out her image. She shoots an enraged face, a cocked baseball bat, a body being pushed to the ground. She shoots Boetell with his mouth gaping and flat-palmed hand in the air, trying to trace the sign of the cross. She shoots four Teamsters holding a terrified Canal freak up above their heads, ready to launch him into the sky. She shoots an *Intercourse Is Abuse* placard, liberated from its owner and being used to smash in the windows of a discount appliance store. She shoots a wave of charging looters hauling stereos, televisions, microwave ovens from the store window. She shoots the arrival of the first of the Bangkok Park gangs—the Grey Roaches—jogging in to see what can be scored and picked out of this explosion of unexpected opportunity.

And then she's knocked to the street. She doesn't even see her attacker. She instinctively cradles the camera into her chest as she goes down full on the knees. Before she can get up, someone behind her starts screaming, "Cops," and she pivots on her behind and brings the camera back to her eye in time to see a line of police racing the Roaches to the already ravaged appliance store. She shoots a bunch of frames of the charge. She freezes a gangboy swinging a fungo bat at a masked cop. She nails the cop knocking the bat from the kid's hands with an arcing swing of his nightstick across the gangboy's arms. She captures the breaking of the kid's elbow, the free-fall to the street.

Suddenly, she's making little movies, cinema reduced to its minimal essence, series of shots, four and five frames to a complete sequence. And all of it pure violence. Everyone is fighting everyone else and there's very little sense of allegiances, of side against side. What appears to have started out as a classic protest event—amplified speeches setting cause against cause—has almost instantly degenerated into a fine definition of anarchy. Every man for himself and God against all. There's blood everywhere and the Roaches have managed to set fire to the appliance mart.

Sylvia finds a pocket of clearing and runs across the street, gets her back against the wall of Herzog's and starts focusing in on the flames. From the glass-shattered entryway of the mart, a cop and a Roach come rolling into the street, locked in a full-body clench, the cop trying to secure a hold around the Roach's neck, the Roach squirming low, grabbing the cop waist-level and throwing short jabs to the groin. They spin out into the street, the cop rolling at the right moment to settle into an upright position on the Roach's chest. And then he starts in with a cut-down billy club, first battering the kid's head until the body goes prone and then grabbing the club with a hand at either end and coming down on the windpipe. Sylvia should be screaming and running into the street. But she's just keeping her right index finger on the shutter release. Cementing the image. Exposing this suffocation to chemical-treated paper. Freezing the horrible instant.

Until the scene through the viewfinder goes black and the camera gets smashed back into her face and she's back down on the sidewalk and now she's screaming and looking up at another, younger cop, his face both terrified and furious. He's hovering over her like he's not sure what to do for a second, then he reaches down and grabs the camera, but Sylvia doesn't let go, she's got both hands on the shoulder strap and it's five seconds of a pathetic and absurd tug of war and she doesn't know why he hasn't just let loose with his club again, but before the idea can occur, one of the Palace bouncers tackles the cop and before Sylvia can stand back up, someone has her under the arms and pulls her hard, backwards, her legs dragging across the sidewalk, back through a doorway and inside to the lobby of Herzog's.

Then she's released and she stays on the ground but rolls over onto her knees. She looks up to see a large man with an enormous bald head which he bows toward her as he extends a hand to help her to her feet. She gets up on her own, dazed and just starting to feel the pain in her right eye.

"I'm afraid," the man says, "you are going to have what they once called a shiner."

Sylvia brings a hand up to her eye, tries to touch it gingerly, then she brings the hand down to her chest and says, "My camera."

The bald man nods and says, "My people will try to retrieve it. We'll see what we can do. Are you from the *Spy?*"

She looks up at him, suddenly feeling shaky and nauseated.

"Are you going to be all right?" he asks.

She tries to say *no,* but all she can do is take halting breaths.

"Come," he says. "It's all right. You are safe now. Come to my office. You'll be fine. We'll wait out this incident upstairs."

He takes her by the arm and she lets him guide her through the center of a wide lobby and up a curving staircase that opens to a balcony. They break left down a corridor and finally turn through a set of double doors and into a large, airy, brick-walled room where he deposits her on a black leather couch.

She leans forward, tilts her head down near her knees, focuses on her feet. She tries to ignore the growing pain in her eye and concentrate on her breathing. After a minute she's able to look up and ask, "Is there a phone?"

The man is at the front window, hands clasped behind him. Without looking back he says, "The phones are out of service," and for the first time Sylvia realizes there's an accent, possibly German.

She puts her head in her hands and says, "I should have listened to Perry."

With this the bald man turns to face her.

"Your husband? He warned you against traveling to the Canal Zone? Yes?"

"Not my husband. But yes, he warned me."

He walks to the couch. "And you argued that it was part of your job. That you owed the risk to your paper."

"My paper?"

"Who will be more angry? he asks. "The boyfriend or the editor?"

"I don't work for the newspaper," Sylvia says.

He sits down on the couch next to her.

"You're not the photographer for the *Spy?*"

She shakes her head *no* and the nausea surges. She lowers her head again. The man gets up without a word and walks back to the window.

"The foolish bastards," he says, rubbing a large hand over the crest of his skull. "I called them a half hour ago."

"I'm sorry to disappoint you," she says. "But thank you for pulling me out of there."

He turns and stares at her, his face expressionless. Then he crosses the room again and says, "Trust me, Miss. You are far from disappointing."

He bows modestly and adds. "I am Hugo Schick. Welcome to me theatre."

"You own this place?"

"For quite some time now. Have you ever been inside before?" he leans down toward her and squints his eyes a bit. "Feel free to lie."

It's a second before she realizes he's joking.

"Just once," she says. "About two years ago. My boyfriend and I came. You know, just to see what it was like."

He straightens up and frowns. "And you didn't care for it? You didn't like the film?"

"No, it was fine," she says, too defensively. "It's just, you know, you see one of those . . . I mean, it was funny. It was all right."

He stares at her and then shrugs and starts to walk back to the window, saying over his shoulder, "I think we may be stranded here for some time. The police are having quite a time restoring order down there."

He moves to a cabinet behind his desk and Sylvia hears a clink of glass. He returns to the couch and hands her a miniature crystal champagne glass filled with a green-colored liquid.

"Absinthe," he says softly. "I get it from some dear friends in New Orleans. They keep a close eye on the wormwood content. Drink. It will calm you."

She swallows it down and for the first time sits back on the couch and breathes normally. He sits down in a matching chair and crosses his legs.

"I'll do everything in my power," he says, "to retrieve your camera."

"That's very kind of you, Mr. Schick."

"Please, Hugo. And I can call you?"

"Sylvia," she says, somehow embarrassed by the sound of her own name. "Sylvia Krafft."

"A wonderful name. A very dramatic name. Yes. I will say it suits you."

"I'll take that as a compliment."

"As it was intended," he says. "Now tell me, Sylvia. If you are not from the paper, what are you doing down here, pointing a camera around in the middle of this tumult? Is this a hobby for you, finding war zones and recording them?"

"I was just walking through here," she says. "I was just heading home after an errand. This thing just broke out around me. I stopped for a second to hear Boetell speak—"

"Boetell?" he asks, straightening in his seat.

"The preacher. The guy on top of the Cadillac with the microphone."

"Of course," he says. "Of course. Go on."

"That was it. I stopped for a second and all hell broke

loose. It was like someone put a match to a gas tank. One minute the crowd is all mumbles and sneers, the next they're tearing each other apart. I've never seen anything like it."

He looks at her doubtfully. "Please, Sylvia. Who is so innocent today?"

"I mean up close," she says. "It's different than TV. It's different from seeing pictures in the paper. I mean, to feel it on your body. It's a completely different thing."

He nods agreement. "But the camera—"

"I usually have a camera on me."

"So you are a photographer?" he says, slightly excited.

She takes another sip of absinthe, finishes the glass. "That depends," she says, "on who you ask. Do I take a lot of pictures? Yes. Do I make a living at it? Absolutely not."

"Do you wish to make a living at it?"

The question hits her, but somewhat differently than when Perry asks it. "I really don't know. It's a strange thing. I feel kind of like once you start doing it for money . . . Jesus, listen to what this sounds like."

"Yes?" he says, barely repressing a smile.

"It's just . . . It's a little hard to explain. I feel a little like if I started to sell my pictures, I'd start taking different pictures. Like I couldn't help it, you know? Like it would happen subconsciouly. I don't know. It's difficult to explain. It sounds so . . ."

"Mystical?" he offers.

She laughs. "I was going to say pretentious."

He dismisses the word. "Not at all. I have to tell you, I have a very clear idea of what you're saying here. I've struggled with this myself. The prostituting of the muse. The schizophrenia of commerce and art."

"Well, that's not exactly—" she starts, but he continues.

"It's the nature of the time and the place we work in. The breach is symptomatic of something much darker. I know exactly what you are saying here, Sylvia."

She doesn't say anything. She wishes he'd offer another drink.

"I think," he says, "that it's fortuitous we met today. In the way we did. I promise you neither of us will forget it, yes?"

"You really saved me out there," she nods. "I owe you one."

"Think nothing of it," he says, a hand flat on his chest. "All things in good time."

He reaches over and takes the glass from her hand, gets up and moves to the window. "They're turning fire hoses on the crowd," he says.

Sylvia gets up from the couch to look, then decides she doesn't want to. Instead, she glances around the office. On the wall behind Schick's desk are seven framed movie posters. They look like every other movie poster except that all of them show semi-naked people wrapped into various lewd poses. The titles are *El Jefe & the Whip, Night of the Amateur, Wynona's Tree Duck, My Solitary Diamond, Flo's Happy Ending, The Wolf Inside Sharon* and *Don Juan Triumphant.*

"I've made hundreds of films," Hugo says, now sitting on the window ledge and watching her study the posters, "but these are the ones which will last. These are the works I will be remembered by."

He seems lost in thought for a second, then walks over and says, "It occurs to me, Sylvia, while you're here waiting, perhaps, if you're feeling up to it, of course . . ."

"Yes," she says, trying to prompt him.

"Well, I wonder if possibly you might enjoy a tour of the theater."

She's not sure how to answer so she says, "Thank you, Mr. Schick, really, that's—"

"Hugo, please."

"Thank you, Hugo, that's kind of you, but I should probably just wait here until—"

"You do know the history of this building, don't you? It's the oldest functioning theater in the city."

"Yes, I've heard that, but—"

"Built by Hans Herzog in 1935. At a cost of the entire family fortune. Do you know the Herzog tragedy? Are you familiar with the story?"

"I may have read—"

"Acht, *read,*" he says, disgusted, it seems, with the printed word. "Come. Up now. Come with me, Sylvia. Allow me to give you the tour. I'll show you things that will make the incident outside a vague memory."

It's clear he won't hear *no,* and she does owe him for pulling her to safety, so she gets up from the couch and follows him to the doorway. He gestures her into the corridor and closes the door behind them and asks, "Where are you from originally, Sylvia?"

"I was born right here in Quinsigamond," she says as they start down the hall.

This seems to surprise him. He looks at her for a second as he continues to walk, then says, "Is that right? Most of my people, the people I work with, they come from somewhere else. I'm not sure I've ever met anyone who was originally born here."

"You're kidding me."

"Our line of work," he says. "We are a mobile people."

They come to a stop back at the balcony area that looks down on the lobby. It's an impressive sight. The ceiling rises up about twenty feet and the floor runs about forty or fifty feet long. The walls are curved so dramatically that when viewed from above like this, the foyer has the feel of a huge bowl. Everywhere there are mirrors and gold leaf, marble and bronze edging. It's genuinely one of the most beautiful buildings Sylvia has ever been in.

"God," she says, staring at the patterns in the tile floor, "you would never know—"and then she stops herself.

But Hugo tilts his head and smiles and finishes for her. "That they showed dirty movies inside, yes?"

"No, I just meant—"

"That's exactly what you meant, Sylvia," he says, but he doesn't seem upset.

"It's just," she tries, "I mean, I knew, I've read, that it was a significant building, you know, historically—"

"I thought you visited," he says. "With the boyfriend."

"I did, but, I don't know. We were self-conscious. We just bought our tickets and ran inside. I didn't look around."

He nods, maybe a little patronizing. "I've been attempting to restore it. Very gradually. One project at a time. As the money becomes available."

She looks back down on the lobby. "You should get the historical society down here. You should get some grant money."

He barks a laugh that fills the whole gulf before them. "The city fathers," he says, "will tolerate me as long as I stay fairly quiet and remember them at fund-raising time with an anonymous donation. I'm afraid, my dear, the care of this marvel has been left to Schick alone."

He puts his hand on the brass railing and takes a tight grip. "She is sixty years old. Designed for a year by a protégé of Donald Deskey himself. Young man named Rejlander. He used all the new materials—aluminum and Bakelite. Spent over three million dollars. This when money had a value that we can no longer comprehend in our shabby age."

He takes her by the arm and steers through a set of huge double doors into the theatre proper and Sylvia looks up to see enormous naked people coupling on the screen.

"I hope you don't mind," Hugo whispers in her ear. "The customers were already in the house when the rioting broke out. We're rerunning the feature until it's safe for them to leave."

"It's all right," she whispers back, but she's completely unprepared for this display.

She stares at the acrobatics while Hugo continues to whisper. "One thousand floor seats of symmetric Moderne perfection. Another two hundred up here in the balcony. And nine private owner's boxes running above us."

He leads her to the balcony railing. She looks down from the screen to the floor and is shocked to see the theater half-filled in the middle of the day.

"The stars that have played in this room," he says. "W. C. Fields on opening night. Mr. Ray Bolger. The Flying Wallendas. Chaplin was here. Never performed, but he was in the audience. A personal favor to Herzog himself. The next day a peasant from the *Spy* had the gall to call this treasure, this Xanadu, a *vulgar curiosity*. Can you imagine, Sylvia? It was too much for the arbiters of taste to comprehend. *Vulgar curiosity*. They say those two words broke Herzog's heart. That he never got over the affront. The moment he read that review was the beginning of his decline."

Sylvia listens to his words, but she's watching a woman having sex with three men simultaneously. It's broad daylight and she's standing in what must be the most luxurious pornographic theatre in America being lectured by a bald Viennese man as she watches graphic sex acts on a three-story screen.

"I would put my Palace," Hugo says, "up against any of them. The Pantages. The Avalon in Chicago. The Fox in Atlanta. Even S. Charles Lee and his Los Angeles. They may be larger, perhaps more ornate. But there is a feel here. An aura and an atmosphere that is unsurpassed."

He lowers his voice and adds, "Of course, I am a bit prejudiced."

"It's a stunning building," Sylvia says.

His eyes turn to the screen. "I hope you're not offended by our feature."

For some reason she wants to laugh. "This isn't exactly how I planned the day."

"Surprise," Hugo says, "is the essence of life, Sylvia. Didn't anyone ever tell you that?"

"I thought that was variety."

Before he can respond a voice behind them says, "You want to keep it down," and Sylvia flinches. They look up to the last row to see the only person in the balcony, sitting up directly under the beam of the projection light.

Hugo puts his hands on his hips and says out of the corner of his mouth, "Speaking of variety," and then, "Come with me, Sylvia. You'll love this."

She follows him up the steep stairs to the second to last row where they slide in to face this audience of one. It's a woman, about Sylvia's age, dressed in a silk, rose-colored bathrobe, but she's got her feet resting on the chair in front of her and her robe breaks away to reveal her bare legs up to her thighs. She's got blonde hair and even in this light Sylvia can tell she's got killer skin. There's a bucket of popcorn in her lap and as Hugo comes to a stop in front of her, blocking her view of the screen, she throws a kernel at him.

"Ever the narcissist," Hugo whispers, brushing at his jacket.

"Learned from the best, Schickster."

Hugo angles awkwardly in the aisle and says, "Sylvia Krafft, I would like you to meet Leni Pauline."

Sylvia reaches over and shakes Leni's hand, brings her own back wet with butter.

Leni ignores her and says to Hugo, "That's it boss, keep recruiting the amateurs. God, you couldn't do a cost analysis if your life depended on it." Then she tilts her body to the side to try to see around Hugo and says, "Honey, don't you sign a thing until you and I have a long talk."

"Once again," Hugo says, "your instincts couldn't be more wrong."

Leni throws another kernel of corn and says, "We'll see." She looks at Sylvia and says. "So are you a fan? How do you like my work?"

"Your work?" Sylvia repeats and Leni gives a huge smile and points to the screen.

Sylvia turns and looks and realizes that the woman up on the screen, the naked woman enlarged to three stories high and currently having a jar of honey dripped on her by a very tall man, also naked except for a chef's toque on his head, *that* woman is *this* woman. That woman on the screen writhing under the coating of golden liquid is Leni Pauline.

"You're very . . ." Sylvia starts and when nothing comes to her, she says, "you have beautiful skin."

Leni looks from Sylvia to Hugo and says, "What is she, a cosmetologist?"

Sylvia doesn't know whether to laugh or be annoyed, but it's Hugo that responds.

"In fact," he says, his accent seeming to get thicker, "Sylvia is an artist."

Leni tosses a kernel above her head and makes a production of catching it in her mouth.

"That right?" she says.

Sylvia starts to say *no,* but Leni continues. "I'm an artist too." She juts her jaw out and says defiantly. "Can you do *that?*"

They all pivot and look at the screen in time to see Leni writhing on a flour-covered tabletop in the midst of what looks like a large restaurant kitchen as she's doused with olive oil by a swarthy young chef.

"My God," Sylvia hears herself whisper and then hears Leni behind her say, "You still think you're an artist, sister?"

Hugo leans to Sylvia's ear and says conspiratorially, "Leni is our current starlet and raging prima donna."

Leni hits him with another popcorn kernel and mimics

his voice, "And Hugo is our current washed-up, never-made-it, almost-broke, can't-get-it-up porno king."

Hugo keeps his composure and says, "Your gratitude is humbling, my child."

"My gratitude," Leni laughs and looks to Sylvia. "What do you think, honey, should I be grateful here for the chance to hump the sandwich boy in this scene?"

Sylvia glances over her shoulder and there's Leni, spread out on a long table surrounded by luncheon meats and a roasted turkey, piles of sliced tomato and bulkie rolls, loaves of rye bread and croissants and French sticks, dishes of mustard and mayonnaise.

Leni mutters, "I was picking parsley out of my hair for a week."

Sylvia turns to Hugo and hesitantly asks, "You made this movie?"

He smiles, closes his eyes and bows his head.

"I thought you owned the theater?"

"Hugo," Leni says, "is a man of many talents."

Another piece of popcorn bounces off the huge skull and leaves a shine in the blue light from the movie. Hugo ignores it, folds his arms, stares at the screen and whispers, *"Glutton for Ravishment II* was something of an indulgence for me. I'll concede that to the critics. But I simply felt there was more to be said after the first film. I just wasn't done with these characters. They hadn't released me yet. And though I quake at the thought of further expanding her swelled head, Leni *is* genuinely breathtaking here. Truly astounding. I took us both to the brink and tore that performance out of her. But, as you can see, it was worth it."

On the screen, Leni is using a plastic spatula to smear mayonnaise on the chests of two over-endowed waiters.

Hugo puts his mouth next to Sylvia's ear and says, "You'd be amazed how little editing was required. She can be miraculous when handled properly."

Sylvia feels a second set of lips at her other ear and she flinches and turns to see Leni up out of her seat and leaning across the chair that separates them.

"Tell me you're not a bored little rich girl from Windsor Hills," she says. "Tell me you weren't jogging past *Casa Schick* when the bald one offered to teach you about art. Please, Sylvia, tell me."

Her tone annoys Sylvia. They shift so they're eye to eye and Sylvia says, "I work for a living."

Leni doesn't get angry. Her voice stays even and she looks to the screen and says, "You don't think *that's* work, sister?"

No one answers and she goes on, maybe a little conciliatory.

"I was just trying to warn you. Hugo's been known to go into anyone's wallet for financing. We've emptied out more than one trust fund to sustain his career."

She says the last word like it was obscene.

A beam of light hits Sylvia in the eyes and then moves on to Leni and Hugo. They all squint to see one of the bouncers from outside.

"Turn that off," Hugo hisses and the bouncer complies, slides into the aisle below and whispers to Hugo that things have calmed down out in the street.

Hugo nods and takes a deep breath.

"All right. Go tell June to get the lawyers and Counselor Frye on the phone. Set up a conference call. Then have Ricco get down to the *Spy* and find out exactly what happened. Have him tell Starkey I'm very disappointed."

The bouncer trots off and Hugo turns his attention to Sylvia. He takes her right hand and holds it up in front of him.

"It looks like you can venture home now, my dear. The rabble has been dispersed."

"Tremendous," Leni says, sliding out of her row. "I'm

late at the masseuse." She stops in the aisle and says, "Always a pleasure meeting my public."

They all nod agreement and watch her run down the balcony stairs.

"I guess I can go," Sylvia says to Hugo, suddenly feeling awkward and frightened.

He squeezes her hand, gives a tight-lipped smile and a nod.

"Schick," he says, releasing the hand and fishing in his coat pocket, "is a true believer in the strange ways of fate."

He pulls out a business card and extends it toward her. She takes it and says, "I want to thank you again. If you hadn't pulled me inside, I don't know what—"

He cuts her off with a wave of his hand.

"We were meant to be brought together, Sylvia. The method is always inconsequential. I feel a genuine connection here. I feel a kindred outlook, a mutual way of seeing things."

Sylvia laughs and brings a hand over her mouth. Someone from down below in the audience shouts, "Shut the hell up."

Hugo shakes his head and whispers, "We must walk amongst the ignorant. That is one of the costs of our art, yes?"

She shrugs and says, "Honestly, thanks again. You saved me."

He smiles a long minute, then says, "I'm throwing a party, Sylvia. Really, a working party. After seven years of toil, we are filming the finale of my great albatross—*Don Juan Triumphant*. I would love for you to attend. We are filming this Wednesday night. I think you'd find it fascinating. You'd get a chance to see the final flourishes in the creation of a masterpiece. And you could bring a camera."

He's caught her off guard. She stammers, "Oh, I don't—"

"Wednesday night," he says. "Give it some thought. As they say, sleep on it."

She simply nods and whispers, "Thanks again."

She makes her way out of the seats into the aisle and follows Leni's course out of the balcony without waiting for Hugo. When she gets to the corridor she looks back and when Schick doesn't appear she guesses that he's stayed to watch the rest of the movie.

She comes to the end of the corridor, to the huge stairway down into the lobby and as she's about to turn the corner onto the stairs, something catches her eye. Just an instant, just a momentary flash of image. She stops and stares at a print that's framed and mounted on the wall. She steps back to get her focus. It's a black-and-white shot. Stark. A little frightening. A Madonna and Child shot. A decaying landscape hosting the mother and infant.

It's a Terrence Propp.

II

Sylvia can remember, with an almost visceral, at times uncomfortable clarity, this late-fall afternoon, a Friday and a day just like today when she was walking home from Ste. Jeanne d'Arc and all the old men down Duffault Ave were out in the gutters with their ancient wooden rakes pushing leaves into piles and lighting them on fire, back when it was legal, and the wind was picking up and just engulfing her in the smell of leaf-smoke. And it was after three o'clock and there was about an hour of sunlight left to the day. The sky was already this same slate color, this exact ghostly feel to it, low clouds but a kind of brittle clarity to the air. And after Elsie Beckmann turned off at Jannings Hill, Sylvia was walking alone and she knows, she's certain, she was daydreaming, completely into some imagined world, though she no longer had any remembrance of what it was. She does remember being brought back to Duffault Ave, though, by the awful weight of her schoolbooks and by the coating of sweat that had broken out under her uniform. She can remember thinking how strange it was, perspiring in the middle of this October wind.

By the time she made it up the driveway to her back door, all her strength was gone and she sat down on the back stoop and just put her head down on her knees. She has no idea how long she sat there before her mother lifted her and carried her up the rear stairway to the apartment and put her on the couch.

For the next forty-eight hours, Sylvia sweated out the worst flu and fever of her life to date. She mumbled and cried every time the cold washcloth on her forehead was changed. Sylvia has no recollection of those nightmares. She doesn't even have much of a picture of her recovery beyond eating Campbell's chicken noodle soup off a tray in bed, while watching some old forties movies on the little black and white TV that Ma propped up on the dresser. Sylvia was well again by Monday and back at school on Tuesday.

And now, for whatever reason, that Friday afternoon, walking home from school, after the first symptoms of fever came over her but before she collapsed on the back stairs, those moments comprise the most haunting memories of her childhood. She has no idea why, but the feeling of light-headedness, the smell of the leaves being burned, the unnatural clarity of the darkening sky, the warmth building up under her arms, the heaviness of her feet inside her shoes—all of these sensations continue to be as real and strong to her as the day they first happened.

And it's how she feels now, at this exact moment, walking down Verlin Avenue, as if locked in slow motion in comparison to the people passing by. She's a block from the Skin Palace. When she came down to the lobby, another bouncer directed her down a long, dim corridor toward a red exit sign and she emerged out the rear of the building. When the sun and air hit her, she lurched into that same light-headed, slowed-down state as that Friday afternoon fifteen years ago.

It's not exactly an unpleasant feeling, though there's almost a latent fear that sickness will come. It's more this otherworldy pocket, this dreamy, growing warmth that's threatening to go out of control from the start. There's a tightness to the joints, but at the same time an almost loose feeling to the skin, to the whole head. She knows that she needs to be hailing a taxi or calling Perry. But it's as if her knowledge of this has little or no connection with her inability to make her body comply, as if the center of her intellect has shifted and is now located in her legs and feet. They're pulling her along Verlin, keeping her in motion, though she doesn't know where it is she's heading. This isn't the way out of the Canal Zone. It isn't the way back to the apartment.

She walks another half-block. The feeling seems to begin to dissipate one second and reassert itself the next. She suddenly wonders if maybe she was hurt worse than she thought in the skirmish. Maybe she's got a slight concussion. She forces herself to stop walking and leans up against a lightpost. She takes some deep breaths and closes her eyes. She stands completely still for a few minutes and starts to feel better, then puts her hand up to her cheeks and forehead and they feel normal to her. It's probably just the shock of the past hour, she decides.

She stands up from the lightpost, gets her balance, and glances across the street to see Der Geheime Garten. The café Mr. Quevedo mentioned. The place where she can find the story of Terrence Propp.

And then she's moving across the street and in the front door. The café is narrow but deep. The ceilings are ridicu-

lously low as if the restaurant had been contract-built for
the sole enjoyment of dwarfs. The lighting is dim and the
deep red walls don't help. Against the far wall is a short
marble bar backed by a mirror that has naked, Reubens-
like women painted on it. There are maybe a dozen or so
tables, only one of which is currently occupied, by a gan-
gly, pale, anemic-looking boy with large ears that wing out
from his head. He doesn't seem to notice her standing in
the entryway. There's a fat paperback titled *Zoopraxogra-
phy* spread open on his table, but he's engrossed in a spiral
notebook, chewing on a blue pencil.

A small man with jet black, slicked-back hair and what
looks like a greasepaint mustache, just this tiny dark line
above his lip, comes out of a back room carrying a tray,
sees Sylvia, smiles and moves toward her. He's dressed in
a suede-looking dinner jacket that matches the color of the
walls. He's wearing a silver earring in the shape of an
American Beauty rose.

"A table?" he asks and she nods.

He looks back over his shoulder at the almost-empty
room and says, "And will there be anyone joining you?"

She doesn't like the remark, though she thinks it was
fairly innocent. And she's hoping the guy can lead her to
Rory Gaston. So she says, "No thank you," and he grabs a
single menu from the top of the maître d's station and says,
"This way, please."

He seats her in a rear corner of the place. He places the
menu over a chipped-up china setting, a kind of antique
ink-blue plate trimmed with tea roses around the edge.

"Could I get you something to drink while you study the
selections?" he asks.

She's about to shake him off when her mouth opens and
she hears herself order a Pernod.

"Very good," he says, his spirits seemingly brightened
by her choice, and he marches off to the bar.

Sylvia sits still for a long minute and collects herself.

She runs her hands through her hair a few times. She looks around the walls for a pay phone to call Perry but doesn't see one. And then she realizes that she doesn't want to call Perry. Because she knows he'll be crazy when he hears about what's happened. It would be an appropriate reaction. She leaves the house. She walks down to the border of the worst part of the city. She sits down and drinks tea in an erotic bookstore with an elderly, blind Latino that she'd never laid eyes on before. She walks into the middle of a goddamn riot and wrestles with a cop, for God sake. She loses a camera. And she waits out the balance of the storm in the most beautiful pornographic movie theatre in America watching scenes from *Glutton For Ravishment II* with the director and starlet. How would she end that phone call—*Be home soon, Perry. Just having a cocktail in the Whorehouse Café* . . .

The waiter returns with the drink and puts it down on the table. "Does anything appeal to you?" he asks and when he sees her confusion he eye-motions to the menu.

"I'm sorry," she says, "I haven't had a chance to look."

He nods and goes to turn away and she says, "Hold on," and picks up the menu, thinking maybe she should put something in her stomach, maybe it would settle her down and help her think.

The entire menu is just one printed page and as she scans it she realizes every offering is some variation on oysters. And she's never heard of one. They feature names like *Oysters Delluc Piquate* and *Oysters L'Herbier in the Half-shell, Cavalcanti's Oyster Bisque* and *Feyder's Saucy Oyster Canapés* and *Fried Oyster Epstein.*

She looks up at the waiter and says, "Your specialty?"

He gives a little pleased-with-himself smile and says quietly, "Food of the gods."

She smiles back. "And the goddesses, I hope."

"Of course."

"Why don't you surprise me," she says.

He takes the menu and moves off before she can broach the subject of Mr. Gaston. And then as she watches the waiter disappear into what she assumes is the kitchen, an awful thought occurs to her—what if there isn't any Mr. Gaston? What if Mr. Quevedo was putting her on or just being cruel? She has no reason to think this is the case. But then she had no reason to think that Jack Derry's Camera Exchange would vanish overnight. She had no reason to think that a walk to the edge of the Canal Zone would degenerate into a riot. And she had no reason whatsoever to think that she'd spend part of today watching hard-core porn on a thirty-foot screen.

The images come back now. The woman, Leni, on her back on that long wooden table. The young guy, wearing only a white apron around his waist and then not even that. The older Asian man, the dishwasher, approaching the two of them, bouncing from a badly feigned shock to full participation in about ten seconds. Bulkie rolls, sliced tomatoes, a jar of olives all falling to the floor as the threesome's convulsions escalated. Leni, grabbing a handful of the dishwasher's hair with one hand, a load of rye bread with the other. And her face as she looked into the camera, looked out of the screen and at Sylvia, closed, then opened, then closed those beautiful eyes and bit down on her bottom lip.

Sylvia takes a long sip of her drink and it occurs to her how curious she is about Leni Pauline. Even in the dim light of the balcony, dressed in a bathrobe and her hair hanging, munching popcorn for God's sake, the woman was gorgeous. And Sylvia realizes this contradicts everything she's always assumed about porn stars. She doesn't know where the assumption came from, but she's always thought the women in those movies looked like retired strippers gone to seed. The image doesn't even add up since she knows, has read, all about the teen runaways who end up before the camera, the sixteen-year-olds who use fake IDs to get the job.

Leni didn't fall anywhere near either of those categories. She's got to be twenty-five or so. And she's got the look of some hip, urban model. Nothing retro or cheap. Sylvia thinks of her image there, in person, in the flesh, not the woman on the screen. She thinks of her in the balcony, without makeup or camera filters or kind angles. Leni looked like she could be the choice paralegal down at Walpole & Lewis. She looked like she could be the manager of some Newbury Street boutique in Boston, some place where Sylvia would have to get the nerve up just to go inside and browse. And Leni was quick with a line. The woman could more than hold her own against a personality like Hugo Schick's.

Though Sylvia hates thinking in terms like this, she can't get around the reality of the fact that from day one, a woman with a face and body and nerve like Leni Pauline starts off about five steps ahead of everyone else. So how did Leni end up on that screen? What series of events could have brought this woman in front of Schick's camera? Sylvia has no idea why it intrigues her so much, but she genuinely wants to know Leni's story. And it annoys her that she probably never will.

She fingers the glass. She brings it up to her mouth and holds it there a second, taking in the smell. Then she takes another sip. It goes down warm and makes itself known all the way to the stomach. Then it settles in and radiates. It's doing its job. She feels much better already.

The waiter returns, puts a steaming plate before her, and asks if she needs anything else. Sylvia tells him no, then grabs his arm before he can leave and asks, "Maybe a glass of wine? What would you recommend?"

He brings a hand over his jaw and stares at the plate. "For this particular delicacy?" he says. "I would probably suggest a Benoit-Levy Chardonnay."

"Sounds perfect," she says and he disappears again. She looks down at what he's presented—a wheel of fat, beige spokes of oyster drizzled with a heavy-looking, rust-colored sauce.

She spears one of the oysters with the fork and puts it in her mouth. She tastes the garlic and the lemon and the Worcestershire, lets the oyster rest on her tongue and its juices run down and into the well of her mouth. It's fantastic. She's not even this big oyster fan, but this is tremendous, the kind of food that justifies words that normally seem pretentious or clichéd when you read them in magazines—*succulent, savory, delectable.* She can't believe the *Spy* has never done a write-up on this place.

The waiter brings the wine in a flamboyant glass, shaped, of course, like a rose in full bloom. She takes a sip, lets it pool around her tongue for a while before swallowing. She's immediately overwhelmed by taste, by shadings and gradations she didn't think she had the capacity for, and she wants to laugh. She's feeling giddy. She's thinking, not really seriously, that the blow to the head has transformed her, thrown switches that have been shut down since childhood. It's like some archtypal comic book story, the eternally boring and noble scientist caught in the lab explosion, knocked to the gleaming floor underneath the shards of her equipment, broken test tubes and splintered Pyrex beakers, green smoke rising up to the ceiling, the whole room bathed in an ultraviolet glow. And then she emerges from the rubble, larger than before, her muscles forcing the seams of her lab coat to burst, her eyes now bulging just a bit from the sockets. And a slightly mad smirk across her lips.

Sylvia closes her eyes and fixes her mouth around another oyster. She sucks on it, refuses to swallow right away, puts all her concentration into discovering flavor. And then she senses someone standing next to her and gets embarrassed, as if she's been moaning over the food. She opens her eyes and swallows and says, "Absolutely wonderful."

But it's not the waiter. It's the kid with the big ears who was reading the notebook when she came in. He just stands there, awkward and hesitant, smiling, nodding his head.

"Oh, God," she says, "I thought you were the waiter," then adds, "Is there something I can do for you?"

"I'm glad you like the food," he says and she picks up an accent she can't place. "Papa will be happy to hear."

She's annoyed. It's not often you get the kind of enjoyment she was pulling out of this lunch and this kid has just stepped on it. It simply isn't going to be her day. She stares at him and waits for his pitch.

"Marcel's in the kitchen," he says.

Sylvia looked at him like she doesn't understand.

He flinches just a bit and says, "Marcel," and jerks his thumb toward the kitchen door. "The waiter."

"You must be a regular," she says and then she could shoot herself for extending the conversation.

"It's a quiet place to come," he says. "A good place to work. Undisturbed."

"That's good to know," she says, resigned to the interruption now. "I take it you're a student?"

He shakes his head *no,* seemingly embarrassed, starts to fish around in every pocket of his suit. "I just wanted to give you . . . I seem to have left my cards . . . forgive me, I'm not very good at this. I'm a filmmaker."

Sylvia's stomach churns with the last word, but she steadies herself.

"I'm glad for you," she says, picking up the wineglass. A beat goes by. The boy looks from her face to the kitchen, but he doesn't seem to know what to say.

"Well it was nice meeting you," Sylvia tries, but he ignores the words and bulls ahead.

"You like film?" he asks.

She doesn't want to prolong the interruption but she can't help asking. "What's your name?"

"Jakob."

"Jakob," she says, "have you ever met anyone who didn't like film?"

He doesn't seem to understand the question and when he pulls out the opposite chair and sits down she realizes she's made a big mistake.

"My father," he says, challenging, "he hates the cinema. I doubt he's ever been to a movie in his life."

"He's indifferent," she says.

"Excuse me?"

"He's indifferent. It's not that he actively dislikes movies. Film just isn't a big part of his life. He's indifferent to it."

"No," he says. "This is not the case. Not in this instance. I have to disagree."

She sighs and says, "Well, I guess you know your old man."

Either the kid is genuinely lame or he's playing the part to avoid leaving the table. He smiles and shakes his head as if she's putting him on and they both instinctively know it.

"What about yourself?" he says. "Are you an enthusiast?"

She thinks about just ignoring him, but decides that's actually more work than giving in and talking.

"I don't get out as much as I used to," she says. "But I used to go a lot when I was younger."

"I knew it," he says. "What are some of your favorites? Who would be your favorite director?"

"Fritz Lang," she says, spearing an oyster and remembering Dr. Jessner from *German Giants* class in college.

It's a mistake. Her answer sends Jakob into something approaching a spasm.

"Lang," he says, voice too high. "Really, Lang. You're a

Lang devotee, yes? I knew it. I *knew* this. How many people even know Lang today? Unbelievable. I saw you walk in, I said, *film woman,* yes, I knew it."

"Film woman?"

"Who else? Please. Who really *does* it to you?"

It's strange. Having someone ask her opinion.

"Murnau," she says, "Dupont—"

"A weakness for the Germans—"

"—Herk Harvey, Browning, Dovzhenko—"

"A buff," he says. "You're what they call a buff."

"Oh, c'mon," she laughs, protesting like some easy prom date. But suddenly she doesn't mind him sitting at the table.

"I bet you don't mind going to the films alone. Correct? Yes? They say a real buff never minds going alone."

"That's in the book," she says. "That's one of the definitions."

"How about Schick?" he says. "Do you know any Schick?"

It stops her cold. She puts down her wineglass and stares at him.

"What is the matter?" he says, sticking his neck out.

Sylvia doesn't know what to say. She feels like she should be angry, but she's mostly confused. Did Schick send this kid down here as some kind of joke? But Jakob was here before her. He was sitting in here reading when she came in the door. Schick couldn't have known she'd be coming here because *she* didn't know she was coming here. Maybe the kid saw her come out of Herzog's. Maybe he saw her leave the Skin Palace and ran to get here first. But again, how could he have known she'd come in here?

She knows she should just get up now and leave. Put some money on the table and get the hell out. There's no need for her to be here. She shouldn't be drawn here in the Zone in the first place. What's happened today just proves that.

She throws down the rest of the wine in one huge gulp and starts to push away from the table.

"What's wrong?" Jakob says, sitting back.

"I've got to go," she says and stands up.

He gets close to panicky. "Forgive me, please. What did I say?"

Sylvia nods goodbye and moves around the table, but Jakob stands up, mortified by some unfathomable social mistake, and starts to follow her to the door. She reaches for the doorknob and he puts a hand on her shoulder and says, "Hold on, please. What is the matter?"

She doesn't turn around. She twists the knob and in as even a voice as she can manage she says, "Get your hand off me now or I'll scream."

He removes his hand from her shoulder and grabs her at the elbow. She tries to yank the door open but it won't budge. Her heart and her breath go crazy and she wheels around to push him, but someone's beaten her to it. A bearded man has Jakob by the shoulder and is yanking the kid backwards. Jakob lets go of Sylvia's arm and his eyes go huge and he starts to stammer, "I did not do anything. I did not do a thing. We were just talking. Please, madam, tell him, please."

The man looks to Sylvia for an explanation and she in turn stares at the fear and confusion on Jakob's face and says, "It's all right, you can let him go. It was just a misunderstanding. I'm not feeling well. I've really got to leave."

She turns and tries the door again and realizes it's locked.

The man looks her up and down, then lets go of Jakob and steps forward to turn the deadbolt and open the door.

Jakob says, "We were talking. She looked perfect for the part of the waitress. We were just talking." Then his voice dissolves into a gasped breath and he runs out of the café and disappears down Verlin.

"Are you all right?" the bearded man asks. "Did he hurt you at all?"

"No," she says, suddenly feeling flushed from the wine and the upsetting. "No, it was a misunderstanding. He didn't ... I should really just get going. It's been an awful day."

"Would you like me to call you a cab?" he asks. He's got a very soft voice and he's dressed in kind of old-fashioned lounging pajamas, that same deep rose color as the walls and the waiter's jacket. They look as if they're made of silk. Sylvia looks down to see he's got slippers on his feet and she'd think that he recently rolled out of bed if it weren't for the fact that his hair looks just washed and combed.

She thinks about walking out of the Zone or waiting for a bus and she surprises herself by saying, "Could you? I'd really appreciate that."

"Of course," he says, looking like a concerned doctor, gently taking her arm and leading her back to her seat.

"Why don't you just sit down and relax for a second. I'll be right back. There's a phone in the office."

Sylvia watches him walk away and though it's probably a stupid thing to do, she takes a long drink of Pernod. She'd not tell Perry anything about today. She's going to chalk the whole thing up to some bad misjudgment and let it go. She doesn't know what she was thinking of, coming down here, alone, following Quevedo into his store, walking into the middle of the crowd outside Herzog's. As soon as the cab drops her home she's going to shower and change and cook dinner. Something nice and warm. Something Perry likes. Maybe some meatloaf and baked potatoes. Something kind of hearty that her mother would cook. She'll tell Perry she's changed her mind about the camera. That she doesn't need the money. That they can buy something else. Or they can bank it. They can start the house fund like he wants. Maybe they'll talk houses over dinner. Where they want to live, what style of house they agree on. Features they want. She hopes the cab comes quickly. She just wants to be back in the apartment, to lock the door and take a steaming shower, put on some tea and listen to some music. Maybe she'll call Perry at work, ask him to come home a little early. Ask him to pick up one of those real estate magazines at the supermarket. Tell him she's sorry about last night. That she just hasn't been feeling well. That she misses him.

The man comes back to her table and says, "They'll be a few minutes." He gestures to a chair and says, "May I?"

She nods, sips the last of the Pernod.

"Jakob gave you a little scare? I apologize. The boy has no sense of social grace. The owner's son. He comes here to read and scribble in notebooks. I'm sure he intended no harm."

"You're not the owner?" she asks.

He looks surprised. "I'm sorry. My God, I've been contaminated by Jakob. My manners appear in remission." He extends a hand and says, "Rory Gaston. And I'm the manager."

She shakes his hand. "Sylvia Krafft."

"I've never seen you in here before, Sylvia."

"First-time customer."

"Well, I hope this little incident won't discourage you from coming back. And as an incentive, allow me to pick up the check."

"No, really—" she starts to protest, but he won't hear any arguments.

"Too late, Sylvia. *Fait accompli,* as they say. Please, I'll sleep much better tonight."

They stare at each other for a moment and then, without any preamble, she hears herself say, "So what can you tell me about Terrence Propp?"

She's jolted him. He literally pulls back in his seat and swallows and seems to consider his words until finally, in a hushed voice, he says, "Who sent you?"

Sylvia's got a small buzz going from the wine and the liqueur and maybe that's what makes her want to start laughing. He sounds like he's delivering a line from any number of campy B-movies. But he's serious. He suddenly looks nervous and distracted, as if she's just accused him of something.

"Quevedo," she says.

"Quevedo?" he repeats.

She nods and lets the silence build.

"Who's that?" he says and starts to crack his knuckles.

"You don't know Mr. Quevedo?" she says, letting her suspicion show.

"Never heard of him."

"Well, he knows you. He sent me to this place. Told me to ask for Rory Gaston. That is your name, right?"

"Look, Ms. Krafft, I'm telling you I don't know a Mr. Quevedo—"

She cuts him off and asks, "Well, why would he send me here and mention your name?"

He turns in his seat and looks at the front door, then turns back and says, "I'm sure I have no idea."

They stare at each other until she says, "Could you just give me Propp's number? I'd rather set something up directly with him."

Gaston laughs out loud, immediately sucks his cheeks in and says, "I'm afraid that's impossible."

A horn sounds and they both look to see a red cab has pulled up out front.

"Your ride," he says, folding his arms across his chest.

She stands up and takes a step toward the door, stops next to Gaston and says, "I might have something that belongs to Mr. Propp. If he's interested in getting it back, have him call me. Tell him I'm in the book."

She heads for the door and as she pulls it open, Gaston says, "Tell the cab to go and give me fifteen minutes."

"You'll put me in touch with Propp?"

"Fifteen minutes," he repeats.

She debates it for a second, then yells to the cabbie that he can leave. He stares with his head cocked, then gives her his middle finger and pulls away from the curb.

She turns back to Gaston and says, "You've got fifteen," but he doesn't seem consoled by her decision.

He moves to the door and relocks the bolt, pulls down a floor-length shade. Without a word he turns and walks to the bar, grabs the bottle of Benoit-Levy from an ice bucket and returns to Sylvia's table.

She moves back to her seat and Gaston refills her glass.

"We're in an awkward situation," he says.

"How's that?"

He takes a drink from the mouth of the wine bottle, then raises it in toast, shrugs his shoulders and says, "I take it you want entrance?"

Sylvia stares at him.

"To the group," he adds.

"That depends—"

"No," he barks, adamant, suddenly annoyed. "We'll have no fence-sitting. You give yourself over or you don't. You've heard the call or you haven't. There's no in-between."

She picks up her wineglass, stares into it. She swallows, tries to stay calm and says, "I didn't mean to offend—"

"And I didn't mean to be rude," Gaston says, lowering his voice. "It's just . . . this is such a crucial time for the Proppists. There's so much infighting lately. And so many rumors. Finding the right direction, staying on the right path, keeping the eyes open and clear. The stress is increasing daily."

Sylvia looks up at the ceiling and stares at an intricate mural of a Renaissance-style bedroom scene where a ghostly young virgin is preparing to surrender her maidenhood to what looks like a hulking incarnation of Pan.

She looks back down at Gaston and thinks, *this guy has*

seen too many Sydney Greenstreet movies. "I think I've
heard the call, but I'm ignorant. I have no idea where to go
from here. I need some information and I was told you
could give it to me."

Gaston rocks his chair back on its rear legs as if the
process will help him think. A smile comes over his face
and he says, "You're toying with me, aren't you? Did
Camille put you up to this?"

"I don't know a Camille," Sylvia says, "just like you
don't know a Quevedo. That makes us even. So why don't
we do each other a favor and stop trying to outmaneuver
one another and just tell the truth."

It's a pushy move, but it's all she has left.

"What if you don't like the truth?" Gaston asks.

"I'm an adult," Sylvia says. "I'll survive."

He nods, seems pleased, takes another hit of wine and
says, "Okay, Sylvia. The truth is I have no idea who Terrence Propp is. None of the Proppists do. I have no idea
what the man even looks like. I'd walk right by him if I
passed him on the street."

Now Sylvia's on the verge of furious. "So this is all a
huge joke," she says. "I've wasted my entire day down
here so someone could have fun at my expense. You——"

He cuts her off. "Calm down. Please. Believe me, we
were once as anxious to know as you. We've all tried to
follow the man's trail. None of us has ever been successful. I can give you a kind of sketchy history. But eventually
it dissolves into vapor. The one thing we can be completely
certain of is that Mr. Propp takes his privacy extremely seriously. If we were forced to speculate on the causes for
this I suspect we'd regress into endless debate. There are
some known facts. At some point, though we can't completely confirm the years, Terrence Propp certainly lived
here in Quinsigamond. We've narrowed down his residence to three or four likely addresses. All of them walk-
ups here in the Canal Zone. And though dozens of the local

raconteurs claim to have known Propp, the only person we give credence to is Elmore Orsi over at the Rib Room diner."

The Rib Room diner.

Where Sylvia found the ad for the Aquinas.

"And these days, Orsi's started to recant," Gaston says. "He now claims he's never met Propp. That it was all a stunt. He thought it would help his restaurant business. In any event, here's what we know for certain."

He gets up and walks to the bar, reaches underneath and returns to the table with a small pamphlet or magazine which he rolls up and hands to Sylvia without any explanation.

"First," he says, "there are currently forty-nine known Terrence Propp prints in existence. Second, most of the known prints were taken in or around Quinsigamond. And third, exposure to and study of these works leads the viewer to a deeper, fuller understanding of their own sensual potential."

Sylvia stares at him for a second, then shakes her head and says, "You talk about this individual as if he's not only a first-rate artist, okay, but as if he'd moved beyond that status. Like he's some kind of visionary. You might disagree with my phrasing, but your whole group here feels a little cultish. I don't mean to be insulting. I'm just asking why, until very recently, I'd never even heard of Terrence Propp? Never seen any of his work. I've never read an article about him. Never heard him mentioned anywhere in the media. And I'm not exactly an uninformed person."

Gaston keeps a poker face and says, "We each come to Propp when we're ready. That's the beauty of the whole phenomenon."

"That's an answer?"

"I don't expect you to understand yet," he says. "And I may have made a very large mistake bringing you in ahead of time—"

"I don't want *in.*"

"But in fact, you made a statement earlier—"

"A statement?"

He looks at her oddly, squinting his eyes.

"You said you had something that belongs to Propp."

Did she say that? Sylvia can't even remember now, but she must have. She doesn't want to mention the Aquinas prints, so she shakes her head and says, "I thought that would get me a name, you know. I thought it might buy me a connection. I lied. And it worked."

It's clear Rory Gaston doesn't like this answer.

"I've just seen a few things," Sylvia says. "I've just discovered a few pieces. Yesterday. For the first time."

"And where," Gaston says, "was your first exposure?"

Sylvia hesitates, then says, "Excuse me?"

She feels him tensing up.

"You just said you'd never seen any of Propp's work until yesterday," Gaston says.

Sylvia nods.

Gaston's hands come out into the air, questioning. "Where did you see Propp's work? Where were you?"

She meets his stare and says, "The Skin Palace."

He looks confused. This wasn't the answer he was expecting.

"Herzog's," she says. "The movie theatre."

"You saw a Terrence Propp in Herzog's?"

Sylvia nods.

Gaston starts to shake his head and says, seemingly to himself, "I've made a huge mistake here."

He walks to the door and unlocks the bolt, pulls the door open, turns and stares at Sylvia.

"What's the problem?" she says.

He doesn't say a word, just stands next to the door waiting for her to leave.

And the light-headedness returns, as if carried in on a draft of air from outside.

She gets up, a little wobbly, moves across the room and says, "Look, I'm sorry if I—"

"Just get out," Gaston whispers, "before someone sees you in here."

IZ

The back door is open. Sylvia comes into the kitchen and sees the bottle of Dewar's, uncapped, sitting on the counter. She can hear the TV from the living room but she can't make out the words. She takes off her coat and hangs it over the back of a chair, walks down the hall and finds Perry sitting on the edge of the old leather hassock that had been her mother's. His suitcoat is tossed on the couch. He's leaned forward staring at the screen, a fogged-up water glass between his hands. His hair is a mess and his shirt is half-untucked. He's squinting at the TV screen, looking like he's trying to decode hieroglyphics.

He's so intent, she feels like she shouldn't interrupt him, like he's in a state of frantic prayer. She's never seen him looking this way in front of the television. Usually he's just the opposite, close to narcoleptic, one eye on a game that he lost interest in a half hour ago.

"Perry," she says from the doorway.

"Jesus," he flinches and rears back, tossing some of his drink into his lap.

"Shit," he yells, standing up, trying to get his balance, pulling at his pants with his hand.

Sylvia starts to go to him but then she gets a look at his face and stops. He's furious. His head is bobbing in that way that she knows means trouble, means he's beyond annoyed and deep into a full-blown temper tantrum. They could have some wall punching any minute.

"What," she says like a scared kid, like she's broken curfew for what will absolutely be the last time.

He's sputtering, he's so mad. He starts biting in on his top lip and his arm comes up and starts pointing at the screen. She steps to the side a bit and looks to see this morning's riot outside Herzog's.

"What the hell happened?" he snaps, but instead of answering, Sylvia just stares at the screen. It's an unsettling experience. She's seeing everything she just lived through about five hours ago, but she's seeing it from another perspective. The riot's been filmed with a hand-held camera and the picture has that feeling of ongoing immediacy, that voyeuristic aura that's spliced with both attraction and repulsion, as if anything is not only possible but probable. And as if you're in the eye of a maelstrom, adjacent to disaster but chronically protected. She's seeing all kinds of things that she missed the first time around. She's seeing more small pockets of skirmishing, more people trading punches and losing blood. And she's hearing noises that she never picked up. Dozens of screamed exchanges studded with a censor's *bleep,* voices at differing distances from the microphone creating a cacophony that tells more than any narration could.

Perry plants his now-empty glass down on the floor and picks up the remote control. He hits a button and the images on the screen start to race by, obscured into a hyperriot, bodies now flying at speeds more laughable than tragic.

"You taped this?" is all she can think to say.

He doesn't respond, but squints down at the screen and then at some right moment, he thumbs down on another button with such emotion and emphasis you'd think he was launching warheads from hidden silos. The picture calms back to normal speed and clarity and there's Sylvia, wrestling with the cop over the camera.

"Oh, God," she mumbles.

"That's it," he says, head still wobbling over his neck, face flushed to a murky red, "Oh, God, huh?"

She looks from his face back to her own image on the screen and in the most sarcastic voice she can summon, she says, *"Sylvia, are you all right? Were you hurt? Is there anything I can do?"*

His arm shoots up and a finger is pointed out at her. "Don't do that," he says, trying and failing to get a grip. "Don't turn this around. Don't try and put this on me. You didn't even call me. It's been hours, for Christ sake. I called the hospitals. I had Ratzinger phone the police station. You didn't even call me, Sylvia."

"How was I supposed to know I'd be on TV?" she says but it's weak and they both know it.

"I've been pulling my hair out of my goddamn head—"

"You're right," she says, suddenly feeling guilty and wishing they could end the argument immediately. "I should've called."

"Should've called," he roars and she knows they've got some bad hours to go through. Maybe some bad days.

"What the hell happened, Sylvia?" he says, wiping his face with his hand and trying to calm down.

Sylvia extends her arms toward the TV.

"You saw what happened, Perry. I went down there to pay for the camera and the next thing I know I turn a corner and the street is filled with all these people—"

"You're fighting with a cop, Sylvia. Look at yourself there. For God's sake, you're fighting a cop."

She looks at the screen. He backs up the picture and they watch it again. The cop grabbing the camera. Sylvia grabbing back. The picture cuts away to another brawl before she's pulled inside the Skin Palace.

She looks at him. She doesn't know what to say. She

doesn't want to say anything. She wants to take a bath and throw down a drink and go to bed for the next two days.

"What were you doing home?" she finally says and knows it's a mistake as the words leave her mouth.

"That's not an answer," he yells, then continues, "I wasn't home. I was in my office with the FUD people having a planning session when Ratzinger buzzes me to come upstairs. He's sitting on the edge of his desk playing this as I walk in. He was watching the local news at noon. When he saw the fighting, he popped a tape in for our personal-injury people. Then he spotted a familiar face. He gave me the goddamn tape, Sylvia. Ratzinger taped the thing."

"I'm sorry, Perry," she begins, feeling like she's going to start crying which is the last thing she wants to do right now.

"Are you hurt?" he finally asks. "Did you get hurt at all? Did you break anything?"

"Not a scratch," she says, too low.

"You're sure?" he demands, and before she can re-answer he says, "Were you arrested? Did they arrest you?"

"I wasn't arrested," she says. "They had their hands full."

"I can see that," he says and they both stare at the screen as he plays it all over again, her now famous dance, her ten seconds of fame. He mutes out the sound and the silence almost makes her sick.

After a minute, he sits back down on the hassock and looks up and simply says, "How, Sylvia?"

She swallows and says, "Does it look like I planned this, Perry? Do you think I woke up today and said *I think I'll cause some civil unrest down in the Zone?*"

"How many times," he says, showing his strained patience, his heroic restraint, "have we talked about you going down there? How many discussions have we had about that part of town, Sylvia?"

"I'm an adult, Perry."

"Yeah," he says, "that's what this looks like. You being an adult."

Her nerves are shot. The toll of the entire day is shorting her out and all her hurt is starting to mutate into anger. "Thanks for the concern," she manages to say.

He bolts to his feet and screams, "I sat here for hours not knowing whether you were dead or alive. You didn't even call me—"

She screams back, "You're pissed off that I looked bad in front of your goddamn boss. That's the extent of your goddamn concern, you bastard."

He rears back and heaves the remote control at the television. It misses the set and sails into the wall, explodes into a rain of black plastic and batteries.

"Your aim is off," she says. "I'm over here."

He stands fuming, hands on his hips, his chest pushing out.

"I don't know what's wrong with you," he says, then he adds, "I'm going out," and moves past her, down the hall and out the back door with a slam.

And now the tears come and she folds down on herself, slides her back down the wall and sits on her feet and just lets it happen. She doesn't know what's wrong with her either. She doesn't know why she didn't call him. She doesn't know what she was thinking of, following Mr. Quevedo, hiding out in the Skin Palace, walking into Der Garten. She honestly doesn't know how today happened. She feels as controlled as the TV set, as if someone she can't see is holding another kind of black box, that they're thumbing down buttons that make her move in ways she can't understand.

She looks up at the TV and into the eye of the Skin Palace riot, finally advanced past the point of her walk-on, her public insult to Perry's career. She watches the jumpy, off-balance shots of chaos, the bouncing pan of frenzied upheaval. It's as if the TV is plugged into her head instead of the VCR, as if the images ricocheting across the glass are a reading of her brain, an X ray of the inside of her skull. And she's watching it through the blur of her water-logged eyes so everything's obscured just that much more.

She pulls herself up from the wall and goes into the bathroom. She turns on the water and cups her hands under the faucet, lets her palms fill up with a pool, leans down and soaks her face. She repeats this several times, then she opens the medicine cabinet, takes down her mother's old Valium prescription, ignores the expiration date and swallows a couple.

She towels her face dry and moves out into the kitchen, opens the refrigerator and grabs a half-full bottle of white Burgundy, pulls out the cork and takes a long draw from the mouth of the bottle.

She walks out the back door and leaves it open. She walks down the stairs to the cellar and locks herself in the darkroom.

She turns on the safelight and the room goes red. She sits down on the step stool and just closes her eyes and takes another sip off the bottle. She takes some deep breaths and tries to calm down, but she starts to get dizzy so she opens her eyes and puts the wine bottle down on the ground. It dawns on her how much she's had to drink today—the absinthe in Schick's office, a Pernod, then a glass of wine at Der Geheime Garten, and now the Burgundy. She never drinks this much, especially not during the day. She realizes she has no idea what time it is. And that she doesn't really want to know. She doesn't want to do anything right now except sit here in this darkroom and be alone.

Of course, finally, she looks up at the pictures. She lets herself stare ahead, at the drying line, at the photos still hanging there in front of her. The Madonna and the child in the ruins. She looks at the whole run of photos, takes them in together, as a whole, a set, a series of connected images. She wonders if she laid them on top of each other and then fanned them fast with her thumb would she detect any movement of the figures? Would she get any sense of motion, something minute, a barely shifted arm or leg? And if she did, what more would this tell her?

She stops looking at them as a series and focuses individually, left to right, down the line. And in this way they remind her a little of the Stations of the Cross, of going to the Stations with her mother when she was maybe seven or eight years old. How many Stations were there? More than seven. There was all that singing, that chant-like song. Kind of a dirge, really, *Stabat Mater.* How did that translate? She can still hear it, the mournfulness of it. The sadness inherent in that sound.

What are these photos? The Stations of what? What did Terrence Propp want me to see when I stare at them like this? Or am I an idiot thinking he had that much of a plan, that extensive a design? Maybe it was just instinct. Classic artistic inspiration. Maybe Propp just let the mood of the day hit him, move him. Maybe he simply set the mother and child up in this awful, broken-down setting and started shooting film. Maybe he wasn't thinking beyond the next exposure, beyond the click of the shutter. Beyond the image at that instant.

Maybe Terrence Propp wasn't thinking about me at all.

She gets up off the stool and moves over to the dry line. She stands with her face about a foot away from her first photograph. She brings her hand up to touch it, but stops herself. She wants to make up her mind—what's the first thing that strikes her about the picture? What's the premier image? What is it that first draws and holds the eye?

She wants to say the Madonna's shoulder, the smoothness of its slope, the tone of the skin, so white. Or maybe it's the relationship of the shoulder to the neck, the sleekness and the perfectness of the bend. Whatever the dynamics of the attraction, it's the Madonna's shoulder.

But then there's the infant's hand, so small and yet so absolutely detailed by the focus. It reminds her a little of pictures she's seen in magazines and on billboards—hyperclear shots of a fetus inside an amniotic sac, parts of the body still vague and unformed, the eye looking a bit fishlike, but other parts, like the hand, the fingers, the fingers specifically, so absolutely developed, the fingernails already visible. The infant's hand in Propp's shots reminds her of those fetus shots, it's so stark somehow, so intricately delineated, out there in the air as if it were waving to her, as if it were signaling the viewer, *look closely, take notice.*

She takes a step to the side and stands in front of the second photo and now it isn't the shoulder or the hand, but the rubble of the floor in the background. It's the lack of focus here that does it, makes for a maddening obscurity, makes her wish she could change the focus of the photo herself, at this late date, bring the emphasis off the humans and onto the inanimate clutter of the ground. She wants to sweep the earth for clues as to exactly where the photograph was shot. She wants to zoom in until she can see recognizable evidence, signs of a time period and a location. She wants to turn the dim glint in the far right corner into a Kennedy half-dollar that dropped from Propp's pants pocket as he scouted the setting. She wants to be able to follow the old support columns up to the roof and nail them as Doric or Ionic. She wants to know why here, why this field of disintegration.

And as she studies the third photo, she focuses on the lighting itself, the way it descends from the top of the shot, the way it shines in beam-like shafts and catches faint storms of dust without eclipsing the sharpness of the mother and infant.

She gives up. She walks back to the step stool and remounts it. She wishes that she could have been there the day Propp did this shoot, that she could have just stood to the side, maybe even out of sight, behind one of the columns, just watching and listening. She'd love to know what he said to his subjects, what directions he gave. Did he tell the mother to drop her shoulder a quarter inch, to loosen her shawl and expose more skin, to pull the infant closer and let it suckle? What was his voice like, low and encouraging or bossy and bullying, intimidating the Madonna into the perfect position?

Or maybe he didn't use his voice at all. Maybe it was all gesture and signals. She can imagine that. She can accept how perfect the silence of this setting would be, Propp's decision not to violate it, the only noise being the murmur of the infant and the ongoing click of the shutter invading the cool, decayed silence of the hall.

And maybe gesture wasn't even necessary. Maybe Propp and the mother knew each other in a way that precluded the need for instruction, the way longtime band members intuit each other's musical changes. Some photographers work with the same models for years. This could be one of those arrangements, artist and subject drawn into an instinctual sense of one another's needs and wants, something like telepathy constantly in the air around them.

Sylvia has never known anyone in that complete a way. Except maybe her mother. And she's more than a little doubtful that Perry and she will ever get in sync. She thinks about his face at the moment that he threw the remote and the tears well up again and she puts her hands in her jacket pocket and touches the magazines that Gaston gave her.

She pulls it out and holds it in both hands. It's a small journal, about six by eight inches, but pretty slick, center stapled, with good quality paper and professional typesetting. She thumbs through it to the end. There are only a dozen pages, but all of them crammed with two columns of

small print. She turns back to the cover. The letterhead
reads

Underexposed
A Journal of Terrence Propp Studies
Published bi-yearly by Propp-Aganda Ltd

and underneath it there's a line drawing of what looks like
an old Brownie camera. She opens to the table of contents
and reads a few article titles. *Trajectories of Longing in the
Bleicherode Exhibit. The Zurau Flea Market Find: Trick-
ery of Treasure. Of Curves and Slopes: The Physics of the
Early Nudes.* The last item listed on the contents page is
Through My Viewfinder: a Column by Rory Gaston.

She turns to the last page of the magazine and there's
a small photo of Gaston in the upper right corner. It's
a close-up head shot and he looks more professional
than sensual. Under his byline, in italics, are the words
an ongoing explication of what we know so far. She starts
in:

This week's mailbag brought yet another attempt at sub-
terfuge by one more dim-bulbed prankster with too much
time on his or her hands and access to a camera. I'm
forced once again to beseech and admonish the faithful
regarding the lending of *Underexposed.* Clearly, back issues have fallen into the hands of some barbarians who
have no hope for conversion. I can't waste my time worrying about their loss of primal sensuality. I'm neck deep
in the evolution of my own carnal sensibilities. So I ask
you once again to guard the magazine and when you're
done reading, either destroy it or keep it under lock and
key.

I don't want to have to spend another morning like
last Thursday when someone other than my letter carrier
deposited a plain brown manila mailer through my door

slot. There were no markings on the packet and though I attempted to prevent myself from feeling that rush of dizziness at even the remotest chance that contact had been made, my heart surged with both longing and fear as I ran my letter opener along the seal and extracted the contents: a single Polaroid photograph, taken, I'm quite sure, by a Spectra model.

I stared at the image until my eyes went weak. A very simple composition. A portrait. An upper-body shot of an individual posed before the brick wall background. The sex of the subject is undeterminable. S/he is dressed in what appears to be a medieval jester's costume. The head is encased in a shiny silver fright wig. The face is decorated with oversized red wax lips with two enormous faux buckteeth extending down toward the chin. The eyes and nose are covered with a brand of "Groucho Marx" eyeglasses and mustache. The cheeks are rouged into a clown's apple-red caricature. A white-gloved hand is in the forefront of the shot, held up and partially obscuring the chestal area. The hand is bent into an obscene salute, the middle finger thrust skyward and directed, unmistakably, at the viewer. Some miniature graffiti was noticeable but unintelligible on the brick background until Wilhelm and the boys down at Duyfhuizen Labs blew me up an 11 x 14 study shot which allowed me to decode the doggerel

> I'm an absentee artist
> which fills you with strife
> but you'll never possess me
> so go get a life

Charming. I'm not sure of the prankster's intention this time around. Did S/he expect me to swoon and blow the trumpet, announce to my people that Propp has touched down, has deemed to send us a communiqué no matter how seemingly cruel, has consented to show his face, no matter how grotesquely distorted? I have no way of deciphering the buffoon's designs. But let the hoaxster know this if they happen to appropriate yet another issue of *Underexposed*: I've spent a good bit of this lifetime studying the work of a singular genius named Terrence Propp. I have spent the majority of my waking hours immersing myself in study of the master since that first day when, at age thirty-three, I chanced to view *Infant & Mother: Deep Sleep & Dark Shadow* hanging in the men's room of Orsi's Rib Room. I have been a devout apostle. I have honed my skills. I have tracked every lead, however ephemeral, catalogued every confirmed and unconfirmed piece of work, and assembled the first group on the planet to zealously pursue the ways and means of Proppiana. And so know, without doubt, that it is a waste of both time and effort to attempt to make a fool out of me. If and when Terry Propp chooses to return home, I will know with an unflinching certainty that will confirm the worth of my faith that he has breached the silence, that he has reached out finally and definitively.

Until that day comes, I will happily endure the nonsense of overindulged children who are somehow aroused by adolescent pranksterism. Take off your clown suit, Imposter. No one is buying. And let me use this incident to remind my colleagues that our only assurance of purity in ferreting out all things Proppian is evidence from the *official record:* that which can be confirmed with physical documentation and counterchecked by secondary material. And so, as the title of my column says, let us review what we know so far.

Terrence Propp was born either in Mollusk Cove, New York, or Quinsigamond, Massachusetts, in either 1937 or 1929. It is almost certain that he derives from some arm of the fairly prominent Propp family who had arrived in America at least by 1694, settling in and around the area of Pittsfield, Massachusetts, in the shadow of Mount Greylock, though there is a dissenting opinion that Propp's ancestors moved south almost immediately after their arrival in the New World and began a pattern of nomadism that eventually brought them to Mexico by the early 1800s, where they established either a string of homeopathic hospitals or a museum to catalog and house native Mexican artwork. I, personally, find this school of thought quite unlikely, based for the most part on far-flung conjecture and self-styled theory.

As a side note, I will mention that we are fairly certain that Propp's maternal great-great-granduncle was one Balthus Nixford, a once notorious and now, sadly, forgotten painter who in 1837 was charged, according to documents kept in Quinsigamond's own Center for Historical Bibliography, with "the creation and dissemination of lewd, obscene, indecent, and un-Christian pictures designed to incite wicked and lacivious yearnings into the minds of the populace." All of Nixford's work was burned in the "October Bonfire of '38" and the artist was driven from the city and banished "for the duration of his natural life." And so we see, apostles, history, that relentless nightmare, repeats itself with a tasteless vengeance. And now, all these years later, we have been given a new artist to drive underground with the abundance of our ignorance and intolerance.

The source of Terrence Propp's primary education is lost to us, but we believe his undergraduate years were spent, at least partially, either locally here at the College of St. Ignatius, or at Cornell University in Ithaca, New York. There is one recently bandied theory that he pursued a now-defunct correspondence school whose application materials were once offered on the flaps of matchbooks dispensed at Orsi's Rib Room Diner. Transcripts at both St. Ignatius and Cornell are either sealed or missing.

There is conjecture, sponsored by the presence of a series of five Southern Pacific landscape pieces, that Propp served in the navy as a signalman shortly before or after his undergraduate education. I should point out that there is also a small pocket of vehement protest that the "Melmoth Island Shots," as they have come to be known, are talented forgeries. Propp finished his formal education sometime in the late 1950s and either remained in (or came to settle in) Quinsigamond. It is possible, some would say likely, that for a time during this period he supported himself by selling balloons to children in Salisbury Park.

Certainly, it is during this time, in the early sixties, when his work began appearing in local galleries such as f.46 and the Riis. Before his death, gallery owner Nigel "Naggy" Moholy, in an interview, recounted that he never actually met Propp face-to-face and that the artist insisted on an elaborate scheme for the delivery of his work. Moholy said he would receive a phone call, at times in the middle of the night, and the caller would simply declare, "Say Cheese!", and Moholy would then have to hurry down to Gompers Train Station, walk to a specific trash can and reach inside where he would find Propp's latest offerings wrapped in "a kind of white wax paper, like the kind they use in the butcher shops for wrapping meat and fish."

As the years went on, however, the late-night phone calls grew less and less frequent and, ironically, as Propp's work began to receive more and more acclaim and attention, his output, or, we should say, his publicly presented output, became minimal in number if not quality. There has been no confirmed sighting of work by Terrence Propp for over a decade now. There has been no confirmed sighting of or communication with the man himself in at least that long.

Rumors, of course, proliferate in the absence of concrete fact. And we here at *Underexposed* are committed to quashing rumor and proliferating truth. And all for one simple reason that is, ultimately, our credo: Terrence Propp's work is the most perfect key we have found yet to unlock the primal, sensual, carnal heart of humankind, to halt and reverse the devotion taking place in each of us. Godspeed.

13

Even on Musuraca Avenue they're a strange sight: Jakob and Felix Kinsky leading a single-file parade of Grey Roaches. The Roaches are all dressed in requisite gang colors, a loose facsimile of the standard uniform from a century ago in the Talmud schools of Old Bohemia— black-on-black wool suits, white cotton shirts, the thin black ties that Felix has had customized with a print design of tiny grey cockroaches. Jakob is dressed similarly, and he's got his ever present Seitz 16 mm up on his shoulder. Felix can't stand the old style of dress. *We live in this country now,* he thinks, *we should act like the natives.*

"Are you nervous?" Felix asks, feeling smug and a little wired.

"I hate to disappoint you," Jakob said, "but there's always the chance he got the money together."

Felix gives a barking laugh. "I can see why your father has left collections to me. He won't have the money,

Jakob. It's not going to happen that way. You better prepare yourself. You're going to have to use the Roaches tonight. You better be ready to give the word. Or find someplace else to sleep tonight."

Jakob stops at the corner, looks at his cousin through the Seitz, shoots a few seconds of film.

"Don't worry about me, cuz," he says. "I always do what I have to do."

They cross the street onto Ruttenberg, the Roaches staying in an ordered line like some sacred and retro fire drill. They're the oddest muscle in Bangkok Park these days, but they're proving themselves as disciplined and dangerous as any of their rivals. They're more quiet than the Granada Street Popes. More stable than the Tonton Loas. Free from the internal strife that seems to constantly grip the Castlebar Road Boys.

The Roaches are led by Ivan "Huck" Hrabal, a sixteen-year-old refugee out of Poric just before the plague and the blockades. Huck lived for a month in the hull of a freighter, subsisting on tins of bootleg caviar and a found sack of half-rotten oranges. He's a confirmed knife man, could give the city's chief pathologist a pang of professional envy. His only weakness is his barely concealed passion for his second in command, Vera Gottwald. No one seems to know a thing about Vera G's past. She simply showed up at the St. Vitus one night; Papa Hermann gave her a meal of beetroot soup and smoked curd cheese and turned her over to Felix.

Huck and Vera supervise a flock of eighteen sanctioned meatboys, grooming them into a cadre of warrior monks for the day when, as Felix promises, the city will exist solely for the benefit of the Family Kinsky. For now, the Roaches keep busy with a routine of standard gang-biz: extortion, black marketeering, pharmaceuticals, and the usual hit-and-run work necessary for making and occasionally expanding the Kinsky territory.

"Jakob, admit to me that you don't have a clue," Felix says, goading his cousin, aching for him to reject tonight's errand. "You've never done this before."

Jakob mocks himself and says, "I've seen movies."

"You and your goddamn movies," Felix yells and grabs his cousin's arm, jerking them both to a stop. He spits on the ground, stares at the Roaches as they go rigid and look to their feet.

"This isn't some movie, you little putz. You're going to have to draw some blood tonight. Look at you. You brought your goddamn movie camera. What the hell are you thinking, Jakob? What is wrong with you? Your father is offering you everything. A year from now we could be ready to knock over the Iguarans. What is your goddamn problem?"

Jakob stays silent for a second, staring at Felix's face, then he starts to nod, and, without any trace of anger or humor, says, "You would make a tremendous character actor, Felix. Honestly. The loose cannon. The simmering pot. The audience watches, knowing from the start he'll explode. The cog the script could always pivot on. You know the type I mean? A James Caan, perhaps. If Caan were born in Maisel. And dressed badly."

Vera can't help but laugh, a throaty squeal that erupts and vanishes in a single breath. And though Felix doesn't turn around to glare at her, Huck knows she's made a terrible mistake. Because though what Jakob has said is funny, it's also true. And at some later point, when this tiny incident has been forgotten by all, Felix's button will get pushed. And then he'll decide to act on Vera's disrespect.

Felix stares at Jakob and says," Do you want me to hold your camera?"

Jakob smiles and says, "I don't think that will be necessary."

They walk a final block to their destination. Felix motions Bidlo and Krofta around to the rear of the storefront. Huck and Vera separate and move to opposite corners of the street to watch for the unlikely arrival of any independent muscle. Jakob takes a moment to focus the Seitz on the gorgeous neon marquee hanging out above the sidewalk:

Citizen Jane's **Underground Videos**
The Best in *Noir* **Entertainment**
Tonight's Discount: "Gun Crazy" (1950)

Then he moves his focus to the door of the shop, which has been entirely papered with hand-out flyers asking for any information concerning the disappearance of the little girl named Jenny Ellis.

Felix taps him on the shoulder.

"The owner is 'Sweet Jane' Firbank. He's a real head case. Dresses in the women's clothing. He's a month late in collections. Papa said he clears his account tonight or we let the Roaches loose. You understand that, Jakob? You think you can follow this?"

"Felix," Jakob says, "there's a point you honestly shouldn't push me past. You don't know me anymore."

"I know all about you, Jakob. You wouldn't know real life if it bit into your skinny little ass."

Jakob rests the Seitz back on his shoulder, then slowly, gently, he touches his cousin's face, brushes a thumb against Felix's cheek as if dusting something away.

"Maybe," Jakob says, "you're more Elisha Cook Jr. Especially around the eyes."

He turns and enters the video store, leaving a confused Felix saying, "Who are you calling *Junior?*"

Jakob stands inside and lets himself be shocked by the detail and imagination that's gone into the store's decor. The small rental shop perfectly mimics its product. It's as if the best noir set designers of the forties had gathered and pooled their talents to make a shrine to their chosen genre. The lighting is stolen straight from German Expressionism—artificial, harsh, and capable of throwing monstrous shadows. There's a row of metal, conical fluorescents suspended from the ceiling, perfect interrogation beams, looking like they'd been stolen from the most brutal police sweatbox in history. Like they came with a gross of rubber hoses. The fat venetian blinds hung in front of the windows are somehow backlit, so that even at night they toss a grid of sliced illumination across any inhabitant's face. The black cast-iron shelving that serves as display racks for the videos gives the feel of prison-issue furniture. The floor is a cold, urban red-brick. There are neon signs, electric blue-white numbers, mounted and glowing at the top of each display case to show the films are grouped chronologically. Jakob walks to the first shelf and picks up the display box for the 1927 release *Underworld*. He closes his eyes and tests himself—directed by von Sternberg, lensed by Bert Glennon—opens his eyes and looks on the back of the video box to prove himself right. He walks to the opposite wall and picks up the most recent release in the store, *Castle Oswald*, but before he can close his eyes, a voice sounds.

"Trust me, darling. You don't want that self-indulgent pap."

He turns to the sales counter, where a huge man dressed in elaborate drag is leaning on the cash register staring out at him.

"All style and no story. Rain and smoke and urban squalor. Just gorgeous. But what about character? What about conflict?"

The guy has to be close to six six, with sunken eyes and a yellow complexion that he's rouged up. He's got on a blond, wavy wig with bangs in the front, red lipstick, a pair of old sunglasses. He's wearing white silk lounging pajamas with flounced sleeves and a pair of classic, kitschy mules on his feet.

He comes out from behind the counter and approaches Jakob, saying, "You're new."

"I just found out about this place."

He puts his hands on his hips, looks Jakob up and down and says, "Are you passionate or just a dabbler?"

Jakob stares at him.

"About the genre, honey. About the medium."

"Oh, of course. I'm passionate. I'm a real zealot."

"That's what they all say. Let's try you out," and he begins to turn in a circle, saying, "Who am I tonight?"

Jakob watches this private fashion show and cringes a little at the thought of Felix and the Roaches walking in. The drag queen comes to a stop and raises his eyebrows.

Jakob starts to shake his head and the guy gives a disappointed sigh and says, "I'm Phyllis Dietrichson, for God's sake."

The name clicks.

"Of course," Jakob says, "you got it. You have really nailed it. Barbara Stanwyck."

The original noir woman."

"Double Indemnity," Jakob says, trying to redeem himself, "Nineteen Forty-four."

"Directed by?"

"Billy Wilder."

"Produced by?"

"Joseph Sistrom."

Phyllis/Barbara leans forward and crosses his arms over his chest, lowers his voice and says, "Art Director?"

Jakob takes a breath, lets a smug grin come over his face and says, "Hal Pereira."

The man is delighted, grabs Jakob's hand and starts to pump it, saying, "You pass. I'm Jane Firbank, the owner of Citizen Jane's."

"I'm Jakob," dropping the last name.

"That," Jane says, indicating the Seitz, "looks like a classic."

Jakob hands it to him. "It's an antique," he says, "they didn't make too many. If I told you who it originally belonged to, you wouldn't believe me."

Jane lets out a laugh-cum-growl.

"Take a look at me. I'll believe almost anything."

Jakob nods. "Well, you picked a real winner to model yourself on."

"Oh, I'm only doing Stanwyck tonight. I have a growing repertory. You should see my Veronica Lake."

Jakob gestures to the display shelves.

"Do you do the ordering?"

"I couldn't trust it to anyone else."

"How loose do you play with the semiotics?"

"Oh, Christ," Jane says, face falling as he hands back the Seitz, "You're not an academic, are you?"

"Hack filmmaker," Jakob reassures and as if to prove his claim, he pulls a business card out of his pocket and hands it to Jane who reads

Amerikan Pictures
hyperreal noir for our entropic world
a division of Hungry Artists Group

Jane's smile returns and he says, "Well, I'm not a purist if that's what you mean. I'll stock non-American. I'll go for a good genre-blend. I can tolerate some of the neo-stuff. I'm simple. Give me some crime, cynicism, claustrophobia, a little innocence betrayed."

"And visually?"

"The starker the better. Disorientation. City grime. As much shadow as you can manage without going muddy. I'll take some angles, some mirrors, maybe some silhouettes. But what about you? What do you need?"

"He needs nine thousand bucks."

Felix's voice.

They turn around to see him directing the Roaches inside. His red leather suit looks vinyl under the shop's harsh lighting.

"We got bored," Felix says to Jakob.

"I can handle this," Jakob tries, but Felix makes a face that cuts off debate.

"Oh no," Sweet Jane says. "Don't tell me you're with these animals."

Felix walks up to Jakob, puts a hand on his chest and softly pushes him backward.

"Film *this,* cousin," he says. "You might find a way to use it one of these days."

Then he wheels around and backhands Jane across the face, breaking skin to the corner of the mouth and initiating a trickle of blood that clashes with the Barbara Stanwyck lipstick. He pulls the shop owner into himself by the lapels and says, "We've been letting you slide, queenie. Now where's my goddamn money?"

Jane looks at Jakob, more disappointed than terrified, as if he's been through this drill before. Jakob wants to tell him Felix is serious this time, to just hand over the payment and get the Roaches out of his life.

"Turn the goddamn camera on, cuz," Felix yells. "I'll show you how to make Papa proud."

He drives a knee into Jane's groin and the shopkeeper drops to the bricks, sucking air.

Felix points to the door and Vera turns the deadbolt. The Roaches start to circulate, knocking over shelves, smashing neon with broomsticks. Emil Krofta takes out an Urquell Malt bottle and heaves it against the wall, where it shatters and fills the store with the smell of gasoline.

"You know why he needs the money, Jakob?" Felix asks, driving a boot into Jane's side. "He wants to get himself castrated. Honest to God. He's saving for some operation."

"Sidney Lumet," Jakob mutters, "Nineteen Seventy-five."

"What?" Felix says, staring down at the bleeding lump of Jane.

Jakob puts the Seitz on the floor and watches the Roaches destroy the place, tear posters from the walls—*I Wake Up Screaming, Scarlet Street, Fear in the Night*. He watches them rip the tape from videocassettes—*The Naked City, Street of Chance, The Big Gamble*—making a growing pile of curling, twisting lace on the bricks.

He steps back to Felix, puts his hands on his cousin's chest and mimics the original push, adding just a fraction more of force. Felix is shocked and then amused.

"What do you think you're doing, Jakob?"

Jakob gets ready to grab for the Seitz and swing at his cousin's head. But from foot-level, Jane croaks, "I've got the money. Stop it, please," and they both look down as the drag queen attempts to stand.

Jakob reaches down and grabs an arm, tries to haul Jane up.

Felix continues to stare at his cousin, the smile all gone, but he says, "Go get it," and the Roaches halt their rampage for a moment.

Jakob holds the stare and says to the room, "I'm Hermann Kinsky's son. We are done here. All of you get outside."

The Roaches don't know what to do.

"You don't move," Felix yells.

Jakob turns to Huck, "Hrabal, take them out of here. Or I'll tell my father to cut you loose."

"No one moves," Felix screams, top of his lungs.

And then a shotgun blast blows a crater in the ceiling and comes close to shattering every eardrum in the small shop. Half the Roaches hit the floor and cover their heads. Jakob and Felix turn, both crouched to see Sweet Jane Firbank positioned behind the sales counter, leveling a 12-gauge pump at them.

"You've got five seconds," Jane says, "to get the fuck out of here."

"Go," Jakob yells at the Roaches.

Felix stares from the gun barrel to his cousin's eyes, takes a single brush at his jacket and says, "Okay, kids, let's kill the freak."

He stands up slowly and the Roaches mimic his movement.

"I swear to God," Sweet Jane screams.

Emil Krofta and Little Jiri Fric are the first to pull their pieces from their suitcoats.

Sweet Jane settles on Fric, pulls the trigger and lets the recoil carry him backwards to the ground.

Little Jiri takes the load midsection, goes to the floor the worst way, gut-shot, torn open in the belly and fully aware of what's happened.

Emil Krofta extends his arms over the counter and unloads his Butterbaum automatic, putting nine lead-tipped rounds into Sweet Jane's head and chest before the shop owner can manage to repump. Sweet Jane is already dead by the time Huck Hrabal and Vera Gottwald line up next to Krofta and turn the transvestite's body into the most prestigious target in this surreal shooting gallery. When the trio's magazines are emptied, Jane Firbank is an unrecognizable mess of shredded flesh and bone wrapped in the remnants of Barbara Stanwyck's pajamas.

Jakob's ears are locked in a loop of ringing vibration and his lungs are caving in to panic, gunpowder, and the asbestos fragments that drift down from the hole in the ceiling. But he manages to crawl to Jiri Fric and pull the smallest Roach into his lap.

"Call Doctor Seifert," he yells to Felix.

But his cousin ignores him and instead yells for his gangsters to evacuate the scene.

"Hrabal," Jakob pleads, "help me carry him out."

Huck takes a step in Jakob's direction, but Felix screams, "Leave him. He's a casualty."

Hrabal turns from Kiri to Felix, watches as Felix motions to the door with his pistol.

"Outside," Felix snaps. "Right now."

"Go ahead," Jakob says and after a second, Hrabal runs out of the store.

Jakob sits on the floor, his pants and shirt already saturated with Jiri Fric's blood. He stares at his cousin, struggles for some air.

"This," Felix says, "is all your fault."

"You," Jakob says, "are a dead man."

Felix holsters his gun, steps into Ruttenberg Road, and takes off after the Roaches in the general direction of the Bohemian wing.

r≪l two

A camera is a gun.
An image taken is a death performed.
—Thomas Pynchon, *Vineland*

14

Sylvia sits inside the Snapshot Shack and does the film inventory. She counts boxes of Kodak and Fuji and Konica and the generic stuff that nobody buys. She arranges box after box in their shelving slots, organizes them by brand name, film speed, number of exposures, black-and-white or color. At ten o'clock the brown panel truck pulls up and delivers the morning's prints. It's a light load, a half-dozen envelopes full of vacation shots, birthday shots, half-focused cookouts that have been sitting in the camera since Labor Day. It seems like there are fewer customers every week.

By ten-fifteen she's phoned them all, told them their prints are ready and they can pick them up at their convenience. She says, "Thank you for using the Snapshot Shack," in this robotically sweet voice. It's the only way the words will come out. By ten-thirty she's so bored and tense she's grinding her teeth and replaying every moment of yesterday until she's got a headache that no amount of aspirin is going to relieve. And it bothers her how much she wants a drink.

She came up from the darkroom sometime before dawn. The kitchen door was still open the way she'd left it, but the Dewar's bottle was empty in the sink and Perry was sound asleep in bed. She lay down on the living room couch, dozed off at some point and woke to find Perry gone. He'd left a note underneath her Ansel Adams coffee mug—

> Sylvia,
> I'm sorry. I'm stupid. We've got to talk.
> Hated to see you on the couch.
> I'll call from work.
>
> P.

She thinks, *what is it we've got to talk about, Perry?* Yes, she was wrong not to call. And if the situation was reversed, maybe she'd have been furious. She should have called after she left Herzog's. She should've just found a phone and dialed the number. Told him what had happened. Assured him she was all right. But what she knew yesterday and what she knows right now, the thing she just can't change, is the fact that she didn't want to call Perry. She may not be sure of why that is, of all the different factors that might have kept her from the phone, but she knows she just couldn't do it. She couldn't hear his voice at that particular moment.

After she showered this morning, as she was standing in the bedroom, brushing her hair in the mirror, she looked down to see a manila file that Perry had left on the bureau. She stood there, hesitated maybe for a second, then opened it and paged through the contents. It was filled with clippings and notes and memos, all of them ink-stamped with dates and the words *FUD: File # 01-602.* There were newspaper articles on censorship battles in various parts of the country, political position papers, summaries on ballot referendums, excerpts from speeches given by Reverend Boetell.

She put her comb down and randomly read some of the Reverend's words: . . . *and a crusade means blood, brothers and sisters. A crusade means staining the land scarlet as we war against the godless, unredeemable enemy. There must be a purity to our thoughts, a surety to our purpose, and a godly persistence to our resolve. For we battle against the filthiest of foes, the beast who uses the Lord's natural urge toward loving procreation and subverts it into unspeakable perversion. But have stout heart, my chaste crusaders, and keep safe the gift of your modesty, for as he struck down the writhing infidels of Sodom and Gomorrah, so too will he bring his vengeance to the land of Quinsig-amond. So too shall he vanquish the wicked of this soulless and sinister town . . .*

At one point, a drop of water ran from her hair and fell on the page she was reading. She brushed it away immediately, but the paper was marked. She stuffed everything back into the file, got dressed quickly and left for work, but this feeling of nervousness had already set in, this sense of tension hidden just under the skin, a little like the way she used to feel back in college after she'd stayed up all night watching movies, drinking a full thermos of coffee. Exhausted but wired. Depleted but incapable of sleep. The images just rushing through the head, as if they were powered by some external force.

And now that feeling is still with her and she knows it's not helping that she's trapped for the next six hours inside this shoebox with only two cans of Diet Coke and an AM radio that keeps fading out. She should have brought a book or magazine, but she just wanted to get out of the apartment. She wishes that somebody would come by to pick up their pictures. She just wants to talk to a stranger. Say all the banal, trivial things they expect. *Would you like a new roll of film today? We're running a special on Snapshot Shack 200 speed. Remember, Thursday is doubles day. Here's your change. Thanks for using Snapshot Shack.*

She picks up the first envelope of new prints. She stares at the name for a while. It sounds familiar to her, but she can't place it: *Mrs. Claudet.* She doesn't recognize the telephone number. She puts the envelope down on the pile of new deliveries. She looks out on the empty parking lot. Then she picks up the envelope and opens the flap and pulls out the pictures.

They're summertime shots. Two and three months old. The first photo is a beach shot, a woman about Sylvia's age in a one-piece royal blue bathing suit. The woman is standing on an outcropping of jetty, water rushing around her feet. There's a huge smile on her face. She looks a little bit embarrassed. She's got a great figure. Probably someone who does aerobics four or five times a week. Maybe this is Mrs. Claudet. Sylvia has never seen her before.

She fingers through the stack. She sees the same woman straddling a bicycle, eating an ice-cream cone, washing a car and seeming to threaten the photographer with a hosing. She sees the woman in the arms of a man with a bushy mustache. Their pose says *boyfriend* or *husband.* Sylvia sees the man patting a dog, a small shepherd with a tongue hanging over the bend of its mouth. She sees the couple together in a restaurant and she imagines the woman asking an agreeable waiter to take the shot. She sees the man sprawled in a mesh lawn chair, wearing a tank top and shorts, raising a beer bottle in the direction of the camera.

They're smiling in every picture. They look like they're having the summer of their lives. The woman looks like a definition of the word *vibrant.* She looks like she's placed a ban on all variety of problems. She looks beautiful and she looks like she knows it.

And Sylvia finds herself thinking *I want your life, Mrs. Claudet* when she hears the tapping on the glass. She jumps and the photos fly into the air and rain down around her. She looks up, ready to find the aerobic goddess staring at her, spying on her as she envies the record of a perfect summer. But it's not Mrs. Claudet. It's Leni Pauline. And she's holding Sylvia's camera.

Sylvia slides the window open and Leni says, "God, I'm sorry. I didn't mean to scare you."

"I was just inspecting," Sylvia says. "Checking the pictures."

"Quality control," Leni says, maybe sarcastically, then "I brought your camera," holding it up in the palm of her hand, waitress-style.

"God. Thank you. Thanks so much. I thought I'd never see it again."

"Hugo got it back last night," Leni says. "He asked me to drop it off to you."

"How did you find me?"Sylvia asks.

Leni shrugs. "Hugo gave me the address. I thought you'd given it to him."

Sylvia takes the camera from her and says, "Not that I remember."

"Yeah, well, yesterday was a little confusing, you know."

"How'd Hugo get hold of it?"

Leni gives a laugh. "Hugo can get hold of anything if he wants it badly enough. Coco calls him *the Evil Santa.* "

"Coco?"

"One of the girls," Leni says. "Down at the Palace."

The camera looks perfect, looks like it's been sitting in the darkroom all night. Not a scratch.

"How can I thank you guys?" Sylvia asks.

Leni stops herself from smiling and says, "Listen, here's a little tip. Never say that to anyone in my profession, okay?"

Sylvia laughs and then realizes Leni's not joking. Leni takes a step back from the window, looks up and studies the Shack. She's wearing jeans and a burgundy silk blouse, ankle boots and a leather bomber jacket that's cracked and fading from chocolate to dusty white.

She shakes her head and says, "You like sitting in this thing all day?"

"It's not bad."

"It looks bad."

"You get used to it."

Leni walks back up to the window and says, "You can get used to anything. That doesn't mean you like it."

"It's a job. I don't have to think."

"You have something against thinking?" Leni says.

They stare at each other until finally Sylvia shakes her head *no*.

Leni changes the subject and says, "Hugo said to tell you there was no film in the camera when he got it back. He said sorry about that."

"Dammit," Sylvia says. "I had some great shots of the riot."

"There'll be other riots, Sylvia."

"Not for me."

Leni says, "That's because you're stuck in this goddamn camera-thing all day. Honest to God, I'd lose it in there. I'd get claustrophobic. I hate small places like that."

"It gets pretty annoying sometimes. The day can go by pretty slowly."

"See, my days, they fly. They're gone. I get up, I get out, I do things. I walk around. I see people."

"What about work?"

Leni shakes her head. "It's not like I work every day. Average week, I work maybe three days. Nights a lot. Hugo loves shooting at night. He says people are more relaxed at night. I don't know. Everyone's different."

"What do you—" Sylvia starts and then stops herself, embarrassed.

"What do I make, right? That's what everyone wants to know. That's the big question."

"I didn't mean to be rude—"

"It's not rude," Leni says. "If I didn't want to tell you, I wouldn't tell you. I do all right. I've got an arrangement with Hugo, so I'm not really the norm. I've got kind of this contract thing with Hugo. So I'm a little different. But the average is four, five hundred. The guys make more, right."

"Five hundred a week," Sylvia says.

Leni gets a big kick out of this. "A day, Sylvia. Five hundred a day. The real names, the women who headline, they can go up to a grand a day, a few go higher. Once you're up there you can put together a more complex package, you know? You can have contingencies. You're a name, you might take back a point or two after the net."

"That's over a hundred grand a year."

Leni leans on the lip of the window's counter. "You're assuming you work fifty-two weeks a year, Sylvia. You know what you'd look like, you worked fifty-two weeks a year?"

Sylvia's embarrassed but too intrigued to shut up. "She can't help asking, "How did you get into this business?"

Leni pushes her hair off her face and says, "How'd you end up sitting inside a camera, Sylvia?"

"I just needed a job."

"There you go."

"It's a little different, Leni."

"Why's it so different?"

"I don't know. You didn't just answer some ad—"

"That's exactly what I did."

"C'mon."

"That's how everyone I know got into it. You answer an ad."

"What? You open a newspaper and it says *woman wanted to get naked and be filmed having sex with strange men.*"

The words sound insulting after they're out there, but Leni just smiles and says, "It's a little more subtle than that."

"Like what? What does the ad say?"

Leni takes a long breath and says, "You're really fascinated by this, huh?"

Sylvia feels defensive. "It's just really foreign to me."

"Honey," Leni says, "you don't know foreign. You've never even seen foreign."

"You make that sound so depressing."

"You hear it that way. It isn't anything to me. It isn't one way or another."

"How long have you been working?"

Leni doesn't answer. She leans down and actually sticks her head inside the window and looks around.

"It's incredible to me that you sit in here all day," she says. "It can't be healthy."

Sylvia shrugs. "I've got a radio. I bring a book. I can read. I get a lot of reading done."

Leni stares at her and says, "Listen, you're so curious, what're you doing for lunch? You must eat lunch. They let you eat lunch, right?"

"Yeah, they let me eat lunch. I usually just just run down to that convenience store and grab a yogurt."

"A yogurt," Leni repeats and Sylvia nods.

"You want to go to lunch?" Leni asks. "I know a place. We'll have something. I'll give you the lowdown."

"Thanks, but I can't leave."

"You just said you run to the convenience store."

"That's like five minutes. You can leave to go the bathroom or on a quick errand—"

"Aren't they generous."

"Really," Sylvia says, "I've got to stay here."

"Yeah, I know," Leni says. "You're just so busy. The lines are backing up here." "Business is dead. I'm amazed the place is still open."

"Sylvia, no one's going to miss you for a half hour. I know a place five minutes from here. You'll love this place."

"Leni, I can't just—"

"You have to, Sylvia. It's not healthy in there. You've got to trust me on this."

"I can't. They'll be furious."

"What will they do, huh? They'll fire you? It'll be really tough picking something up this stimulating. And I'm sure the money is tremendous, right? You said yourself the place'll probably close up in a month—"

"I never said—"

"—and will they give a damn about you when it does? This is crazy, Sylvia. Do something fun for a change."

Ten minutes later, they pull up next to Kunitz Tower at the top of Behrman Hill and just sit there for a few minutes looking at the thing. It's a sixty-foot tall, two-and-a-half story monument built of boulders and cobbles and designed to look like a mini feudal castle. The structure is acutally two towers joined together by an open-air archway.

Sylvia lives less than five miles from the Tower, but she's been here exactly twice—on a grade school field trip and in high school, parking with a boy names Bobby Fenton on their first and only date. She wonders now what ever happened to Bobby.

The Tower is surrounded by a circular gravel road that in turn is surrounded by a scrubby, overgrown woods that covers the hill. Supposedly the view from the top of the Tower is tremendous, but to get there you've got to walk up these dank and grungy stone stairwells that always stink of urine. The rumor is that during the day the drunks and the gay hustlers share the place peacefully, but at night it belongs to the teenage punkers whose malt liquor bottles get tossed from the observation parapet. Today, the place appears empty.

Sylvia looks at Leni and raises her eyebrows for an explanation.

"The Floating Kitchen," Leni says and climbs out of the car.

They walk to the stairwell opening and start up.

"It's a hit-and-run operation. The owners haven't scored a restaurant or a license yet, so they jump around. They've been using the Tower for about a week now. No signs. No advertising. They get by on word of mouth. It's a family operation. The Zumaeta clan. From a village called Puquio in Peru. Everybody works. The old man, Jorge, he came north about six years ago. Worked as a cabbie and a barkeep. Put in like a hundred hours a week. Work and sleep. Lived on coffee. Brought everybody up one at a time. Soon as he had enough cash—bang, here comes son number one. Six months later, bang, here comes a daughter. The last to come was Maria, the wife. She held the fort back home until they'd all hit the road. Jorge sets them all up with work. Same deal, they work till they drop. Then six months ago, Daddy gets the idea for the restaurant. Keep everyone together. Capitalize on Maria's fantastic cooking skills. Only they can't afford to buy a place. So Maria comes up with the idea of the Floating Kitchen. They find empty spaces, move in and set up shop. And as luck would have it, the Zumaeta's moveable feast is now the hottest trend in the Zone."

They emerge out onto the top platform and Sylvia walks to the edge and leans on the capstones. She can see miles in every direction. In the center of the concrete floor is a round wooden table with four mismatched chairs grouped around it. A stooped and withered old woman emerges from the opposite, twin tower with a broom and starts to sweep around the table. She's dressed in a quilted mechanic's jacket over an old fashioned cotton housedress.

Leni pulls out a chair and says, "That's Gramma. I'll introduce you to the whole crew."

They sit down and Sylvia says, "How do you know these people?"

"I know everybody," Leni says, then smiles and shakes her head. "I'm their big booster. I bring everyone up here.

Except Hugo. Hugo refuses. Hugo would have a food taster on payroll if he could find someone willing."

She starts to study the chalkboard menu that the old woman is now holding and Sylvia looks out again at the view and keeps asking herself questions like, *what about the cops* and *how do you cook in this place.*

When she turns back, Leni is staring at her.

"Isn't this a little better than the torture booth?" Leni says. "That place just wasn't *right,* Sylvia. Bad juju. You were drowning in there."

"Little melodramatic. Leni."

"This is where you're absolutely wrong. It's the little stuff that gets to you. Always. It's the stuff we don't pay attention to. Our environment is hitting us on a hundred levels every second and we don't even recognize it. But inside we're growing tumors and making plans to buy assault rifles."

"Assault rifles," Sylvia says.

Leni brings her head across the table. "You walk down the street in a big American city, okay? You walk by block after block of these big towers, these monster rectangles, that just shoot up forever. They're just enormous blocks of glass and steel and concrete. No design. No angles. No color. No real variation. You know what those buildings are saying to you when you go by?"

"The buildings?"

"They're saying—*you're worthless. You're powerless. You're a peasant. Your time here has no meaning.* They're saying *you'll never know what goes on in here.*"

They stare at each other for a second and then Sylvia shakes her head.

"What?" Leni says.

"Nothing."

"No, what?"

"I just can't help . . . I'm just . . . Do all of Hugo's actresses talk this way?"

Leni sits back in her chair and says, "A. I'm not a possession of Hugo Fuckhead Schick. You've got to watch your terminology there, Sylvia. And B. No, the actors I know are like everyone you know. They're all over the board. I work with stupid people. I work with really savvy people. I work with an occasional neurotic and I work with a lot of just average, boring stiffs. I did my last film with a girl who had a master's degree in anthropology—"

"Get out of here," Sylvia interrupts.

"You come down the Palace, I'll introduce you to Miriam."

A teenage girl comes to the table with an order pad in her hands. She nods and smiles at Leni, who says, "How are you doing today, Alejandra? I think I'm in the mood for Cuy. Maybe some Papas Arequipena. And a house coffee with the shooter on the side."

"What's Cuy?" Sylvia asks.

"She'll have the same," Leni says to Alejandra, who scribbles on the pad and walks away.

Sylvia opens her mouth to protest and Leni says, "Trust me here, all right? You'll love it, okay?"

If Perry pulled something like this Sylvia knows she'd be annoyed for the rest of the day. But something makes her want to give over to Leni. Sitting here with her might mean forfeiting the Shack job. But so what. Leni's right. You can always get another job. And maybe the Shack *was* doing something to her. Maybe sitting inside that big camera all day was getting to her in ways she couldn't perceive.

Alejandra comes back with two mugs of coffee, black and looking thick. The mugs are only about three-quarters full and next to them she places two shot glasses filled with a clear, slightly green liquid.

"Uh-uh," Sylvia says. "It's too early in the day. And I drank way too much yesterday. I felt horrible this morning."

"It was the thought of going to that hut out there. God, just the thought of it." Leni imitates a full body shiver and picks up the shot glass.

"No, really—"

"Here's what you do," Leni says. "You take half of it in your mouth and hold it there. Let it roll around the gums. Tremendous. It heats up. Then you dump the rest into the mug, swirl it once, take a big sip of coffee and swallow the whole thing down."

Sylvia gives her a skeptical look. "What is it?"

"Hootch. Their native moonshine. They won't tell me the real name. No liquor license, you know."

Sylvia watches the routine, then follows Leni's lead, fires half the shot, dumps, swirls, and swallows. Then she sits back. The rush comes in about five seconds. It's like she applied Ben-Gay to the inside of her throat and chest. It's like her lungs have been soaked in mentholated muscle rub.

Leni is looking over at her, a huge grin breaking on her face.

"Isn't that great," she says.

"Does it let up?" Sylvia asks.

"Who wants it to let up? God, your whole face is flushed," Leni says. "Gives you great color. You look gorgeous right now."

"I feel like I've just breathed ether."

"This is better than ether," Leni says, straight-faced.

"I'm not going to be able to eat."

"Three minutes, you'll be ravenous."

"Any other side effects I should know about?"

"Well," Leni says, looking from side to side as if checking for spies in their little watchtower, "it doesn't short-change the libido."

Sylvia stares at her, finally says, "Am I ever going to know how much of what you say is the truth?"

"Sooner or later," Leni says, "everything I say is the truth."

Alejandra brings three bowls, one filled with what looks like potatoes mixed with eggs, olives, and red chilies, another with an unidentifiable meat dish, and the last filled with Ritz and saltine crackers. Leni takes a handful of crackers indiscriminately and crumbles them over the top of her food. Sylvia leans down and smells garlic and maybe mustard.

She lifts up her mug to take a sip of coffee and Leni says, "You're going to want to make that last."

Leni starts stirring her lunch with the concentration of a jewel cutter. Sylvia picks up a spoon, starts to make the same motions, moves her food in slow circles, reversing direction, cutting through the middle, pushing the top layer down to the bottom. She feels a little like a precocious monkey.

"So you want the big story," Leni says.

"Huh?"

"My life. You want the unabridged version. You want triple X, right?"

Sylvia doesn't know what to say.

"You're curious," Leni says. "Don't worry about it. That's how we learn, right?"

Sylvia takes a mouthful of meat. There's a sweetness she doesn't expect, nothing cloying, but a definite sugary tang.

"I was born twenty-four years ago," Leni begins and right away Sylvia doesn't believe her.

"My mother was originally from around here. Couple towns out. Came from a family used to work the apple orchards, you know, out on route 34. She married at, I don't know, maybe seventeen. Guy was a salesman from an auto parts company. That's what she used to tell me. He moved her out to Indiana right away. I think it was Lafayette. She was pregnant with me in the first year."

Leni stops, takes a sip of coffee.

"You're hoping I'll cut to the chase, right?" she says, then before Sylvia can answer she adds, "Sorry, you have to sit through the previews before the main attraction. Remember that. There's got to be buildup."

"Is your mother still alive?"

Leni shakes her head *no* and swallows. "The old man took off a month before I was born. Never heard from again. No letter. No phone calls. Just gone. He was a sweetheart, huh? Mom had to come back here. And though I only know her side of it, her people weren't exactly sympathetic. A little *I told you so* going on there, I guess. She moved in with her older sister and her family. That's where I lived for the first six or seven years. Then there was some huge blowup. I've got no idea what it was about. But we left and moved here into the city. Mom got us a little apartment on Froelich Way. You know those row houses over there? I actually loved it there. Great place to be a kid."

"How'd you get by?"

"You're an intuitive woman, Sylvia, aren't you? You know the right questions to ask. You should've gone into law, you know that? Mom got a job at the old Viceroy Theatre. She sold tickets. She sat in a little booth just like you've been doing."

"The Viceroy," Sylvia says.

"That's right," Leni says. "The bells go off. One of the city's first adult theatres. I mean the features were pretty soft-core compared with today. This was early seventies. I think they still called them 'nudies' back then. That was before the industry really took off."

"She couldn't get anything else?"

"You mean a job? I don't know. Maybe she didn't want anything else. It got complicated. She started dating the manager, a real, original greaseball, you know. One of these dicks who always wanted me to call him *uncle*. I couldn't stand the bastard."

"Was there a problem——"

"Abuse question, right? No, it was nothing like that. The guy was just a jerk. Mort Greneway. Never forget his name. He used to slick his hair back. Had terrible breath. He treated my mother like shit. But after my father's little act, you know, I think she felt kind of desperate . . . I don't know. She started drinking. Old story. She aged like crazy. Looked twenty years older than she was. I think about it now . . ."

She breaks off and Sylvia picks up her mug and holds it to her lips without drinking.

"Things went progressively downhill. We changed apartments a lot. They got smaller and smaller. By the time I hit high school it was all over with Morty and Mom was out of a job and nursing Johnnie Walker for breakfast."

"What did you do?"

"C'mon, Sylvia. Think about this. Where did you meet me?"

"I mean, how did it happen? How'd you end up making films?"

Leni plants her spoon in the remains of her lunch, pushes her bowl away from her, and wraps both hands around her coffee mug.

"I was about fifteen, sixteen. I wasn't getting to school much anyway. I dropped out. Went down to the Zone one afternoon. This was back when a few of the factories were still open and they had those strips of bars down on Grassman. This was just before the first boho kids moved in. I got a job waitressing at this little dive called the Wintergarden. Year later the owner sold out and they changed it to a topless place called Lodge 217. The new guys asked me if I wanted to dance. I said sure."

"Dance?"

"Yeah, dance, Sylvia. You know what I'm saying. They put in a runway and wrapped the bar around it. Doubled the price of the drinks. Hired half a dozen dancers and hung red and blue spotlights from the ceiling. We're talking a tacky place here. The runway was made of little mirror tiles and they'd chip and crack but nobody would replace them. Cheap. These guys—Doug and Jerry—these were very cheap guys. And no business sense whatsoever."

"How did you learn how to dance?" Sylvia asks and sips some coffee. She wants the whole story.

"What's to learn?" Leni says. "This is not the Bolshoi, okay? It's pretty rote. You've never seen a strip show?"

Sylvia shakes her head.

"Piece of cake. You'd learn it your first time out. It never changes. You go across the whole country, okay, you'll see the same setup. Only the accents change. The 217 had this three-dollar cover charge, then you could stay as long as you wanted. The bar seated maybe twenty-five people and there were a dozen or so cocktail tables beyond it. I'd do five sets a night. Six if it was a weekend night. You're on a total of about two and a half hours."

"What did you do the rest of the time?"

Leni raises her eyebrows. "Well, you'd have to put some time in during the breaks hustling foam. Not what you think. That's what we called this horrible booze they sold by the bottle. This industrial carbonated shit. They called it Schmitz Champagne, but it was like this blend of grain alcohol, club soda, and pink food coloring. Unbelievable. They brought it off the truck at twenty bucks a case, made us sell it for twenty a *bottle*. Just shameless. It's an old-time scam now, but back then Douggie thought they were so innovative."

"Who'd you sell it to?"

"The droolers. You'd find some schmuck just couldn't take his eyes off you. Then when you'd break you'd ask him to join you at a back table and once he sat down you'd ask him to buy you a bottle of Schmitz. They always went for it. Really sad. But when I wasn't dancing or hustling foam, I was reading."

"That explains it," Sylvia says and then regrets it, but Leni isn't going to let the comment go.

She says, "There's a real attitude there, Sylvia. It's the only unattractive thing I've seen about you so far."

"I didn't mean anything. It was a compliment—"

"No, no," Leni says, "don't hide behind that. You find me intelligent and confident and you couldn't figure out how a slut like me came to have a brain. Have opinions and ideas and everything."

"You're overreacting," Sylvia says. "I didn't mean to sound condescending. You said you'd dropped out of high school and—"

"There are all kinds of classrooms if you look for them, Sylvia. I'd sit in the dressing rooms down Lodge 217 and I'd always have a book with me. I hit the library every morning on my way down the Zone. I read everything I could get hold of. The owners teased the hell out of me. Stupid grunts."

"You were supporting your mother at this point?" The question comes out somehow harsh.

Leni nods. "For a while. She didn't last long. But what you really want to know, Sylvia, is—did she know? Did my mother know how I was earning a living? Right?"

Sylvia just shrugs.

"The answer is no, Sylvia. She never knew. She was beyond caring about things like that anyway. If you haven't lived this kind of thing, you haven't lived it. What can I say?"

Sylvia sits back and thinks about her story. "I don't mean to be obtuse," she says, "but I just can't get past the fact . . . I mean, you walk in off the street, you're what, sixteen years old—"

"I was a mature sixteen years old," Leni says. "In every way."

They stare at each other for a few seconds, then Leni breaks eye contact, reaches into her pocket and pulls out a roll of bills, peels off a few and slides them under her shot glass.

"Finish that," she says, gesturing to the mug, and Sylvia drains the last of her drink.

Leni slides out of her seat, yells goodbye to the Family Aumaeta and heads for the stairs. Sylvia follows along and says, "I think I did need to get out of that booth for a while."

They exit the Tower and as they start to thread their way through a cluster of zombie-like drunks that's materialized during lunch, Leni says, "Sylvia, I think you met me just in time."

15

Sylvia wants to think that there will be a point maybe five or six months from now when this blur, this weirdness of the last few days becomes understandable. She wants to imagine some fixed point in time, some day up ahead when the apartment is quiet and she's come in from work and it's another hour or so before Perry gets home and she's sitting at the kitchen table drinking a club soda or an iced coffee, leafing through the *Spy*, looking at what movies are playing at the colleges, maybe reading her horoscope. And then she'll think back on the day she went in to buy the Aquinas. And she'll follow her steps through, she'll be able to see herself move from location to location, meeting these people she's never seen before, going to these places she never knew existed. Behaving in ways she never did before and never will again. And the distance from these events will give her some perspective. She'll sit there and sip her coffee, take a melting ice cube into her mouth and suck on it, and she'll come to an understanding of why she did those things, why she fought with Perry and prowled around the Zone and walked into a riot and sat in a sex theatre. She'll just naturally, easily, come up with answers, like remembering some math forumla that orders all your components and solves the equation. A will equal B and B will equal C. Maybe she'll laugh at herself there alone in the kitchen. Maybe she'll just shake her head and still feel uncomfortable with the memories and go back to scanning the paper, finding out if this is a good day for Moon Children.

She wants to have faith that a day like that will arrive.

But the problem is that she's felt this way before. Dislocated. Strange to herself. Motivated by forces that she can't name. After her mother died and she was living on the couch, subsisting on breakfast cereal and cookies and every Rita Hayworth movie ever lensed, she knows she tried to tell herself the same thing—that a moment would arrive like something destined by prophecy, and everything would be made clear. That she'd be straight about her mother's death and her own decline. That she'd receive this innate explanation of why the only things she could tolerate were Chocolate Chip Clusters and another showing of *You Were Never Lovelier*.

But that instant, explanatory moment just didn't arrive. There was no epiphany. No second of pure satori. Life simply changed. She just got better and moved on, left the couch. She found a job, found Perry, integrated herself back into the flow of the normal majority.

And she's had days when she's sat at the kitchen table, listening to pop songs from her years in college, thinking about what to make for dinner, chopping vegetables for a salad. And she's gone back three years, regressed so completely that she could feel the harsh wool from her mother's sofa against her face, could feel her eyes glaze up with the third watching of *Cover Girl*. And she's expected the answer to roll in with the next second. She's expected that this time, her recall will give her that clarity that's just beyond her reach.

But it's never happened.

Sylvia doesn't know why she sank in the way that she did. She doesn't know what was going through her mind during those months she was tethered to her dead mother's apartment. She doesn't know why she couldn't just shake loose and move on. Do something. Save herself. She just knows that at one point she couldn't. And at another she could. Life changed. The wheel turned. Things altered. But there was no wisdom earned in the process. Just raw experience. And to this day it feels like a useless wound.

So maybe next summer, she'll be checking the times on the feature at the Cansino Drive-in. Maybe she'll be at the kitchen table making sandwiches to take to the movies. And maybe as she slices the bread and pushes the sandwich into the little plastic bag and folds the flap secure, she'll suddenly flash on this moment with a porn actress named Leni Pauline, driving through the Canal Zone in a Citroen, taking in air and trying not to be sick, woozy from booze and weirdness. Maybe she'll be able to call up this exact scene with photo-clarity.

But she doubts she'll understand anything about what she's been doing. She doubts the memory will hold any meaning or tell her something that's been previously hidden. It will just land there for a minute, in her brain. Behind her eyes. It will just remind her how odd things can turn at any given moment.

They come around the corner onto Watson and Leni hits the gas and Sylvia's stomach lurches. They screech to a stop in front of the Skin Palace, hop the curbstone and come to a stop at a tilt, two wheels in the street, two up on the sidewalk.

Leni kills the engine, raises up in her seat and gives a horrible, shrill whistle. One of Schick's beefy spandex-men comes out the front entrance, glancing up and down the walk, still wary from yesterday's rumble. Everything's fairly quiet though and Leni climbs out of the car, tosses the keys through the air and says to the bouncer, "Be a gentleman and park it for me, huh Franco?"

He mimes a kiss at her as she passes and then looks at Sylvia to see if she's going along for the ride. Sylvia takes a breath and stumbles out to the sidewalk, stands still for a second to get her balance. She looks up at the theatre and the wave of dizziness comes over her again, so she tries to ignore it and follows Leni into the lobby.

Inside there's an old man slouched on one of the lounges, sound asleep. He's deep into it, locked in REM-stage right here in public. His eyes and one of his hands are twitching, just like the way you see dogs quiver and kick out an occasional limb when they dream. An usher moves past the old guy and ignores him.

Sylvia hears the rumbling sound of corn popping and walks around the corner to the concession stand where Leni is behind the counter scooping newborn buds into a stiff paper cup that has the Skin Palace logo stenciled on it.

"You want some?" Leni asks as she pours salt over her corn.

"I'm supposed to be back at work," Sylvia says.

Leni seems to stop and think for a second, then puts the popcorn down, comes forward and leans on the counter.

"Look," she says, "I brought you back here 'cause the boss wants to see you." She pauses, then adds, "I just hate running Hugo's errands, okay?"

"What errand? You mean bringing back my camera? I could've come down—"

"Look, Sylvia," Leni says, "Hugo wants to make you a job offer."

Sylvia gives her a look and Leni finally smiles and says,

"It's not what you think. He's looking for a photographer. But don't let on I told you, all right? He likes to do these things in his own way."

"What kind of photographer?"

Leni picks up her popcorn and moves out from behind the counter.

"What kind do you think?" she says. "He needs publicity stills. Poster shots. You know."

"Nudes?" Sylvia says.

"For Christ sake," Leni says. "You are unbelievable. Wake up, will you? Look where you are. This is what we *do* here. This is our business. *Nudes?* What the hell do you think he wants?"

She heads for the grand stairway and not knowing what else to do, Sylvia follows her, but once they're upstairs, instead of going into the theatre, Leni turns left, heads down the corridor to another stairway and keeps ascending to a third floor. And like some dim apostle, too confused and maybe scared to walk away alone, Sylvia tails behind. At the landing, they swing past a huge metal door at the top that has the words *Editing Suites, Do Not Enter* stenciled across it in red block letters. Leni cuts a sharp left and starts jogging up a narrower spiral stairwell made of some black, cold metal. It empties into a small foyer with high ceilings and walls painted scarlet. Hung on the walls is a series of framed and matted old movie posters. Sylvia recognizes *Diary of a Lost Girl* and *Pandora's Box* and *The Last Laugh,* but then there are a couple in German that she's not familiar with. The far wall of the foyer is a set of huge, wooden double doors. Near the top of the left door, in the same red lettering as downstairs, it reads *Studio A,* but someone has spray-painted a fuzzy black line through this and written *Henrik Galeen Memorial Studio* underneath in this childish, cursive scrawl. The lettering ran before it could dry and each word drips downward toward the floor. Above the doors is tacked a cardboard sign that reads *Hot Set.*

Leni says, "Get ready for the screaming," then without waiting for any response she walks up, shoves a door open like a storm trooper, and charges inside.

Sylvia hears Hugo scream, "Son of a bitch," followed immediately by someone else yelling, "Cut, cut it now, hold up," and then a general chorus of moaning and cursing.

Sylvia looks back to the stairwell, but hears Leni say, "Oh, God, I did it again, didn't I?" in this barely sarcastic voice.

"Get over here," Hugo's yelling. "Someone take hold of her. Bring her over to me."

"Let's break for ten," a new voice sounds, followed immediately by Hugo shouting, "Who said break? Hans, what do you think . . ." and his voice trails off and for a couple seconds Sylvia gets only mumbling and an undercurrent of machine-ish noise, kind of a whirring hum, like her mother's old refrigerator used to make. Then half-naked bodies, a half-dozen of them, two men in short terry robes and four women in campy lingerie, walk out of the studio, ignore her, pass by and start down the spiral stairs.

A guy in jeans and a workshirt emerges with coils of thick black cable slung over his shoulder. He says, "They want to see you," as he passes.

She steps into the studio and is startled by how big it is. The cramped foyer didn't prepare her for this cavernous loft. It's like an old-time gymnasium. A lot of wood and brick and a musty smell. The ceiling rises up about two stories and the far wall seems like a football field away. But the place is junky, a museum to disorder. It's as if someone decided to build a maze out of found trash but got bored halfway through the project. There are clusters of furniture sets and tilting racks jammed to bursting with hanging clothes. There are tables covered with power tools and ragged sheets of plywood stacked against every free piece of wall space. There are ladders and step stools and mismatched chairs, camera tripods mounted on makeshift dollies, microphones hanging from their leads, suspended from ceiling girders. And lights. There's lighting equipment everywhere and most of it looks like it's been salvaged and repaired. Everything's nicked up and dented and heavy-looking. There are reflectors and deflectors and all kinds of filtering equipment.

She's surprised when she spots three old Panaflex cameras. In this age of high-definition videotape, Hugo sticks with bulky and expensive film. He marches over now, already half-bowed as he moves. It's weird, there's this stiffness and oiliness to him at the same time. He grabs Sylvia's hand and lifts it to his lips, plants a kiss and says, "Forgive my outburst. I didn't realize we had company."

"I didn't know you actually filmed here. I thought this was just the theatre."

He seems to like her confusion. "We're a self-contained package," he says, gesturing with his hand at the room in general. "I insist on control and I learned long ago that the only way to have it is simply to *have* it."

He gives a conspiratorial wink as if she's supposed to understand what he means and continues, "I don't like dealing with middlemen. Landlords, agents, distributors. The Palace had ample room, so over the years we've become more and more self-sufficient. I have my own contract players perpetually on the payroll. Would Jack Warner have spent time chasing after this week's megastar? Would Louis Mayer? You sign them young, support them, develop your own talent. It's an investment."

"So every film gets made right here?" she asks.

He takes her arm and leads her toward a floral couch out on the set itself. "We sometimes film on location, though I dislike outdoor work. It's a difficult balance, finding the control of the studio without getting too visually boring."

"And you even market the final product?"

"We have a small holding company. Pretori Distributors. It's a separate corporate entity."

"God," Sylvia says. "It's amazing. You do the whole show. Soup to nuts."

"So to speak," he says, suddenly amused.

"I wanted to thank you," she says. "For finding the camera—"

"Say no more," he holds up his hands. "I'm just sorry that we couldn't retrieve the film. But you'll take other pictures. You'll do even better work, I'm sure."

She looks out and for the first time she notices what must be today's set, the place they were shooting just minutes ago, before Leni ruined the shot. It's a huge bedroom. It looks a little like an old hotel room and it has a vague, undefinable style to it, kind of a pseudo-deco. Everything in the room is cut in sharp angles. In the middle of the set is an enormous bed, larger than king-size, maybe custom-made.

"You have to remember," Hugo says, seeing her studying it, "we can manipulate perspective. Within the frame of the camera, I can make this room do anything I want. It looks much smaller with your own eyes. You'll need to see the finished product on the screen."

And it suddenly comes home to Sylvia that as she stood out in the foyer, people were lying on this bed, having sex under these lights, being recorded by Hugo's old cameras, moaning for the benefit of the hanging mikes, sweating and grinding and groping while she stood in the next room.

And then they walked out past her as if they'd just left their desks at some anonymous bureaucracy, as if they'd just broken off from some clerical report to grab a little coffee down in the company cafeteria.

"You know," Hugo says, "it's fortuitous that you came to visit today. Yes, it's actually kismet. I was going to give you a call tonight."

The job offer. She thought Leni might have been putting her on.

"You were going to call me?" she says.

He nods, brings a hand up to stroke his chin.

"Yes. Absolutely." He stands up, paces to the set, turns to face her. "All my career I've trusted my instincts. And rarely have they let me down. Surely never when the hunch has been this strong."

"The hunch," she says.

"Now, I realize I've never actually seen your work. But as always, my need for a feeling, an intuition, is much stronger than my need for physical evidence."

"Very simply, Sylvia, I need some photographs taken. I need a photographer on the staff. Someone with both taste and flair. Subtlety and a sense of originality."

"You're offering me a job?"

"Exactly. Yes. A position. There's an opening in the organization and I'm extending it to you. You could learn quite a bit. I'm sure we could work out the financial particulars."

"I don't know what to say." Something makes her want to take his offer.

Sylvia's life this far should have exempted her from this entire situation. She's getting a job offer from an Austrian pornographer. She doubts anyone she grew up with or went to school with can make this exact claim. And on the heels of this she realizes that maybe there's something inherently subversive within her. Maybe something that's been there all along. Because as much as she thinks she wants to get things right with Perry, to get back to the normal routine, there's this other desire, this other knowledge that it would be a very real and very potent rush to sit opposite Perry over dinner, over that boring chicken and rice dish he loves so much, and somewhere in the midst of their lazy supper conversation, sometime after he's run down everything that took place at Walpole & Lewis that day, she'd love to casually take a sip of wine and let it wash over her tongue and then clear her throat and look at Perry's face and say, "Honey, I just took a job on a pornographic movie crew."

"I'll tell you what to say," Hugo says, "you say 'yes.' Or at the very least you say 'I think it over, Hugo.' "

"But, honestly, you've never seen anything I've done—"

He cuts her off. "Sylvia, please. You have to understand how I operate. When I'm in the restaurant. When I'm in the shopping plaza. When I'm in the balcony of the Palace's lobby on two-for-one night and all the college boys and girls are walking in laughing and embarrassed and thrilled. And when I spot that face, that young and genuine countenance. That look that captures me, that sets off the alarms. Do I stop and say, 'but can she act?' Do I hesitate and wonder, 'are there any unsightly blemishes I haven't yet seen?' No. Never. I approach them on the spot and I make them the offer. I tell them I'm a director. I tell them I wish to put them in a film. I may be rebuffed or even slapped. This has happened often. But that is fine. I've made the attempt. I've acted on the impulse. That is the nature of my work. The impulse. The instinctual sensation. I'm correct much more often than I'm wrong. Trust me, Sylvia, I don't need to see your work."

She shakes her head. She looks again at the set. The goddamn bed is so big you could get lost in it.

"Don't you ever worry about the police?"

He gives a smug and icy smile.

"Shall we say," he laughs, "that is but one line on the budget sheets."

"You pay them off?"

Now he really lets loose with a laugh. "I will never lose my love of that innocent American bluntness."

"I'm sorry," she says.

"Not at all," he says, then adds, "but my arrangement with our city fathers has nothing to do with your position."

"Right. Of course," she says. "What exactly would be my position?"

"We have a small portrait facility over in the Willi Forst Studio—"

"Willi Forst?" she says.

"Studio B," he says. "On the other side of that wall. I sometimes film simultaneously. I pop back and forth between the two sets. I find it stimulating, keeping the story lines separate."

She wants to ask *what possible difference could it make if the story lines get confused.* Instead she says, "So I'd be doing portrait work?"

"Believe me," he says, "you can get very creative. I need poster shots for each film. Publicity stills of my stars. Marketing pamphlets for the conventions. This type of thing. You'd pick it all up very quickly, I have no doubt."

"Mr. Schick—"

"Hugo, please."

"Hugo, I really appreciate your offer. It's really very nice of you. But the thing is, I just don't have a lot of experience doing portrait work. I'm much more a landscape person. Street scenes, that kind of thing."

"Like the incident yesterday."

"Well, no," she says. "Not really. That was a fluke. I happened to walk into it. And I happened to have my camera."

Hugo sighs and smiles at her. "If you can stand in the middle of that tumult and focus in on individual scenes, my God, Sylvia. You can do my work in your sleep."

"But there are very different techniques. You have to be good with people to do portrait work. You have to put them at ease, bring out their best face. Keep things natural. I'm not great in that area," she pauses and adds, "especially not when the people are naked."

He looks shocked. "Oh, that," he says. "One hour, you won't notice it. Trust me, it becomes irrelevant."

"I find that hard to imagine."

"Don't decide yet," Hugo says. "You go home. Sleep on it. Whatever you're making now, I'll increase your wage. And I'll pay a bonus on your acceptance."

"Hugo, really, you're making this very tempting—"

"That's my job," he says with a nod.

"But I just don't get it. There are a lot of photographers out there. You must know dozens who are already connected with your field. But you seem intent on hiring me, even though I'm not connected. You met me yesterday, for God sake. You don't know if I'll fit in. And you've never even seen my work."

He sits and seems to consider what she's said. Then he leans forward, clasps his hands together and balances the weight of his doughy body onto one knee. He lowers his voice and says, "I view your innocence, your industry-virginity, if you will, as a virtue rather than a deficit. I'm always looking for a new vision, Sylvia. A new way of taking in the image and a new way of giving it back. I think you can do that for me, Sylvia. And I know that if you choose not to I'll be terribly disappointed."

He seems so goddamn sincere. She's ready to cave in right here in front of him. She's ready to sign on with Team Hugo. She's ready to load up the Aquinas and shoot a whole parade of naked bodies.

She says, "I promise I'll give your offer every consideration."

He sits back, sinks into the couch and crosses his legs. He holds his arms out in the air and says, "I suppose I can't ask for more than that."

As if on cue, Leni comes up from behind and puts her hands on Sylvia's shoulders.

Hugo cocks his head back, looks up at her and says, "I'm very upset with you, Ms. Pauline."

She leans down, hands still on Sylvia, and kisses the top of his bald skull. It's possible she's left the red imprint of her thick lips, but from this angle Sylvia can't tell.

"You can spank me later," Leni says and Hugo looks around with semi-mock exasperation.

The actors and crew start to file into the studio. Two men disrobe as soon as they're in the door and start to walk toward the couch. Sylvia tries to stare at the floor.

"You're welcome to stay and watch me work," Hugo says, standing up.

Sylvia gets up and says, "I've really got to be going."

He takes her arm and walks her to the foyer, then with almost a fatherly stroke, he gives her cheek a soft brush with the back of his hand and in a low voice he says, "I'll wait for your decision, Sylvia. I know you'll fit in perfectly here at the Palace."

Without waiting for a response, he turns on his heels and heads back inside. Sylvia walks down the spiral staircase on shaky legs, thinking suddenly about what she's going to make for Perry's dinner.

ıᐃ

In the basement of the Hotel St. Vitus, Little Jiri Fric is laid out on top of a dusty Ping-Pong table. He's covered by two black wool blankets that bear the white words *Property of the Diocese of Quinsigamond.* The boy's entire body is quaking, vibrating in a constant, ever-growing shiver. Even in the dimness of the cellar, Jakob can see the glow of sweat running off the forehead.

Dr. Seifert is at a tool bench, repacking his duffel, shrugging in Jakob's general direction and trying to hide his theft of a rusty pair of needle-nose pliers.

"There's nothing more I can do," the doctor says. "Even if we could get him to a hospital, it would make little difference."

Jakob suspected the diagnosis from the start. Jiri lost so much blood on the way back to the St. Vitus that the doctor's questionable medical background is beside the point.

"Jakob," Seifert says, "if your father learns that I've come here—"

"Don't worry about Papa, Herr Doctor. I will take full responsibility."

"It's just that, you know his rules about treating gang casualties. He—"

"I couldn't let him die on the street," Jakob interrupts, then fishes in his pants pocket, pulls out a hundred, shakes Seifert's hand, pressing the bill into the old fraud's palm. The rumor is that Seifert was just a second-rate meat cutter back in Maisel. But he speaks the old tongue and he knows all the superstitions, so he's the only acceptable doctor for most of the Bohemian wing of Bangkok Park.

Seifert starts to climb the stairs to the kitchen, stops halfway up.

"If someone should see me—"

"Tell them," Jakob says, "I ran out of the camphor injections."

He turns and looks at Little Jiri, the youngest of the Grey Roaches, not sure if the boy is called "Little" because of his age or the deformed right leg that helped determine his stature.

Jakob moves to the old soapstone wash sink, takes his handkerchief from his back pocket, turns on the spigot and soaks the rag. Then he walks to the Ping-Pong table, sits down on the edge of it. Jiri is moving his mouth, trying to give words to the pain of his last dreams. Jakob leans in, brings lips near the boy's ear and whispers, "It's all right, I'm here, I won't leave you alone."

He holds the handkerchief above Jiri's mouth and squeezes just a bit, lets water trickle onto the lips. Jakob folds the cloth and lays it on the Roach's forehead, takes the boy's hand and simply holds on.

And he finds himself thinking of Felice Fabri.

At the moment she touched him—in the back row of the Kierling Theatre, at that exact instant on-screen when Ralph Meeker, bigger than life, crushed the hand of some craven and greedy pathologist—Jakob's life turned a sudden, dislocating corner.

If Jakob's existence up to this point was to be viewed as an ongoing film—and, in fact, this was the primary way he viewed it, a piece of celluloid looped into a Mobius strip: a film about a boy who lives only to watch film—Felice's hand falling between his legs was a plot twist he never could have anticipated. A story-curve that took the narrative of his life in a completely new and unknown direction, that employed techniques and stylistic innovations he had never dreamed of.

Passionate to this point only about movies, the heat of sexual initiation propelled Jakob into a realm where the entire city of Maisel became a fiction he could simply ignore. He stopped hearing his father's harsh voice drone on about this promised land titled *America*. He became oblivious to Felix's increasingly detailed descriptions of hit-and-run thugdom in the alleys off Kaprova. He failed to even comprehend the frightened babble of the neighborhood fishwives as they gossiped over their washlines about the now daily street-beatings or the bombing of the Altneu Synagogue.

None of the miniature pogroms could impact him in any way. The images of the Hasidim being harassed and shoved to the ground could not compete with Felice's body. The stoning of Rabbi Meyer on Moldau Lane just could not rival the power that ran along the surface of Felice's skin. The burning of Hilsner Kosher Meats, just a block from Papa's shop, simply didn't penetrate the heady realm of pubertal, animal passion that culminated between Felice's legs.

Everything boiled down to the essentials—the mysteries of Felice Fabri's body and the images projected day and night on the screen of the Kierling Theatre. And, importantly, those two elements were tied together in a primary, fundamental way. The films led into Felice and Felice led back into the films. They were almost one and the same: *Sanctuary. Satisfaction. Epiphany.*

And so, of course, all their consummations took place inside the Kierling. The theatre, always a holy place, now became the altar for the sacrament of their coupling. Jakob became a kind of high priest prone to visions by way of ecstasy. He wished to consecrate as often as possible. And Felice, enraptured by this insatiable mystic she'd created, obliged him to the point of an aching, wonderful exhaustion.

Their affair lasted for a month, though it was never so much an affair as it was a bizarre, insatiable pilgrimage into the limits of the carnal. They both found it particularly exciting to move slowly, settle into their back-row seats, begin by simply feeding each other candy and popcorn, the dispenser's fingers occasionally being sucked by the ingestor's mouth. They attempted to enforce a limited fondle for the first reel of film, allowed a more rigorous groping through the second reel. And finally, if discipline was possible, surrendered to consummation only during the movie's final moments. They copulated while watching *Nightmare Alley* and *Peeping Tom* and *Kiss of Death* and *Kiss the Blood off My Hands* and *Kiss Tomorrow Goodbye.*

For four rapturous weeks, Jakob left the Kierling with his lungs in a sweet pain and his head dizzy with sensation and vague, racing impulses. Felice would pull him to a favorite bench across the street in Dvetsil Park where they would embrace in a post-coital, post-cinematic warmth. Within the soft heat of this embrace, Jakob allowed himself to fantasize an idyllic future beyond anything he could previously imagine, an Eden where he and his lover would purchase the Kierling from Yitzhak Levi-Zangwill, restore the entire building, and fashion a honeymoon apartment out of Yitzhak's Zionist work-office. The boy gave full berth to these vivid dreams of a coming paradisaical time when his lungs were restored to normalcy by the power of love and the inhalation of fresh celluloid stock, an era when Maisel would supercede Hollywood as the motion picture capital of the world. When the Kierling would be seen as the crowning jewel of film institutes and archives everywhere and he would have to hire workmen from the Schiller ghetto to pour a long cement walkway so actors and actresses could forever come to leave their hand-and-footprints as testament to the ultimate seat of imagistic power.

Holding Felice in Dvetsil Park, yards from the soft glow of the Kierling's marquee, during the happiest month of his life, Jakob even allowed himself to imagine transforming the theatre's unused second floor into a working studio, a great hall full of heavy black equipment, cameras, lights, boom microphones, pulleys for lifting and placing scenery, mirrors for applying makeup, and a wooden canvas-back chair inscribed with his name in flowing, scripted letters.

This would be his holy land—*I'm sorry you can never understand it, Papa*—and so, he named his dream-studio *Amerikan Pictures*.

He whispered these dreams into Felice's ear as they sat on their bench on Dvetsil Park. He spoke of new camera angles he would try, pointed out interesting passing faces he would like to employ in specific roles, joked irreverently about remaking *Citizen Kane*. Mainly, Felice would nod and murmur a vague approval while running a hand lightly over his chest, beneath his coat. It was only when Jakob offhandedly mentioned that he was thinking of changing his name that Felice pulled away, let her body go stiff in his arms, and said, "Remember, Jako, you can only break the rules once you know the rules. And you can only cut away your past when you truly know your past."

Jakob had no idea what she meant, but he was unnerved by the comment anyway and they parted that night with an edgy final kiss that, on his walk home, the boy could only think of as *suspicious*.

And the next night at the Kierling, this suspicion was still present. They had gone to see an experimental feature, a one-night-only event whose title Jakob has never been able to recall. He cannot remember the plot or the actors or the director. He cannot envision the settings or the wardrobes or the musical score. This is the only film in his life that has evaded him in this complete a manner. And weeks later, on the first day of his arrival in Quinsigamond, Jakob opened his notebook and wrote:

> All I can remember is the image of a man being pursued through dark, decayed streets by a sea of eyes, human eyeballs, an audience of some sort, preying on this man, hunting him down for the marrow in his bones, the marrow in his soul. And this is simply an impression. A trace memory. Nothing I can verify or concretely describe. But instead of receding, the image is more and more relentless. It does not get any clearer. But it will not leave me alone.

Over the next three years, Jakob would attempt to find out what film this was. He would spend hours in the public library, poring through every cinema reference available. And he would be entirely unsuccessful.

But on that night, while the movie unreeled and the

stark, grainy images were gunned onto the screen, Jakob and Felice made love in the back row, and that particular coupling proved to be the most violent and intense session of both their lives.

When the lights came up, they exited the Kierling and walked to Dvetsil Park in silence, both of them trembling, both almost worried about the prolonged intensity they'd just subjected themselves to. They took their bench, fell into each other's decompressing embrace and, very likely at the same instant, looked out at the Pietá to see that the unconscious body of Yitzhak Levi-Zangwill had been draped into the arms of the weeping stone mother, another doomed child to cry for. Yitzhak had been beaten unconscious, but it wasn't until Jakob and Felice ran to the statue that they discovered the real nature of the theatre owner's wounds. Into his forehead had been carved the word *Zionist*. And below the dripping letters, his eyes had been gouged out.

"Are you out of your mind?"

The voice comes like an unexpected slap, like an open hand thrown full-force across the cheek, exploding the recipient out of a long sleep.

Jakob leaps off the Ping-Pong table and Little Jiri stirs and lets out an awful moan. Felix is at the bottom of the cellar stairs, an arm extended, a finger pointing at the gangboy's quaking body.

"You brought a casualty to the house?"

"I couldn't—" Jakob begins and Felix waves the excuse away, furious, his hand coming back to his face and rubbing over his eyes as if he could make the sight of Jiri Fric dying before him vanish.

"Do you have any idea the consequences this could have?" Felix barks. "Have you not heard a word your father has said? You brought a gang casualty back to your father's home. My God, Jakob."

Jakob looks from Little Jiri down to his feet, mumbles, "Well, he's here, now."

Felix rushes at his cousin, tackles him at the waist and they go to the floor. Jakob throws his head forward, smashing the bridge of Felix's nose and drawing blood. Felix is shocked with the pain and in the instant his distraction allows, Jakob gets both hands around his cousin's neck and begins to close off the windpipe, his thumbs pressing in on the throat with a power neither of them anticipated. Felix starts to choke and Jakob bears down harder, enraged, three years of repressed anger flooding from his adrenal gland like a tidal swell.

He leans down to his cousin's face and spits, "You don't know me."

But Felix jerks to the side and throws a knee into Jakob's groin. Jakob loses his breath, hunches into himself and absorbs a kick in the ribs that rolls him onto his side, fetal and gagging.

Felix grabs the edge of the Ping-Pong table, pulls himself up, then plants a boot on his cousin's neck, but doesn't apply any pressure. Through gritted teeth and faulty breath, he says, "You stupid little bastard—"

Then he backs off and Jakob can hear him sucking air. After a second, Felix moves into a shadowy corner of the basement and the noise of Jiri Fric's labored breathing is displaced by the sound of careless rummaging, trunks being shifted, forgotten crates shoved roughly to the side.

Jakob gets to his knees, pulls himself to standing and looks to see Felix holding a small, threadbare throw pillow over the face of Little Jiri. The smallest Roach gives no sign of suffocation, beyond a sudden and horrible twitch of his deformed leg. Jakob shifts his vision from the slightly jerking foot to Felix's eyes.

The cousins stare at each other in silence until Jiri Fric's leg falls motionless.

17

Sylvia takes the Waldstein Ave bus to the westside, transfers and takes the #14 to Hoffman Square. As she's walking the last two blocks home, she realizes that she left her camera in Leni's car. But that's the least of her problems. That feverish feeling from yesterday is starting to come back. Her legs are beginning to feel rubbery and her head is throbbing. She doesn't want to think about anything beyond climbing up the stairs, writing Perry a note that she's sick and getting into bed. She wants to sleep for the next two days. She wants to squirrel down under the covers, keep the shades drawn and just go under for the next forty-eight hours or so.

But when she opens the back door of the apartment, she can hear a chorus of unfamiliar voices coming from the front room. She walks as far as the doorway and looks in as all the talking stops.

"Honey," Perry says as he gets up from the couch, knocking a stack of papers on the floor. "You're home early."

"I wasn't feeling well," she says.

Perry's flustered. He hesitates between picking up his papers and coming over to her, then says, "We're having a meeting here."

"Sorry to interrupt," she says.

There's a moment of horrible quiet until Perry finally comes over next to her and starts introducing people, though she already knows who most of them are.

He gestures around the circle, all of whom, except for

Boetell's silent assistant Fernando, have manila folders at their feet and in their laps. The Brazilian kid is sitting on the floor in the corner, his head buried in a Bible. He doesn't look up at Sylvia. She wants to ask him if he ever gets tired of wearing that stupid white robe.

"You know Candice, of course," Perry says, "and this is District Attorney Meade. Reverend Boetell you heard speak the other night. You remember Brother Fernando. And this is Paige Beatty of the Women's American Resistance," his head bobs and he says, "This is Sylvia."

"Pleased to meet you," she says, wondering why the hell they're not doing this thing at one of their big walnut conference rooms downtown.

"I'm sorry you're feeling ill, Mrs. Leroux," the Reverend says. "Perhaps we should relocate—"

"Krafft," she says.

" 'Scuse me, ma'am."

She can feel Perry stiffen next to her.

"My last name is Krafft," she says. "Perry and I aren't married."

"Pardon my confusion," Boetell says, though no one here thinks for a minute he was confused. "Perry, let us clear out of here and we can reschedule for tomorrow."

Sylvia puts her hand on Perry's arm and says, "No need for that. I'll just be in the next room. It was nice seeing everyone."

"Excuse us for just a second," Perry says and follows her into the bedroom. He closes the door and Sylvia sits down on the bed and looks up at him.

"You okay?" he says in a modified whisper.

"My head," she says. "It's just killing me. I'm just going to take some aspirin and lie down for a while."

He nods.

"Sorry about this," he says, edgy, looking at her face as if he was trying to figure something out.

"It's all right," she says. "I just want to lie down for a while."

"It's just," he starts, then restarts, "Ratzinger thought it would be better if the group gets together outside of the office. He sort of volunteered my place."

"The group," she says.

He jerks his thumb in the direction of the living room.

"Technically," he says, "Eddie Meade isn't supposed to be here. It's weird."

"Look," she says, "go back out there. You can tell me all about it later."

"Can I bring you anything?"

"I'm all set. I'm just going to sleep for a while. I'll be fine later on."

He gives her a nervous shake of his head and says, "Just give a yell if there's anything I can do.

She nods back. He comes forward and plants a kiss on her forehead, then goes back to the group.

She takes off her shoes and massages her feet a little. She gets undressed, grabs a T-shirt out of the drawer and pulls it on. Then she climbs under the covers and curls up, all fetal and cold. She wants the room pitch-dark. She climbs out of bed and turns off the wall switch. She squats down next to the door and puts an ear to the crack. She hears a woman's voice, probably Candice's saying, "We can go over to my place if you'd like. It's not far from here."

There's some mumbling that she can't make out, then Perry says, "It's fine, really, It's not a problem. Let's just continue."

She sits down on the floor, pulls the door open just a bit more. Someone gets up and walks past, out into the kitchen. She hears the faucet run for a second, then footsteps returning to the living room.

"My people and I," Boetell says, "are still very uneasy about the nature of Miss Beatty's march. I think we need to hear more about this stunt. I think we need to be allowed to review these films she plans on showing."

"The march has nothing to do with you," Paige Beatty responds. "It's our statement and we'll take the consequences. I'll make that completely clear to the press, Mr. Boetell. You don't have to be worried about being soiled by associating with us."

"I think we're getting way ahead of ourselves," Perry says. "We've got a lot of work in front of us tonight and we need to be methodical here—"

"If this is going to run into the evening," Boetell's twang interrupts, "perhaps we should order a little supper. Does anyone else enjoy Chinese?"

"Can't do it," Meade says, "I'm meeting Welby back at the office at four."

"Candice," Perry says, "why don't you run down the notes we compiled at lunch."

Sylvia hears papers shifting and Candice says, "Can I have that green folder," a pause and then, "Basically, this is the prep-work that Perry and I assembled over the past month. We've put together a summary and analysis of all the Herzog initiatives going back ten years. We looked at licensing hearings, zoning board debates, letters and editorials written in the *Spy,* council speeches. Every two to three years cleaning up the sex trade becomes a hot issue for less than a season, then gets forgotten. The usual pattern is for a candidate or church group or community organization to make some up-front noise. The paper throws out some perfunctory headlines and op-ed fire. The council chambers fill with two sessions' worth of yelling and podium bashing. And then the dust settles and Schick and his compatriots quietly continue to go about their business."

"It's *going* to be different this time," Boetell promises.

"I've taken an informal survey," Perry says, "through very informal channels—"

"You bought lunch down at Valhalla," Meade interrupts and Perry gives him a forced laugh.

"The problem is basically twofold. You need the newspaper to keep the fire up, which they won't do. And you need to kill debate, get some real legislation out of committee and voted on. A single local ordinance could change the face of Watson Street in a year. Six months if the real estate started to look good to anyone."

"What we want to avoid," Candice says, "is a First Amendment circus. The last thing we want is a free speech debate. That could lead to outside funding and even ACLU targeting. You don't want to get inside a courtroom where anything can happen. Our recommendation is that the best course of action would be to cement the appropriate support, then move quickly from all sides."

"We need to determine exactly who's doing business with Schick and company," Perry says. "We need to follow the money and see whose pockets it's flowing into. Then we need to make that information public. Put some photos on page one."

"Basically," Candice says, "we need an icon. We need a face to stand for filth. We need a big bad guy. And Schick is perfect for the part."

"He's a naturalized citizen," Perry says. "So we can tap into the whole xenophobic current. We can have this city hating him in a month. We can build up a real passion in two, depending on our budget for media."

"Schick's theatre is the biggest," Candice says. "The grandest. It's enormous. It's excessive. It's over-the-top. It's perfect for our purposes. We make it the epitome of the evil pornograhic empire. We allude to other connections."

"That would be my department," Boetell says. "I've got a whole suitcase of stump speeches I can tailor to the Kraut—"

"He's Austrian," Beatty says.

"We hammer home child abuse, drug dealing, satanic

activity," Boetell says. "The satanic stuff plays real well. My boys back home have done the stats. Satan's good for a ten to fifteen percent upswing in any given night's gate."

"Thanks, Reverend," Perry says without a trace of humor in his voice. "We'll definitely keep that in mind."

"Every chance you get, you want to pull Lucifer into the stew," Boetell says. "That's what I tell my protégés, 'hit 'em with the beast till they howl for mercy.' Right, Fernando?"

"If there's any way at all," Candice says, "that we can capitalize on a satanic connection, rest assured we will. I'll make a note for a *Spy* leak at some later date."

Perry begins, "We'll also want to—" but he's cut off by Boetell who says, "There must be something amusing that I'm not privy to."

"Look," Paige Beatty says, "I'm willing to do whatever it takes to bring down Schick and all of Watson Street. But don't expect me to take your fire-and-brimstone rants seriously, Mr. Boetell."

"People," Perry says, trying for authoritarian and missing, "we already talked about our individual differences. About uniting for a common goal—"

"You find something *comical* about the beast, dear lady?"

"Let's just say I'm not ready to lay the blame of ten thousand years of female abuse and oppression on Beelzebub."

"Well, now," Boetell says, the politeness of his voice somehow insulting, "whether you're a believer or not is hardly the point here, is it? I think what we're discussing tonight is manipulation. And as one with a Duke law degree and two years as a senior account executive at Ogilvy & Mather, I know just a little something about manipulation."

"Well, I'm sorry, Reverend," Beatty says, almost mimicking Boetell's tone, "but as a woman who's been manipulated half her life, I can't help feel that Satan gets enough of a bad rap. And that lets the real criminals off the hook."

"The real criminals?" Boetell says.

"The testosterone nazis," Beatty says.

"We're off track here," Perry says. "We're losing focus."

"I'm sorry," Beatty says, "but I'm not about to put my efforts into tearing down objectifiers like Schick if it means I have to toe some white-trash, Bible-thumping, patriarchal, reactionary, bullshit party line—"

"Young lady," Boetell explodes, the voice high and slow and threatening as if he's gathering strength for a real lambasting. But nothing follows and the room fills up with a silent tension until Candice says, "If we break down into internal squabbling, we can kiss this campaign goodbye."

"Perry," Meade says, "I'm really going to have to get running if I want to catch the mayor."

"Why don't we do this," Candice says. "Why don't we break up for dinner and meet back at my place around seven-thirty, eight o'clock. We'll all be refreshed and we can work into the night. Try to build a head of steam. Perry and I would really like to show you some of the strategies we've put together this week."

"I'm free," Beatty says as if it were a challenge to Boetell.

"I cleared the whole evening," the Reverend responds.

"I should be able to shake loose from Welby by eight," Meade says. "Write down your address for me."

"Okay, great," Perry says. "Everyone go soak up some coffee. We'll have a real study session. Seven-thirty we'll meet back at Candice's."

There's some throat clearing and mumbles and bodies rising from chairs. Sylvia jumps back into bed and turns her back to the door. She hears them pass by the bedroom and for some reason she stays perfectly still, practically holding her breath.

It takes a while for Perry to see them out, then the bedroom door whines open and he's sitting on the edge of the bed. Sylvia rolls to face him, feigns like she had just started to doze. He brings a hand to her cheek and then her forehead.

"You feel warm," he says.

"I'm freezing."

"I think maybe you're coming down with something."

She gives a small nod.

"You should sleep," he says.

"I guess so."

"Can I bring you anything? Maybe you should have some soup first? Put something hot in your stomach."

"No thanks," she says. "I'm kind of queasy."

He nods, then in a low voice he says, "I don't know what's been going on the past few days."

"It's been weird," she says. "I've been feeling lousy. It's me."

He pulls the blankets up to her neck and says, "I don't know. I've just been tense, you know. I've just been caught up with things at work. I've just wanted this partnership so bad."

"Well, you got it," she says, trying to sound upbeat and ill at the same time.

"What we need to do," he says, "is pick out a weekend and get out of here. Head out to the Berkshires maybe. Just go to dinner and talk all this out. Maybe a long drive to Stockbridge. You know what I'm saying?"

"I'd love it."

"We'll just clear some time. We'll make it a three-day weekend. Leave on a Thursday night. Stay at that place you liked."

"I think it's a great idea," she says.

"Soon as I get the ball rolling with the new clients."

"Just let me know," she says. "I'm always ready."

"You think you can get out of the camera," he says with a big smile, referring to the Snapshot Shack.

"I think I can manage."

"I don't want to fight anymore."

She nods her agreement.

"Unfortunately," he says, "I've got to work tonight. I might not get in till really late. So you just roll over and get some sleep. I'll try not to wake you when I get in."

"Don't worry about that," she says.

"We'll work everything out, honey. I promise."

He leans down and kisses her again on the forehead, then walks out of the room closing the door behind him. She lies still and listens to him gathering things together. She hears him mumbling, probably making a phone call. But she can't hear what he's saying. She hears the refrigerator open and close. She hears the toilet flush. After about five minutes, she hears him go out the back door.

IX

Café Arco reminds Jakob of one of the little coffeehouses down on Rossmann Lane back home in Maisel, one of those tiny, low-ceilinged storefronts that functioned more as minuscule libraries than pastry shops. Originally built in the sixteenth century as dormitories for the alchemists of "Mad" King Reinhardt, the cafés were warm cells of communal solitude where one could step out of the rain and read the latest journals while snacking on a piece of palacinky and sipping any number of Slavic kavas.

So too, the Arco is a mysteriously calm port within the noise and glare of the Canal Zone. Carlo, the shift manager, is always indulgent when it comes to loitering over a single cup of coffee. And last month he accepted Jakob's gift of a framed marquee poster for the 1947 Warner Brothers release *Dark Passage* and hung it on the café wall. Oddly though, the Arco is not a Bohemian enterprise but is operated by a Chilean named Sarmiento. No matter, more and more, Jakob is finding it a perfect place to work on the screenplay.

Tonight, he takes his usual corner table with his back to the door, orders a kakao and a potato dumpling that will take him a half hour to "fletcherize," and opens the *Little Girl Lost* notebook. He removes his red editing pen from his jacket pocket and begins to read.

LONG SHOT -EXT. CINÉ DADA -NIGHT -LOWEST POSSIBLE ANGLE (shoot from the gutter)

The movie theatre, seen through swirls of mist, looks haunted. Half of its marquee bulbs are burned out, though we can still read the title of the last feature -*The Lady from Shanghai*. Vandalism and the elements have taken their toll on the building. (Is The Ballard available? If not, can we appropriate for a night? Talk to Hrabal). From an alleyway across the street, the Doomed Man appears. At the moment of his appearance, distant sirens are heard. (Dub Note: Use the low-pitch horns of the July Sweep).

TIGHT SHOT -FACE OF DOOMED MAN

panicked, strobed in repeating flashes of light and dark. Fade sirens slightly and bring up diseased-lung loop.

MED SHOT -SORTINI AVENUE

as the Doomed Man dashes across the street, the clip-clop of his feet on the pavement terribly loud. He runs into the alley adjoining Ciné Dada.

LONG SHOT -THE ALLEYWAY

as the Doomed Man climbs up a decayed, rickety, iron fire escape. At the top, he uses his elbow to break open a window. He climbs inside the movie theatre.

For three years, since he arrived in America, Jakob has used the world of film to shield himself from, at times to obliterate all together, the ugly questions of what his cousin has called *real goddamn life.*

Right now, the question Jakob wants to avoid is—*If I have to, can I kill cousin Felix?* The reason for the avoidance is that he hates both possible answers. If the response is *Yes,* then he's become that thing he's resisted from birth. A gangster rather than an artist. A wheezing mirror of Papa the mobster. A moral vacuum that knows only the creed of acquisition and power. And the joke would be that he's become this creature by virtue of the resistance itself, as if in marshaling all his strength in opposition to the Family mold he somehow damaged any chance of immunity from an inherited brutality.

MED SHOT -EXT CINÉ DADA

as a police car screeches to a stop in front of the boarded-up doors of the theatre. (Favors from Papa's friends on the force?). ERNST "THE INSECT" BROD steps out of the squad car into the horribly quiet street. He is followed a moment later by his gunmen, POLLAK and WERFEL. The police car drives away. The Insect removes his gloves, pockets them, snaps his fingers. Pollak and Werfel draw long-barreled guns from their coats, move to the theatre entrance and kick in the doors. Their weapons extended before them, they rush inside.

TIGHT SHOT -BROD

alone, the movie theatre backing him, he removes a spool of piano wire from his overcoat pocket and begins to twine it about both his hands. He turns and walks boldly into the theatre.

But if the answer is *No*, then there's still no hope of breaking away. Papa and Felix won't allow it. It's a version of the future they're incapable of accepting. Papa will never stop pushing for an inheritor who will grasp the Schonborn with pride and ceaseless ambition. And Felix will never stop pushing until there's a definite vacancy at Papa's right-hand side.

MED SHOT -THE BALCONY

as the Doomed Man crawls on hands and knees toward the rear wall of the theatre looking for another exit. The balcony is jammed with broken seats, projectors, electrical cables, film canisters. Suddenly, a few lights in the theatre snap on with a loud, echoing, mechanical noise. A moment later, the sound system is activated and the cinema fills with the heavily accented voice of Ernst Brod.

He edits the questions, looks at it from a different angle. What if this was a movie? What if this time in his life was transformed into 170,000 frames of film? How would he conceive the resolution to the central conflict?

Obviously, he's the hero, Jakob as protagonist, the audience's identification figure. He's the icon whose job is to carry all the desires and fears the audience can squeeze into two hours of passive observation.

Doesn't the ending have to be the hero's triumph, that moment of swelling music and dam-breaking emotional satisfaction when the audience's boy overcomes every inner and outer weakness and plot-wrenching long shot to capture his heart's dearest wish?

BROD (O.S.)
(in a singsong chant)
Come out, come out,
Wherever you are.
(speaking)
We will not hurt you, little man.
(awful laughter)
You won't feel a thing! Babykiller!

The Doomed Man panics and begins to scramble for the far wall, knocking over a klieg light, which ignites and fills the balcony with brilliant illumination.

Not in noir. Jakob knows the makeup of the noir film too well, maybe better than he knows himself. In noir the hero can be crushed. The audience's boy can turn out to be the audience's enemy. In the noir film, you just never know if you're going to get the resolution you've been trained to want.

LONG SHOT -INT. THEATRE PROPER

as Pollak and Werfel wheel around, aim their guns high and begin blasting an assault at the balcony.

Jakob looks up from his notebook. He pushes his dumpling away and runs his hands over his face. Things were so much easier back in Maisel. Growing up back home, he and cousin Felix had managed to overlook their innate difference, had been able to care for each other despite yearnings that were perfectly opposed.

It's as if in coming to America everything became too defined, overly manifest, as if on the day he and Felix stepped off the boat and onto the American shore their vision became hyper-focused, instantly and painfully sharpened to the point where neither of them can now fail to see

the threat the other has become. This new country has
turned the Kinsky cousins into an either/or proposition.

MED SHOT -THE BALCONY

as a rain of bullets explodes around the Doomed Man, ripping up seats, ricocheting off metal. The Doomed Man, a
frantic animal, scrambles, clutching at the velvet curtain
that lines the rear wall. He yanks the curtain back to reveal
Ernst "The Insect" Brod, framed in the exit doorway, holding out the garrotting wire and grinning maniacally. The
Doomed Man reacts instinctively, tackling Brod around
the waist. The two men fall to the ground and the surprised
Brod begins to wildly maneuver the wire around the
Doomed Man's neck. Doomed Man shifts weight and the
two roll down the balcony stairs to the railing.

Jakob grabs hold of the notebook and begins to tear out
random pages, crumples them, jams them into his suitcoat
pocket.

He swallows the last of his kakao and wonders what Felice Fabri would say. The love of his life, his mentor and
his protector and his initiator into the mysteries of flesh
and of film, what would Felice advise?

And he hears her voice, from the dark of the Kierling,
that throaty, buttery whisper.

*"Remember Jako, it will be your film. Yours alone. Not the
studio boss, not the producer, not the investor. Not the bullying method actor and not the spoiled and sulking starlet. You
don't let any of them touch your work. Your eyes. Not even the
audience, Jako. Not even the fickle, hateful audience."*

But Felice, he thinks, *this is not a film. This is my life.*

He picks up the red pen, turns to a fresh page in the notebook and begins to write.

TIGHT SHOT -BROD AND THE DOOMED MAN STRUGGLING ON THE FLOOR.

Brod manages to right himself, climbs on the back of the Doomed Man, leans forward and secures the piano wire firmly around the victim's throat.

TIGHTER SHOT -FACE OF THE DOOMED MAN

as he begins to choke, his eyes bulging in agony and terror, color draining from his skin.

MED SHOT -BALCONY FLOOR

as, with his last burst of will, the Doomed Man rears up, his skull crashing into Brod's nose, blood exploding. Brod, shocked, lets go of the garrote, staggers to his feet, at the same time pulling a gun from a shoulder holster inside his suitcoat. A bullet from below catches him in the chest, wheels him around. He drops his pistol to the floor.

> POLLAK (O.S.)
> (screaming)
> Hold your fire! You've hit the Insect!

The Doomed Man pulls the garrote free from his neck. Stunned, close to blacking out, he tries to stand, grabs at the legs of Brod, pushes him forward. Brod loses balance, screams, falls over the railing. CAMERA follows body's path as Brod crashes to the floor far below, breaking his neck.

Jakob feels a hand on his shoulder and immediately jerks and wheels around in his seat, pulls the pen into his fist and raises it like a makeshift dagger.

Carlo, the shift manager, jumps backward and yells, "Jesus, what the hell—"

"I'm sorry, Carlo," Jakob says, "you startled me."

"I was just going to clear your table—"

"I apologize, I'm so sorry, I didn't see you there."

Carlo nods, shakes his head, grabs the pie plate and the mug and moves back behind the counter, mumbling.

LONG SHOT - THEATRE FLOOR -FROM BALCONY

Brod's lifeless body spread prone at an awful angle, streams of blood beginning to flow randomly. Pollak and Werfel run to their boss. Gunfire sounds. Pollak and Werfel clutch their chests, collapse in a pile near Brod.

REVERSE SHOT -THE BALCONY

as the Doomed Man, bleeding slightly around the throat, lets a smoking pistol wave in his hands, then allows the gun to drop down onto the bodies below him.

Carlo returns with the bill. He puts it cautiously on the table and Jakob closes his notebook, pockets his pen and reaches for his wallet.

"Delicious as always," Jakob says.

"Can I get you anything else, Mr. K," Carlo says, "something to go, maybe?"

Jakob smiles and shakes his head as he picks cash from the billfold.

"I'm full to bursting," he says, getting up. "I couldn't take another thing."

19

When Sylvia wakes up, it's dark in the room. She feels like she's slept for a week. She lies in bed for a while, takes some deep breaths, stretches her arms and legs and realizes she's feeling a lot better. She's still kind of foggy but the aching and nausea have vanished and she's got some energy back.

She sits up, kicks off the covers. Perry isn't here. She stands up and goes to the bedroom window and looks out. The streetlights are on and she can see the moon low over the church tower.

She walks out into the kitchen, closes her eyes and turns on the light. She opens the eyes slowly into a squint, goes to the table. There's no note, no sign that Perry's been back to the apartment.

She moves into the living room, grabs the remote, which Perry has Scotch-taped together, and turns on the TV. She stares at the weather channel for a minute with the sound off. A young guy with a mustache is in front of a map of the United States. Semitransparent swirling clouds move in a choppy pattern across the screen, left to right, as the weatherman gesticulates, points and sweeps these big hands all over the country. It's an unsettling image and she shuts it off and goes into the bathroom.

She turns on the light and without thinking, moves to the tub and starts to draw a hot bath. She dumps in several capfuls of essence of rose bath oil, pulls off her T-shirt and tosses it in the hamper, then climbs into the tub and sits down and lets the water fill up around her. It looks like the color of the developer chemical. But it feels wonderful. It never fails that on the rare occasions when Sylvia does take a bath at night, she asks herself why she doesn't do it every evening, why she doesn't unwind in a steaming tub while Perry reads briefs or watches a game. She could bring in the radio and turn on a good station, maybe read something, one of those articles she's got crammed in the desk, something she clipped from the art magazines and forgot about.

The water finally edges up near the top of the tub and she turns it off. The room is filling with steam, getting kind of misty, the mirror getting totally smoked over. She leans her head back and thinks about what Perry said before he left. *I don't know what's been going on the last few days.*

You don't know the half of it, Perry.

She's got no explanation for her behavior. The fact is, the things that have happened, the external things, she can accept, write them off the way you'd dismiss a slump, a couple days of bad luck. She's just had a patch of weirdness, a run of strange hours. The outside events—the camera shop closing down, the riot outside the Skin Palace—don't really concern her. Everybody's got some story to tell about the day things went off-kilter. But what she really can't get a handle on is her reaction to the weirdness. Instead of being repelled, it's like she's been sucked in. She's sought these things out. She followed a strange old man into a pornographic bookstore. She walked into Der Geheime Garten on her own. She accepted Leni's invitation to lunch at an unlicensed, hit-and-run Peruvian restaurant. She nodded her head *yes.* She moved her own feet. She was operating under her own influence and control. And now, sitting here in the tub, she's got no rationale for why she did these things. There's no precedent for it in her past. She's never sought out these kinds of experiences before. For the most part, she thinks she's lived a fairly narrow existence. Maybe more narrow than most. It's as if for twenty-five years her brain has been functioning in this standard, middle-class, linear way and then one night, maybe while she was asleep, maybe in the middle of a boring and nonsensical dream, some switch just got thrown, some neurons just started firing in a different manner, a different pattern. And she woke up as this other woman, as this stranger, like in one of those late-night cable movies. Like in Don Siegel's *Invasion of the Body Snatchers.*

She props her feet up on the faucet and looks at them. These are the feet that brought her into Jack Derry's Camera Exchange and Brody's Adult Books and Herzog's Erotic Palace. The feet look the same as they did a week ago. But something's changed.

And she wishes she could pin down the cause. Even if she couldn't reverse it and get back to normal, she wishes she could simply know what's brought her to this point. She doesn't know why she thinks this would make things better, or somehow more acceptable.

A week ago, the Snapshot Shack was not only tolerable but actually inviting. It was stable and simple and she loved locking herself up in that booth and running through the boring routine of every shift—counting boxes of film, phoning up customers to say their pictures were ready, handing change through the sliding window/lens like some toll collector on a highway people rarely travel anymore.

Now, she feels like Leni's right, like the place is a prison and she'll go crazy if she sits inside it one more time. But she's got to do something for work and there's no way she's going to hire herself out to some studio that'll have her running after wedding parties every Saturday.

There's always Hugo's offer. She could just let the feet bring her down to the Skin Palace every morning and shoot roll after roll of naked people groping each other. Perry would love it. *Honey, you know the porn king you're trying to shut down? Well guess who my new boss is.*

She just can't imagine looking through a viewfinder and

focusing in on, say, Leni and one of those actors she saw this afternoon, caressing each other and looking at her while she yells out these inane commands like *tilt your head up* or *could you flex for me a little?*

She looks down at her own body sort of shimmering and enlarged through the oily water. She'd like to lose maybe five pounds. She'd like to tone up a little. Maybe get into an aerobics class. Nothing ridiculous, just a couple hours a week. She's sure she'd feel better. She wishes her breasts were just slightly bigger. It's not a huge problem, not like she'd go for surgery or anything.

Before Leni, Sylvia never knew a woman who was satisfied with her body. At best, back in college, she knew some who just never complained or joined in when the subject came to body image. But that's no real indication of satisfaction.

She looks at her body now, rolled out here in front of her, magnified a little by the rose-colored water. She wonders what it will look like in another ten years. And then she thinks suddenly of the pictures down in the darkroom. Propp's pictures. The Madonna and child in the ruins. How old is the woman in that picture? Sylvia is convinced the Madonna is lacking any body neurosis. And Sylvia knows she's reading into the photo. She has to be. There's nothing in those shots to indicate that kind of knowledge. You can't even see the Mother's face. Beyond the play of light on her back and shoulder and breast, the rest of her is in silhouette. So how can Sylvia be so sure, more certain the longer she dwells on it, that the Madonna is wholly content with her body?

There's got to be something in the pictures that she's not recalling. She pulls the plug from the drain and stands up, grabs the towel off the radiator and starts to dry herself. She goes into the bedroom and turns on the lamp on the nightstand. She grabs her jeans, holds them out to step into them and catches her reflection in the mirror above the bureau.

She tosses the jeans back on the bed, opens the bottom drawer and paws through T-shirts and pajamas and nightgowns. And then she feels the lace and pulls out what she's looking for. It's a full-length English nightdress, all sheer cotton trimmed with Battenburg lace, with this deep V-neck that can be secured by buttons at the neck, and long, ruffled cuffs and a flounced hem and a thigh-high side slit. It's probably the most elegant thing she's ever owned. It was a present from Perry. Way back. Near the beginning, when they couldn't keep their hands off each other.

They went away for a weekend. It was near the end of winter and they drove into the Berkshires and stayed at this ancient Victorian inn. They were the only guests and they arrived around midnight. The woman who ran the place had left the door open and the room keys on the front desk along with a note that told them to lock up. They climbed a double-wide staircase past walls lined with dark oil portraits of people long dead. They moved down a narrow corridor until they found the Rose Room, small but with a huge brass bed and complimentary brandy in a crystal decanter. Sylvia went into the bathroom and Perry went for the bags. When she came out, he was still gone, but there was a gift box on the bed wrapped in thick floral-print paper. She sat down next to it and opened it slowly, folded back all the thin, white tissue paper and pulled up this nightgown. She remembers staring at it for what seemed like too long, running her fingers over the lacework around the collar. She remembers gathering it up against her chest, going to the door and peeking out into the hallway, looking for Perry and not finding him. Then she went back into the bathroom and put it on and it fit as if she'd picked it out herself. She stood in front of the mirror. She actually combed her hair for a few minutes. She remembers putting a single drop of perfume on her wrist. When she opened the bathroom door, Perry was sitting on the edge of the bed with just his jeans on, facing her, holding a cognac in one hand and a small bouquet of sweetheart roses and baby's breath in the other. He held them out to her and says, "I was afraid they'd freeze in the trunk." But they hadn't and she took them from him and didn't know what to say. He stood up and whispered, "Do you like it?" and she just nodded. Then he took the bouquet out of her hand and put it on the bureau, took her hand and led her over to an antique chaise longue in the corner of the room, this heavy velvet lounge chair that Sylvia just sank into. He stood back and looked at her and smiled and nodded, held up a finger to say *one minute,* went over to the camera bag and took out the Canon. Sylvia started to shake her head and made herself stop as Perry focused the lens, then stopped, put the camera on the bed, stepped forward, and raised the hem of the nightgown until it was just above her bent knee. His hand lingered a second and she remembers how it felt as he let his fingers touch the back of her thigh, still innocent, just above the knee, but on this soft part of her skin that sent a wave through her, jangled the rhythm of her breath a little. Then he stepped back and slowly shot off an entire roll of film. And halfway through the roll, without any provocation from Perry, Sylvia pulled the hem just slightly higher on her leg. And Perry stopped for a second and closed his eyes, then went back to shooting. When he finished, he moved to the other side of the room and re-bagged the camera. Then he stood up and stared at her as he pulled off his jeans. Sylvia sat there and stared back. There was a long moment after his pants were on the floor and neither one of them was moving, this wonderful, one-time, aching tension, this palpable atmosphere that, even as it engulfs you, you know you'll probably never capture again.

Perry came to the lounge, lifted her up, set her down on

the brass bed, but never removed the nightgown, simply raised it above her waist.

They made love that night in a way they've never repeated. Not an athletic endurance or a primal, dank kind of fierceness, but more a kind of trance state, filled with an intensity and a surety, an absolute correctness and a limitless empathy as if each knew exactly when to move and when not to, when to stroke, kiss, breathe. As if for the whole of that night in that room, they couldn't make a mistake. They couldn't be less than flawless for each other.

Or at least that's how Sylvia remembers it.

She doesn't know what Perry's memories are. They haven't discussed that night, as if they have a shared understanding that words could easily damage it.

The pictures never came out. And Sylvia knew they wouldn't at the time Perry was taking them. He hadn't used a flash and the speed wasn't slow enough to compensate for the dimness of the room.

She's glad those pictures don't exist. She still has a very clear, very sharp idea of what she looked like in this nightgown. She loves that image of herself. It's the only instant, the only image she has of herself as totally desirable. As completely sure of and comfortable with her own sensuality. And she knows more than half that idea, that image, is imagined. It's a story. It's a fabrication, more altered then true, more created than any airbrush could manage. And she wants to hold onto it forever.

She slides the nightgown on over her head. She pushes her arms down through the sleeves. She buttons the three pearls at the neck. Then she goes to the closet instead of the mirror, searches until she finds a virgin pair of white ballet slippers and slides them on her feet. She goes out to the kitchen, takes the key off the nail on the side lip of the molding, goes out the back door, locks up behind her, and replaces the key.

She heads down to the cellar, down into the darkroom,

trying to keep the nightgown from touching the stairs or the rock and mortar walls that are covered with a hundred years of soot and grit. She gets inside the darkroom, turns on the white light, gathers up all the Propp pictures and spreads them on the worktable. She pulls the step stool up to the table. She grabs the magnifying glass and the softest dust brush she's got. Then she bears down. She leans in over the first photograph until it fills her field of vision. She tried to break down the shot, divide it into separate quadrants, first by simple mapping, what lies to the upper right, lower left. Then by the fall of the light in the photo. Then by the shifting fields of focus. Then arbitrarily, wherever her eye takes her, she seizes on that section of the photograph. She looks at each small piece under the glass. She takes her time, burns the image in. She looks again, immediately, with her bare eye, her face less than an arm's length from the paper. Then she climbs up onto the step stool and looks down from above. She changes the position of the light. She cuts the glare. She adds some glare. She brushes the shot clean. She rebrushes it. She gets up, takes it to the drying line, clips it steady and stands in front of it, six inches away, two feet away, four feet away. She squats down and looks up at it. Finally, she turns it upside down, rotates it on the drying clips at different angle stops until she's come a full circle.

Then she repeats the process with photo number two. With number three and number four.

Time blurs until she hears the noise. It sounds like a cat scratching its claws over something harsh. Like a wire screen. She thinks for a second that it might be the furnace. Perry fills it with water once a week for Mrs. Acker. But the furnace still makes a knocking or rumbling sound.

Sylvia steps outside the darkroom, immediately hears it more loudly, turns to the cellar window and sees a face staring in at her. She keeps herself from screaming but starts to run for the stairway when she hears her name and stops. She looks again and now the face is exposed, lit up by a flashlight at its chin, and she sees Leni Pauline shaking her head and laughing.

Sylvia goes over to the window and looks. The frame is nailed shut but she can hear Leni say, "Lemme in. I'm bored."

Sylvia points to the rear of the building, then shuts down the lights and closes up the darkroom. Leni's at the back entrance wearing an oversized mohair sweater, tiger-stripe spandex running pants and those old burnt-orange construction boots. Sylvia steps back to let her in and Leni motions for her to come outside.

They go out onto the back landing and Sylvia's surprised at how mild the night is.

"God," Leni says, "you're gorgeous."

Sylvia's forgotten she's wearing the nightgown and suddenly she's feeling too stupid and embarrassed to ask what Leni's doing here. She tries to think of an excuse for why she's got the nightgown on, why she looks like she just stepped off the page of some elaborately illustrated fairy tale, but nothing comes.

"C'mon," Leni says. "It's perfect."

"It was a gift," Sylvia says. "From my . . . from Perry."

But Leni's not listening. She's taken hold of the gown's hem and is holding it out from Sylvia's legs and studying the beading in the glow of the moonlight.

"What Hugo could do with this number," Leni says, almost to herself.

Sylvia pulls the hem away and Leni looks up at her with this self-satisfied smile on the lips. And for some reason Sylvia feels as embarrassed as if she was standing here naked.

"What are you doing here?" she asks.

"I brought your camera," Leni says, bringing it out from behind her back. "You know, you're pretty careless with your gear."

"It's been a bad week."

"You're too tense, Sylvia. It's not right, someone your age being this stressed out. Ten years from now, you'll be looking for organ donors."

"Real pleasant, Leni."

"I'm trying to help you out here, kid," though they're most likely the same age, "You need somebody——"

"I've got somebody," Sylvia says.

Leni nods, "Sure. The guy that bought the nightgown."

"That's right."

"So where is he?" she asks, looking past Sylvia at the stairs. "I'd love to meet a guy who can walk into a store and score something this campy."

Sylvia's taken back. "You think this is campy?" she says, looking down at herself.

Leni retreats immediately with a shrug. "Don't get me wrong, Slyvie," and Sylvia realizes no one has ever called her *Sylvie* before, "it's honestly gorgeous. It's really beautiful but in this, you know, retro-way. This Victorian decadence thing. White on white. All cotton. Just screaming purity. But then there's the plunging neck. And the slit up the side. The color and material say one thing. Then the cut and the fitting contradict it all."

Sylvia's flinching from self-consciousness but she doesn't stop Leni.

"It's the kind of thing I'm always trying to get across to Hugo. Less is more. The tease is everything. It's the covered pot that'll boil with the most intensity. You know what I'm saying. I *know* you know. The greater the repression, the more over-the-top the revolution."

"You think I'm repressed?"

"God, Sylvia, you take everything I say as an affront. This is a compliment, all right? You look like a dream. You're more erotic right now than a year's worth of centerfolds."

Sylvia folds her arms over her chest. Leni hands the

Canon to her and says, "I threw a fresh roll of film in there," then turns to leave and says, "Get back upstairs to the boyfriend and revel in it for God's sake."

"He's at work."

Leni stops and pivots but doesn't say anything.

"He's in the middle of a pretty important project," Sylvia starts and then can't believe she's trying to justify Perry to Leni.

"One question," Leni says. "Were you wearing this when he left?"

Sylvia shakes her head *no*.

Leni looks her up and down again. "So why did you put it on?"

Sylvia starts to shrug, then says, "You said one question."

"Turn around," Leni says.

Sylvia squints at her.

"I want to see the whole thing. Turn around."

She feels funny, but does it, a full circle with the gown flowing around her legs.

"Come here," Leni says, no play in her voice. She steps off the landing into the backyard.

Sylvia hesitates and Leni says again, "Right here, Sylvia. Come on. Let's go."

They walk down onto the grass. Everything's silent but for their steps on the leaves. Leni looks around a little, concentrating, then without saying a word she comes over and takes the camera, takes Sylvia by the arm, leads her to an old catalpa tree and positions her in a shaft of moonlight that falls next to it.

"You've got a good eye."

"Keep quiet," Leni says, lifting the camera to chest level and looking down at the settings, then up at her subject.

"You've got to let in all the light you can," Sylvia whispers. "Try opening it up all the way."

Leni twists the exposure, brings the camera up to her

eye, and fires the shutter a few times, then lowers the camera and asks, "How's it feel to be on the other side?"

"Awkward."

"You're a natural," she says. "Do me a favor. Unbutton the top button. Just one."

Sylvia shakes her head, but as Leni focuses and starts to shoot, she complies.

"Lean back against the tree."

"I'll be in shadow," Sylvia says and Leni *shushes* her and says, "Just do it."

Sylvia doubts the pictures will come out and she realizes this disappoints her. She feels the tree against her back, wonders if she's staining the nightgown.

Leni comes in closer. "Slide down till you're sitting on the ground."

"It's cold."

"Don't whine," she says, a little harshly, and Sylvia moves down until she's seated.

She lowers the Canon from her eye, bites her bottom lip for a second, studying the image.

"It's hard," she says and Sylvia just nods back at her, pleased with the comment.

"Okay, bring the hem up just a little. Maybe mid-calf. You think?"

"Your call," Sylvia says.

"Try it. No higher."

Sylvia raises the hem of the nightgown from her ankles up her leg. Leni seems to take forever focusing. Sylvia keeps quiet and waits until finally she hears a single shutter release. Then Leni walks over and hands the camera down.

"That's it?" Sylvia says.

Leni nods, extends a hand and helps Sylvia back to her feet, then casually reaches up to Sylvia's face and gently pushes some strands of hair back behind the ear. It seems like this unconscious, almost motherly gesture and it sends a lick of cold down from Sylvia's neck. Without a word, Leni turns and starts to move toward the street.

"Leni," Sylvia says.

Leni stops and looks back.

"I was just . . ." Sylvia takes a breath. "I mean, do you have plans? You want to come in and watch a movie or something? There's this Peter Lorre festival."

Leni smiles, bends her head back, looks up at the sky. She walks back, takes Sylvia's hand, says, "C'mon, I'm parked out front."

By the time they park down on Dupin, Sylvia's still putting up a fight. "I'm not dressed. I can't go to a party dressed like this."

Leni kills the engine.

"You ever go to the Zone's Halloween block party? It's an annual thing, Sylvia. You've seen the pictures."

"You're sure it's tonight? Halloween's a week away."

Leni opens her door and says, "Sometimes this thing can run on, you know. Everyone will be in costume, honey. You'll probably take home a prize. Will you stop worrying. Think of the shots you're going to get."

"I only have this one roll of film," Sylvia says, pulling the camera into her lap and checking the meter.

"Then you'd better pick and choose very carefully."

They start to walk down Dupin toward a pocket of light and noise at the intersection of Aragon. The air is fairly mild. Sylvia looks down at her feet to see the slippers going black from the filthy asphalt. On either side of the street, large and small packs of people are running to get to the block party. They're dressed up as apes, vampires, gunfighters, Elvis Presley, Charlie Chaplin, Marilyn Monroe, and other more subtle icons, too vague to name at a glance. There's a trio of Diana Rosses in matching pink sequinned gowns doing a passable version of "You Can't Hurry Love" and even after they move by her, close enough to smell their Chanel, Sylvia still can't decide if they're men or women or some combo of the two. She sees a guy simply wrapped in an American flag jogging next to a woman who may or may not be going for a Little Orphan Annie look. She sees a werewolf in a leather jumpsuit, an obesity case in a pseudo-loincloth and with his hair in a topknot looking like a non-Asian sumo wrestler, some young women in yellow hard hats, T-shirts, work boots, chewing on cigars, spitting and catcalling at passing men, doing a lot of exaggerated crotch-grabbing. She hears singing and spots a small band of men completely attired in old Howard Johnson's-style waitress uniforms, all orange and white with aprons and order pads. Some wear hair nets and all but two hold brown plastic serving trays over their shoulders while the duo with free hands carry aloft a banner that reads *Verlin Ave Cross-dressers' Lodge*.

A parade of bikers on Harleys slides past her and she can't tell whether they're foregoing costumes or, in fact, they're faux bikers, daytime accountants or orthodontists who blew a wad on one elaborate night of dress-up. And the same question arises when she sees a group of hookers high-heeling it around the corner of Waldstein.

"How do you tell who's real and who's not," she asks Leni.

"Tonight," Leni says, "it doesn't really matter."

They round Waldstein and come into the hub of the block party. The Canal Zone treats Halloween like some high holy day in a fanatical religion. Sylvia has never been to the festivities before. In the beginning, the *Spy* used to run a big feature the morning after the madness with a page of great shots, but as the costumes got progressively more lewd and graphic and just over-the-top weird, the paper left the coverage entirely to the Zone's own free hand-out rags. Now, Sylvia feels like that might have been the right decision. The width of Waldstein Avenue is swelled to bursting with a Mardi Gras scene as directed by Fellini, a shoulder-to-shoulder circus of fire-eaters and tuxedoed stilt-walkers, snake-dancers and gypsy tarot booths, spontaneous crap games and doorway magicians and a tribe of roller-skating women in bridal attire. There are men dressed as women and women dressed as men and at least one accordion-wielding-hermaphrodite. There's a reggae band playing from the top of the Radcliffe Building, drowning out these slightly annoying Renaissance chamber singers who are all swaddled in dark velvets and feathered hats doing an a capella number about good King John being dead by his own hand.

The whole scene reminds her of the first street carnival her mother took her to, one of those traveling trailer shows of wobbly cart rides and rigged games of chance that move into town for a week or two, then move out in the middle of the night leaving a muddy vacant lot covered with popcorn and powdered sugar and ticket stubs. The Halloween Block Party is much more free-form and wild than that second-rate carnival of her youth, but standing here now in the swirl of it she's getting that same kind of virgin rush of being outside at night in the cool of the October air, just engulfed in flashing lights and noise, just washed over by hundreds of disparate, clashing sounds, and with no idea of what's about to happen.

She wishes she could see the whole thing from up on a roof, get an overview that would allow her to estimate the size of the crowd and how far down the street the party extends. She catches herself wishing this and wonders why she'd want that. Why does she have such a need to see the total picture and analyze its meaning? Why can't she be like everyone currently bumping into her, lost to herself, going with the moment and the surge? And suddenly she wants to thank Leni for bringing her down here.

But she doesn't know where Leni is. She turns a full circle before she realizes that she's already lost her driver and guide. And she panics just a little, starts to move through the crowd for the sidewalk, but it's like fighting an ocean wave whose undertow keeps growing. She's moving against the flow of the crowd, smacking into a fireman, a mummy, a vaguely biblical character with a braying sheep lodged up on his shoulders, bent around the neck. She turns and tried to move for the opposite sidewalk, jumps out of the way as one of those huge, old-fashioned unicycles comes rolling too fast in her direction, the pedaler honking a red rubber squeeze horn over and over.

How could Leni leave her like this? She searches for a familiar face but she's pummeled with a nonstop rush of rubber masks and veil-hidden eyes. It's like a cargo truck full of stage makeup exploded moments before she arrived here. People are rouged or pancaked into caricatures, into mutants, into distant relations of what's recognizably human.

She starts to make her way down Waldstein by turning sideways, ducking, sidestepping. Once she picks up the rhythm, she begins to make more progress. She comes upon a toga-wrapped Romanesque couple and it dawns on her they're probably going for a Caligula-and-Drusilla act. They're huddled with three burly men dressed in the old-time full habits of nuns. They're all standing at the mouth of an alleyway with their necks craned back, focused up at the sky. She pauses long enough to see a tightrope walker with classic balance pole wavering midway between two rooftops, then she hurries on before the aerialist can either regroup and complete the crossing or free-fall into the blue trash Dumpster below him.

Sylvia moves past an organ grinder with a spastic monkey, a sleight-of-hand man manipulating cards and coins above a huge leather satchel, a small squad of unbelievably risqué cheerleaders doing a raunchy pep-routine for a drunken circle of old men.

And she's just starting to catch the buzz of the night, to go with the communal adrenaline of the street, when she

turns a corner and spots the woman she saw on the screen
of the drive-in, Mrs. Ellis, the woman whose daughter is
missing. Mrs. Ellis is trying to stop people as they run past,
to press posters and flyers into the hands of the revelers.
But she's not having much luck. The people who do take a
hand-out drop it to the pavement without giving it a look,
most likely thinking it's one more come-on for a club or a
concert. But the missing girl's mother persists, machine-
like, as if there was no other option but to stand in the
midst of these speeding, carousing celebrants and distrib-
ute the photocopied face of a ten-year-old daughter she
may never see again.

Sylvia turns away, takes a quick left, comes to the food
kiosks, dozens of carts and wagons emitting a wind of
slightly diverse but collectively greasy smells and the
overall sound of meat sizzling. Oldish, kerchiefed women
hunch over butane-fed flames or beds of glowing charcoal,
poking at potpourris of sausage, onions, peppers,tomatoes.
She spots a compact and swarthy old man in a snow parka
concentrating over what looks like a cast-iron black caul-
dron—that's the only word for the enormous cooking pot
he's stirring at the corner of Goulden Ave. And his wooden
stirring utensil looks like an oar from a canoe. He's an apparition from some malevolent children's fable and Sylvia
walks up to him and looks inside the kettle and sees a
sweet smelling goulash bubbling like mad, as if the contents were about to come alive, metamorphose into some
sentient creature of her nightmares and jump into the fray
around them looking for children. The old man glances up
at her, reaches inside a deep pocket of his parka and offers
her a tin mug for dipping. She shakes her head *no* and
starts to move off, then, totally on impulse or instinct, she
pivots back toward him, brings her Canon up to her eye,
pulls this dark-skinned warlock into an exact focus and
clicks off three shots: the face, this now-wonderful, crease-
lined, eye-drooping face, captured forever in the vapors

rising up from his mystery stew. When she takes the camera down he's smiling and blowing a kiss at her. She mouths a *thank you* and moves onto Goulden.

She walks past a half-block colony of tentatively erected shacks and makeshift plywood counters selling a mishmash of used junk—costume jewelry, buttons, bubblegum cards, dog tags, jackknives, chipped china teacups, old newspapers and magazines, devotional candles, bags of marbles, and at the last shack, crumpled old pinups, once glossy cheesecake pictures of long-dead starlets whose names no one remembers. Surprising to her, all these little wooden booths that look like they were thrown up minutes ago have mini TV sets flickering on the counter with the sound shut off. She lingers in front of the last booth, scans the leggy eight-by-tens clipped to a hanging wire run wall to wall. One of the photos—a willowy blonde stretched out on a sofa—has a faded imprint of full lips lipsticked below the model's signature. Sylvia thinks about buying the pinup from the Asian behind the counter, but the clerk's attention is consumed by the television and besides, she doesn't have any money on her. Instead, she wades into the street, waits for a break in the crowd and clicks off a shot of the booth. Through her viewfinder she notices the proprietor is watching a Peter Lorre movie. She stands for a second and watches Lorre framed inside her camera, framed again inside the TV. It's the central scene from *M*, where Lorre and his niece walk past Grosser Mittagstisch and then stop to look in the shop window. The niece notices the chalk-marked letter *M* that's been imprinted on Lorre's back. She tells him he's all dirty. He turns sideways to look in a mirror and we see him in three-quarter profile. Then the camera tracks in until we've got a tight shot of just Lorre's panic-stricken face, the reflection of his face in the mirror, and the condemning letter *M* on his back. Peter Lorre's eyes give Sylvia an honest, awful shudder.

She looks away from the screen, pans to her left, beyond

the sales strip, and sees an old Thunderbird convertible that looks like someone abandoned an attempt to turn it into a punkish parade float. There's graffiti sprayed across the length of the body, a line she thinks might have come from Picasso—*good taste is the enemy of art*. Two mannequins have been positioned in the rear seats, manipulated into a state of awkward coupling. And a big Liberace-like candelabra is mounted on the hood with all its red candles aglow. Before she realizes how much she likes the scene, she's already shooting it and wishing she'd brought a starburst filter to fracture the dozens of small flames into mini-novas.

She's getting charged up now. She flies through the mob to the Thunderbird and climbs inside, stands up on the front seat and faces out to the street and immediately lets her instinct start picking and choosing, lets her fingers find that unison with the eye, lets her eardrum relish the vibration of the shutter's click-sound. She finds a topless, co-ed tribal dance around an impromptu bonfire and she nails it. She finds and captures the passing face of the 1931 Karloff monster with perfect neck-bolts and facial scarring, sad mouth and anguished eyes. She swings high and traps the pinched features and wrinkled forehead of a middle-aged woman in a dark-colored bathrobe leaning out the window of the brick tenement across the road, maybe wishing she could get some sleep.

A speeding bulldog hauling a severed leash in its mouth and threading through the legs of the crowd.

Click.

A trio of teenage boys, all in camouflage pants, bearing toy carbines up on their shoulders, huddled around a pack of firecrackers exploding on the ground between them.

Click.

A limp toddler helplessly falling into sleep inside the arms of his wobbly mother as mommy drops quarters to the pavement trying to buy cigarettes from a vending machine that's been pushed out onto the sidewalk.

Click.

The more she looks, the more images come, as if her only limitation is the speed of her shutter finger.

She gets out of the Thunderbird and starts to walk down Goulden. She sees a line of people in black-tie filing into the red-brick arc of the Renger-Patzsch Tool & Die Company. She crosses the street and joins onto the tail of the group, but when she gets to the door a bouncer says, "Your invitation, ma'am?"

She stares at him and he adds, "This is an invitation-only event, ma'am."

She lifts up her camera and shoots a couple frames of his beefy face, lowers the camera slightly and says in a strained-indulgent voice, "I'm from the *Spy.*"

He immediately steps back to allow entry and says, "Love your costume," and suddenly she realizes that she hasn't been conscious of wearing the nightgown since she lost Leni.

She moves inside the factory, which has been closed down for almost a decade but which still houses an awful lot of heavy machinery, big green and black oil-guzzling, ear-rupturing warhorses. The machines look like they've been arranged to transform the dance floor into a kind of industrial maze, a heavy labyrinth of cast-iron partitions. Somehow, it's a little disturbing, watching impeccably groomed people ballroom dancing through these corridors of obsolete grinding monsters that were once gluttons for loose human fingers. Men looking like some elite cadre of movie ushers and women who could give new definition to an overused word like *glamour* are together in each other's arms, gliding through a gauntlet of metal hulks that have stubbornly outlived their usefulness.

There's an enormous banner stretched across the far wall that reads

**The Bella C. Memorial Dance Marathon
to benefit
The Fund for the Preservation of Dangerous Art**
shake your booty to break their balls

and underneath it is a digital clock with huge red numbers showing, Sylvia guesses, the elapsed time since the start of the marathon. The room is well lit by the hanging fluorescents so she maneuvers to an uncrowded corner and gets ready to start shooting.

She watches new dancers report to an aluminum picnic table under the clock and banner where a d.j. is sorting through piles of tapes and CDs. The contestants crouch down as they present their invitations, as if they were second-string ballplayers thrilled and scared at their imminent insertion into a crucial game. The officials behind the picnic table give all the entrants some sort of punchcard to clip to an accessible part of their clothing. Most of the dancers arrive together but there are a few solo entrants leaning anxiously against a side wall, waiting for a partner. It's this crew she starts shooting, zooming in close on the faces, on the palpable excitement and underlying anxiety. She shoots a husky young guy with ridiculous sideburns as he unconsciously snaps and unsnaps his cufflinks. She locks onto an almost-pretty woman, a little younger than herself, dressed in a fifties-style prom dress that, unfortunately, isn't enough of a put-on. The woman's eyes are turned all the way to the left and her tongue is running a chronic circle trying to keep the inside of her mouth moist. Sylvia finds the focus and she's about to release the shutter when a man dressed like a cross between Zorro and a drug-dealing bullfighter suddenly steps into her line of fire and begins to approach.

She lowers the camera and glares at the guy, but he keeps coming toward her. He looks the right part for the costume he's wearing—jet-black hair and a trimmed mustache that appears genuine. Sylvia thinks of Errol Flynn in *Captain Blood* if that movie were remade in, say, Argentina. He comes to a graceful stop just far enough away to bow toward her. He's done up completely in black—matador shirt tucked into real leather pants, pointed-toe boots with spur straps, tapered gloves, a heavy-looking cape of some kind, draped over his forearm rather than his shoulders and, the crowning effect, a simple Lone Ranger-style mask to cover his eyes.

She's about to sarcastically thank him for blowing her shot when it clicks in that he's given her a more dramatic image than the jilted wallflower in the distance. He holds out a hand, palm up, and says, "Shall we?"

She brings camera to eye and starts twisting her focus ring and says, "Shall we what?"

"Take home the prize for best costumes."

"Sorry," she says and shoots him, "I'm working."

But there's no way he's giving up this easily. "This isn't a night for work," he says.

"It is for me."

"Your dress says otherwise."

"I like to blend in."

"Is that what you're doing?" he says. "Blending in?"

"What I'm doing," she says and hits the shutter, "is trying to take some photographs."

She lowers the camera and leans forward, smiles and says, "Look for yourself tomorrow in the arts and leisure section."

He moves quickly, reaches in, and before Sylvia can grab it, he's got the Canon in his hands, then up at his masked eye, focusing in on her.

"For Christ sake," she yells.

"Relax," he says and fires off a frame. "How does it feel? Being on the receiving end."

She stays calm, extends her hand and says, "Look, that's an expensive piece of equipment. Just hand it back to me."

Another shot and he says, "It's a very intrusive art form, wouldn't you say?"

"Give it back," she says and a little helplessness bleeds through the mounting anger.

"You can see," he says, intent, rotating the camera and firing again, "why the Indians despised it so much. The way it captured the soul and all."

"What do you want?" she says. "You don't like your picture taken? Fine. We won't run any prints of you. Is that—"

"You don't work for the *Spy,*" he says in a matter-of-fact tone.

"What do you want?" she repeats, getting nervous.

He takes his time for another shot, pulls her in and out of focus, tries a variety of angles until finally something he sees pleases him and he clicks off a shot, lowers the camera and says, "I want to dance."

"I don't dance," Sylvia says.

He stares at her through the felt mask.

"One dance," she says.

He nods.

"Give me the camera."

"After the dance," he says and deposits the Canon into some interior fold of the cape, then secures the cape around his shoulders. He takes her hand and leads her to an open spot next to an oil-scarred grinding machine up near the picnic table. Then with his free hand he gives this flourish of a signal to the d.j., who immediately fills the loft up with tango music.

Sylvia looks up at the guy and rolls her eyes and says, "I don't know how to dance to this stuff."

He throws an arm around her waist and pulls her forward and says, "After tonight, you'll never forget."

She says, "Be careful of the camera and let's get this over with."

He starts to lead and it's clear this is no bluff. The guy knows what he's doing. He could be some kind of profes-

sional instructor, for God sake. And within minutes this an-
noyance starts to turn into something fun and wonderfully
different.

She's getting warm and just slightly out of breath. They
dodge behind one machine, zigzag past another, and somehow he's willing her into matching each of his turns. Then
they're off the dance floor entirely, their arms locked
straight out and their hands intertwined and they're moving all the way to the rear of the building. He stops once
and they pivot to the side and their speed seems to increase
as they come right again and move forward.

In front of them, a double fire door is half-open and the
cool outside air feels tremendous as it gulfs around
Sylvia's legs and neck. And then they're headed for the
door, moving out the door and into the alley in the rear, the
music now starting to fade and her partner's face suddenly
grazing at her neck, her neck getting wet, his hand suddenly releasing her waist and taking hold of her behind and
she starts to push him off but he half-dances, half-carries
her farther away from the factory and they collide into a
chain-link fence and he turns her until her back is pinned
against the fence and now his hands are all over her, trying
to pull up the hem of the nightgown, and he tears it in the
process. Sylvia starts to scream but her voice just dissi-
pates into the total noise of the block party. Then suddenly
his whole body vaults into and off of her and she slides
down the fence onto her behind and Zorro's on the ground
and it's *his* voice she hears screaming alongside her own.

And now, standing sideways in front of her is another
man. But this one's got a baseball bat in his hands, choked
up high in his fists, and Sylvia looks down to see Zorro-
the-rapist bleeding like a son of a bitch from his head and
trying to cover up.

And all Sylvia can scream to this bat-wielding stranger
is, "Don't break my camera."

But the stranger doesn't seem to hear her. He moves in

on Zorro and pokes at him hard with the end of the bat, let-ting the tango-master get clear on what's happened and maybe what's about to happen. And despite the possible concussion the message gets through and Zorro starts to do a panicking scamper from side to side, tries to get to his knees, but each time the guy with the bat knocks him onto his backside with a harder blow until finally Zorro gives up and cowers in one place trying to cover his head. The standing man looks down on Sylvia, then swings the bat up to waist level, hesitates for a second, then chops down one last time onto one of Zorro's ankles and snaps it into a sickening right-angle to the rest of the leg.

There's a blast of screaming which the stranger ignores, turns to Sylvia and says, "Are you all right?"

She edges her way up to standing, runs to the cape and pulls out the camera.

Someone yells, "Marco? Are you all right?"and Sylvia looks to see two figures framed in the fire door. Then the man with the bat is reaching for her, grabbing her arm so hard she almost drops the Canon. He jerks her forward into a run and heads for a smaller connecting alley, moving away from Goulden Ave, making turns and rounding cor-ners as if they were threading their way through a brick maze that narrowed with each directional choice. Finally, they turn right and dead-end into a trash-filled alcove, a tiny mini-alley between two identically nondescript buildings.

The man lets go of Sylvia's arm, hunches forward onto his knees for breath and, staring at the ground, says, "Are you all right?"

She leans back against the wall, only now being hit by the facts of what just happened to her.

"I was dancing with him . . ." she starts and trails off.

She looks up to see him staring and fishing in a back pocket. "You're safe," he heaves. "And the bastard isn't going to be doing any dancing for some time."

And suddenly Sylvia's terrified. She's alone in a de-

serted alleyway with only one exit, with another strange
man who's holding a baseball bat over his right shoulder.

"I'm not going to hurt you," he says and takes a step
backwards, pulls from his pocket a keychain weighted
with dozens of keys and moves to a tiny doorway near the
dead-end wall.

Sylvia starts to edge backwards toward the opening of
the alley. The man looks sideways at her, expressionless as
he fiddles with a door lock. He says, "You can go if you
want," and she nods and keeps stepping backwards until he
says, "but I'd like to know why you've been asking so
many questions about me."

And she stops.

"About you?"

He finds the right key and opens the door, stands up
straight, runs a hand through his hair and nods at her. They
stare at each other for a few seconds. It's the first chance
she's had to get a look at him and right away there's something familiar. He's small and wiry, with a broad forehead
and salt-and-pepper hair that's grown too long. But the feature she locks on is the cool, pale blue of his eyes.

"C'mon, Sylvia," he says. "I don't have all night."

He knows her name. And she's hit with this awful surety
that she knows his. And she makes herself open her mouth
and say, "You're Terrence Propp."

ZO

They move through basements that connect to secondary
basements, cellars that lead to subcellars. They follow the
yellow beam of Propp's penlight, though Sylvia gets the

feeling he could find his way in complete darkness. They're silent except for the short yell that slipped out when the first cobweb blanketed her face.

They climb through small portholes that have been sledgehammered out of brick walls. At some point the ground turns from concrete to loose earth and Propp slows to a halt. She hears him take a long breath through his nose, then he shines the light on her, lets it play on her face for what seems like a long time, finally asks, "You okay?"

"Where are we going?"

He swings the light up to his own face and says, "Home."

He shines the beam in front of them and Sylvia looks ahead to see the tunnel they've been walking through has started to narrow down, the floorway rising and the ceiling lowering until they intersect at two heavy wooden crossbeams, these fat, dry, dense-looking timbers, like logs used in building a cabin. The beams are fitted into an X and they create an inept barrier.

"We've got to squeeze through here," he says. "The beams are thorny, be careful you don't tear your gown."

She looks in the direction of his back and thinks he must be kidding. Her *gown* turned into an expensive cleaning rag when they entered the first basement. She follows him and ducks and twists until she manages to slide past the posts and ends up huddling down in a crawl space, pushed up against Propp's shoulder. She hears him fiddling with rusty metal, then he seems to lean back against the crossbeams and kick his feet out. A half-door, like a metal hatchway, swings outward and a dim red glow of light reveals a much larger tunnel beyond.

"You'll have to go first," he says, "so I can resecure the door. Just edge over the side here until your foot touches the rung. It's a short climb down. Less than ten feet."

She does what he says. She comes forward on her behind until she can dangle her legs out and her heels hit a metal ladder rung. She reaches down and takes hold, lifts herself out into the air, pivots around until she's facing the ladder and climbs down.

He follows, shuts the hatchway, comes next to her, takes her arm and says, "Not far now."

They start to walk down a small incline that empties into a railroad bed. They're in what looks like a kind of primitive subway tunnel. There's an old bulb-eyed red railroad light mounted on the wall on the other side of the tracks. Propp motions to it and says, "It's always on. No idea what powers it."

They head down the middle of the tracks and Sylvia says, "What is this? What were these tracks for?"

For a second she doesn't think he's going to answer, then he says, "You know, the Canal Zone wasn't always just a nightclub for dilettantes."

He picks up the pace a little. "Quinsigamond used to be one of the biggest manufacturing centers in the Northeast."

"So I've heard."

"You've heard the truth. The city's first industry was a paper mill. Early 1800s."

She can't believe she's getting a history lesson here. She's in a storybook nightgown, walking with a myth-figure through an underground railroad bed. And he wants to lecture about the industrial revolution.

"Everything from wooden wheels to hoopskirts got shipped out of here at one time. Bail wire, industrial wrenches, furnace chambers, drill presses . . ."

His voice drifts off and he stops walking, turns and points to a break in the opposite wall. A huge shaft is visible, like a loading platform, a shadow box whose floor is a flat apron of cement that juts out slightly from the facing wall and is covered with a kind of metal grid, a big mat of iron slats. It looks like an empty prison cell with the front wall of bars removed, a square room of three facing walls and a floor, but no visible ceiling.

"Old story," he continues. "We all know some part of it. The city thrives. Goes into a kind of hyper-life. The need for cheap labor is filled by European peasantry. The population explodes and Quinsigamond grows into a kind of gritty, redbrick metropolis. You can picture it. Teeming streets. Tenements popping up. More factories. Bigger mills. For a time, everything congregated here."

He turns and kind of dramatically points down the tracks in the direction they've just come from.

"The raw materials came in this way by handcarts," he turns again and faces the loading platform up the embankment. "Got off-loaded to the appropriate building and then," he makes his hand into a thumbs-up sign, "hauled up into whatever factory where it was transformed into ball valves or skiving knives or gearboxes or grinding wheels—"

"I get the picture," Sylvia says.

He nods and continues, "—then it was lowered back down below the street, loaded onto an outgoing freight cart and sent on down the commerce highway."

"Till the need for skiving knives started to wane—"

"And the climate in the South started to look better and better—"

"And the railroads started to groan and die."

He says, "You know where this track leads, don't you Sylvia?"

She looks past him into the darkness and tries, "Gompers Station?"

He nods and starts to walk again. She moves up next to him and says, "You really are Terrence Propp, aren't you?"

"Why've you been looking for me, Sylvia?"

"How do you know my name? And how do you know I've been looking for you?"

"I guess," he says, "we both have a lot of questions."

"You said we were going home. You live down here?"

His voice goes lower. "Here in the tunnels? Of course not."

"Doesn't anybody know these tracks still exist?"

The track bed begins to curve to the left and a new red bulb lights their way.

"If you mean the DPW, probably. It's still on their maps, though it doesn't tie into any currently relevant sewer or power lines. If you mean the little leather bohemians writhing around above us, they don't know their affected asses from their affected elbows."

"Sounds like you hate your own devotees."

"I never asked for devotees of any kind, Sylvia."

"I'm not exactly a devotee," she says. "I never heard of you before this week."

"Then your luck took a change," he says, sounding unoffended.

"For better or worse?"

"That remains to be seen, doesn't it."

He stops, shines his penlight up at the rounded ceiling to show a series of cracks in the masonry, veins that spread wider and wider where the concrete has separated from itself.

"The '53 earthquake," he says. "June nine. I don't think anyone in this city even realized we were sitting on the O'Toole Fault until it hit. You're about to see the most pitiful casualty of the quake."

He clicks off the light and pockets it, takes her hand, and as the tracks begin to incline toward street level, Propp veers to the right and crawls up an ash and gravel embankment and then squeezes through this horrible manmade corridor that looks like it's been hacked out of the earth and stone by pick ax and shovel. They have to walk sideways to fit through, Propp leading the way, and thankfully it's only a short path, maybe ten feet, but long enough for Sylvia to get a little claustrophobic, especially when she feels the cold of the rock face behind her narrowing in.

But then they're in the open again and the space is lit by two hanging plastic lanterns throwing bluish light and she's standing staring and not believing the vision in front of her: In this brick-and-stone cave, this crater-like hollow, this dank earth floor chamber, covered with silt and dust and ash, but still recognizable, there's a classic Quinsigamond Lunch-car Company diner, one of those little boxy restaurants that look like stationary train cars. It has no windows and parts of the barreled roof are missing and the walls are cracked, but it's sitting there like some petrified museum piece. And it's *underneath* the street.

She looks to Propp for an explanation and he looks pleased.

"I told you we were heading home," he says.

"This," she says, "is where you live?"

He points to the ceiling. "We're directly below the lower level of Gompers Station. Where the tracks broke left, the handcarts would have been coming up into the station."

She nods and stares at the diner and waits. He pushes his hands into his pockets like some barely shy date, self-impressed but trying hard not to show it.

"It's called St. Benedict's," he says. "It sat for years down on the lower level of Gompers. Owned and operated by a family named Guttman. It was mainly frequented by the trainmen and the freight crews. The passengers, the travelers, they all ate upstairs at the Grand Pavilion."

He walks up to the structure and brushes at the outer wall with his hand.

"It's a small diner comparatively. Could only seat forty-nine bodies at full capacity."

He turns and faces her. "In '53, when the quake hit and the fault opened, the old wooden columns just buckled, snapped like twigs, the flooring beneath the diner gave way and the whole thing fell through and came to rest down here."

"Which is?" she asks.

"Some kind of subcellar vault the rail company had built. For storage, I suppose. There are dozens of them under the station."

She looks past him to St. Benedict's. "It's amazing the thing wasn't completely destroyed."

"A testimony to their construction. The damage you see, I don't even think it happened during the quake. I'm fairly certain it was during the attempt at salvage."

"They tried to pull it back up?"

He nods. "A logistical nightmare. How do you get a crane inside Gompers?"

She shrugs.

"You don't," he says.

"I can't believe," she says, "I didn't know about this."

"You didn't know about me either."

"But this must have made the papers and—"

"The *Spy* did a huge spread. Amazing photographs. But this was what, Sylvia, a good fifteen years before you were born."

"Still, you know, over the years, a feature article or something."

He shakes his head and mimes a laugh.

"The Guttmans took their insurance money and left town," he says. "I've heard they thought the city was cursed. The P&Q Company cemented over the hole and then the rail line took another painful twenty years to rust over and turn into a freight service. Everything gets forgotten, Sylvia. Your first important lesson of the night. And that fact can be as wonderful as it is horrible. But I don't mean to offend a history major—"

"Fine arts," she corrects him and then freezes. "Jesus Christ, what else do you think you know about me?"

"There'll be time for all that," he says. "C'mon in. I'll make some coffee."

Inside is beautiful and somehow cleaner than she expected. There's a marble counter running the length of the diner and a half dozen mini-booths attached to the front wall. Above the counter hangs a mesh hammock strung from wall to wall and beyond it, in what was the open kitchen space, are crates and cartons of what must be supplies piled on top of grills and steam tables and cutting boards. Propp steers her to the first booth and clears clutter from the table by sweeping it to the side with his arm. Then he moves behind the counter and squats down till he's out of sight and in a second she hears the soft machine-purr of an engine.

His head pops back into view and he says, "Portable generator. Makes all the difference. There are still a lot of gas lines running down here that I could tap into, but why worry."

He starts to work at what it takes her a second to recognize as an espresso machine. And not one of those home models but a traditional, ornate, industrial job.

"I don't believe this," she mutters. She brings the camera up and pans around the place once, then puts it down on the table and stares at Propp.

With his back to her he says, "They don't let you live in the Zone without an espresso machine. It's a law."

"How did you—"

"It nearly killed me, getting it down here. But it's been worth it. Good espresso is such a small pleasure in the end, right?"

"How does the generator run?"

"Gasoline," he says. "I do a little siphoning about once a week."

"Siphoning?"

"Dupin Boulevard's the best. I try to stay as far away from Bangkok as possible. But these days—"

"Wait a second. You steal the gas? Out of people's cars?"

He turns around holding two coffee cups in his hands

and with a smile on his face. "I'm sorry, Sylvia, does that offend you?"

"Forget it," she says.

"I'm just curious," he pushes. "My stealing a couple gallons of gas bothers you. But Hugo Schick and his vile little circus down on Watson Street give you no problem."

She stares at him and when it's clear he's not going to continue, she tries to keep her voice even and says, "Okay. So you know everything about me. And I know nothing about you. Are you enjoying this?"

He gives her a slow shake of his head that says *no*, turns back to the espresso machine and says quietly, "Stay away from Schick, Sylvia. You have no idea what he can do to you."

His words come out more as a plea than a threat and she stares at his back, unsure of what to say. But then her eyes drift to the stainless steel shelves above his head and she sees a line of ragged books. She reads some spines—*The Phantom of the Poles. Soleri's Arcology. The Journals of C. R. Teed.* On the next shelf, she spots what look like old-time silver film canisters stacked side by side and bearing their titles in black ink on what looks like white adhesive tape. And she wants to laugh as she reads them off.

"Get out of here," she says and he turns with a surprised look, then follows the focus of her eyes.

"Yes, of course," he says, sort of relieved, "the film fanatic."

"This is ridiculous," she says. "There's no way . . ."

He folds his arms over his chest and widens his eyes, then reaches up without looking, pulls down a canister about the size of a fat pancake and frisbees it to her. She grabs for it and makes an awkward catch, runs her finger over the tape that reads *Greed—von Stroheim (1924)*.

"I've got all twelve hours," he says.

"Ten," she says. "It ran ten hours."

"Trust me," he says. "It's twelve."

"This is impossible. It doesn't exist."

"You're holding it in your hand, Sylvia. 'Course it's been reduced to sixteen millimeter."

She's just shaking her head and he clearly loves this reaction, so he throws another canister and she catches it and reads *The Other Side of the Wind—Wells (1984)*.

She looks up. "But he never finished it—"

"He finished it, Sylvia."

"—and what prints there were are in some bank vault in Iran."

"Not anymore," he says.

Sylvia is stunned. She looks up to the shelf and reads *Further Ecstasy—Machaty, (1934), The Godless Girl's Daddy—de Mille (1930), Berlin Melody of 1936—Reifenstahl, Norma Jean & the Camelot Kids—Hoover (Compilation), The Day the Clown Cried II—Lewis (1972), Last Love Scenes from the Bunker—Braun (April, 1945)*.

She wants so much to believe this isn't a prank. None of these films are supposed to exist. They're all just wishful rumors, fever-dreams of movie nuts everywhere.

"How do you . . ." she says, "I mean do you ever . . ."

"Screen them?" he helps her out. "Of course. You know the old Ballard Theatre? The Loftus Brothers just bought it. They're reopening next week as Impact: The Car Crash Cinema. But I know a way in. Would you like to—"

"Would I *like* to," she says and Propp laughs.

"Calm down," he says. "There's time for everything."

He brings their cups over and slides into the booth opposite her. They both take sips. She burns her tongue, ignores the sting and says, "You're really Terrence Propp?"

He sits back. "Who else?"

"And you really live down here?"

"Where else?"

She sits back, matches his posture and says, "How'd you find this place?"

He shrugs. "Exactly how you'd think. I was out at night,

prowling, looking for shots. I used to do that. Take some speed and just wander all night. Find a way into the old buildings. Shoot the old machines. Shoot angles. Abandoned cars. Then I started to get hooked on old furnaces. Old boilers. Peerlesses. American Standards. Even a few industrial Marville—Negres. The bigger and greasier and more sinister looking, the better."

"When was this?"

Another shrug. "I don't know anymore. No, really. You see any calendars hanging on the walls? Time gets fairly irrelevant down here."

"I know that feeling," she says.

"You do?"

"You were shooting furnaces," she says.

He agrees to move on. "I discovered I had a talent for getting into any building. So I spent nights moving through every basement underneath Verlin and Aragon and Waldstein. Must've shot a thousand prints—"

"Could I see them?"

He just shakes his head *no,* without any emotion. "I destroyed them all. One big bonfire—"

"The negatives—"

"Of course, the negatives. That was the point."

"It's just—"

"Please, Sylvia, don't say it. They were horrible. Agonizingly boring. Who wants to look at a thousand prints of heavy machinery? What kind of man would take a thousand shots of old furnaces? One night I just woke up and realized what I was doing. Got disgusted with myself. And just started walking."

"Underground."

"It was chance. I just kept moving. I simply didn't care where I ended up or just how lost I got."

"And you ended up here," Sylvia says, looking around the diner again.

"It wasn't in this condition, believe me. But the moment

I came upon it, I knew it was the end of the line. I just *knew*, it, you understand, in that way we all hope to know something. With that kind of certainty."

"Can I ask," she asks, "where you lived before this?"

"No place dramatic," he says. "I moved from rooming house to rooming house. The weekly hotels. One room. Pay as you go."

She leans back in the booth and stares at him.

"What?" he says.

"It's just . . ."

"Go ahead."

She takes a breath and says, "Why?"

He stares back at her as if trying to decide which of several possible answers to give. As if his decision will be determined by the look on her face.

"I like my solitude," he says.

"So join a monastery."

"Too many monks. And they've got that awful requirement these days."

She raises her eyebrows and says, "Celibacy?"

He picks up his cup, self-satisfied, and says, "Faith."

"You're not a believer?"

He puts the cup down, comes forward on his elbows and suddenly looks exhausted.

"I believe in a lot of things," he says. "I believe in my own mortality. I believe in sleeping when I get tired—"

He's getting cute and she hates it. "Why did you bring me down here, Mr. Propp?"

"God," he says, "such formality. Propp will do, Sylvia. Just Propp."

"Why am I here?"

He looks down at the table, lifts his cup almost absent-mindedly and throws the remains of his espresso out the window. He looks up at her and says, "I heard you had something that might belong to me."

She doesn't want to give anything away.

"Who did you hear that from?"

"Oh, Sylvia," he says, "you know how the Zone is. You just hear things."

"From Rory Gaston?"

"Gaston?" he says, amused. "I've never met the man but I'm told he's an idiot."

"He holds you in pretty high regard."

"Case closed."

"Was it Quevedo?"

"Who the hell is that," he says.

"You don't know Mr. Quevedo? From Brody's?"

"Brody's?"

She stares at him, annoyed. "Okay, fine. You never heard of Brody's. Good."

"I'm not trying to be difficult, Sylvia. I swear to you. I know it doesn't seem that way, but it's very . . . it's extremely difficult."

"Maybe I should go," she says.

"If you want to leave," he says, now seeming to hold back a genuine agitation, "I'll take you back up to the street. It's possible, it's entirely possible I've made an enormous mistake here."

"Then maybe that would be best."

He pulls his bottom lip in and chews on it. The action seems to calm him down. He says, "First just tell me. You've got something of mine, don't you? What did you find, Sylvia?"

They stare at each other over the length of the table. Though they're locked on each other's eyes, Sylvia can see the fingers of his right hand flexing out and retracting, doing this awful, nervous fidget that Propp might not even be aware of. She should probably be terrified at this moment. She should probably be preparing herself to ward off some kind of attack, to defend herself in whatever manner she might find available. But she simply doesn't feel any threat.

Instead, she senses a queasy desperation breaking over this man's entire body, an engulfing wave of dread, as if he has a small window of opportunity to say and do the exactly correct things, to enact a specific response from her. Only she doesn't know what that response should be. She doesn't have any idea how she figures in this moment, in this bizarre life. But she does seem to matter here. Terrence Propp, reaching out now, taking her wrist in his hand, running his tongue over his lips as if he was about to propose marriage to her, as if he was completely unsure of her answer, Terrence Propp came looking for *her*. Was waiting for her. Knew an uncomfortable amount of information about her small life.

Clearly it's not chance that brought her to this diner booth. It feels like forces are acting *upon* her. It feels like since the moment she took that camera, that Aquinas, Propp's Aquinas, into her hands, coincidence and familiarity and boring routine have been vacuumed out of her life and replaced by things a lot less benign.

But that doesn't mean she doesn't want to be down here, ten, fifteen feet below the surface of the street, in the ruins of St. Benedict's Diner, the only human to have made recent contact with the myth of Terrence Propp.

She looks away from his face when she realizes that what she's feeling isn't shock or reverence or even fear. None of those things that would normally be accorded to myth. What she's feeling is something like pity. And she doesn't know why.

"I bought a camera," she says, "in an old store down on Waldstein. An old Aquinas."

He takes a long inhale. "Where is the camera now?"

"At home," she says. "It's safe."

He nods.

"Someone," he says, "told you it might be my camera.

She nods.

"What do you think?" he asks.

And she decides, at that moment, not to mention the seven prints she developed.

"I have no idea," she says. "On Monday I walked into a camera store and brought home a camera. The store owner told me it was a consignment sale. He mentioned your name. He says you were losing your eyesight—"

He doesn't raise his voice but he cuts her off and says, "That's a lie, Sylvia. Jack Derry never mentioned my name."

"Oh," she says, "you know Mr. Derry? I could've sworn he mentioned your name. Would you know where he might be? I still owe him some money."

"Derry never mentioned my name," he repeats.

"I guess I've got it wrong then."

He's frustrated. He shifts in his seat and says, "Have you taken a look at the camera?"

"Not really. Been so damn busy—"

His head falls back, bumps the Naugahyde. He says, "Please, Sylvia. Don't be this way."

She shakes her head. "Look, I don't know what you expect from me, but you've got a hell of a lot of nerve. You want something from me, fine. It's possible I can help you, I don't know. But stop jerking me around—"

"That's not what I'm trying to do, Sylvia—"

"Good. Great. Then just start telling me how you know so much about me. How you know where I've been and what's happened to me. Why you were watching me at the dance back there—"

"Damn good thing I was—"

"You're a hero, Propp," she says, now furious. "So noble of you to stop a goddamn rape. How do I know that son of a bitch Zorro wasn't working for you? Beautiful way to get me down here—"

He pounds down on the table. Her cup falls over and coffee spills and he yells, "I don't believe this. I don't believe you just said that."

He slides out of the booth and exits the diner without looking back and Sylvia slumps and realizes she's made a mistake. She lets a second go by for both of them to calm down, then she slides out and goes after him.

But he's nowhere to be seen. She walks a full circle around St. Benedict's but he's not in the cavern. And then a thought hits her and before she even looks back inside through the windows, she knows it's true—her camera is nowhere to be seen on the tabletop. Propp has taken it.

She stands still and listens but can't hear any footsteps, any noise at all beyond the soft hum of the generator back inside. And the impact of where she is and the fact that she has no idea how to leave suddenly hits her and she wants to run but keeps herself from moving, stands still and calls for Propp.

But there's no answer.

ZI

Sylvia retraces her steps. She moves through the opening to the diner's cavern, squeezes down the narrow path. She starts down the gravel embankment, slips and slides to the rail bed on her behind. She's back in the dark except for the red lantern glow that barely makes it around the bend of the tunnel. She knows the way back to the Zone is left, in the direction of the red light. She knows if she just follows the tracks, eventually she'll come to the hatchway that leads up into the Canal cellars.

She also knows that if Propp was telling the truth, turning right and following the tracks that lead away from the

Zone will bring her up into the remains of Gompers Station.

She stands in the middle of the rail bed for a second, trying to think. They took so many turns on the way down here that it's doubtful she could remember them all. On the other hand, Gompers Station, with its packs of wild dogs and junkies and drunks and gangboys is not someplace you want to stroll through at night, especially when you're wearing a shredded nightgown.

But she can find her way home from Gompers, so she turns right and starts walking. Within five minutes the track bed starts to incline upward and she climbs toward an arc of moonlight and emerges in a huge pavilion. The roof of the station is almost nonexistent and enough light is getting through to give her some bearings. She's only been inside Gompers once and that was over a dozen years ago. She'd stayed too late at the Girls' Club one Saturday and, afraid of missing the bus home, she took a shortcut through the station. It had already been closed down for a good ten years and natural erosion combined with perpetual vandalism had made some awful headway by then. She ran through this blighted, bombed-out temple as fast as she could, but the image of the place stayed with her for weeks.

And now, looking around in this weak moonlight, in these dim, soft beams of light that reveal all the dust and grit just hovering in the air, it's like her childhood memory has come to life. But it's more vivid and decayed than anything her imagination could have estimated and provided for. All she can think of is grainy black-and-white landscape shots she's studied, the aftermath of world war bombings, pictures of places like Berlin and Dresden, the ground just a jumble of various-sized craters and mounds of earth and brick and stone, buildings half-slouched into each other, their walls knocked down, windowless, chimneys toppled into useless heaps, and everywhere these indiscriminate tangles of something like wire and iron and scraps of cloth and metallic shards, just clumps of recombinant junk whose origin is unknown, plunked down like a shower of meteorites from space and now sitting mute and useless like clusters of industrial weed.

This is the remains of Gompers Station. This is what's left of one of the most stunning architectural wonders in New England. It's now a monument to entropy, an embarrassing hulk whose only purpose is to admonish the ego of a community. It's an arc of cracked and ash-caked vaulting walls, grand stairways that degenerate halfway to their destination into simple mountains of hacked-up bedrock, Greco-Roman columns that lie sideways in cinder beds and are covered with neon gang graffiti and now serve only as marble bull's-eyes for the spray of dogs and forgotten reprobates.

Sylvia thinks there's something wrong with her for looking on all this decay and thinking only *I wish I had my camera.*

Maybe that's why she came this way. Because she thought Propp would come this way. And Propp has her camera.

She looks around the perimeter of the pavilion for movement, for some sign of another presence. She should be looking for exits, ways out to the street and out of downtown. But what her eyes settle on, across the hall, for some reason bathed in a brighter, more direct shower of moonlight, is what at first looks like a huge, white-ish boulder. As she moves across the hall toward it she realizes it's the bottom half of a massive support column that's been knocked down and broken at its base. The odd thing is that the main shaft of the column, the bulk of its mass, is gone, is nowhere in the vicinity. Someone must have hauled it away and she can't begin to imagine how much the thing could have weighed. What's left here is the base, about three feet tall and maybe three feet in diameter, this ribbed pillar that looks like solid marble, a creamy white-gone-yellow but shot through with dark veins that in a better light she'd take to be scarlet.

And as she comes to stop in front of it and puts her hand out to touch it, to take in the coldness that she imagines it retains, Sylvia is instantly struck by the fact, by her absolute surety of the fact, that she's seen this broken column before, that this is the specific pedestal that the Madonna and her infant are posed on in the seven photographs she developed.

This is where Terrence Propp shot the series. This is the precise point where the shadowy mother with the achingly tender shoulder and her half-shrouded infant with its hungry mouth sat and were exposed, at least seven times, to the open eye of the camera.

She touches the pedestal, feels grit under her fingers.

A light flashes, strobes at her from above and she flinches.

Then comes Propp's voice.

"Sit down, Sylvia."

She looks up in the direction of the flash and is hit with another burst of light. He's somewhere up in the balcony that rims the pavilion, up in the clubby loft where old men once drank brandy and smoked cigars while waiting for a train out of the city.

"That's my camera," she yells up.

Another flash.

"Yes," he says, no yell, but his voice carries, "I seem to have misplaced mine."

He's moving around up there, probably on his knees, crawling under the cover of the balcony wall.

"I'm leaving," she says, her voice slightly lower.

There's a pause and then, "No, you're not."

She waits for a flash but nothing comes.

"I think," he says, "you want to know who she is. I think you want that too badly to leave."

They both know he's right. She wants to know who the woman in the seven photos is. She wants to know what the woman was to Propp. She wants to know what the infant's name was, what became of them. She needs to know why the pictures came into her life.

"Why don't you sit down, Sylvia," he says and she pivots to the left to follow the voice. "I want to take your picture. Do you know what some people would give to have me take their picture?"

She doesn't like the arrogance and says, "I'm not a fan, Propp, Remember?"

He ignores her. "There are stunning similarities," he says, almost a whisper that she has to strain to hear, "between you and she."

This stops her and she hates the fact that he knows how to manipulate her with this kind of ease.

She says, "Similarities," knowing, as the words come out, that he'll let her hang. And he does.

So Sylvia does the only thing she can do. She climbs up on top of the pedestal and tries to arrange herself into the pose of the Madonna. She tilts her face upward and gives her profile to the direction of the last camera flash. She leans her body forward until half of it is cloaked in shadow. She doesn't know what to do with her arms. There's no baby to hold onto. So she puts her hands awkwardly on her knees and thinks, though she's not sure, that she hears a whispered *thank you* from up above.

There's a long wait and she begins to imagine that he's gone, that simply getting her to assume the pose was enough to satisfy him. But then a single flash shoots down on her and she hears him bumping into something, the noise of clutter being scattered, a bottle rolling down an incline. She wants to squint and look up but she makes herelf stay still, wait for direction, instruction. Maybe some answers, some kind of story.

"Could I see the shoulder, Sylvia."

She's not sure what to do, but before she can think too much, she simply brings her hands up from the knees to the neck, unties the small silk bow and unfastens pearl buttons until she's given herself enough room to slide the nightgown off her left shoulder—it was the Madonna's left shoulder, wasn't it—and bring her skin out into the cool air of the pavilion. And it feels odd but wonderful and immediately a series of flashes erupt, four or five or six in a row, and she tries to remember how many shots could be left in the camera.

"You're perfect, Sylvia," and flash, "You're beautiful. You're absolutely perfect."

He's moving up in the balcony. He's jogging from spot to spot like a quirky, self-possessed dancer, dodging, with a semi-gracefulness, from one instinctual point to another, planting down, landing steady for a second, hitting the shutter, exposing a shot, taking in her body in this ragged gown, her face, her naked shoulder lit by the dusty light of the moon piercing through the gaps of the station's roof. And he's doing the standard, actually chichéd photographer's patter, spieling away at her, a riff on David Hemmings in every photographer's favorite movie. But Propp is wonderful at it and, incredibly, somehow sincere, somehow putting across to her the feeling that each moment that she sees the explosion of light that allows her image to be cemented onto film, that each of those microseconds, is inherently *important* to his life, to his reasons for being. His movements up in the balcony are beyond some idea of love of craft. They're beyond any notions Sylvia's ever had about art. It feels more like Propp is making a connection, with her and with himself, that few people ever get to live through.

"The shoulder, Sylvia, more shoulder," and she unhitches two more buttons.

Another flash and another and suddenly Sylvia doesn't want to leave. She doesn't want to move off this pedestal. She doesn't even want to talk, to ask any questions. She wants to pray he has pockets stuffed with film and enough energy to move until dawn.

Then there's a noise, another din of junk clattering under a tripping foot. But it doesn't come from the direction of the flash and suddenly it's as if she senses Propp's mood being shattered in the instant that the noise explodes into the air, a palpable flinch. And as the clatter echoes into silence, there's this surge of ignited tension that blows down across the space between them and immediately infects her.

"All right, you little bastards," she hears Propp say, his voice low and genuinely threatening, "I see you."

There's a rumble of incoherent whispering from halfway around the balcony area.

"You want to watch me work, fine. But any noise and I'll shoot into the whole goddamn pack of you."

She pulls the nightgown back up onto her shoulder and starts to climb down from the pedestal and Propp screams, "No, Sylvia, don't."

She looks up and tries to see who he was talking to but all she can make out is a cluster of shadows that wave in and out of visibility.

"They're harmless," Propp says, "I swear to you."

She wants to run.

"They're children, Sylvia," his voice lowering but still fighting a panic. "They're just lost children. They live here, Sylvia. We're in *their* home."

She turns her head to try and see Propp and he repeats, "They're harmless. They only want to watch."

And he lights them up with the beam from his penlight. Sylvia sees a dozen or more small faces, each spotlighted for a second or two, just long enough for her to realize that Propp has told the truth, that they're exactly what he says, they're children, ranging from maybe six years old up through the early teens. In the instant that each face is highlighted for her benefit, Sylvia can take in the horrible facts amended to their raw ages, the sunken eyes that result from too much fear and solitude, the grime-plastered hair that juts from or pastes down to the miniature skulls, the cast-off, filthy, ill-fitting clothing, and more than anything else, the generic look of defeat from faces that should still be too young to know there's a battle.

Has Propp brought her here on purpose for this singular reason? Has every other element of this nightmare—from taking the goddamn Aquinas to posing here as the stand-in Madonna—been subordinate to this *image,* this group portrait of inexcusable tragedy?

The children look down on her as if they were some nest of insects that share a single eye. None of them speak. None of them even move. Looking back up at them is like studying a haunting, inherently demented canvas, something slaved over by a tortured medieval monk with unlimited talent, a man whose life's work was to depict the definition of *abandonment.* They're a half-starved peasant choir, made mute by an endless destitution, angelic by way of a brutalized life rather than an unspoiled innocence.

And Sylvia thinks, in that moment, of her own childhood. And of her mother, of her mother's face, of her smell, her entire presence. Of all the hours spent safely, securely, protected in the warmth of their small apartment.

And she lets the tears come to her eyes, come past her eyes, pour onto and then down the cheeks. But she doesn't let any accompanying sound out and because of this she can hear Propp again. This time he's speaking to the children, whispering, all threat and authority gone from his voice, replaced only by this fragile certainty.

He says to them, "Isn't she beautiful?"

She doesn't want to look up, but her head moves and the landscape is blurred and she wipes at her eyes and blinks until they clear. The children are moving off, disappearing through some small crevice in the balcony's inner wall, until only one is left, maybe the smallest, a child of indeterminate sex, black hair matted, wearing something dark and muted. Propp keeps the light on the child and he or she lingers at the balcony's edge, just staring at Sylvia, as if waiting for her to say something.

And when she doesn't, the child turns and runs, follows the trail of the others like a small, nocturnal animal, something with skittish moves and small claws.

Sylvia brings her hands up to her head and when the camera flashes, she knows that she hates Propp even if she doesn't know why.

ZZ

Things are humming in the Henrik Galeen Memorial Studio at the top of the Skin Palace. The whole Schick company is present, filming what Hugo calls "vital stock," footage of unscripted orgy scenes, graphic serial sex between multiple partners that the director keeps on hand at all times and edits into a film to break up what he calls "the necessary evil of the talking heads."

Jakob Kinsky is both exhilarated and exhausted. Though he'd never admit it to any of his coworkers, he thinks he's expending more energy than the intertwined throng rolling around on a mattress the size of a swimming pool for the benefit of two very old Panaflex cameras. Jakob hasn't stopped moving since he arrived for his first day of work. Hugo keeps the new assistant director shooting around the studio like a pinball, positioning cameras and props, double-checking the sound, taking and retaking light readings, spraying the actors down with an atomizer full of oil and water, rummaging for a fresh can of Rigor mentholated balm, and bringing coffee, doughnuts, and carton after carton of amyl nitrite poppers.

Life is good.

He never thought he'd feel this kind of happiness again. He assumed he'd spend the balance of his life shambling after Papa and Felix and Weltsch, trying futilely to bury his grief over Felice in endless viewings of *Black Angel* and *Touch of Evil* and *Edge of Doom*. He wishes Felice could see him now—eighteen years old, maybe the youngest A.D. working a hot set. So it's three thousand miles from Hollywood, but it's four thousand miles from Maisel. He's getting closer all the time. And if Felice couldn't have appreciated the genre he's found himself apprenticing within, she'd at least have to see how much more satisfied he is. How just the proximity to the cameras, the lights, the boom mikes give him a reason to want more.

What would Felice make of the actresses spread out now before him, not a trace of self-consciousness as they drop robes to the floor first thing in the morning and begin to move through a series of carnal encounters that exceed the average imagination? There's Coco Bing, with her odd, unplaceable accent and Garbo-like aura, asking Jakob in an emotionless voice to wipe her down with a bath towel. There's Miriam Persons, a peerless African queen who accepted the jelly Danish Jakob brought like it was the head of a weak rival. There's China Wiene, always joking, distracted, vulnerable, huddling in her terry robe as if the overheated loft was an icehouse.

And then there's Leni Pauline, who stands apart from everyone, as if she knew the central secret of every life in the Skin Palace, as if she'd found a way in childhood to boost her intelligence to the point where all matter of human concern was little more than a semi-funny joke. The only time Jakob feels nervous is around Leni Pauline. There's something about the woman that makes him want to cultivate her approval. When she asked him to help her with a series of stretching exercises, he thought he'd lose the ability to speak for the rest of the day.

The men are different. Just as each actress seems a specific individual, the men seem interchangeable. They walk around as if the set were a locker room in a high school they'll never graduate from. They never seem to put on their robes, even when shooting ends. Their demeanor gives the impression that there's only one thing in this life that a man should either be proud or ashamed of and it's dangling forever between their legs. Jakob wants to laugh every time he thinks of their names—Herbie Warm, Demetrie Green, Pedro Gallagher, and, the best and funniest man on the set, with his chronically sashaying hips and thrusting chin, a kind of pornographic idiot savant, telling everyone who'll listen that he has an upcoming appointment with the *Guinness Book of Records* people, Udolpho Phist. Udolpho insists that Hugo bill him on the film posters as *Phist, The Gargantuan Freak of Human Nature.*

In a single morning, Jakob has learned film terms that he never knew existed. Things like the *money shot,* the *two-for-six splice,* the *Singapore pan,* and the *Krakatoa dissolve.* He's studied camera angles that were never covered in any of the standard texts. He's followed script structures that go against all the dynamics he's worked so hard to make reflexive. And he's seen actors and actresses do things that not one of the performers that ever appeared on the ripped and patched screen of the old Kierling Theatre in Loew Square back home ever even hinted at.

By midday, the couplings in front of him became like some sort of dizzying geometry problem in the most baffling math class on earth. Angles dissolved into angles that rounded into shimmying circumferences that mutated into flesh-tones fractals of explosive significance. Sounds reduced themselves to an experiment in moaning dissonance and then pivoted and somehow became perfect choruses of melodious, if otherworldly, noises. The loft filled up with a pervasive, alien smell, the stuff of car crashes, old farms, stale candy, talcum, blood, and a hundred other fragrances too strange to name.

In the end, the only way to make any sense of the spectacle was the oldest way Jakob knew—through the lens of a camera. Hugo not only let him man the second Panaflex, but encouraged it, stood over his shoulder as Jakob peered one-eyed into the tube of black metal and glass. Schick whispered, *light and motion, my boy, that's all it is.*

And in that moment, staring at this scene, this tangle of human limbs flailing like the branches of a willow tree caught in an unexpected gale, this chambered nautilus of supple coral spiraling itself to death, Jakob thought *this man may well be a genius,* and then, *my father is about to destroy him.*

Jakob sits in the front row of the theatre in the aisle seat. Something is wrong with the sound system and Hugo's had to close the box office for the night. The cast and the crew are all on supper break so Jakob has an hour to himself. He opens his work notebook, squints in the dim light and flips pages until he finds the strip of photos pasted into the rear cover. Four tiny black-and-white pictures. Two-inch-square head shots from the arcade machine in the lobby of the Kierling. Jakob and Felice, faces pressed together. A happiness that stretched beyond the province of imagination.

"Not hungry tonight, son?"

He slaps the notebook closed and looks up at Hugo, not knowing what to say, feeling like he's been caught doing something embarrassing if not necessarily wrong.

Hugo slides into the first seat on the opposite aisle and says, "Neither am I," then he tilts his head back and rubs his eyes for a time, opens them and stares up at the enormous white of the screen.

"This is church for people like us, Jakob," Hugo says. "I

find the blank screen relaxing. It eases the mind. It slows down the images."

Jakob's not sure if he should answer. He's a little uneasy, worried that Hugo will try to pump him about Papa's motives and methods.

Hugo takes a handkerchief from his coat pocket and pats at the top of his head.

"It's shocking," he says.

"Sir?"

"How well you know your way around. You'd think you grew up on a soundstage."

Jakob shakes his head. "If only," he says.

"Clearly," Hugo says, "you have the passion. And the talent. This is to be your life's calling, I take it?"

"I just love movies, Mr. Schick," Jakob says. "I always have. I've never wanted to do anything else."

"It frightens me a bit," Hugo says. "How common that is, I mean. Cinema has taken over in a way I never quite thought it would."

Jakob stays quiet but nods.

"Did your mother love the movies?"

"I never knew my mother, Mr. Schick. She died soon after I was born."

"I'm very sorry, Jakob. Your father then. Did he instill the passion for film?"

Jakob's laugh fills the room.

"My father never went to the movies. He was busy. Working. It was very difficult in Maisel."

"So I've heard."

"I had a," the boy pauses for just a second, "governess. A kind of nanny. She took me every day and night. The Kierling Theatre. A beautiful building, even in its decay. Most of the movies were in English. Subtitled. We went until I began to learn the language. Then we kept going."

"Is she still back in Maisel? The nanny?"

"She's dead also," Jakob says. "Maisel has a very high mortality rate."

"Apparently," Hugo says, repocketing his handkerchief.

There's a few minutes of silence until Jakob gathers the nerve to say, "Ms. Persons says you worked with Fritz Lang?"

"*Ms. Persons,*" Hugo repeats. "How precious of you."

"Is it true?"

"What do you think?"

"Coco says you were second-unit camera for von Stroheim."

Schick likes this one.

"My children," he says, "love to tease."

"Miss Wiene says you ghostwrote part of *Citizen Kane.*"

"This one I had not heard."

"And Leni—"

"Yes?" Hugo says, grimacing a bit. "What does Ms. Pauline say?"

"She says you did surveillance work for some government man named Mr. Cohn. She says you secretly filmed some meetings."

"One day, Jakob, I will kill that woman."

Jakob wants to bite his own tongue out of his mouth. Hugo senses the explosion of regret and says, "Relax, son, Schick is only joking."

Jakob mutters, "She's amazing."

Hugo nods and says, "Unfortunately, she is," then he gets up out of his seat and walks to the right, climbs the stairs to the stage and comes to the lip in front of Jakob. "But never forget, son, she is just another actor. My good friend Hitch called them all *cattle*. But I think they are more like a common venereal disease. You can always pick one up without very much effort. So sad really, that *this* is who will carry on my gospel once I've exited the stage."

He stares down at the boy, expressionless, hands clasped

behind his back, his safari jacket straining over his belly. He leans his head forward a bit, smiles slightly, and says, "So, when are you going to show it to me?"

"Show it to you, sir?"

Hugo nods.

Jakob tried to think what he could mean and comes up empty.

"I'm afraid I don't—"

"The script," Hugo explodes, his voice booming through the cavern of the theatre and echoing back.

"The script," Jakob repeats.

Hugo sighs, arches his back, says to the ceiling, "You know, at some point, coyness becomes an insult."

"I'm sorry, Mr. Schick, I don't—"

"Are you trying to tell me you don't have a screenplay, son? Is this what you would ask an old man to believe? Please, Jakob, think about how long I've been around this industry. I've seen the prodigies come and go and end up schlepping industrial training strips in Newark. Please, don't presume to tell Hugo that you haven't written a script. That you don't think it is the greatest thing since *Chinatown*. That you never for a moment considered using your father's influence to foist it on me."

"My father," Jakob yells, coming to his feet, "has nothing to do with my screenplay."

A huge, smug smile fades into Hugo's face. He folds his arms across his chest and says, "So there is a screenplay."

Jakob wants to leave, wants to be back upstairs trying to find a tape measure for Udolpho Phist.

"Would you at least tell me the title?" Hugo asks, now sounding apologetic.

Jakob looks down at his feet, sniffles, mumbles, "It's called *Little Girl Lost*."

"I like it," Hugo says.

"That's just a working title for now."

"Of course," Hugo says.

They both let a minute pass.

"I never intended to give it to you," Jakob says, knowing how false this will sound before the words leave his lips.

"I would be delighted," Hugo says, "no, honored. I would be honored to read this *Little Girl Lost.*"

"It's not really done yet."

"They're never done, Jakob."

Jakob shakes his head.

"I swear to you, Mr. Schick, my father doesn't even know I've written a film."

"Jakob, relax, please, Hermann is my banker now. If he wants us to make your movie, I'm sure we can find—"

"My father," Jakob yells, "doesn't know I wrote a movie."

Hugo is taken back. He sits down on the stage between the break in the gold railing and lets his legs hang toward the floor.

"All right, calm now," he says. "There's no need to be angry."

"I do not need nor want," Jakob says, "my father's help to make my film."

"This is good, Jakob. This is wonderful. You surprise and delight me. Upon this rock, eh son? You have the talent and you have the passion. And now I know you have the anger. No one realizes how much anger you need to make a picture. You treasure that anger, my boy. You nourish it until you can channel it into the camera."

Jakob doesn't want to hear any more. He steps into the aisle and Hugo says, "Sit down, boy."

Jakob freezes.

"You still work for me. Now sit down."

There's no threat to Hugo's voice, but a palpable seriousness. Jakob slides back into the seat.

"Now, you tell Schick, who is it you emulate?"

Jakob looks up, confused.

"Who is it you want to be? Tell me. Is it Lang? You mentioned Lang, yes? Kurosawa? Bergman? Reifenstahl, perhaps?"

"I don't—"

"No, of course not. You love the Americans. It's obvious. It's how you learned the language, as you say. Yes, it's got to be Joseph H. Lewis? Or F. E. Feist? Maybe Phil Karlson? Tony Mann? Sam Fuller? Fuller was a local boy, you know."

"Stop," Jakob says. "I don't want to be any of them."

"Who am I missing?" Hugo asks.

"I want to be Kinsky. I want to be an original."

Hugo takes a long and deep breath and manages to suppress the laughter.

"An original, is that right?" he says. "And what does this original want to do?"

Jakob knows he's shown too much of his hand. He can't believe he's done this. It's always been so easy to keep the film-talk inside. He must have inhaled some of the amyl nitrite floating through the studio. He must still be punch-drunk with the sight of Leni Pauline taking an endless shower with Coco Bing and Herbie Warm.

"I want," Jakob says slowly, "to give them the primal image."

"Ah," says Hugo, closing his eyes and nodding, "of course, the primal image."

Jakob isn't sure if he's being mocked.

"And how will you go about that?" Hugo asks.

"If I knew, do you think I'd tell you?"

"Very good, son, I'd certainly steal the technique immediately."

"I didn't mean—"

"Hush, Jakob. Keep still and listen to an old man for just a moment. Indulge me, yes?"

"I'm sorry, I just—"

Hugo brings a finger up to his lips, lets out a long *shush* that in the hollow of the theatre takes on a life of its own. Then, after a testing moment of quiet, Hugo says, "It is not that your primal image doesn't exist. It very much does. I suspect it has since the dawn of consciousness. But hear me now, please Jakob, because I can save you decades of futile and agonizing work. I can save you public failure and a very personal, lingering humiliation. The primal image you want to badly to capture, it is different for every set of eyes. Image is ambiguous. *We* invest it with all its power. We determine whether it will bring us the greater truth or the more shielding lie."

Jakob shifts in his seat.

"Film," Hugo says, "is a collaborative art. No matter what anyone will tell you, son, film is always a collaboration. Beyond this, and I'm sorry, Jakob, I know this is the last thing you wish to hear today, but film is a business. It is a product. It is a commodity to be marketed wisely and often."

Jakob lets loose a condescending sniffle that Hugo ignores.

"The primal image is unique to every eyeball on this planet, Jakob. You can't get around that. It's like knowing about our own death. Facing that fact is part of becoming an adult. And for the filmmaker, facing that fact and continuing to work, that is about becoming an artist."

They stare at each other.

"Let us make this a mutual confession, my boy. Let me tell you what I strive for, what I would hope to realize before the end of this lifetime of work. I tell you this knowing that it will never happen, that my time grows more limited each day, each film."

Jakob is suddenly intrigued.

"Someday it may be possible. We see the first steps already—the morphing, the computer modeling. Someday, the cinema as we know it will be as obsolete as the printed page. A historical curiosity. Eventually, I'm sure there'll be no need for the human actor, not as we know them today. We'll store hundreds of millions of sequences of their movements and mold them together as is necessary. But this hocus-pocus, this nonsense really, isn't what possesses me."

A deep breath, making the boy wait.

"I want the day, the method, the impossible ability to throw each individual's unique movie, their own *primal image*, as you say, up on the screen. I want the very synapses of the human brain to be accessible as my own editing board, the ultimate Moviola. I want a way of establishing a pool of sorts, a floating and infinite library of every imagistic instant ever exposed to light. More images, faster images, all the time. I want a way of tapping into each memory that each nanosecond of celluloid they've ever opened their eyes to. And finally, I want a way of editing any and all of this goulash together—life image, dream image, movie image—and all the cutting choices are mine. What stays and what goes and in what sequence it unravels.

"From the start, reality has had its way with us. Reality has constantly raped us. Attacked us daily and molested us mercilessly. But soon, Jakob, we will rape reality. We will fuck with reality in ways too monstrous to imagine. Won't it be wonderful?"

Another aborted laugh.

"I would call it a Hyperflix of the mind. *Hyperflix.* Incorporated."

Jakob stands up and walks to the stage, his eyes almost parallel with Schick's dangling knees.

"And they have the nerve," Hugo says, "to say I have a psychotic ego. It goes so far beyond ego. You *do* see that, don't you, Jakob?"

The boy smiles and nods in the darkness.

"Clear as can be, Mr. Schick."

23

Outside, they meet on the remains of the stairway that leads to the station's main entrance. Propp is walking, holding the camera in front of him and twisting the rewind crank, spooling all the exposed film back into its metal canister. Over his shoulder, he's carrying a canvas satchel, an old, scarred-up duffel embroidered with a line drawing of what looks like some deformed version of Diane Arbus's face.

Sylvia is sitting hunched over, hugging her knees and looking out at the Bishop Square rotary where a body is lying facedown. She's watching for signs of movement, any kind of drunken twitch or shake. But so far there haven't been any.

Propp comes to a stop next to her and when she shifts her focus to his face, he pops open the back of the camera, tosses the roll of film into his palm and pockets it, then places the camera on the ground between them.

"The film was mine," Sylvia says.

Propp lowers himself down next to her, mimics her posture, cracks his knuckles elaborately and says, "But the image is mine."

For a number of reasons, she's galled by the remark.

"I don't think so," she says.

"It's an old argument," Propp says. "You want to waste the rest of the night replaying it?"

"The night," she says, "is over."

"Is it?" he says, overtly patronizing. "And why is that, Sylvia?"

"Because I'm tired and I'm cold and I want to go home."

"Is Perry waiting?"

"You don't know Perry," Sylvia yells and now the body across the street in the rotary stirs, looks up for a second, then lowers its head again.

"Why did the children bother you so much, Sylvia."

She just looks at him.

"The kids. The kids who live inside. The sight of them really got to you."

She gives him the sign he wants and says, "One of those elemental images, I guess," borrowing the phrase from Mr. Quevedo.

He shakes his head, tremendously pleased, as if she's made his night with her answer.

"That's exactly correct," he says. "What shall we name it?"

She squints at him.

"The image," he says. "The archetype, back in there," gesturing to the station, "the image that just invaded us."

"I thought you said we invaded them."

He ignores the comment and says, "Can we call it *The Persecution of the Innocent?* Or is that too melodramatic? Help me out now, Sylvia."

She doesn't want to indulge him. She wants to walk away. Instead she says, "It's not exactly persecution, is it?"

He shifts on his ass, clasps his hands and brings them up to his mouth and says, "No, I see what you're saying. It's more like they were forgotten—"

"Abandoned."

"Exactly," he says. "Just abandoned."

Sylvia stands up and Propp says, "Don't *abandon* me, Sylvia."

He wants to get her furious and she fights it. She just turns and says, "Why would you want to triviliaze those children in there?"

"Trivialize?"

She holds his stare.

"I think," Propp says, "it's almost impossible to trivialize anything anymore. That implies differentiating, giving greater weight and concern to one thing over another. I think we're losing the ability to do that. I think everything's evening out. We've been assaulted for so long now. Imagery just hitting us over and over. More images. Faster images. All the time. It's a kind of media overfarming. It's the most addictive narcotic in the world. We're choking on images. Our vision has grown toxic with an overabundance. The input is erasing our capacity for judgment. And for empathy.

"It's funny, Sylvia," he takes a breath. "But until ten minutes ago, you didn't know those kids back inside really existed, did you? And for eighteen months I've been the one leaving them food and clothing," now he stands up, his voice rising with the movement, "so before you start to lecture to me, maybe you better run home to the little love nest you and *wunderkind* Perry—"

"What," she yells, her voice echoing through Bishop Square, "do you want from me?"

Propp folds his arms across his chest, pleased, as if he has willed all their words to this specific point.

"I *want*," he says, "for you to spend the rest of the night with me. I want you to reload your camera. I *want* you to see the world underneath Quinsigamond. The other place. At least once."

There's a pocket of silence that builds as they stare at each other. He unzips and slides out of his coat, hands it to her and says, "It's getting cold. Put that on."

And she does. She puts her hand in the pockets and touches canisters of film.

They walk down Voegelin Avenue, straight into the heart of Bangkok Park. She may be a tourist in the Canal Zone, but in Bangkok she's an absolute alien. Except for that one mistaken wrong turn that brought her down here fifteen years ago, she's never ventured into the Park. It's a part of the city that's turned into more of a dark myth than a genuine location, a tenderloin only mapped by fearful rumor and bad-tasting jokes.

But Propp seems to know where he's going and she follows, her camera tucked inside the jacket, making her look pregnant with some harshly angled fetus.

They walk on the Little Asia side of the street, the frontier where the Latinotown border ends. The storefronts are all tiny noodle joints, mini counter-service galleys where maybe ten people can squeeze shoulder to shoulder and eat a soy-based goulash under the blue glow of a wall-mounted television. She doesn't hear a word of English. Propp links his arm through hers like an attentive father.

"Aren't you afraid you might be recognized?" she says.

He laughs, picks up the pace. "Down here? You kidding me?"

"There could be some Proppists, you know, touring the Park—"

He shakes his head. "They don't have a clue what I look like. Even the ones who think they do are wrong. Ridiculous bastards."

"You're so harsh," she says. "These people revere you. They love your work."

They come to a stop at a small booth-like store just crammed from floor to ceiling with electronic gadgets, mostly camera and video equipment. Propp pulls them inside and the guy behind the register nods to him. The clerk is Asian, old and bony and with a crew-cut cover of white stubble on his skull and a large-handled pistol protruding from the elastic waistband of his loose, black, silk pants. He's wearing a red T-shirt with Peter Lorre's face silk-screened on the front and Sylvia wants to ask if there's some connection with the film festival that's on TV all week. But she keeps quiet and Propp takes a twenty from his pants pocket and slides it onto the counter.

"I think we've got enough film," Sylvia says, but they both ignore her.

"Where's Johnny Yew?" Propp says to the clerk who just stares at him and shrugs, rings in the purchase on an old tin register, then tears what look like two green movie tickets from a roll mounted beneath the counter, rips them in half, hands the stubs to Propp, and presses a buzzer mounted under the lip of the register.

Propp bows his head to the man and instead of exiting, leads Sylvia to the red-metal fire exit door at the rear of the shop. He pushes the door open and they walk through to an empty foyer, a cubbyhole of four blank brick walls and another metal fire door, this one painted green. There's a small closed-circuit security camera hanging from the ceiling and it pivots in their direction as Sylvia watches it. Propp holds the ticket stubs up near the camera's lens and another buzzer sounds and they push through the green door.

And out onto a narrow wooden catwalk that looks down on what appears to be a massive warehouse, a huge brick windowless loft area, as big as an airplane hangar. The ceiling must be twenty, maybe thirty feet high and lined with rows of hanging fluorescent tube lighting that gives the whole room this pale white, blanched-out cast like the interior of an alien rocket ship in a bad movie. The floor of the place is divided into a dozen aisles by rows of plywood booths and long picnic-style tables. Behind the tables and booths are people in canvas aprons and kelly green baseball caps. They seem to be salespeople and they're all in varying speeds of motion, using exaggerated hand gestures, explaining and cajoling, bartering and hawking whatever their individual product might be.

The catwalk runs all the way around the interior of the building and at each corner there's a man sipping something from a white Styrofoam cup, looking over the rim of the cup down to the sales floor. They all wear nylon wind-breakers and Sylvia would bet that each has a pistol underneath like the Oriental clerk out front.

"Welcome to the flea market," Propp whispers in her ear.

She follows him down a stairway to the floor. There's no way to tell without windows, but since they entered the electronics shop at street level, half the flea market must sit underground.

Propp takes her arm again and they start to stroll down the first aisle they come to.

"I'll tell you what I feel for the *Proppists,*" he says, continuing the discussion from the street as if there'd been no interruption and saying the last word with a touch of disgust.

"What's that?" Sylvia asks, turning to avoid bumping into a woman carrying cardboard cartons upon her shoulder.

"Pity," Propp says.

"Pity," she repeats.

He shakes his head *yes* and says, "Would you like some cotton candy?"

She shakes her head *no.*

"It's a shame," he says, "that they don't have lives of their own. Because why else would they insist on trying to turn me into something I'm not. Jesus. They run around to their ridiculous little pajama parties. All their semantic bullshit about separating the erotic from the pornographic. That pathetic willed innocence."

She stops him from walking on.

"First of all, by insisting on being the invisible man, you had a big hand in turning yourself into their legend—"

"I resent that," he interrupts.

"And second, I met one of the people, and I may not

agree with his mythmaking, but it goes way beyond you, Propp. It's about something they think you represent."

"Which is?" with this self-indulgent smirk on his lips.

"The erotic impulse."

"The erotic impulse," he repeats, about to break into an insulting laugh.

"That's right," she says, for some reason wanting to defend Rory Gaston and company.

"That's catchy," Propp says.

He turns and releases her arm, reaches down to the table they're standing next to, picks up a figurine and tosses it into the air in front of her face. He moves off down the aisle and she bucks and catches this little sculpted figure, this little knicknack, and looks at it. It's made of some kind of black enamel cut into a human shape. It's male and completely, stunningly, anatomically correct. It's some kind of fertility totem, like a peasant deity with genitalia whose size is almost equal to the mass of the entire body.

"That'll be ten ninety-nine," a woman's voice sounds from behind her. "Or I can let you have three of them for twenty-five."

Sylvia turns to her, a big bruiser of a woman, arms like a linebacker, her green baseball cap pulled way down to the line of her eyes, the smoldering stub of a thin cigar dangling at the edge of her mouth, the head of ash bouncing as she speaks. She waves her hand out and Sylvia looks to see an entire table of these figures, a crowded buffet of fertility Hummels stacked side by side like an army of erect soldiers ready to impregnate some huge village.

"If you can pay in yen," the woman says, leaning across her wares and lowering her voice a bit, "I can work you an even sweeter deal."

Sylvia puts down the statue and walks away without saying a thing. She studies each booth and table she passes and begins to realize that this entire warehouse, this entire *flea market,* is exclusively selling items of the sexual variety. This is a clearinghouse for libido tools, a discount department store for all things carnal or erotic. She sees marital aids and lingerie, lotions and balms and ointments, something called *the booth of dancing eggs,* something called *The French Tickler Showroom,* a Peg-Board displaying thirty different brands of handcuffs. There are blow-up plastic dolls whose polyurethane skin can be selected in a variety of pigment hues. There are demonstrations for the Waxman Vibrating Bed, available in twin to king sizes. There are brochures for institutes of sensual massage and Kama Sutra academies.

And there are the books. Everything from the pulpiest of magazines that look, even from a distance, as if they'd dissolve in your hands after the first reading, to thick and encyclopedic texts with color Mylar illustrations and cross-referenced indexes. Paperback novels. Coffee table art volumes. Erotic comic books. Works customized for the motorcycle enthusiast and the bank clerk and the S&M housewife. Tomes for the gay and the straight and the confused. Bibles of the sensuous for the timid and for the crazed. And hundreds of self-help manuals. A banner hanging above one book booth seems to say it all: *There isn't a variation we don't carry.*

Then, of course, there are the films. Stockpiles of the oldest smokers, grainy black-and-white reels shown at carnivals and men's clubs decades ago. There are bootleg 16 mm spools that purport to hold lewd images of hundreds of your favorite celebrities. There are homemade efforts, husband and wife teams from the heartland whose crude technical skills are promised to be overshadowed by the genuine depths of their passion. There are expensive laser disc spectacles worthy of some sex-obsessed MGM, with big casts, special effects, lush sound tracks, and state-of-the-art decadence. But most of all there are videocassettes, an endless supply whose diversity seems to surpass even that of the book section. The video hawkers all have TV monitors set up on their counters and tabletops, showing a taste of some of their offerings.

Sylvia stops for a second at a half dozen screens and watches a multiplicity of couplings and gropings and longings, combinations and recombinations that go so far beyond her paltry imagination that she's forced to wonder if she's defective in some way, if the world is really just some seething, teeming throng of frenetic and ever sweating partners, engorging and releasing twenty-four hours a day, never tiring, perpetually hungry. And if she's gone unaware of this dripping world since day one.

She looks up from a flickering screen filled with naked sky divers reaching across blue air for their partners and sees Propp munching on a Sno-Kone in the corner and staring at her. He raises his brows theatrically when their eyes meet and, ridiculously, she's embarrassed.

Sylvia walks over to him and he extends the Sno-Kone in her direction. The shaved ice is dyed a deep purple color and she shakes him off and says, "You come here a lot?"

He shrugs, swallows some ice and says, "What do you mean by a lot?"

"The police know about this place?"

He gives an indulgent smile: *isn't this provincial child amusing.*

"And they never bust the place?"   .

Propp looks out at the room in general and says, "The place is sort of a co-op. Every merchant pays a booth fee. Some percentage of the gross goes in the right pocket every month." He looks back at her and says, "Besides, Sylvia, fifty percent of what's in here is legal."

"And what about the other fifty percent?"

"What about it?" he says. "That's not my judgment to make."

She shakes her head, looks at the floor, tries to let him know she expected a better answer from a myth-figure.

"What?" he says. "You want to have the standard debate? You want to take positions here? Spend the night making points? Or do you want to see things you've never seen before?"

"Maybe," she says, looking back up at him, "this subject doesn't interest me the way it does the rest of this room. Or the way it does you."

"Could be," he says, staying loose, possibly trying to bait her. And possibly not. "Interest in sex is a brain function like anything else. Could be some people get too much. And some get too little."

"And," she says, "could be that kind of labeling is both useless and insulting."

"I'm not trying to insult anyone, Sylvia."

"I don't get you. Back at the diner you were warning me away from Hugo Schick and the Skin Palace—"

His tone changes immediately and he snaps, "That's different," and then he realizes he's going to have to explain himself.

"I mean," he says, "Schick, as an individual, is different. Schick doesn't give a goddamn about anything erotic. He cares about money and manipulation. And his own ego."

Sylvia stares at him, shocked, and she gives him a second to turn what he's just said into a joke. But Propp doesn't take the opportunity and Sylvia can't help putting her hand on his shoulder, giving him a patronizing pat and squeeze.

"Money and manipulation and ego," she says. "Yeah, there's none of that sitting in this room."

"You don't know Schick—" he starts.

"Is that right?" she says, wanting to capitalize on his mistake. "And you're the guy who called the Proppists fools because of their willed innocence."

"I didn't—"

"So what's the truth, Propp? Is there a difference between the erotic and the pornographic?"

He calms down, looks behind him and throws the Sno-Kone into a trash barrel.

"There probably is," he says. "And it's probably different for every individual."

"Right. Except some individual's judgment is less valid than others. Like the Proppists. And like Hugo Schick. And like me."

"Maybe," he says, "the Proppists haven't earned their judgment."

"Earned?" she says, really stunned by the road he's heading down. "Earned their judgment? Could you just tell me who makes that determination? Is this what happens to someone when they become a hermit?"

"I'm no hermit, Sylvia."

She can't help smiling at how self-deceived this man is. "You know, my boyfriend has some new associates you should meet. You'd really get on."

"You're misinterpreting everything I've said."

"Just tell me how, exactly, you earned these critical skills that everyone around you seems to be lacking. For God sake, you say Schick has an ego."

"You don't know me, Sylvia," getting angry now, the comparison with Schick pushing his button. "You don't know where I've been, the things that have happened . . ."

"That's right," she says. "That's completely correct. And no matter what you think, you don't know me either. No matter what sources you have. No matter how much you've spied on me or tried to look into my life, you know nothing about me."

A naked, heavily tattooed woman with snakes coiled around her neck walks up to them and starts to display her product, which Sylvia guesses to be the snakes. Propp runs a hand over his face and moves brusquely to the other side of the room and Sylvia follows.

"Have you ever been to Bangkok, Sylvia?" he says, staring ahead as they walk. "The real Bangkok. The city in

Thailand, you know, that this neighborhood is named after."

Before she can answer he says, "You haven't. I know you haven't. Except for college, you've never lived outside of Quinsigamond."

They come to a stop next to a booth where a small, professorial-looking man in a white lab coat is distributing leaflets on something called the Dillinger & Hindenmacher Miracle Implant Clinic in Tijuana, Mexico. On a rickety wooden easel next to the booth is a poster showing what looks like a technical blueprint for a zeppelin.

"I lived in Bangkok for three years. I lived in one room in the heart of Patpong Road. I had one change of clothes, a Nikon, and a Polaroid passport camera. For three hours every morning I shot Polaroids. Visa shots. Immigration shots. Rest of the day and night I shot for myself."

"Look, Propp," Sylvia says, "I've read stories about Bangkok—"

"Listen to yourself. Read stories."

"Fine. It's secondary. It's worse than secondary. It's nothing. I'm carnally illiterate. And you've been *around.* You've taken the big trip upriver to the core of all desire. You saw the best and worst of it. And now you're enlightened. You're *the* maven of all things sexual. And the rest of the world just can't keep up. The Proppists are spoiled children with some storybook dream of this romantic, dewy sensuality. And Hugo Schick is just a cold businessman who knows how to exploit a raw image until it makes a respectable profit. And I guess I'm just a blank slate who hasn't even considered the possibilities. So we've got no right to an opinion, because they're all going to be uninformed."

He rubs at his eyes, looks at his feet. "That's not it at all. That's not what I'm saying at all. Bangkok has no corner on carnality or lust or lasciviousness or whatever. Neither does Amsterdam. Or Forty-second Street. Or this flea market."

"Okay," Sylvia says. "Agreed."

His voice changes slightly, gets huskier, a little tired. "I've spent large chunks of my adult life studying and capturing images, Sylvia. I've lived as a photographer. You know what that is. You know what that does to your eye, how it affects the way you view the world in every second you're awake. And maybe when you're asleep. You frame everything. You weigh every visual against an approaching better one. You do that over a number of years and it changes you. It makes you a mutant. But it happens so subtly that you might not even be aware of your own transformation."

She looks at him and his face seems to be losing color, as if pigment is draining away as he speaks.

"When I became aware of what had happened to me, to my sensibility, I went, very literally after a time, underground. I've been around, as you sarcastically say. And you want to call the results of my experiences ego. That's fine. But I know it has nothing to do with ego. And I'll stand here and judge the Proppists. And I'll judge Hugo Schick and the Skin Palace people. Because I know how wrong they both are. How ignorant. They don't have any idea how deep it goes inside us. They approach image as if it were a theory. Or a commodity. They're on opposite sides of a ridiculous fence, but both groups are fools. I know it, Sylvia. That makes me a fanatic. I don't care."

She takes a breath and says, "What about me?"

"I came for you, didn't I?"

"Why?"

"Because I owe you, Sylvia."

And she doesn't want to ask what he owes her. Why he owes her. She stares at him and she thinks of Hugo Schick's face. And then of Perry's face. Propp steps up to her, leans in and kisses her, so softly, on the forehead. He puts his hands on her shoulders and turns her until her back is to him and she's staring across the aisle at a display for self-adhesive mirrored ceiling tiles. Sylvia looks into the mirrors, sees the quilted jacket zipped over the remains of her Victorian nightgown, sees the white-gone-black slippers still on her feet. And then she looks into her own face, smudges of ash on her left cheek, her eyes bloodshot, dark circles underneath. She knows she looks horrible.

There are similarities between you and she, Propp had said back in the station. Similarities between Sylvia and the Madonna. Was he lying or was that genuinely his view of how Sylvia looked through the camera lens? *You're beautiful,* he said.

Could what they see possibly be this different?

She looks from her reflection to Propp's, his face behind her, back over her left shoulder. He looks equally haggard. Then there's another face next to Propp's and they both turn around to the smile of this old butterball, this pasty-skinned man who looks like a boozy ad man who's finally gone to ruin. He's got jowls and a head of bristly, pepper-colored hair and a brown suit with stained lapels. The fat man nods his head as he smiles and the jowls swing and Sylvia has to look down at the floor.

"Mr. Smith," he says to Propp in this high-pitched voice like a muted horn, "could I have a word?"

Propp gets a little distracted. He looks from the man to Sylvia and back to the man, then says, "Sure, fine, just a second," then pulls Sylvia out of earshot and says, "I've got to talk to this guy for a second."

"Mr. Smith?" she says.

He shrugs. "It's a joke around here. Everyone's Mr. Smith."

"You do business down here, Propp?"

"It's not what you think, Sylvia. Could you just wait for me down in back and I'll be there in five minutes."

And he turns back to the fat man who huddles down and

starts to talk fast. Sylvia moves past them and hears the words credit and fraud. She walks all the way to the rear of the building and comes to a row of what look like glossy, wooden confessionals or maybe those old arcade photo booths where you cram inside on a stool and they spit out four black-and-white head shots on a long, single print-strip. There's a security guard sitting on a stool looking bored next to one of those velvet partitioning ropes that blocks entrance to the booths. He stares at her with his arms locked across his chest. She nods to him but he doesn't move a muscle. She turns to walk away and the guard says, "You Sylvia?"

She turns back and stares at him and he lets a little smile break and says, "Yeah, you're Sylvia," and unhooks one end of the velvet rope to let her through.

She doesn't move and he says, "Booth number seven."

She looks down the rows of booths, finds the one marked 7 and, of course, there's a hand-lettered *Out of Order* sign pinned to its curtain. She moves past the guard to the booth, pulls back the curtain and enters, ten years old again and trying to remember her sins. The booth is pretty stark. There's a wooden stool to sit on, a metal coin box that reads *quarters only* and a mesh speaker set in the paneling next to a plate glass window that's shuttered with what looks like corrugated metal. Sylvia resecures the curtain behind her and stands still in the dark.

There's a second of motor noise as the metal shutter slides up and reveals a darkened, matching, booth-like room on the other side of a thick-glass window. Then blue and red ceiling spotlights click on and Leni Pauline is standing in front of her.

She's dressed in this extremely short, black, see-through robe that she has barely belted around her waist. The floors and walls and ceiling of the booth surrounding her are carpeted in what looks like unusually plush bearskin. Leni clasps her hands behind her neck and does these back arches as if she were about to start into an aerobics routine. Then she bows toward Sylvia and says, "This is a freebie so don't expect the full five minutes."

"Where the hell did you go?" is all Sylvia can think to say.

"Where did I go?" Leni says and starts to laugh.

"Does Hugo know you moonlight here?"

The laughter stops and Leni says, "Hugo forgot to renew his Leni license. I'm a ward of the state now."

Sylvia doesn't want to fight. "I turned around for a second," she says, "and you were gone."

"Yeah," Leni says, "That's my story too. So how'd the night go? Get anything good?"

Sylvia squints at her and Leni makes a face and says, "Pictures, Sylvie. You take any good pictures?"

"Yeah. I think I did."

"Where'd you get the jacket?"

"Long story," Sylvia says. "What the hell are you doing in there?"

"What do you think. It's a peep booth, you know. People get to peep at me."

"No, no. I mean, how did you know I was out there? How did you know I was at the flea market?"

"The flea market?" Leni says.

"Isn't that what they call this place?"

"Not that I know of. And I didn't know you were here. I thought you saw me come in or something."

Sylvia gives her a disgusted look. "Leni, the guy out front called me by name and told me to go to booth seven."

Leni screws up her face as if to say this is ridiculous. "Hey, Sylvia, I make it a rule that I don't talk to the grease-ball toy cops at this hole, okay?"

"Then who—"

"Look, you got about a minute before the window closes, all right? And I've got to tell you something."

"Wait a minute," Sylvia says.

"You need to be at the Skin Palace," Leni interrupts, putting both her palms flat against the window and leaning forward, "at midnight tomorrow. I'll have something to show you that'll clear everything up."

"What is it?" Sylvia says as the window partition starts to roll down.

"Midnight, tomorrow," are Leni's last words before the window is completely blocked and the booth is in darkness again. Sylvia reaches out and touches the coin box and then, without thinking, she starts banging on it with her fist and to her shock the partition begins to roll back up.

But when the window comes clear again and the red and blue lights go on, Leni is gone and the viewing room is empty.

24

Sylvia stays in the peep booth for what seems like a long time. She sits on the wooden stool, leans down on her thighs. She stares out into the viewing room and hopes that someone will walk in and start to talk to her through the speaker, start to explain the last three days as a practical joke or a punishment for sins she doesn't remember committing.

But no one comes in and no one comes to call her out and she just continues to look into this square box, this vault of soft white walls. It reminds her of a school trip she took as a child, maybe twelve years old, when she went to a pathetic zoo about fifteen miles outside the city. The class walked through a nature trail and, except for a timber wolf who was kept chained to a tree, all they saw were

signs hanging on fences and nailed to posts that said the
animals had been *temporarily vacated.* She wondered all
day what that meant. The words carried this vague but definitely threatening aura until she began to think all the animals had been sacrificed in some kind of terrible ritual.
And at the end of the trip they visited the reptile house
which was steamy and dank and muggy. And the whole
class walked single file through a corridor that twisted
every few feet and on either side the walls were fitted with
glass windows, like in an aquarium, only these windows
were all streaked and smudged and you looked in on rocks
and dirt and broken-off tree branches. And you tried to find
the snakes or toads or lizards that were trying to hide inside their tank, under fluorescent lights, trying to blend
their colors with this shabby environment they'd woken up
and found themselves in one morning.

That zoo trip still makes her shiver and she blocks it out
of her mind and tries to imagine lying down on the viewing room floor, just stretching out on that bearskin and
falling into a long and dreamless sleep.

But she can't fully conceive of the sleep. She can only
imagine waking up naked and having the peep booth
crammed with voyeurs who are gawking at her the way she
gawked at those snakes and lizards. Wondering *how the
hell did she end up in this position?*

When her legs start to cramp, she gets off the stool and
stretches. She turns to leave and hears the metal shutter roll
down behind her.

She walks out a rear exit of the flea market into an alley
and finds Propp sitting on the ground, leaning against the
bricks. She moves over to him, looks down on him. She
won't even ask if he knows Leni. If he set up their meeting
in the booth. She doesn't want any more denial tonight.
She doesn't want any more sentences that turn the facts
around and make her question herself and everything that
seemed to be true.

"You finish up your business?" she asks.

He shakes his head and puts out his hand and she pulls him up to standing.

"Things didn't work out exactly as I'd hoped," he says.

He starts to walk and Sylvia follows and says, "You know, you really shouldn't slag Hugo Schick the way you do. You two being in the same union and all."

"I knew you'd think that," he says, "but I'm not a pornographer, Sylvia."

"So what is it you sell to these guys, Mr. Smith?" sarcastic on the last two words. "Tours of the underworld?"

He stops walking and says, "I sell them Terrence Propp prints."

She looks at him, confused, and he just smiles and starts walking again.

"I was supposed to be a dealer with some connections to the mystery man. Only nobody's buying these days. They suddenly think I'm a fraud. They think Propp is dead and I'm trafficking in second-rate imitations."

"That's hysterical,"she says.

"Not when you're trying to buy film on your good looks."

"This is going to sound a little cruel, but don't you find it just a bit ironic?"

He lets out an annoyed sigh and says, "Irony is a constant once you reach my age." Then he just stares at her and when he speaks again the tone of his voice is completely different.

"Don't you wonder why I brought you here tonight, Sylvia?"

Now it's her turn to give a stare. "You live underneath the streets in an old diner, hiding from everyone. I should try and figure out your motives?"

"I brought you here," he says, unchallenged, "for two reasons. The first was simply to show another world, another dimension, that's operating, at all times, separate from your world—"

"You know so much about *my* world—"

"—It's dark and it's hidden. And for a stranger it can seem obsessive. Insular. Unsettling and alienating. Parts of it might even seem brutal and perverse. To someone like you, Sylvia, everything would look angled and shadowed and haunted."

"What's the second reason?" she says.

"That's a little harder. I wanted to show you that within those shadows, inside the brutality and perversion, you can find moments of humanity if you train yourself to look closely enough," he reaches out and touches her camera, "and you can capture them. You can hold them. You can make a rosary of these images."

"A rosary?"

He nods.

Sylvia shrugs, "Why should I want to?"

Propp squints at her like the answer should be obvious.

"To gain grace," he says.

"Grace?"

He makes a kind of awkward, noncommittal shake of his head, pushes his hands in his pockets and takes a step toward the mouth of the alley. Then he turns back and like a teenager impulsively asking for a date he says, "You want to go to the movies?"

She keeps herself from blurting out the immediate *yes* that's answered that question her entire life. She says, "What's playing?"

He holds up his satchel and says, "How about the suppressed cut of *The Wizard of Oz*?"

She stops walking and Propp smiles and looks at her with raised eyebrows, a kind of challange, an invitation to doubt him.

"Give me a break," she says.

He takes a few steps back, opens the satchel and pulls up

a dull silver film canister, just a flash of it, then drops it back down into the bag.

"Suppressed?"

"You never heard of this?" he says. "What kind of film animal are you?"

"*The Wizard of Oz*?"

His shoulders slump, he swings his head in the direction of the alley's mouth and they start walking again, more quickly this time.

"It was the first week of November, 1938. There was some unspoken tension on the set, you know, with Victor Fleming taking over for George Cukor. And this was after Cukor had already replaced Richard Thorpe. You add to that the concern about the aluminum powder—"

"Aluminum powder?"

"They'd had to rush Buddy Ebsen to the hospital. Found out he was having allergic reactions to the Tin Man makeup. They had to replace him with Jack Haley. C'mon, Sylvia, you know all this, right?"

She just gives him a blank stare.

"Anyway, the first scene Fleming shoots is the yellow brick crossroad bit where Dorothy meets the Scarecrow. Only the raven they had sitting on Bolger's shoulder got loose and started flying around the studio. Bergswich, the unofficial MGM animal expert—he was really just an assistant electrician—he wasted a whole day trying to catch the damn bird. So, you can imagine, right, when they finally get down to filming that scene the actors are a little tense, okay? And things got a little out of hand at one point."

"What do you mean?" she can't help asking.

He lifts the satchel up in the air.

"Supposedly," he says, "they burn the offensive scenes. Only somebody, maybe Mervyn LeRoy, maybe Louis Mayer himself, pockets the cut stock and it sits for years in some Beverly Hills vault. But like everything else, Sylvia, eventually it surfaces again. Makes it out onto the gray market. I've had my reel for over a decade now."

This one she just can't believe. "What could possibly be offensive about *The Wizard of Oz*?"

"Any number of things. But this had to do with Dorothy's relationship with the Scarecrow. Wait till you see what was cut from the dance scene. That yellow brick road was on fire. They—"

"No," she says and stops as they emerge back out on Voegelin.

"What?"

"You've gone too far, Propp. There was nothing erotic or sensual or in any way sexual about Judy Garland's dance with Ray Bolger. There just wasn't."

"Not in the print *you've* seen, no."

"Not in any print."

He waits a few seconds, biting off a smile, seeming to study her face, the ever patient patriarch.

"Why, Sylvia?" he finally says. "Because you don't want it to be? Because you've always looked at that moment in that movie, that dance, that image," emphasizing the syllables until they sound foreign, "in a very specific way. And you don't want to believe there could be another way to look."

"That's not it at all," she says. "It's because your story isn't rational. It doesn't fit the context of the movie. There's no reason why they would have filmed that kind of thing. It just didn't happen."

"But it did, Sylvia," Propp says. "And if you want to come to the Ballard with me, they've got a sixteen millimeter projector just waiting to be used."

They stare at each other until Sylvia says, "All right, Propp. You show me," and they turn left down Voegelin and head toward the Canal Zone.

The old Ballard Theatre sits down on Bonnefoy Drive sandwiched betweeen a former paper mill and a nonfunctioning electric company transformer station. It's always been one of the smaller cinemas in town, with less than a hundred seats, but from the start it had a subtle elegance to it. Nothing overwhelming like the Skin Palace. More a quiet charm, an unspoken confidence and a discreet style, from the amber glow of the wooden walls to the coziness of its mini-balcony. There was something about the way the Ballard offered homemade quilts to every customer when the quirky heating system failed every January. But most of all there was the silent and graceful demeanor of the eternal usher, a small, ghost-faced, foreign-looking man in a black suit who remained at the Ballard no matter how often it was bought and sold. The rumor has always been that he lived in the theatre and never went outside. He reminded some patrons of a refugee funeral director, but Sylvia always thought of him as more of a secular monk in the celluloid faith.

The Ballard has changed hands half a dozen times in the last twenty years. Something about the building seems to attract dedicated film specialists whose business acumen is eccentric at best. In the past decade the theatre has been known by a variety of names. There was The Kinetoscope, which revived an endless number of pre-talkies until the IRS rode into town and padlocked all the doors. There was Dragonsbreath, which was dedicated to the martial arts film in all its cheesy glory and blew most of its receipts on a ridiculously expensive, life-size, full-body sculpture of Bruce Lee in a midair assault. There was a single summer of Ciné Flesheater that almost managed to display every variation of the B-budget zombie flick, but tended to dwell on the Spanish-Italian subgenre. And there was The Jerry Lewis House of Mirth which was able to roll everything from *My Friend Irma* through *The King of Comedy* before the proprietor retired to France, a happy, if bankrupt man.

The Ballard's last incarnation was as The Anne Frank Cinema. And the '59 version of *The Diary of Anne Frank* was the first in a series of holocaust movies Sylvia watched down here, followed by *Genocide, The Garden of the Finzi-Continis, Sophie's Choice, The Night Porter, Playing For Time, The Last Metro, Kapo, Diamonds of the Night, The Wannsee Conference, Judgment At Nuremberg, In a Glass Cage, Shoah* and *Hotel Terminus.* She doesn't know exactly what did in the Anne Frank, but at the final screening, a double bill featuring *The Sorrow and the Pity* and *Night and Fog,* the only two people in the place were she and Shel Singer, the neighborhood mayor of the Jews. At intermission, Mr. Singer got up from his seat in the last row and sat next to Sylvia, brought her a box of popcorn. For the last hour of the Anne Frank Cinema's life, Shel held Sylvia's butter-streaked hand, nothing erotic in the act, just a touch, human flesh brought together for a short time. Then as the credits rolled, Mr. Singer got up and left without a word. And that night they bolted the doors of the Ballard and cleared the marquee.

Now, six months later, the Loftus Brothers have decided to take a stab at the movie business. Tonight, the front of the Ballard sports a new, pricey sign made up of hundreds of blinking lightbulbs that are patterned to read Impact: The Car Crash Cinema.

"I guess the idea," says Propp from the roof of the building looking down over the transformer lot next door, "is they'll edit out everything but the crash scenes. They'll dump the rest of the movie and just leave the smashups. If there's a good chase scene preceding the crash, they might leave it in. But if a chase doesn't end in a crash, no good."

"They've got a lot of material to work with," Sylvia says.

Propp nods, kneels down and starts to open a skylight. "And you're probably just thinking of theatrical releases, right?"

"I'm thinking H. B. Halicki," Sylvia says.

"Very good," Propp says. "I'm impressed. Halicki, the Patron Saint."

"Gone in 60 Seconds," Sylvia says. "Ninety-three cars destroyed in forty minutes."

"How about *Grand Theft Auto*?" Propp says.

"Eat My Dust!" Sylvia says. *"Smash-Up on Interstate 5."*

"The Seven-Ups. Dirty Mary and Crazy Larry."

"White Line Fever. Freebie and the Bean. Le Mans."

"The *Cannonball Run* series," Propp says. "My God, you could get through the first three months on Burt Reynold's oeuvre alone. But the rumor is they're going to use industrial films as well. Stuff out of these Detroit labs where they test cars. And underground video stuff borrowed from state police files. There's supposed to be some Autobahn footage where you can see a head come right through a windshield."

"You think they've got a shot?" she says.

Propp smiles at her and says, "I don't see how they can miss."

He opens the skylight back on its hinges and gestures for her to climb in.

"No alarms?"

"Not that I know of."

Sylvia moves into the opening and lowers herself, then lets go and drops down to the floor in a squat. She gets up and steps back and Propp joins her, agile for his age and looking like he's done this a lot in the past.

They're in the balcony of the theatre, about a dozen rows pitched at a steep angle. Sylvia's always loved the seats in the Ballard, old-time rockers covered in plush maroon velour and plenty of arm room so you're not in constant battle with the person next door. Sylvia and her mother used to come to the Ballard a lot when Sylvia was young. They saw a lot of Disney stuff here, a lot of movies starring Kurt Russell. Sylvia hoped her first boyfriend would be like Kurt Russell—clean-cut, square jaw, well intentioned.

"You pick the seats," Propp says, "and I'll go fire up the projector."

He climbs back to the projection booth and she surveys her choices and settles on the front row center where they can put their feet up on the railing. She sits down and gets comfortable and looks around at the decor, all natural wood and soft velour. And the sight of it all makes her hate the mall theatres even more—the little bowling alleys with their back-ache chairs and tiny screens and bad sound systems.

Last year Perry and she went to a Friday night late show of *Castle Oswald* and when the lights went down and the previews came on they thought there was something wrong with their eyes. The people on the screen were just ghost-images. If you squinted hard, you could barely see a man and a woman running through a park. They waited for someone else to get out of their seat and find an usher but no one did. So Sylvia got up and went out to the concession stand where all these teenagers in polyester jackets were busy trying to pick each other up. And she asked them if there was a problem with the movie. The assistant manager put down his massive tumbler of soda and explained with strained politeness that, in fact, one of the bulbs in the projector had burned out and that she could get her money back at the box office if she wanted. He turned back to the popcorn girl and Sylvia asked why they didn't just change the bulb. The boy's patience edging toward rupture, he told her the bulb was too hot to be changed now, that it would be changed tomorrow morning. Then he pursed his lips and breathed through his nose waiting to see if there was anything else she needed. Sylvia asked him if anyone else had requested their money back and he seemed pleased to tell her she was the first one. On the drive home she can remember Perry saying, "It's no big deal, Sylvia. I'm not crazy about the movies anyway."

And now she stares out at the huge old screen in front of her as the heavy blue curtain starts to roll back and she wonders *how could I end up with a guy who isn't crazy about the movies?*

Propp does a fast trot down the inclined aisle, braking against gravity, slides in next to her and says, "Exactly where I'd have sat."

"Glad you approve."

They watch leader strip fill up the screen, a scratchy-looking test pattern that shows a color spectrum.

Propp leans into her shoulder and whispers, as if the theatre were filled and they might disturb someone. "Remember, the reduction to sixteen millimeter is going to be painful. I'm pretty sure this was done on the run. And the sound track isn't quite in sync."

"Please," Sylvia says, "don't build my expectations so high."

He gives her elbow a playful shove off the armrest and they turn their attention to the screen. An old-time clapboard comes up that reads 11/5/38, then the marker is pulled down out of the shot and they're watching Judy Garland looking beautiful in spite of the start of all the diet pills and bad advice.

The sound track is a mess. Ray Bolger walks into view done up in full Scarecrow costume. As a child, Sylvia's favorite of the three traveling companions was Bolger and at the end of the movie, when Dorothy tells him she's going to miss him the most, Sylvia instantly wanted her to stay in Oz. Forget Auntie Em. Forget Kansas. And now, watching the Scarecrow lean over and whisper in Garland's ear, making her laugh with some secret no one will ever know, she feels Dorothy's making a huge mistake all over again. You can't go home again, girlfriend. So bag the thought of a dicey balloon trip with the faux wizard. And forget the heel-clicking mantra of Glinda, the little overachieving cheerleader. Hit the road with the Scarecrow and go assume the mortgage on the Witch's castle. You can train those flying monkeys to keep house and do the cooking. And you and strawboy can head out every night, dance and get weird in the deepest part of that haunted forest.

There's an awkward cut and the film goes dark for a second and when the light comes back, the Scarecrow is up on his post at the fork in the yellow brick road. His voice gives Dorothy confusing directions a few seconds after his hands point down the proposed path she should walk. It's unsettling watching this—the images mimic, almost perfectly, the images that Sylvia's known from this film most of her life. But *almost* is a crucial word. There's something just a hair off at all times, something that doesn't exactly line up. Something beyond the out-of-sync sound track.

Sylvia has watched this movie at least once a year since she was five or six years old. More, once it was released on video. That means she's seen it over twenty-five times, enough to have the nuances, the inflections of voice, the exact manner of movements, down to a reflexive memory. It's akin to that instinctual, really helpless way you know a pop song note for note after you've heard it a hundred times. You sing along in your head and you know, without thinking, without even being *aware* that you know, when the singer's voice is going to alter, to drop or rise or quiver. It's a buried surety, a certainty that's grown so innate it's like breathing air.

And now, watching Bolger and Garland, Scarecrow and Dorothy, play out movements that *almost* match up to what she knows should be happening, but don't quite, it's akin to hyperventilating. It's an awful confusion. Because she can't even identify what's wrong. She just knows something is off. Scarecrow's arm might move an inch beyond the length it extended in the standard version of the movie. Dorothy's voice might rise just a bit higher. The choreography is the same. The words are the same. But their presentation is just a millimeter away from what she's come to memorize. And as the differences continue between what she sees each moment and what she expects to see, she begins to feel a kind of vertigo, a dizziness, a sense of displacement, an apprehension that the whole world has just slipped out of a balance that she thought was inviolable. If the Scarecrow can act in a different way than he's always acted, then science and religion are destroyed. Then anything can happen to her life.

And yet she can't take her eyes off the screen. She watches as Dorothy bends the nail that has trapped the Scarecrow on his post in the cornfield for an eternity. She watches as the Scarecrow slides to the ground, tries to stand on rubbery legs, slides into "If I Only Had a Brain."

She stares at the screen as Dorothy tells him her hopes for salvation in the Emerald City. And she focuses in tight as these two innocents join forces and break into this skipping promenade down their chosen pathway while reprising "We're Off to See the Wizard."

It's possible that some offscreen voice, maybe even Victor Fleming's, calls, "Cut," but Sylvia doesn't hear it. She knows for certain that the next scene should be the bullying apple trees. But Garland and Bolger are still in front of the cornfield. The music crashes into this dissonant confusion for a second or two, then returns in another form, something far removed from the light innocence of "If I Only Had a Brain." Now they're hearing a king of jazzy swing, but there's no way to tell is this is part of the original sound track or was dubbed in at some later date. The music seems to fit the movements of the two figures on the screen, but it deviates enough for doubt.

The Scarecrow has taken Dorothy's hand and is whirling her in and out of his arms, spinning her outward and retracting her into his straw-stuffed chest like a yo-yo. He catches her in an aggressive embrace and they start a polka-ish hoedown trot, circling around the perimeter of the yellow-brick dance area. Clearly, the film has broken free of any connection to the images of Sylvia's memory. It's a brand new world now, a place where she has no idea what's coming. And she likes it a lot better. The vertigo, the inconsistency between what should be and what is, has vanished and all she wants to do is watch.

She gets a good look at Dorothy's face as the screen dancers loop by their closest point to the camera. The girl from Kansas is howling, loving this moment, seemingly set free and basking in the spontaneity, the unscripted abandon of the Scarecrow's improvisation. Here, in this moment of deviation, there's no worry about budget or time schedules. There's no fat-faced studio boss hollering about gained weight or contract clauses. There's only the Scarecrow's flying, steering arms and their intermingled, convulsing laughter.

They mutate their form into a tango, pivot at the far point from the lens and stomp back, cheek to cheek. Dorothy's eyes closed up with laughter, until they're grotesquely close to the screen and someone yells, "watch the camera" over the music. Scarecrow does a slapstick pratfall as if tripping over some unseen equipment and laughter erupts everywhere. He pretends to drop unconscious on the bricks and Dorothy stands over him for a minute, arms across her stomach, then hand up to her mouth to cover the uncontrollable laughter. With her back to the camera she steps over him, straddles the prone straw body and bends down, the pleats of the farm dress spreading across her rear. She begins to help the recovering Scarecrow up and he suddenly springs back to full-bodied life, bounds to his feet, sweeps Dorothy into the air. She lets her head fall back, her hair swinging in the rush, new waves of hilarity playing over her mouth.

Then Scarecrow goes into her neck, his floppy hat sailing away to the ground, a vampire-like flourish to his maneuver. The offscreen noise turns to hoots and whistles and the music shuts down. But a curious thing occurs, totally unexpected from the context of everything that's led to this moment. Dorothy's arms, limp in the air behind her one second, swing up and forward and wrap themselves around Scarecrow's neck. And the strawman's lips move and find the farm girl's. And suddenly, instantly, in one bolt of adrenal fluid and muscular expansion, startling as the change from black-and-white to color, the playacting is over.

Sylvia is removed from the image before her by over half a century. But she's absolutely certain that a change has taken place. The Scarecrow and Dorothy are French-kissing and the joker running the camera pulls in for a tight close-up and there's a shocked electricity that passes from the now probably dead movie crew through the screen and into the Ballard Theatre and into Propp and Sylvia. The unmistakable charge of sexuality has exploded unexpectedly between the eternally virginal Kansas schoolgirl and the man made of straw and cloth. Mouth on mouth and eyes closed, their heads twist and the audience of two can feel the warmth that has to be expanding beneath the skin of the actors, inside their legs and stomachs, making their breath come faster and harder. And in that moment, Sylvia lets herself act without thought or preparation, totally and completely on instinct and impulse. She reaches down and puts her hand on Propp's leg.

And without a word, he bolts out of his seat and races up the aisle stairs until he disppears into the projection room.

Sylvia closes her eyes and takes a deep breath and hates herslf for her stupidity.

She opens her eyes and on the screen the kiss is over and Dorothy pushes out of the Scarecrow's arms, almost falls to the bricks and then runs out of screen view. And the Scarecrow is left embarrassed, staring at the camera without anything to say, without an explanation, until he too runs off in another direction, leaving wisps of straw drifting in the air behind him.

Oz vanishes and the screen is filled with black leader that has huge white letters and numbers written on it. Sylvia gets out of her seat and walks up to the projection booth. The door is open and the projector is still humming and cranking, but Propp, of course, is nowhere to be seen. There's a square opening in the floor at the rear of the booth. She steps inside and looks to see a spiral staircase which she climbs down into a closet that leads out to the concession stand.

She leans on the candy counter and looks forward at the main entrance of the theatre. The double glass doors are pushed wide open, a set of keys hanging from an interior lock.

Sylvia stands still until her breathing calms and all she can hear is the slap-and-purr sound of the movie reel upstairs, the tail end of the film perpetually revolving on the take-up arm of the projector. She listens until she decides not to turn it off. She pushes her hands into the pockets of her coat to confirm what she already suspects. The film canisters are gone.

Then she moves out the front door and starts to walk home.

25

Jakob loves scouting locations. If some quirk of nature or God were to prevent him from being an auteur, he thinks he could still find a reasonable percentage of happiness as a set scout. He's convinced he could be dropped from a plane into any locale on the planet—urban, suburban, full-blown rural—and he'd be able to find the exactly correct visuals for any hypothetical film in development. And in any art form so dependent on collaboration, scouting requires no interaction beyond that of his inner-eye and his outer eye.

It's a question of determining coordinates, of uncovering real world field-sites that agree with the images already screened in the skull-cinema. You look at the printed page where the screenwriter has written.

EXT. TRAIN STATION -NIGHT

and you know, from the context of the narrative, from the endless number of movies you've seen in your life, from the specific throb in the center of your bone marrow, you *know* what this train station must look like.

It must look like *this*.

Like Gompers Station, Jakob decides, exactly like Gompers Station once the correct angles are established and the lighting is battled out and the dry-ice machine has pumped the perfect balance of smoke and water into the air.

Jakob is sitting fifty feet above the ground, his legs dangling toward the fastest lane of the interstate. He's perched on the small lip of steel staging that supports an enormous billboard that reads

Aldrich Brothers Opticians
in the lobby of the Justman Building
"Because We'll See You Through"

From this height and distance, he can get a beautiful wide-angle of Gompers and he knows, if he can make it haunting enough, this is the shot he'll use to both open and close his film.

Jakob has been sitting up on the billboard lip for almost an hour. He keeps staring out over the train station with his bare eyes, then lifting the Seitz and staring all over again through the camera's eye. Something is troubling him, but he's yet to discover what it is. It's an absence of some sort, a missing component to the total picture. It's something he knows, instinctively, in his gut, that he can correct. It's a hole that needs to be filled, some kind of minor element like a truant wine bottle that should be in the rail bed, a pane of glass that needs to be broken. If he's patient and sits long enough, the gap will reveal itself. Sometimes there's nothing else you can do.

It would have been easier in Maisel, he thinks, but ease is not what makes a great film. *Quinsigamond is a deranged stepmother with very sharp claws.* But this is why it's the perfect place, the only place, to film *Little Girl Lost.*

He takes in the night air, thick with the rain that keeps threatening to fall, arches his shoulders backwards and wonders how Felix will dispose of Jiri Fric's body. Then he pushes the thought away and lifts the Seitz back to his eye, peers through, aiming down at the station. And, for the first time all night, he sees movement.

He zooms in and adjusts his focus manually. There, poking out of one of the Saville Co. Storage cars. And she's gone before he can shoot any film. He shifts the camera up on his shoulder, points it skyward, looks over the whole of the lot. He brings the camera back, aims at the storage car, waits ten seconds. Waits another twenty. There, again, the head edges out beyond the door, furtive, like an animal aware of an unseen predator.

The head lingers this time. It's a young girl, preteen. She takes another look around the yard, then shifts her body, throws her legs out the door and eases herself down to the ground, in an anticipatory crouch. Then, as if a switch is thrown, she bolts toward a waste Dumpster across the yard, hauls herself up by climbing a pile of scrap metal next to the bin, and rolls like a gymnast down into the trash, disappearing from the frame completely.

Jakob's heart is racing with epiphany. This is the face he has been looking for, the saint that will bless his film. This is, without doubt, without any equivocation, the face that will fuel every inch of celluloid he'll expose. This is the *Little Girl Lost.*

All he'll need is a single, perfect, still shot. Something he can blow up to wall-size for the chancellery interrogation scene and integrate into the newspaper mock-ups. Something he can transpose, full-screen, a ghost-image, over the anti-hero's final moments.

And then he's climbing, racing down the struts of the billboard like some arrogant prince of a traveling circus who has nothing but contempt for gravity. He leaps the last five feet to the breakdown lane of the highway, cradling the Seitz like a baby pulled from a burning tenement. He dashes across the interstate, ignoring the awful horn blast of the refrigeration trucks barreling down on him. He jumps over the guardrail, does a graceless, full-speed dance down the embankment that rolls into the perimeter of Gompers. And then he freezes, not sure how to proceed. If he rushes her, he'll panic her back into hiding and lose his central image forever. But if he calls out to her, gives her warning, she'll have even more time to cut and run. So he decides the best thing to do is probably keep his distance, but follow her, wait for her to appear in some random shaft of light, and shoot as much film as he can without her ever knowing.

He moves as quietly as possible, positions himself behind an Elias Freight boxcar. He gets on one knee, brings up the Seitz and finds his focus. And then he finds the girl. Incredibly, she's even better in closer proximity, matching, almost too well, the rough sketches he made in the back of his notebook. She has the kind of eyes that make dialogue irrelevant. The flowing blonde hair, matted now in places, that gives her a vulnerable but feral look. She's dressed in filthy clothing that looks like cast-off rags.

Jakob watches as she begins to chew on something found in the Dumpster, maybe a crust of bread. She tears into it with her teeth, pushing it into her mouth until the cheeks bulge like those of a squirrel. Her skin is smudged with ash and dirt and Jakob thinks it could be deliberate, a crude camouflage or war paint.

The girl makes a hard swallow, stuffs a pocket with something unrecognizable. Then she climbs back to the ground, stunningly agile, and makes a beeline for the interior of Gompers. She enters through a low window hole that's been halfheartedly boarded over. Jakob gives her a few seconds' head start, then follows.

But he finds he can't fit through the gaps in the plywood, so he circles around the side of the station and finds a hole that's been smashed through the marble wall. He gets down on his knees, blankets the camera inside his jacket, and climbs through.

Jakob enters the main chamber of the station and stops, stays motionless and tries to get a fix on where the girl has gone. He smells smoke, hears the sound of running feet from above. He sees the remains of a huge support column to his right and crawls toward it on all fours, then eases himself into sitting and withdraws the Seitz from the fold of his coat. He brings the camera to his eye and pulls back to a medium shot, then begins to scan the balconies that rim the main chamber.

At the far end of the hall, he fixes on a small bonfire. He pulls in slightly, finds faces illuminated in the glow of the fire's light. They're all children, both girls and boys. In the center of the group is his star, the engine of his movie, the face that will only appear in reproduction, a still, fixed image. But, Jakob knows, even in this ridiculous dimness, that the power of this child's face will certainly outshine every scenery-chewer slated to walk across the screen.

The little girl is handing out to her compatriots whatever she scavenged from the Dumpster outside. She works deliberately, with a seriousness of purpose far beyond what her age should allow. Every now and then, she stops to rub her eyes or bring the back of her hand across her nose.

This lighting isn't going to work, Jakob thinks. And the distance is too great.

He's going to need to shoot her during the day somehow. And to do that, sooner or later, he's going to have to approach her. He comes back up onto his knees and starts to move for a closer column, but his hand hits something cold and metal and sends the object rolling down a slope of broken concrete. The noise echoes through the chamber and the children up in the balcony immediately scatter, one of them dousing the fire with tossed liquid.

Jakob cringes and curses himself. He stands up, shoulders the Seitz, looks through the lens and sweeps across the balconies. And he's shocked to find himself staring up at a young boy, barely a teen. But as Jakob starts to sharpen his focus, the kid pitches a rock. The stone impacts at Jakob's feet, but it's just the initial assault in what suddenly becomes a barrage. From every angle above, rocks and bottles and lengths of pipe come hurling through the air down around Jakob. An old boot catches him across the forehead and he falls intentionally to the ground and starts to crawl for shelter.

But there's no safe place to run. The children are fanned out and seem to have the whole of the main hall covered from every direction. They make no noise beyond the striking of their missiles. They appear to have an endless supply of rubble to use as ammunition.

Jakob tries a crawling run from column to column. Scrap metal and stones and rail spikes and small shafts of wood rain down around him. He flinches, takes a hard blow to the shoulder and sees he's been hit by an unopened soup can. He rolls to the side, still trying to shield the Seitz, and a chuck of marble falls inches from his head.

"Please," he tries to yell. "I'll leave you alone."

There's a moment of amnesty and he takes it, climbs to his feet and starts to run for the hole he used to enter the station. As he approaches his exit, the attack begins again and as he squeezes through to the yard outside, he takes several blows to his back and head.

He falls outside bleeding, but he thinks the Seitz is unharmed. He gets up, starts to run toward Ivano Ave. He makes it a block, to the intersection of Polito, then lets himself slump against a street lamp and catch his breath.

Across the block, a crowd of hookers loitering in front of the Occidental Lounge seem to turn their collective attention his way. He tries to think of the fastest way back to the St. Vitus. Then he hears the screaming from behind.

Kidnapper. Murderer. Child Killer.

He turns back to Gompers Station, sees a small figure at the edge of the station's roof. It's pointing down in his direction, the voice so much larger than the stature should indicate. It's the little girl from the Dumpster.

It's him. He took Jenny Ellis. He killed Jenny Ellis.

A crowd starts to empty into the street from the Bangkok clubs and alleyways. And Jakob realizes what is about to happen.

He killed her. He killed the little girl.

He straightens up, hears voices being raised. One of the hookers starts pointing across the intersection toward him, yelling, "That's him. That's the son of a bitch who grabbed that little girl."

He doesn't wait for another word. He turns and bolts back down Ivano and knows the crowd is going to follow.

And they do. This drug-steamed parish of the night instantly transforms itself into the classic angry village and begins its pursuit. Jakob knows he could run faster if he dropped the Seitz, but that just isn't a possibility. From the sky behind him, from the rooftop of Gompers Station, a child's voice of unthinkable power explodes, an alarm bell ringing into consciousness an instantaneous mob mentality. And this mob is comprised of the citizens of the meanest tenderloin imaginable.

The babykiller. The babykiller is here.

Jakob runs across Haller Road, hangs a left onto Mac-Donald. The noise behind him is increasing and drawing nearer. There's an awful taunting quality to it. He can't make out any words, only a threatening babble. The sound track to a brutal demise born of blood-lust and a chronic, indiscriminate rage. He throws himself through a series of interconnecting alleyways and comes out on Polito. He's run a full circle. Across the street is the opposite border of Gompers Station.

He starts to hesitate, but the sound of barking dogs drives him across the road and through a gap torn into some rusted cyclone fencing. He picks the first open boxcar he sees and climbs inside it. And only then does he realize how badly his head is pounding. His lungs begin to seize up on him and he claws at his pockets for his medication, but comes up empty.

He rolls onto his stomach, lets his head rest against the floor of the boxcar, thinks he might be able to pass out. He can no longer tell if the noise of the mob is growing fainter or drawing nearer. He touches the Seitz, strokes it, keeps his hand on the grip.

Some time passes. A series of minutes filled only with the sound of his decayed lung expanding and contracting like a sputtering motor consuming its last drops of fuel.

And suddenly Jakob realizes that he's lying on a blanket of white paper. The entire floor of the train car, every inch, is carpeted with "Missing" flyers.

He rises up on his elbows, lifts his head, blinks to clear

his vision. He looks down to the floor of the train car and reads

Have You Seen This Child?

He stares at the words as if they might mutate into a parade of insects and march off the page. He stares until the words lose their meaning.

And only then does he let himself look at the photo beneath the words. The picture of Jenny Ellis. The picture of the little girl from the Dumpster.

You escaped, he thinks, shocked at his envy as much as his discovery. *You escaped as I wish to escape.*

He gets up on his knees, picks up one of the flyers, runs a hand over the photocopied visage.

I would never have told them, Jenny. I understand completely. As only I can understand. I only wanted your face.

He folds the flyer and slides it into the inner pocket of his coat.

There is no need to fear me, Jenny. I only wanted your picture.

z△

Walking through the city at night, this night, is like walking through a serial dream, a slightly gauzy mirage where, though specific images repeat on a regular basis, the whole of the landscape never gets very clear or recognizable.

The apartment is about five miles from the theatre and it's after four in the morning when Sylvia finally walks up the back stairs, still dressed in the remains of the Berkshires nightgown and Propp's coat. Her hand on the back door, she pictures Perry sitting at the kitchen table, still in his suit though the tie will be pulled loose from his throat and the top button may be undone. Will she even try to offer some explanation? Or will she just stand still and wait for the yelling to dwindle so she can crawl into bed and try hard to fall asleep and pray that there's some way to go back to the day before the Aquinas, before the seven pictures that have melted her life into this unrestricted chaos?

She takes the key from the molding lip, unlocks the door, replaces the key and heads into the kitchen. She flips on the light, puts the Canon down on the countertop and she's both relieved and surprised that Perry isn't there. She closes the door quietly and walks to the bedroom. The bed is empty but the red light on the answering machine is blinking in the dark. She hits the playback button and after the rewind comes Perry's voice, hushed but clearly drunk.

"Syl, good, don't get up, stay there, it's me. I'm at Eddie Meade's place. It's about one A.M. and we've had a few, we've had quite a few, you know, drinks. After the meeting. After we finished the meeting. So I'm in no shape to drive home and I'm just going to sack out here on Eddie's couch. Okay? You sleep. Hope you feel better in the morning. You sleep. I'll talk to you then. We'll talk in the morning."

She sits down on the edge of the bed and puts her head in her hands. She's too tired to laugh. She pulls the slippers off her feet and throws them in the wastebasket. She thinks about pouring some wine, going into the living room, flipping on the tube and seeing what Peter Lorre is up to. She unbuttons Propp's coat and shrugs out of it, holds it in her lap and realizes it would be hard to explain if Perry saw it lying on the bed in the morning. She gets up, goes to the closet, opens the door and stares into Rory Gaston's terrified face.

It's his eyes that keep her from letting out a scream that

could wake up Mrs. Acker. Gaston's eyes are so wide and flinching he looks like a child on his second trip to the dentist. He's hunched in on himself, trying somehow to disappear, a deer that's suddenly sensed a predator in close proximity. He starts shaking his head *no* over and over and Sylvia's first wave of shock and fear is replaced by anger undercut by just a little pity.

She steps back and says, "Get out of my closet."

He complies and starts to walk past her for the bedroom door. She grabs the back of his sweater and yanks him to a stop.

"Where the hell do you think you're going?"

He turns around to face her.

"I'm so sorry, Sylvia," he stammers. "If there was any other way. I'm begging you, please don't call the police."

"You broke into my goddamn apartment."

"I didn't take anything. I swear to you. You can check. I didn't take a thing."

"You broke in, you bastard."

"Please, Sylvia, try to understand our position—"

"I don't see anyone here but you, Gaston."

"You left the key over the door—"

"That gives you the right to come into my apartment."

He stares at her, prematurely ready to give up. He says, "You're going to call the police?"

"Are you going to tell me why I shouldn't?"

He looks around the bedroom, pulls on his beard. "I wasn't going to take them," he says. "I just wanted a look. I just wanted to see, to confirm for myself . . ."

"See what?" she says.

"The pictures." he says.

"And confirm what?"

He looks at her, suddenly more confused than afraid.

"That they're Propp's," he says in a soft, kind of reverent whisper.

Sylvia stares at him and refuses to speak for a while.

Then she steps over to the telephone on the nightstand and lets her fingers rest on the receiver. Gaston looks from her hand to her face and back again.

Sylvia says, "You look different when you're not in your pajamas."

"For God's sake," he says, "I didn't even find them. I didn't disturb anything. Can't we just leave it be?"

"No, we can't just leave it be. You broke into someone's apartment, Gaston. That's a serious breach. That's a crime. You can't let things like this go."

"Please, Sylvia," his voice breaking and his eyes starting to blink too fast.

She lets him struggle for a few more seconds and then steps away from the phone and says, "Let's go in the kitchen."

They sit at the table with glasses of tap water in front of them and stare at each other.

"Why did you come here tonight?"

"I told you," Gaston starts, "I only wanted—"

"No," Sylvia says, "I mean what makes you think I have any Propp photos. I told you the only place I've ever seen a Propp was at the Skin Palace."

He draws in a doubtful breath and says, "Please, Sylvia—"

She cuts him off and says, "Mr. Gaston, you're not in a position to dictate how this discussion will go. We're not sitting in Der Garten tonight. You want to screw around with me? I can have the police here with a phone call."

"All right," he says. "Calm down."

"Quevedo told you the story, didn't he?"

He shakes his head. "I told you before, I never heard of a Mr. Quevedo. Call the damn police if you want. I don't know the man. Nobody in the group knows the man."

"Please, Gaston," mocking him.

"We know this much. We know you were the last person to visit Jack Derry's before he stripped the store and ran.

We know you left the store with a camera. An Aquinas. And we know you showed up at our door the next day."

She takes a sip of water and gets overwhelmed with a metallic taste. She gets up and goes to the sink and dumps the glass.

"Back up. How do you know Derry? How do you know I went to the store?"

"Jack Derry has been in the Zone for years—"

"So has Quevedo."

"I don't *know* a Quevedo," he snaps.

"All right," she says. "You don't know Quevedo."

"Look, Sylvia," he says. "We're like the apostles after the crucifixion, okay? The group tries to live on faith. We look for signs, little traces that Propp's still around. That there might be more—"

"More what?"

He looks at her, either annoyed or confused. "More images. More clues. More messages."

"What the hell are you talking about?"

"We can't get enough, Sylvia," he says. "There have to be more pictures. We go on in the hope that there are more pictures."

"Look, we're getting off track here—"

"What would you think?" he says, kind of a challenge. "A stranger comes to Der Garten. She asks questions about Propp. She's evasive about her reasons and her existing information."

"I'd think that she wasn't telling me everything. That maybe she knew something I didn't."

"Exactly," he says with a little pound of his fist on the table.

"But I wouldn't necessarily break into her apartment."

"But then," he says, "you haven't been infected as long as I have."

"Infected?" Sylvia repeats.

"After a time it's more of a burden than a joy. That's

probably true about every obsession. But it's worse with Propp."

She comes back to the table and sits down.

"Did you ever think," she says, "that maybe Propp wouldn't want all this devotion?"

"Did you ever think," he answers, his voice on the edge of a sneer, as if she's the fool for trying to reason with a fanatic, "that perhaps that doesn't matter?"

She lets a beat go by and then changes the subject.

"So Derry's been a link to Propp information in the past."

He nods. "A very tentative link. But at times he's all we had. You have to understand that there are a lot of shysters in this area. People who will lead you on, tell you they know of someone who knows of someone, that there are rumors of a print in Europe. It's like pulling teeth and it's always expensive. More often than not it all leads to a dead end or a forgery."

"But that wasn't the case with Derry?"

"It never appeared to be. Once or twice he grudgingly supplied us with a tip. A phone number. An ad in a catalog. Nothing ever materialized, but it wasn't a case of fraud or deceit. Things just blew up in our faces. People didn't show up for meetings. That kind of thing."

"Do you think Derry personally knows Propp?"

"Now that," he says, "supposes that Propp is among the living."

"So it does."

"What do you think, Sylvia?"

"I'm new at this, remember?"

"Tell me you've got some prints, Sylvia."

The look on his face is so earnest and really almost desperate that there is this sucker part of her that wants to take him by the hand and lead him down to the darkroom and hand him the salvation or narcotic that's hanging on the dry-line.

"I wish I could, Gaston. But I've got nothing. Yes, I knew a little more about the myth than I let on at Der Garten. And yes, I bought a camera from Jack Derry. But that's all I bought. I'm more in the dark than you people."

He looks down at his lap and says, "You know I don't want to believe you."

She gets up and crosses to the back door and opens it.

"I've got to get some sleep now."

He sits staring at her, finally rises out of the chair with a weary effort, walks past her out to the back hall, then stops and turns back and says, "I'm sorry, Sylvia."

She doesn't say anything and he moves down the back stairs.

In the cellar, Sylvia sits on the step stool. Her head has started to ache again. Her eyes are so tired and dry that each blink brings a sting like a wound. But she looks out on the line of pictures. She keeps looking at the pictures. She keeps staring at this woman and this child and this cavernous ruin.

She thinks about a Friday night long ago, attending the Stations of the Cross with her mother down at St. Brendan's. She thinks about the Stations, the carvings, hung on the walls of the cathedral, hung in a specific order, each a story unto itself, and yet, each one connected to the next, connected by a ceremony, linked by a chain of interrelated events, and telling a larger story, the sum greater than the parts. And now the drying line is like the Stations of the Cross, hung this way, seven stories, seven segments of one story: Sylvia's Stations.

She rubs her eyes, opens them, stares at the photographs.

Here are the things she knows.

No, here are the things she believes she knows: *There is nothing erotic about these photographs in front of her.*

She understands how subjective a judgment that is. She

realizes that there are individuals who could find the erotic in a landfill or an ad for mouthwash, people who could manage to insert some idea of eroticism into any image they happen upon. But she believes that the majority of people, confronted with these seven pictures, would not attach the adjective, the concept, of *erotic* to them.

There is something extraordinary about these photographs.

She knows what they aren't. But it's something else entirely to define what they are. They are ethereal, but at the same time rooted in an earthy, actually grimy, setting. They are tender, and yet that tenderness feels overlaid with a fear, a vague conviction that something malignant is within reach. They are tragic and yet the more she looks at each one, the more she's convinced of this unexplainable, unjustifiable sense of endurance emanating from the mother figure. Maybe even from the infant. More than anything, she wants to say the prints are haunting, like touchstones for memories that could unseat someone's entire sense of the world. The pictures scare her, and yet she can't turn away from them. They sadden her, and yet she can't get enough.

There is no way to be sure these prints were taken by Terrence Propp.

Or, for that matter, that the man she spent this evening with, the man who took her to his underground lair and the flea market and the movie theatre, the man who photographed her at Gompers Station, there is no way to know that *that* man is Terrence Propp. Terrence Propp could be Jack Derry. He could be Mr. Quevedo. He could be dead and buried. He could be continents away, having renounced photography and his own past. He could be an empty legend created by a slick entrepreneur with the eye of an artist.

Whoever the man was tonight, he posed me in the same manner as the Madonna in these pictures.

Which means he must know about these pictures. Which suggests that it's likely he *did* take these pictures. Which suggests that the Aquinas was placed in her hands on purpose, that the events of the past several days are much more than coincidence, are likely part of a plan, a strategy, a system for manipulating where she goes and what she thinks.

Someone wanted me to have these pictures.

She gets up off the stool and unclips the last print in the series, brings it to the worktable and holds a magnifying glass over it. She bends down, peers over the print, focuses on the mother's face, stares at the shadow that obscures her features.

Propp's voice comes to her.

There are stunning similarities.

She drops the magnifying glass. She walks to the dryline and steps in front of each photograph. She looks at the mother. She looks at the infant. She looks back to the mother.

She doesn't want it to hit her, but of course it does, with the kind of vengeful, crippling intensity that can only pass over you once in a life span. She sinks down on the floor below the seven pictures and she begins to weep. Her arms and shoulders start to shake slightly and her nose begins to run. She tries to stifle any noise and manages only a soft keen, like a small animal caught in an even smaller space.

Epiphanies of this nature don't grow out of a logical progression of facts. They don't evolve from a rational chain of deduction and analysis. They simply appear, unexpected and uninvited, like a car out of control that changes the life of every person it collides with.

She cries even though she knows that it's a waste of energy to try to fight this kind of knowledge. This certainty. This simple but horrible idea. It comes at you with the kind of suddenness and persistence you've chronically feared in your dreams. It rapes you with a kind of shocking but undeniable certainty. It takes your body, without warning or explanation, and hurls you brutally across a chasm of protective doubt, across the impediment of absent proof. And it lands you with a bone-rattling crash that no amount of time will allow recovery from.

She hears her throat and her tongue form the word out of the remains of her crying.

Mother.

The last things she's sure of are the most awful of all.

Terrence Propp is my father.

The Madonna in the pictures is my mother.

And I am the infant at her breast.

reel three

The visual is *essentially* pornographic . . .
—Fredric Jameson, *Signatures of the Visible*

The sound of a dog barking wakes Sylvia sometime before dawn. She gets up off the cellar floor and locks up the darkroom without looking at the pictures. She goes back up to the apartment, climbs into bed and falls asleep for another three hours, then showers and gets dressed and walks to the Snapshot Shack.

Now, sitting in the tiny booth with a half hour till opening, there's no way to stop thinking. The radio is no distraction and Cora's crossword magazines are all filled in. So she stares out the bubble window at the plaza in front of her, at the whitewashed glass and the realtor's rental signs and the trash that's collected on the walkway.

There is no reason to believe that twenty-five years ago, her mother bundled her in a blanket and took her down to an already abandoned and decayed train station. That her mother took a seat on a broken marble pillar and tilted her face toward the man who was her husband and Sylvia's father. That her mother posed for seven photographs as Sylvia fed at her breast. That the man with the camera deserted them. And that for the next twenty years, up to the time of her death, mother never told daughter a word about any of these events.

There is not a single fact to suggest the validity of this particular story. And yet, Sylvia knows it's the truth. She

knows that this is exactly what took place. She knows the
real fiction is comprised of the few details her mother did
tell—that her father died before Sylvia was born, that the
father was a milkman for a local dairy, that Sylvia had no
family to speak of beyond her mother.

And so what does she do with this knowledge? She
thinks about Propp fleeing the Ballard last night and
cringes at how close she came to violating the oldest taboo
in the world. But should she seek him out now? Go back
to Gompers or the Canal Zone cellars and try to find her
way to St. Benedict's?"

On the walk to work, low clouds rolled in and it's been
threatening to rain for the past hour. The air almost has that
pre-tornado feel to it, a false stillness, as if this lack of
breeze was just an ambush tactic. Sylvia looks at the strip
of connected stores again and tries to picture what would
happen if a tornado did touch down here. She can imagine
the Snapshot Shack itself being torn off its slab and spun
into flight, spiraling above Quinsigmond, just like Dorothy
Gale's farmhouse. She can imagine her head stuck out the
bubble window, seeing people blown past her—Perry
doing an off-balance air-swim, losing all the papers from
his monogrammed briefcase, Leni Pauline bumping and
grinding into the yonder, tassels revolving with the force of
the twister, Hugo Schick maniacally grinning at this spectacle of nature, a hand-held camera filming the flight path
of his own demise. And Terrence Propp just letting the
winds take him, an ambiguous look on his face, neither terror nor contentment, just a nod in Sylvia's direction as he
passes.

She kills the fantasy and realizes she's staring at Mrs.
Ellis, Jenny's tormented, agonized mother. The woman has
her ever present "Missing" posters tucked under her arm.
She's dressed in the same clothes she was wearing when
Sylvia saw her at the Halloween block party. The woman's
hair sticks out in every direction. She's walking slowly

past the plaza's empty stores, trying to peer inside each one through the whitewashed windows, as if her daughter sits inside some bankrupt footwear shop, playing with abandoned laces and shoeboxes, just waiting for her mother to find the correct location and take her home again.

Mrs. Ellis walks up to an old man sitting on a slatted wooden bench at the end of the walkway. She begins to go into what must by now be an automatic spiel, the incomprehensible story of how random evil came to her door one day. The old man nods sympathetically and takes one of the flyers, studies Jenny's picture. Then he gestures to the Snapshot Shack and, after some discussion, leaves Mrs. Ellis and begins to move across the parking lot toward Sylvia. He walks with a slight limp, leaning down on a cane. Halfway across the asphalt, Sylvia realizes that the figure is Mr. Quevedo from Brody's Adult Books.

She slides the bubble open and waits for him to approach.

"You're a long way from your shop," she says before he can speak.

He comes to a stop directly in front of the window and stands formally with both his hands on the top of his cane and his milky eyes staring out at nothing in particular. He's dressed in a slightly worn and very dated brown suit with a yellow and brown paisley tie.

"I decide to take a stroll," he says, "before the weather turns."

"I think you'll get caught on your way back."

"I won't melt," he says, then both of them are quiet for a few seconds and the awkwardness blooms. She should have expected to see Quevedo, sooner or later.

"I went to see Rory Gaston," she says. "He swears he doesn't know you."

Quevedo seems to think for a minute. He blinks a few times and then says, "I don't believe I've ever been introduced to Mr. Gaston."

"You're the one who told me to go see him."

"I provided you with a name, Miss Krafft. I never said I knew any of the Proppists personally."

A small, annoying smile comes over his face and prompts her to say, "What is it I can do for you, Mr. Quevedo? Do you have some film to drop off? We're running a sensational price on Snapshot Shack brand when you drop off an exposed roll for processing."

"I don't take pictures, Sylvia," he says.

"Well then," she says, "it was good seeing you. I'm sure we'll run into each other again."

"My child," he says and she flinches. "This is no way to treat an old man."

"I'm sorry, but I'm having a very tough day. And the morning shipment is due any minute."

He shifts his stance and looks up at the darkening sky and she wonders just how much he can see.

"I'm not your enemy, Sylvia. Out of all the men in your life, I'm not the one you should fear."

Before she can think she says, "There's only one man in my life."

"Would that be Mr. Schick or Mr. Propp?"

"That would be Mr. Leroux."

"No," he says, shaking his head and pushing his pale, cracked lips out as if he was trying to whistle, "no it wouldn't."

So far, she's more angry than fearful. She yells, "Who the hell are you, asshole?"

"Vulgarity doesn't flatter you, child."

"All right, just knock it off with the *child* shit. Jesus."

She wants to climb out of the booth and knock the blind old bastard on his ass. He remains unfazed. He touches the small knot of his tie and says, "I'm not here to anger or annoy you, Sylvia."

"So why are you here?"

"Very simply," he says, "to be of assistance. I know you

currently feel that there's no one you can trust. And I know what a horrible feeling that can be, Sylvia. Please believe me."

"And why," she asks, coming back to control, "would you want to help me?"

He smiles as if the answer should be obvious. "I'm a displaced person, Sylvia. Before I settled in Quinsigamond, I was often a transient. Often a victim of some very brutal forms of repression. Buffeted by forces I could not always see. Forgive the pun."

"Go on."

"You are not the only frightened person in this city. I am not a free agent. I have compromised to the point where I owe allegiances and favors to a multitude of conflicting clients. To everyone but myself. People seem to think I'm the nexus where they can find satisfaction. Attain some unattainable artifact of their desires. Believe me, Sylvia, I know what it's like to be scared and confused."

"You haven't given me a single reason why I should trust you."

"I'm not sure," he says, "what I could give you that would be adequate. That would make you believe my intentions are simple and benign. I've lived in Quinsigamond for a number of years now, Sylvia. I was here before you were born. But I'll always be a foreigner in this city. The advantage of that fact is that I see a good many things the natives miss. And I'm a blind man, so I hear much that the sighted are deaf to. I'm a receptacle of information. Much of it is rumor and gossip. But some percentage of it is of value."

She studies him, this awkward, slightly bent old man with odd, papery skin, long fingers, brittle, white, birdlike hair. Flanked this way, by the deserted plaza in the distance, the sky looking like it was about to press down on him, all she can think is what a wonderful picture he'd make.

"Last night," she says, "I met a man who claimed to be Terrence Propp. Was he telling the truth?"

There's no hesitation. He says. "He is what he claims to be. Don't judge him too harshly."

"I never said anything about judging him at all,"she says. "He tried to warn me away from Hugo Schick. Is that good advice?"

"Schick," he says, seeming to consider his words, "is a megalomaniac. He is also a man of some talent. But then, there is no law, natural or otherwise, that says artists have to be ethical people. Schick may be a pathological liar. And he appears to consume all but the strongest individuals in his path. To be honest, Sylvia, I can't see the benefit of an association with Mr. Schick."

"Which one is running me through the maze, Quevedo?"

"The maze?"

"You want to help me? Then answer some of my questions. Like who made sure I got the Aquinas? Why was I supposed to find those pictures? What happened to Jack Derry? How did Propp know I'd be at the Halloween block party?"

He waves his right hand, a kind of fluid stop sign.

"Slow down, Sylvia," he says. "Yes, I want to help you. But understand, my child—I'm sorry, excuse me—understand that, like everyone else, I'm at the mercy of my age and my culture. I may well know a bit more than you about both Mr. Schick and Mr. Propp. And I confess that I can't prevent myself from making certain judgments concerning their behavior, their attitudes, the wreckage both seem to leave in their wake. A man of my particular sensibility might use phrases like *irresponsible cad,* like *self-consumed scoundrel.* Possibly, I could use a word like *deviant* or perhaps, in some case, even *pervert.* These words might be applied to one or both of the men in question. But

Sylvia, they are not limited to those men. The world is full of callous and cruel men."

"You have a problem getting to the point, Mr. Quevedo."

He closes his eyes, nods. "Perhaps," he says, "your greatest threat does not come from either Schick or Propp."

"I found Rory Gaston in my apartment last night—"

"He's a sad and deluded figure, but not a dangerous one."

"Should I be afraid of you, Quevedo?"

He lets out a quick blast of a laugh, a high-pitched, one-syllable bleat. "I'm an old man at the end of a tiring life, Sylvia. Admit the obvious."

"You're saying Perry. You're saying you know something about Perry."

The white eyes just stare at her and she knows he's got nothing more to say.

"Perry would never hurt me," she says. "He's not even aware of what's been going on in my life."

"I must get back to the store," he says, gives a little bow, turns on his heel and starts to walk away across the lot. Sylvia doesn't try to stop him. She doesn't say a word. When he gets to the edge of the plaza, the rain begins to fall and she watches him turn up the collar of his suitcoat before he disappears around the corner.

She turns on the radio. She searches the drawers for an eraser so she can rub out all of Cora's crossword answers. She picks up one of the romance novels that someone's always leaving behind in the booth, opens it randomly and reads a page.

. . . Yes," Simone said as she turned away from the sight of Pierre disappearing down the beach, "if I can't have you, my love, I can still paint you!" She picked up her palette and straightened the canvas on the easel. She began to mix the colors once again, swirling shades to-

gether the way she had been taught so long ago in Paris,
but now her eyes began to fill with the sting of tears and
the dabs of bright paint spread out before her began to blur
and . . .

She throws the book in the trash bucket. The courier
truck pulls up to the window and she slides the bubble
open. She's never seen this driver before. He doesn't say
hello. He's writing furiously on a clipboard which he suddenly heaves at her, almost hitting her in the face. She
signs for the delivery and hands him back the board and
the courier passes her a fat packet of film envelopes held
together with thick rubber bands. Then he drives off, leaving the Shack engulfed in a cloud of carbon monoxide.
Sylvia closes the window completely, which she hates
doing even when it rains. She unbands the envelopes and
sits them in her lap and starts to alphabetize them.

The phone rings and she jumps and the envelopes fall
onto the floor. She starts to scoop them back with one hand
and answers the phone with the other.

"Snapshot Shack, this is Sylvia. Can I help you?"

"A heart and lung machine and total forgiveness would
be a start."

It's Perry. She knew the call would come but she's still
dreading the next three minutes.

"You survived," she says.

"Barely. You just can't do this after you turn thirty. I'm
going to be hurting for a week."

"Well, you couldn't let the district attorney think you
were a lightweight."

"Eddie's out of my league. Never again. I'm just not a
Scotch drinker," a pause, then, "How are you feeling,
Syl?"

"Much better," she says. "I just needed some sleep."

"You were gone when I got in this morning."

"I got to work early. I wanted to beat the rain."

"I'm really sorry, Syl. That was really juvenile last night. I'm an idiot."

"It's okay. I understand. The new law partner doesn't say no when the D.A. is buying the drinks."

There's a second of silence and she wonders if he thinks she's being sarcastic, but he comes back with a new tone to his voice, all low and serious. "We've really been strangers all week. It's worrying me, Sylvia. I don't—"

She cuts him off. She doesn't want to do this. "It's been a bad week, Perry," she says. "It's been bad for both of us. It's the moon or something."

"We need to do some major talking, honey. You know. We need to just sit down and clear the air. Start fresh. We've got to get things straight again—"

"Oh, God, wouldn't you know it," she says.

"What?"

"I've got a customer at the window. I'm going to have to run."

"Call me back, Sylvia."

"Okay, I'll call. I've gotta go now."

"Call me."

She hangs up the phone. She doesn't know why she lied to him. She doesn't know why she couldn't talk to him. She reaches down to pick up the last of the dropped pictures and the phone rings again. She stares at it, thinking about letting it ring, thinks that it might be Cora checking on her and picks up the receiver.

"Snapshot Shack, Sylvia speaking. Can I help you?"

"In more ways than you can imagine."

It's Hugo Schick.

"Actually," he continues, "I think we can very likely help each other."

"If you're calling about the job, Hugo—" she begins, but he cuts her off.

"Did this morning's delivery come yet, Sylvia?"

This throws her and she looks down at the black plastic envelopes in her lap. "Yeah. About five minutes ago."

"I'm hosting a working party tonight, Sylvia. I need for you to be there. It's going to be a major event. I'll be filming all evening and into the morning. I'll be completing my meisterstück. Tonight, we finish years of work on *Don Juan Triumphant*. I need you to document it all, Sylvia. I need your eyes."

"I'm not coming to the party, Hugo."

"We'll be taking down a wall and using both studios. Bring your equipment, Sylvia."

"I won't be there, Hugo."

"You'll want to talk to me. And if you come, I promise I'll make time. We'll steal away at some point."

"I'm sorry, Hugo—"

"In this morning's delivery. A package for a Mr. and Mrs. Jones. Not much technique, but you have to credit their imaginations. You take a long look at their pictures, Sylvia. And then you decide about tonight."

"Look Hugo," but he's already hung up.

She replaces the receiver. She shuffles the envelopes and looks at each name sticker until she comes to one that reads *Jones*. She puts all the other envelopes to the side and holds the Jones's in her hands. She breaks the seal and pulls out the prints. They're 4 x 6 color shots. Of Perry. And of Candice Haskell. And they're having dinner in a restaurant that could be Fiorello's. And they're walking in what looks like a public park, holding hands. And then they're seen from a distance, through the window of some nondescript room, kissing each other. They're touching each other. They're on top of each other. Perry on top. Candice on top. There are shots of them on some leather couch, necking. Shots of them half-clothed, bent over Perry's desk at Walpole & Lewis.

Shots of them in Sylvia's bed, completely naked, sitting up, in motion, chest to chest, both sets of eyes closed as if they were straining against the force of some imminent explosion.

ZX

Mr. Quevedo moves down Waldstein Avenue striking the sidewalk with his cane, tapping out the beat of a song from his childhood, "La Tablada," a tango by Vincente Greco. He's pleased with his recollection, though the song holds no sense of nostalgia for him, no longing for an unretrievable past time. Quevedo is simply happy and surprised that his memory is not only intact at this advanced age, but seems to be somehow improving. Images he hasn't pulled up in decades are now being screened daily behind his ever worsening eyes. The candy store on Tucuman Street where the *guapos* bought their mermaid playing cards. The garden in Palermo where grandfather practiced his topiary. The old-book smell in the basement of the library at Montevideo.

We go back to the past, replay the familiar in slightly different ways, with new shadings and colors that give what was once mundane a new aura of excitement, and sometimes, of meaning. There's no harm in this reconstruction. Like everything else, its a way to occupy the hours until the true darkness falls. Certainly it's a more pleasant diversion than trying to determine where a schizophrenic camera salesman might be hiding.

There was a time in Quevedo's life when the more complicated transactions were the most worthwhile and when a modicum of precariousness gave an exquisite seasoning to the deal. Those were the days of long afternoons in

Turkish cafés, drinking raki and not having any idea
whether the briefcase being opened by a fat man in a linen
suit contained a stolen Egyptian fertility totem or a 9 mm
Beretta automatic. Fortunes impenetrable to the tax man
were made in Istanbul's spring and squandered by Stock-
holm's autumn. Contracts were sealed with a passing of
the jewel-encrusted hashish pipe and ruptured with a bun-
dle of dynamite underneath the antique Rolls-Royce.

Now, Luis Quevedo is a marble-eyed refugee in a city
abandoned by God. And his lunch hour is spent, not brib-
ing a customs minister with naked photos of Victoria
Regina, but begging for information from trust-fund artists
with brass rings dangling from one or more nostrils. *Lucifer never fell so far,* Quevedo thinks as he unlocks and
opens the door to Brody's Adult Books.

And is yanked inside by Huck Hrabal and thrown to the
ground at the feet of Felix Kinsky.

Felix slaps closed an atlas-sized volume titled *The Suc-
cubus Through History* and heaves it over his shoulder.

"What in the name of God?" Quevedo says and tries to
stand up, but Vera Gottwald steps forward and puts a boot
on the old man's back.

"The only God worth praying to today," Felix says,
coming down on one knee to pat Quevedo's head like that
of an indulged beagle, "is named Hermann Kinsky."

"I've paid this month's service fees—"

"My visit," Felix says, "has nothing to do with our service fees."

Quevedo tilts his head up and squints, as if contracting
the skin around his eyes will do what a half dozen
marathon surgeries at Havana Eye and Ear could not. He
sees the usual ghost-world, the cloud-draped, shadowy
symbols that have instinctively come to represent physical
reality. There are a dozen people in his store. Their posture
alone is disrespectful. They are lounging on his sofa, reclining on his Persian rugs, poring over his wares like dim

adolescents surveying the cheapest skin magazines on the planet.

"My uncle," Felix says in a whisper, "is extremely disappointed in your abilities, Luis."

Luis, from the mouth of this teenager.

"Then your uncle," Quevedo says, unbowed, spitting out the relation, "should have come to see me."

Felix stands up, walks to a nearby shelf, pulls down *Don Juan: The Suppressed Versions* and starts to open to the illustrations.

"If you knew Hermann," he says, "you'd know that he hates to waste time. And you, Luis, have become an enormous waste of his time. And, I will add, of his money."

Quevedo makes another attempt to rise and this time Vera Gottwald climbs on his back, straddles him like a miniature pony at a petting zoo. All the Roaches laugh and Felix says, "Be careful, Luis, she's wearing her spurs today."

Then he snaps his fingers and Hrabal and Krofta and Bidlo get up and wander down different aisles, begin to grab books and toss them in the air, knock them in piles to the ground.

"Please," Quevedo cries, "some of these texts are very old, very fragile."

Felix steps to the first-editions case, runs a finger down a row of spines and pulls out a slim, leather-bound volume.

"*Magdalene Revealed,*" he says to the room. "Tell me, Luis, how much would this item be worth today?"

"Please," Quevedo repeats, only to be answered with the cringe-inducing sound of brittle paper being torn from its binding.

"Five thousand," he yells.

Felix clucks his tongue in the hollow well of his mouth and says, "Jesus, old man, we've been underchanging you."

Quevedo shakes his head. "You must tell Hermann, I am

making progress in the transaction. I am very close to finding Jack Derry. I will have the photographs—"

Another page is torn free and Felix says, "Hey, idiot, I'm not an errand boy here. I'm not some goddamn answering service. I don't know what you were supposed to get my uncle and honestly don't give a rat's ass."

He walks back to the center of the store and slaps Quevedo across the forehead with the wounded book.

"You fucked up, you moron."

"Please, Felix," Luis stammers. "I am asking for time, I am asking for another day. Hermann is making a terrible mistake."

"Hermann," Felix yells, then pauses, lowers his voice, "doesn't make mistakes. Now I don't know what business you two were doing, but something has gone terribly wrong. My uncle thinks you've taken his money. He thinks you've failed to honor your end of an agreement. That's like spitting in his face, Mr. Q. And you just do *not* spit in Hermann Kinsky's face."

Felix motions Vera Gottwald off her geriatric trotter and she jogs to an aisle to join Huck Hrabal. Quevedo starts to stand and Felix gives a short kick to his side, collapsing him to the ground, then grabs the old man by the suitcoat and yanks him up into a wing chair.

Kinsky walks behind the chair, reaches over and puts his thumb and forefinger on either side of Quevedo's Adam's apple.

"I don't like you, Luis," he says, pinching in on the neck. "In fact, of all my customers, I think I dislike you the most. And I'm not completely sure why that is."

He begins to apply more pressure to either side of the throat.

"It could be that smugness, you know what I'm talking about? That nose-in-the-air bullshit coming from a guy who sells smut."

More tension from the fingers.

A gurgle from Quevedo.

"Or maybe it's those fucking eyes. I can never tell when you're looking at me. How much can you really see—"

"Just do it," Quevedo rasps. "Just take out your wire and finish it."

Felix lets go of the throat and pats the bookseller on the head. He walks back around the chair and takes a seat on the couch, opposite Luis. Felix crosses his legs, smiles and shakes his head.

"The Schonborn," he says, then bites his bottom lip and nods. "My uncle's signature. He always uses the Schonborn. It never breaks."

He starts to leaf through a book lying next to him on the couch—*A Manual for Extended Ecstasy*—and he mumbles, "Such a waste of energy."

Felix closes the book and sits back. Out of the corner of his eye, he sees Hrabal and Gottwald at the far end of an aisle, both staring into some thick art volume, transfixed by the image they've found, Huck's arm hooking around Vera's back to massage a breast.

Quevedo leans down, rests his elbows on his knees.

"Please, Felix," he says, "You must speak with Hermann. If he genuinely wants the photographs, I am the only conduit."

Felix sniffs, nods again. He leans back on the couch, seemingly exhausted.

"Luis," he says, speaking to the ceiling, "I don't know from any photographs. And I *never* use a Schonborn. It's so," he closes his eyes, brings a hand to his mouth, then to his chest, "primitive. Old world. You know what I'm saying? All that blood and spittle on the hands. Don't get me wrong, it's fine for Uncle Hermann. He'll die with the old ways."

He reaches inside his green suede jacket, withdraws a pistol.

"This," he says, holding up the gun, "is the American way of business."

And he squeezes the trigger twice, pumps two bullets into Luis Quevedo, one entering through the forehead, the other finding its target and tearing through the left eyeball. Quevedo bucks upward a bit, then the body just slumps to the right and slides down slightly, the head coming to rest at a ridiculous angle. The old man's mouth opens but no sound emerges. Then the mouth closes, but the right eye remains open, its creamy marble interior rigid in its socket.

Felix stands, reholsters his gun, moves to the body and rifles inside Quevedo's jacket, pocketing a wallet.

"Hrabal," he yells down an aisle, interrupting Huck and Vera who are lost in an endless French kiss. Huck pulls away, wipes at his mouth and jogs to the front of the store.

"I want the body lost," Felix says. "You think you can handle that? Or should I assign it to the little lady?"

Huck Hrabal meets his boss's stare but doesn't say a word.

Felix gives a soft snort through his nose, then turns and exits the store.

zy

Sylvia sits inside this overgrown camera and starts to cry. And immediately she gets furious with herself. But the anger doesn't stop the tears, doesn't stop the feeling that floods into her stomach and lungs.

She throws the pictures and they rain down around her until the whole of the booth is filled with odd-angled glimpses of two people in various stages of copulation.

I left my mother's couch for this. I pulled myself out of a world that was confined to the corner convenience store and the sound track from Rita Hayworth movies so I could be assaulted from every possible direction, so I could be confused and betrayed and paranoid. So I could sit in the vault of film and batteries and disposable cameras with my ankles covered by glossy images of my lover lying down with someone else.

And then the thought occurs to her that there's no way the lab would have developed these prints. There are strict guidelines for this kind of thing. They'll print an exposed breast or behind, but no full-frontal nudity and absolutely no sexual activity of any kind.

She fishes around on the floor, picking up and discarding envelopes till she comes to the Jones's package. She turns it over and looks at the order blank where instructions for developing and pricing are located. But the order boxes are blank. The only thing written on the envelope is *Mr and Mrs Jones*. And it's not in any handwriting she recognizes.

So the package didn't come from the normal lab. Schick managed to include it with the regular delivery.

Maybe these pictures are what Leni wants to warn her about tonight. And maybe Leni can explain why Schick wants to do this.

The phone starts to ring again and Sylvia starts to cry again. She turns out the light in the booth and lets herself sob. She misses her mother with an intensity that feels like it will take over, like it will become the only emotion, the only sensation she'll ever feel. She thinks of Ma, alone on that first night, realizing her husband is not coming back, that he's dead or that he's run off, whichever story is correct, it doesn't matter. And for the first time Sylvia understands the true weight of that kind of realization, the possibility that in the instant that *fact* of loss takes hold of you and lodges, permanently, intractably, into the deepest marrow of your bones, you could turn against life and movement. You could turn against yourself. She can picture her mother, she can *see* her, so brutally clearly, twenty-five years ago, looking in on the daughter, in bed, in the dimness of that tiny room, Ma staring at the form beneath the quilting, Ma in the doorjamb, framed, backlit, motionless, a definitive picture of a woman alone, fighting a kind of half-apprehended terror that she senses might never go away, looking down on the responsibility of a child, of Sylvia, in front of her, filling her vision. And all of Ma's innocence, her sense of promise and hope, just dead, just petrified in the emptiness of the rooms behind her. How did she go on for the rest of this imagined night?

And now Sylvia's crying more for her mother than herself. Because she knows that she doesn't love Perry. She's not sure she ever loved Perry. He was a way to move from one point to another. He was someone she needed badly at one time. Maybe desperately. And she's crying because she doesn't know if she'll ever forgive herself for that.

She reaches down and picks up the razor knife she uses to open supply boxes. She lifts up the ringing telephone and puts it in her lap on top of the pictures of Perry and Candice. She grabs the phone cord in her left hand, makes a small loop. She cuts through the cord and the ringing stops, then she opens the bubble window and heaves the freed phone into the parking lot.

This will be Sylvia's last day at the Snapshot Shack.

On the walk home, she keeps expecting to see Mr. Quevedo in the distance ahead, walking like the risen dead, an awkward zombie in a fraying suit. But she doesn't see anyone. The storm has gotten worse and she's completely soaked after the first block.

When she finally gets back to the apartment, she stands inside the entry and just shakes her shoulders and head like a big long-haired dog. Then she un-Velcros the pouch on her anorak and takes out the pictures of Perry and Candice. She thinks about leaving them on the stairway, one on each stair, each picture getting progressively more explicit as you climb to the apartment. A trail of sleazy crumbs leading back to one more boring primal image—*the wronged woman.*

She puts the pictures back in the pouch and runs up to the back door, takes the spare key, lets herself into the kitchen, goes straight to the bedroom closet and pulls it open. And, thankfully, no one's inside this time, so she starts pulling off sopping clothes and dropping them into a laundry pile. The plan is to collect all her dirty clothes, grab a bottle of wine, head down to the cellar, toss everything in the washer, pour the first drink of the day and go into the darkroom. She wants to pin the Perry-Candice pictures on the dry-line. She wants to study them the way a bride studies the proofs from her wedding package. She wants to pick the seven most hurtful poses, the seven most insulting and degrading postures. She wants to clip them alternatively next to the Propp photos. *Madonna and Child* followed by *Perry and Candice* followed by *Madonna and Child.* She wants to see what the positioning will do to her. What it might tell her. She wants to see if the combination of alternating images will have some reaction, like chemicals thrown together in some impulsive and radical experiment.

She slides into her mother's slippers and is belting her robe when she hears a knock on the back door. She puts the pictures in the pocket of the robe, walks out, pulls the door open and sees Mrs. Acker, the landlady standing in her red sneakers and housedress covered by her dead husband's old canvas fishing jacket, feathery lures still pinned to the lapels. The jacket has a detailed picture of a trout embroidered on the back, a huge hook through its mouth and the words *this one's a keeper* written in script underneath.

Mrs. Acker smiles and tries to look into the kitchen. This

morning she's wearing her standard schmear of heavy makeup, layers of some rust-colored rouge from below her eyes to her chin and a bluish, purplish eye shadow that wars with a fire-engine red lipstick that Sylvia has never seen her go without. Last year there was a car crash out in front of the church at three in the morning. Perry and Sylvia ran outside and there was Mrs. A in housecoat and sneakers and full makeup. Someday Sylvia wants to get up the nerve to ask her where she buys her cosmetics.

"Wonderful," Mrs. Acker says, "you're home."

"The Shack's closed. Problems with the phone system."

The landlady's hands go to her hips. "Listen, Sylvia, I wonder if you could do me a little favor."

Sylvia indicates her dripping hair. "I just got out of the rain, Mrs. A, could you give me about fifteen minutes."

"This'll just take you a second, honey. Honest to God. I've got some of Begelman's coffee cake heating," and she's got Sylvia by the arm and is leading her down the stairs.

Sylvia doesn't fight it. She moves to sit at the kitchen table, but Mrs. Acker says, "No, no, the papers are in the living room."

For all her money, Mrs. A hasn't redecorated her apartment since Mr. Acker died in 1969—*we were up late, watching that moonwalk, and I say, Louie, don't those big suits they wear look uncomfortable and he doesn't answer. He's had a coronary right in front of me and the astronauts . . .*

The walls are covered with heavy flock wallpaper but the paper is mostly hidden by plaque after plaque bearing mounted, shellacked fish and the inscribed date of their demise. Mrs. A shoos a half dozen cats off the couch and they jump and run in a blur of different shades of brown and grey.

"Have a seat, dear, I've got the pen here somewhere," and she starts pawing around the coffee table. "You're such a help. Such a nice girl. The one before you, she was as surly as they come. A policewoman, of all things. Now she lives with an asthmatic mailman about a mile from here. I say, good luck to her."

Sylvia looks at the clumps of cat hair covering the plaid wool sofa and sinks into the matching rocking chair. The television is on but the volume is turned down and she sees the Reverend Garland Boetell hopping around a red-carpeted stage in a huge auditorium, waving a Bible and thrusting his microphone around like a stiletto.

Mrs. Acker sees her watching and says, "Isn't he just wonderful?"

"You're a fan?"

"Sylvia, we need a man like the Reverend. We need him desperately."

Sylvia nods agreement and looks back to the TV.

"The Reverend is here in Quinsigamond—" she starts.

"I know," Mrs. A says. "Isn't it exciting?"

Sylvia motions to the television and asks, "Is this a tape?"

Mrs. A raises her penciled-in eyebrows and steps over to a cherry bookcase filled to capacity with books and video-tapes. She puts a hand on top of the case like some bizarre display model and says, "I've got the entire library. Three hundred and sixty-five hours of wisdom. And all the books."

She pulls out a volume and shows the dust jacket. The title is *Tear Out the Offending Eye* and the cover art is appropriately graphic.

"The books are divinely inspired, you know."

"Is that right?" Sylvia says. She can smell cinnamon coming from the kitchen.

"He just sits down and turns off the business of his brain and the words flood into him. That's what he says. They just flood in."

Mrs. A sits down on the edge of the couch and a cat pops

its head out from underneath the fringe and starts to mewl around her ankle. She picks up the cat absentmindedly, puts it in her lap and starts to stroke it. "I've never been a particularly religious individual, Sylvia. But this isn't just about religion. This is about cleaning up. This is about restoring things to the way they should be. We've drifted, Sylvia."

"I guess so," Sylvia says and stares at the cat as its tongue comes out and swipes around its mouth.

"And the time is short," Mrs. A says. "The time is dwindling. It's upon us. The prophecies are all there, plain as day for anyone who'd take the time to look."

The coffee table in front of them is blanketed with crumpled envelopes, manila folders, coffee mugs, a pair of scissors, and a pamphlet with the words *Revelation Can Be Yours* on the front flap.

"You mentioned a favor," Sylvia says, pushing her wet hair behind her ears.

"When your Perry told me he was working with the Reverend, well you can imagine, I just about died. When he told me the man himself was in your living room the other night, I could barely contain myself. It's as if it were destined, don't you think?"

"That's how it seems."

"Perry's told me about the important work they're doing. How our city is going to be the springboard. They talk like such crusaders. Such passion. *Springboard.* Don't you just love it?"

Sylvia's head fills with a picture of a naked Perry and a naked Candice bouncing into the air off a monstrously high diving board. Intertwining during their free fall.

"You have to love it," she says.

"But this morning I saw the forms required a witness—"

"The forms?"

Mrs. Acker nods and leans forward, pulls up one of the manila folders and hands it across the table. Sylvia opens it and reads *Last Will and Testament of Roberta J. Acker*. She looks up and Mrs. Acker is holding a pen out.

"You're leaving all your money to Reverend Boetell?"

Mrs. A smiles and nods, proud and determined. "And the house. And all the rental properties and Louie's antique coins and the greyhound I keep down in Rhode Island, though to be honest, Sylvia, I think his best days are over."

It takes Sylvia a second to realize Mrs. A means the greyhound.

"Don't get me wrong. It doesn't all go to the Reverend personally. It goes to Millennial Ministries Corporation of Macon, Georgia. And there is a small clause for the cats."

"The cats?"

"Perry's assured me they'll be taken care of."

"I'm sure."

Sylvia starts to read through the first paragraph of the will and stops and says, "I can't witness this, Mrs. Acker."

Mrs. A looks confused.

"What's the problem, dear?"

"It's just," Sylvia stammers, "I can't—"

But Mrs. A suddenly ignores her and lunges for the remote control to the TV and the cat leaps over the coffee table and disappears in the direction of the kitchen.

"I just love this part," Mrs. A says, focusing in on the screen, and Sylvia turns to see the Reverend in a brown suit that looks a little like cowskin. The man is furious, worked into a lather that puts his art museum spiel to shame.

The volume on the set comes up and the Reverend's eyes roll back in his head and he slaps a hand on his forehead and falls to his knees, brings his microphone up until it touches his mouth and gets assaulted with spittle. It's as if he's launching into a seizure that will require long-term medical care. His whole body starts to buck like a rodeo rider on a ghost-bull.

"I saw a vision," he screams, in a roar so intense it appears likely he'll rupture blood vessels. "I saw a vision of the coming rapture. I saw the future of the coming war when blood will engulf this wretched planet. And I heard the voice of the Holy One calling down to me, calling down with the mission I could not refuse, calling down, *dauuoown* upon my pitiful human ears. And he said the battle is now upon us, my miserable servant. The battle is here and the time is now. And he says unto me the *tha*-rone of Satan rises in the east. The time of the tribulation screams down to our feet and none can escape the *ravagement* of these horrors. And I saw the son of *may-ann* with seven stars in his right hand and the key of David in his left hand and a *raayzor*-sharp two-edge sword issuing from his mouth. And his face was like the sun shining in full inferno. And I looked upon that face of the Master, seated there in the golden throne, and he showed me the scroll and the seven seals and said, it must be you, Garland, it must be you and you alone who will break open these seals and prepare my people for the coming Armageddon . . ."

Sylvia closes the manila folder and puts it back on the coffee table, but Mrs. Acker doesn't seem to notice. She's fingering the remote control box like prayer beads and Sylvia gets up and leaves the apartment without another word.

Down in the darkroom, she mounts the step stool and makes herself look at the seven pictures.

And all the surety of last night is gone.

There's nothing in these images to suggest that this woman was Sylvia's mother. That Sylvia is the infant in her arms. That a man named Terrence Propp took the shots. Or that the man named Terrence Propp is Sylvia's father.

Playing the idea back now, like this, it sounds ludicrous to her. The kind of thing you can only conceive of at the height of your most outrageous drunk. The kind of thing that in a day's time and sober, you can't imagine having considered.

She imposed that meaning on these photographs. She took the essence of these seven images and imbued them with a need completely specific to her, and yet one that, until now, she's not sure she knew existed.

And if she can do that with random pictures, chance images that happened to come into her possession, she has to wonder what else, what other artifacts, what other identical and meaning-free *objects* she commonly acts on. What other haphazard items does she mindlessly change into something she wants or needs them to be?

The first answer is *Perry.*

And then everything else lines up behind

The Berkshires nightgown.

The Snapshot Shack.

Old movies.

The last answer is *Memories of my mother.*

Last, not because she's exhausted the subject, but because she sees there might be no end at all.

What she needed was for Rita Hayworth to look out from the screen just once, just one time during the tenure on mother's couch, during the Lost Months, the zombie-time. She needed Rita H to turn away from her on-screen co-star and peer into Ma's dim living room and take the cigarette from her lips and say, "The world does not revolve around you, Sylvia."

She takes the snapshots of Perry and Candice from the pocket of the robe. She gets off the stool and walks to the dry-line and pins one color snapshot over each of the Madonna and Child shots. She moves back to the stool and sits down and looks. There's no reaction, chemical or otherwise. No interaction between the two series. Nothing that will give up an answer, a way to act or react.

So, what to do? Confront Perry? Wait for him to come home, be sitting maybe in the living room, silent and coiled the way he was the day of the Skin Palace riot. She could glue the pictures to the TV screen until the whole tube was covered, stay frozen as he walked in loosening his tie, wait until he noticed the new station she's found on the cable band. The infidelity collage network.

Or maybe she could get dressed right now and go down to Walpole & Lewis, march past the receptionist's warning that Mr. Leroux is in an important meeting, throw open the doors on the conference room where Reverend Boetell and the FUD-heads are huddled down with Perry and Candice trying to decide how to rid the world of Hugo Schick and all things lewd and lascivious. She could throw the pictures on their fat walnut table, watch Boetell's face go white and red, see Candice run for the partners' washroom, feel the vibrations of Perry's future crashing and burning around him.

But if she really doesn't love Perry, these photos shouldn't mean much beyond hurt pride and embarrassment. And if that's true then the only motivation for attacking him with the pictures is vengefulness.

Still: three feet in front of her is a photograph, the last photograph in the series, of her lover, the man she's lived with these past two years, the man who supposedly wants to marry her and buy a house together and have kids together. And he's naked, in their bed upstairs, having sex with someone other than Sylvia, with a woman he very likely finds more attractive.

Sylvia wants Rita Hayworth to appear out of the blackness of the darkroom's corner, done up in that dress from *Gilda*. Wants her to step in front of the dry-line and say, "This *is* a place for vengefulness, Sylvia."

But Rita, all of this is taking me away from the more important questions.

Hugo Schick called on the phone to say that the pictures existed. Schick's biggest enemy is Reverend Garland Boetell. And Boetell's point man, his newest tool, his latest creature, is Perry Leroux.

Hugo and Sylvia need to have a talk.

30

Back upstairs Sylvia unplugs the phone, lies down on the couch, relieved the sky is overcast, turns the TV to the Peter Lorre Festival and watches *They Met in Bombay* and *Invisible Agent,* then dozes off halfway through *Hotel Berlin.*

At seven-thirty she gets up and it's dark outside and she's still alone in the apartment. She goes into the bathroom and throws water on her face and pulls her hair back. She puts on jeans, a pair of ankle boots and a sweater. She grabs the Canon off the counter and a new roll of film from the fridge, then pulls a very old yellow rain slicker from the hall closet.

She heads outside just as the Wolcott Street bus pulls up. It's one of the ancient, small and boxy, green-and-red buses with the porthole-style windows and the antiquated exhaust system that belches black clouds every time the driver accelerates.

She gets on, drops the change in the fare box and moves all the way to the rear bench seat. The driver grinds gears and they start to roll downtown. She takes the Canon out from under the slicker, loads the film and sets the speed, brings the camera up to her eye. She starts to focus on the framed advertising placards hung near the bus ceiling. She shoots

Attention Lonely Bachelors
Why go it alone?
We have a wide selection of mail order brides

She moves her focus from the advertisements to the spray-painted graffiti and street art marking every free foot of wall space. And it starts to feel like she's being overloaded, attacked by images, messages, signals, until none of them make any sense and she pulls the camera from her face, closes her eyes and rubs at them. She takes a breath, brings the camera back up, but this time focuses on the backs of human heads. She wonders if the other riders can feel her looking at them, magnifying the rear of their skulls, pulling in the wet, slightly matted hair, enlarging the flecks of dandruff, the patches of scalp that show through the thinning spots.

She puts the camera down in her lap and looks out the window. The rain has obscured everything and as the bus starts to approach the business district, the colored lights from neon signs are fragmented across the windowpane, made to sparkle more, to flare out and pinwheel a bit.

When Sylvia looks back to the other passengers, she comes eye to eye with an old woman who's turned around and is staring at her. The woman is bundled inside a tan raincoat with the collar turned up. Sylvia smiles at her but the old lady just gives this dour, threatening look, then reaches and pulls on the stop-cord and the bus lurches into the curb to let her off.

Sylvia looks out the rear window and finds the woman still staring, standing motionless in the rain, hands pushed into the pockets of her raincoat, waiting for the bus to pull away.

When Sylvia turns back around to face front, three other riders are perched sideways in their seats looking at her. All of their faces have a kind of beaten quality to them. One is gaunt and bony, another puffy, and another bland, nondescript. But all of them seem tired and angry and most of all, worn-out, as if energy has been chronically stolen from them in small doses but over a long period of time.

She looks out the window, watches a black limousine pass on the left, looks back a second later. More faces have joined the trio. They all look malign, like they wish her harm, but they're too listless to actually attack. And yet it's as if their bad intentions were adequate, as if their sluggish malevolence was enough to bring her down and cause her trouble.

"What?" Sylvia blurts out, loud and annoyed and scared. She focuses on one young guy in a leather jacket and bristly flattop and matching ear and nose rings connected by a silver chain. They stare at each other until he lets a horrible grin break slowly over his face.

Sylvia pulls on the stop-cord and there's a frantic moment when she wonders if the driver will let her leave, but the bus cuts in to the curb and she grabs the camera tight and slides from the back bench, runs down the aisle as all the other passengers start to laugh in unison. She jumps to the curb as soon as the doors spring open.

She stands for a minute and catches her breath, then
wipes the rain from her face. She's on Maddox, just a couple of blocks from the Canal Zone. She starts walking
quickly toward Rimbaud Way, rounds the corner and starts
running for the Rib Room Diner. The windows are all
steamed up ad the *Open* sign is glowing in the door.

She goes in, finds a booth midway down the aisle, slides
in, her back to the door, pulls the zipper down on the
slicker and dries her hands on her jeans. Tacked to the wall
of the booth is another *Jenny Ellis* flyer and the huge, black
letters that form the question *Have You Seen This Child?*
feel like they're demanding an answer from Sylvia. She
looks away from the poster, puts the camera on the table
and an old guy with an unruly mane of white hair bounces
up to the booth with a coffeepot in one hand and a mug in
the other. And Sylvia knows from all the photos in the *Spy*
over the years that it's Elmore Orsi himself, owner of the
Rib Room and legend of the Canal Zone.

"You look," he says, filling the mug and sliding it in
front of her, "like you need a mug."

She nods and says, " Thank you," and he smiles and
lingers. Part of the Orsi legend is that Elmore, now in his
mid-seventies by most estimates, still has a weak spot for
the young boho women who hang around the diner.

Sylvia sips the coffee and says, "Delicious."

He's pleased. "Hazlenut mocha," he says. "Pain in the
tush to get, but, you know, anything to keep my children
happy."

She knows that Orsi is thought of as this eccentric god-
father to the art crowd and she wonders how much of his
oddball shtick is genuine and how much is made up. He's
a vision here in front of her, done up in pleated white wool
pants, black silk shirt opened wide to reveal a forest of
chest hair and a fat, gold crucifix dangling by a chain
around his neck, and red paisley vest.

Maybe because she can't judge the artifice factor, she's got no impulse to photograph him.

"You're Mr. Orsi," she says and he takes this as an opportunity to slide into the seat opposite her.

"In the flesh," he says. "And you are *not* a regular. New to town?"

She shakes her head. "I've lived in Quinsigamond my whole life."

"That's wonderful. A real native. That's tremendous."

"Is it?"

He sits back jerks his head to the rest of the booths on the other side of the aisle. "All the natives want to leave these days. Everyone wants to move away."

"Not you."

"They're going to bury me in this town. I want the wake right here in the diner. Two days. Open bar. I know it's a big health code violation, but I'm an old friend of Counselor Campana. There are ways around everything, if you follow."

Sylvia nods her unspoken understanding of the not-so-subtle back-scratching that powers City Hall.

"You've been down here in the Canal a long time," she says.

"Opened the doors on September fifth, Nineteen fifty-seven. I was a goddamn youngster."

"You've seen a lot of people pass through this place."

"The famous and the not-so," Orsi says, thrilled at the chance to bask in his own history.

"I'm more interested in the famous."

"Another pilgrim," he says. "I'm telling you, I'm waiting to be put on the historical register there. That has to be some kind of tax break, wouldn't you think?"

She takes a swallow of coffee, then asks, "I've heard you knew Terrence Propp."

There's no flinch or balk. There's no reaction at all and that's as unsettling as if he'd exploded. He just shakes his head and says, "That's an old rumor that just won't die gracefully, dear. Every now and then somebody comes in here and mentions that name to me. And I'll tell you what I tell them. I don't even know who the hell this Propp son of a bitch is."

"I heard you once claimed you knew him."

Again, no anger, only, "Honey, I'll say anything to fill this place up. I'll tell you Jesus ate the last supper in here if it'll sell more meatloaf and coffee."

"But if someone really needed some information—" she starts and he shakes his head and says, "Then someone would be out of luck. Personally, I don't even think there is a Terrence Propp. I think it's all a kind of hoax. Another way to push some product. Nothing gets more attention. *How could someone not want attention?* Twenty-four hours a day we got people sticking their faces into your television and telling you more horrible crap about their lives than you ever wanted to hear. I wish I'd come up with something like this Propp idea—*the Myth of Elmore Orsi.* Christ sake, they'd be lined up down the block to eat the leftover chili. Put some faded picture of me on the wall, I could spend every day at the goddamn track."

He laughs, runs both hands over his eyes, then refills her mug.

"You seem like a nice girl," he says, somehow without sounding patronizing. "Don't buy into this Propp nonsense. Find your own routine."

He slides out of the booth.

"Routine?" Sylvia says, but Orsi just smiles at her and heads toward the kitchen yelling into the air, "Renata, clear table six."

Sylvia looks up at the clock on the back wall. It's over three hours until midnight and her meeting with Schick. She thinks about going to a movie and then catches herself and wants to laugh. Her eyes fall from the clock down to the huge cork bulletin board that fills most of the back wall. The bulletin board where she found the original ad for the Aquinas. The place where all of this began.

She gets out of the booth and walks to the rear wall. She finds the exact spot where she'd first seen the little 3 x 5 card filled with the black block letters that said PORTRAIT CAMERA. Where she'd yanked out the red pushpin that secured the card to the cork and where she'd felt that rush of delight as she pictured an Aquinas in her hands.

In that same place now is a new index card, but this is a glossy printed ad, like an oversized business card, with raised, multicolored lettering that reads

Lusty Lady Lipservice
"fulfillment is just a phone call away"
picture your dream woman & we do the rest
Call: 555-6628 / 24 hrs a day / 7 days a week
MC/Visa/AmEx

She rips the card from the board, turns it over, turns it back. It's her own phone number.

She pushes the card into the pocket of her slicker and walks out of the Rib Room.

The rain has faded to an occasional mist and Rimbaud Way has filled up with marching women. They're all wearing black armbands and chanting as they parade.

Intercourse is Genocide
Castrate, Castrate
Cut with Pride

their arms shooting into the air like angry cheerleaders. They're being led by Paige Beatty, who's setting the pace of their cry with her red police bullhorn.

An arm reaches out and pulls Sylvia off the curbing and into the throng and the next thing she knows a woman with a hook for a hand is linking arms and yelling, "It's every-one's fight."

Sylvia looks to see a hefty woman with a baby sup-ported against her other shoulder. The child might be about a year old and it's burrowing into its mother's neck, clearly more interested in sleep than political ideology.

Sylvia walks along, though she doesn't chant. She cranes her neck to see everyone carrying white candles shaped like small phalluses. And they all have a small chalkboard, about the size of a dinner plate, bouncing off their chests as they walk, hung around their necks with twine and shoestrings. The boards all have male first names written on them—Sylvia notes *Harold* and *Dennis* and *Karl* and *Antonio.*

She asks the one-handed woman what the story is and her new partner shouts, "Didn't you get yours? You write down the name of the last bastard that abused you."

What if he was anonymous, Sylvia wonders. *What if he was a phantom?*

They swing off Rimbaud and onto Main Street and there's a group cheer at the sight of the City Hall Tower. Through the bullhorn, Paige yells, "Tell Mary and Martha to go check on the sheets," and two women in matching sweat suits break off from the assembly and start to sprint down the middle of Main.

"What sheets?" Sylvia yells and the hook-handed mother gives her an annoyed look and yells back, "Didn't you go to any of the planning sessions?

Up ahead, cars are being detoured out of the way by a cop with a flashlight. Clearly, Mayor Welby and Manager Kenner know how politically hot this thing could turn and they want as little confrontation as possible. Let Paige and Company vent some steam and if it means rerouting a lit-tle night traffic down Main Street, so be it.

The marchers pass unmolested down the center of the road though there are some comments about *dyke bitches* yelled from the doorways of the greasier bars. When they're almost on top of City Hall, Sylvia is shocked to see the building totally surrounded by even more women. They're spilling off the front steps, overflowing on the common and the side pavilion. The halogen spotlights that normally shine down from the Hall's tower have apparently been knocked out and this sea of bodies is lit only by the hundreds of candles that everyone's holding aloft. It gives the whole scene a weird, semi-religious feel and a church-like hush falls over the crowd as Paige leads her platoon through a parting of massed spectators who simply roll back like the Red Sea and clear a path to the front stairway.

Paige climbs the stairs like some cross between a military president and a pope, someone who's moved beyond the boundaries of ego and power and into a realm where the forces of history can be wrestled with and occasionally altered. In Sylvia's small living room Paige gave off none of this larger-than-life quality. She seemed like a smart pragmatist, a savvy deal cutter who'd rely on lawyers and opinion polls. But here, mounting the steps of City Hall with bullhorn in one hand and flickering, penis-shaped candle in the other, she's transformed into an icon, a definition of charisma and strength so vibrant it feels as if she could liberate every soul in earshot with the sound of her voice.

She takes her central position at the rail of the balcony that leads to the building's main entrance. Two lieutenants take their places to the right and left of her. They unhitch a banner that drapes over the rail and reveals the night's motto—*Intercourse Is Genocide*—written in red paint. Paige lets the quiet permeate the midst of this swollen mob, lets its meaning become palpable and fix the depth of her command. She turns her head from side to side, then lifts her candle into the air, to the full extension of her left arm.

Through the bullhorn, she yells, "The purge has begun," and the crowd goes insane for the next few minutes, making it impossible for Paige to continue speaking.

The one-handed mother and Sylvia move up onto a knoll of grass that slopes down from the First Apostle Bank building, Sylvia watches the baby, almost a toddler and of indeterminate sex, shift its head on the mother's chest. It's a pudgy, sallow-faced child and even in this dim light smudges of crusted food can be seen on its cheeks, maybe some form of carrots or squash.

"Tonight," Paige announces from the balcony, re-demanding that attention of the crowd, "is the Night of Short Candles. And it will be remembered for years to come as the first strike in the battle that will free us forever. In a few hours, sisters, we are going to cut down their balls."

Sylvia looks up at Paige Beatty, then around at the crowd. She listens to the escalation of the leader's rage and feels the way it's palpably spreading among the faithful. She turns to the mother and says, "That's pretty extreme stuff."

The new friend is ready for the comment.

"Paige says people are sheep. You've got to hit them over the head. You've got to be extreme. You've got to be visceral. Go for the throat. You have to make them see behind the screens. Make them understand all the signs and signals being pumped out as part of the war against us. All this common junk, you know, from *Playboy* to the beer ads, it's even more insidious by its subtlety."

"Beer ads are porn?" Sylvia asks.

The mother gives a look like she's not sure why Sylvia's here, like Sylvia might be something worse than the sheep. Something like the wolf's collaborator. And Sylvia wants to tell her, this stranger with a metal claw at the end of her arm and a shivering child sleeping at her neck, that she's nobody's collaborator. That she's a free agent. That she's so free she's dizzy with the isolation.

A new wave of explosive cheering sounds and it becomes clear that if Paige wants to get through the speech she's going to have to tone down the inflammatory rhetoric.

"No one can fight for us," Paige's voice booms, hoarse

with the intensity of both her rage and her empathy. "We unite. And we fight. Or we die. Because make no mistake, don't let yourselves be deceived ever again, *they are our enemy,*" spitting out these four words loudly and slowly.

Sylvia leans into the ear of the mother and asks, "What's the baby's name?"

The woman turns and gives a surprised and maybe angry look, then says, "Maria."

"They answer," Paige screams, *"we are your fathers, your sons, your brothers, and husbands.* But no fact of relation can change the nature of the beast. And on that day the species enters puberty, the switch is thrown that regresses the boy back to the swamp at the dawn of time when the code of aggression was imprinted on his animal heart."

"How old?" Sylvia asks Maria's mother.

This time she says, "I'm trying to listen to this."

"See the beast for what he is," from the bullhorn. "He is our oppressor. He is the savage who would enslave our bodies, destroy our minds, and obliterate our spirits. He of the *Y* chromosome. He of the testosterone depravity."

Sylvia stares at the child. She tries to picture, if Perry and she had a child, what would it look like. She can't do it. She can't produce the image.

All she can hear are the amplified words that seem to assault the air around her head.

"The exploitive, objectifying demon. The primal brain that escaped evolution and now strives always to dominate, to victimize, to abuse into submission, to erase our very presence. This is his Final Solution. This is his death camp. The images he makes us into are his ovens. And we will not, we can not, walk into those ovens peacefully. I am calling for an absolute separatism. And I am calling for a holy war. We must rage. We must fight. We must battle with everything we have inside us. There can be no truce. There can be no compromise. We must rise and we must triumph."

The crowd hits its climax and comes together in an

evangelical hysteria. And then Sylvia's being hugged by her hook-sister. After a minute they step back, out of the embrace, and Sylvia sees the water off her slicker has partly obscured the name on the chalkboard. It must have been something like *Benny* or *Barry*. Sylvia reaches out and touches the chalkboard and says, "Did he do that? To your hand?"

The woman nods and shrugs at the same time and says, "Sort of. It's a long story."

Sylvia gestures to the *Intercourse Is Genocide* banner and asks, "Do you believe that?"

The woman gives an earnest nod.

"You don't think sex can ever be okay?"

The woman stares at her for a second, smiles and says, "Not with a man."

Sylvia nods because she doesn't know what else to say and they both turn their attention back to the balcony as Paige Beatty relights the head of her candle with a pocket butane, brings up the bullhorn one more time and says, "Now let's burn down their filthy constitution and let the flames ignite our war."

31

The train lot behind Gompers Station looks like a ridiculously gritty set from something filmed in a ruined city near the end of a particularly vicious war. Gompers itself seems unreal, this crumbling, graffiti-obscured hulk of broken white marble, toppled Ionic columns, charred rosewood, and thousands of splinters of stained glass that once, combined, depicted an idealized tour of the industrial age.

It's almost as if the ruined building was really just a one-dimensional fronting propped up by plywood struts, or maybe worse, an intricately detailed matte painting that could be broken through by a speeding car or a rain of bullets.

The only lighting comes from the moon and the red bug-eye spots near the junction of two freight lines. The ground is a brittle carpet of cinder and ash and gravel. And the temperature has dropped, triggering Jakob's asthma and causing wisps of steam to gust from his mouth with each struggling exhale.

He tries to ignore his lungs, huddles inside the boxcar and looks down on his notebook.

EXT. LOWENSTEIN ROAD -NIGHT

The Doomed Man emerges from an alley in a stumbling lope. Stops to steady himself in front of LASZLO'S CAFÉ. Falls to one knee. Places hand against storefront window. Looks in window at display shelf to see fresh-baked rolls. Looks from rolls to his own vague reflection.

EXT. LASZLO'S CAFÉ

Focus change to show a customer within the café notice the Doomed Man framed in window. Attention of all patrons turns to the window. Slow zoom through window to WAITRESS who lifts head from order pad. widens eyes, lifts arm, points finger and mouths words, "It's *him*," though we can't hear her.

TIGHT SHOT -FACE OF DOOMED MAN

realizing he's been spotted.

WIDE SHOT -EXT. LOWENSTEIN ROAD

Doomed Man turns and begins a pathetic, limping run down narrow, curving Lowenstein. Waitress emerges from door of Lazslo's, runs into middle of street.

> WAITRESS
> (cupping hands to mouth, yelling)
> It's the killer. The killer is here.

Doors open up and down Lowenstein. PEOPLE emerge pulling on coats. Confusion as they all approach waitress at once. Slowly they begin to form into an ANGRY MOB. Din of cries and curses fills the air. Mob overturns trash cans. Arms itself with rocks, broken bottles, iron bars, baseball bats. Whistles are heard. Barking dogs are heard. Police sirens are heard in the distance. Mob begins pursuit.

EXT. THE TENDERLOIN

The Doomed Man hears the commotion behind him. Dashes from street lamp to mailbox to doorway, bumping into and off of drunks and seedy thugs who populate the area. Doomed Man emerges to an open square where there is no place to hide.

TIGHT SHOT -FACE OF DOOMED MAN

as he turns and sees the bulk shadow of the mob moving forward through the tenderloin. Panicking, blinking eyes. Blood, seeping from forehead, obscuring vision.

CRANE SHOT -EXT. OPEN SQUARE -LIT BY HARSH HALOGEN SPOT

The Doomed Man turns around and looks across the square toward the Train Station, where he began this odyssey. He runs toward the Station, falls on his face in middle of square. Sound of the angry mob increases. Doomed Man gets to his feet and desperately runs to the train yard.

"Cuz."

Jakob looks up, unsurprised, unruffled, and smiles.

Felix leans his elbows onto the lip of the car, peers inside.

"We've been worried sick about you," Felix says. "What the hell are you doing out here?"

Jakob closes his notebook. He cradles the Seitz and climbs outside to see all of the Grey Roaches waiting for him.

"I couldn't visualize a scene," he says, "I had to come out here. Look at it again. Up close."

Felix smiles and shakes his head, throws an arm around his cousin's shoulder. "The things you do for your art, huh?"

"What are you doing here?" Jakob asks, staring across the yard at Huck Hrabal who flinches and looks to the ground.

Felix turns to Jakob so they face each other, then he begins to brush down Jakob's lapels like some compulsive valet.

"Well," he says. "It was supposed to be a surprise. Huck had an idea where we might find you. We wanted to have a little party back at St. Vitus—"

"A surprise?"

Felix takes a deep breath, shrugs his shoulders a bit.

"I've talked to your father, Jakob. And it's clear to both of us. Finally. Our way just isn't your way, cuz. You're an artist. You can't help yourself. We've all seen the light. Gustav has even found a way to funnel income to underwrite your career. You are in business, cuz. You can make your movie. And we've got a present for you."

Jakob looks over Felix's shoulder at Vera Gottwald who gives nothing away.

"It's good you brought your movie camera," Felix says. "We should record it all from the start. Some day the archivists will want to look back at everything. Hugo Schick is meeting us here. He'll be turning over the deed to the Skin Palace. To you, Jakob. It's yours from this night on, cousin. Your own studio. Your own stable of actors. Your own crew. Your own theatre. The whole thing is yours."

"But Papa—"

"Your father is a very wise man, Jakob. In the end, he always knows what's best."

The cousins stare at each other, the space between their faces filled with the white clouds of their breath. There's a minute of silence until Felix says, "You don't look very happy, Jakob. This is what you've always wanted. I thought you'd be delirious."

Jakob stares down at the ground, at the crumpled remains of dozens of *Jenny Ellis* posters.

"It's just . . ." he begins and breaks off.

Then starts again, "It will be awkward. Mr. Schick has been very good to me."

"Well," Felix says, shaking his head, tossing his arms out to the side and making a hand signal that the Roaches note and act on, spreading into a circle around the two Kinskys, "everyone has been good to you, Jakob. Haven't they?"

Jakob lifts his camera to his shoulder, pans across the faces of the Roaches and says, "We've all been fortunate, Felix. America has been very kind to our family."

Felix squats down and starts to trace something in the ash with his finger.

"Still," he says, "I lost both my parents in the July Sweep."

Jakob moves the camera to Felix's face, zooms in.

"I know that. And I'm sorry about it every day."

Felix smiles for the camera.

"Yeah, well, like that prayer says, *life's a bitch—*"

"*And then you die,*" Jakob finishes for him. He pans to the left and sees Vera Gottwald take a section of rubber hose from an inside fold of her suitcoat. He turns slowly, keeping the Seitz running. He does an even 360, frames each Roach extracting saps and blackjacks and brass knuckles from their clothing.

"It looks like Mr. Schick is going to be late for our meeting," Jakob says.

Felix lets out a laugh.

"A putz to the end, eh cuz?"

"Mr. Schick isn't coming, is he Felix?"

"No, Jakob, I'm afraid Schick won't be joining us tonight."

"This is suicide, Felix."

"Put the camera down, Jakob."

"You are out of you mind. Do you have any idea what Papa will do to you? There's no way you can pin this on one of the other gangs."

"Put the goddamn camera down."

Jakob refuses. He keeps the Seitz filming and comes back to a closeup of his cousin, who's now holding a long-barrel revolver straight out, pointed at the camera.

"All right," Felix says, "have it your way. Film the whole thing. Your first and last feature, you stupid little son of a bitch."

"Please," Jakob says, "put your gun away."

Felix jerks the pistol into the air and pulls the trigger. A shot explodes, echoes across the train yard, fills the air with a trace of burnt powder.

"It's not a prop, dickhead. It's the real goddamn thing. It's a beauty, isn't it? And there's a bullet in every chamber. You know who gave me the gun, Jakob? Uncle Hermann. Your goddamn Papa who's coddled your wheezing ass since the day we hit this city. You know where it came from, Jakob? Any idea? Huh?"

Jakob stays silent.

"It belonged to the commandant who murdered my mother and father. A man named Teige. One of the great zealots of the July Sweep. Before we left Maisel, Uncle Hermann paid more money than you can imagine to get next to Teige. Then he took out his Schonborn and strangled the bastard, came close to taking the man's head off his shoulders. Literally separating the head. He told me he's never pulled that hard in his life. He hit bone, Jakob. Can you imagine what that feels like, cousin? To pull wire through the skin, through the cartilage and the arteries?

"Uncle Hermann gave me the commandant's gun, Jakob. He gave you your camera there. Belonged to some great director, right? He gave me the pistol that killed my mother and father."

"Felix," Jakob says, "should you hurt me in any way, Papa will manage to bury your head a block away from your body."

"You idiot," Felix's voice dropping low. "Can you imagine how you've disappointed him? I told you the video store was your last chance. I tried to help you. You were in there *talking* to that freak. You were inside talking about *movies*. My God. You should have seen Hermann's face when I told him."

"Felix, I'm begging you . . ."

The Seitz catches Hunk Hrabal, in fuzzy back-focus, taking a step up behind Felix.

Felix levels the gun back at Jakob and says, "I promise we'll bury you with the camera, cousin."

Jakob pulls out to a medium shot and watches Hrabal bring a truncheon down on Felix's arm as the pistol explodes again, this time planting the bullet in the ground. The arm snaps. A quick zoom to show the shock spreading across the cousin's face. Huck throws a kidney punch and Felix crumbles to his knees. Vera Gottwald comes forward, picks up the pistol and carries it to Jakob who puts it in his pocket. The Roaches yank Felix back to his feet. He starts to struggle and Huck saps him in the back of the head.

Jakob detaches a shoulder strap from the camera and tosses it to Huck, then he turns the Seitz over to Vera, saying, "Remember, just keep the red button pressed."

He walks toward his cousin, extends his arms out at his sides, smiles and says to the whole congregation, "I'm as bad as Hitchcock. I promise this will be my only cameo."

He comes face-to-cafe with Felix, stares into the incredulous eyes, bites back the pity and slaps his cousin across the face, drawing blood that steams in the cold air.

"But how—" is all Felix can manage.

"It's not your fault," Jakob says. "It's vanity and greed. It will always blind you in the end. Your problem is you haven't seen enough movies."

He nods to Huck Hrabal and the Roaches force their former leader to his knees, then Hrabal fashions the shoulder strap into a kind of collar and twists it around his deposed boss's throat.

"I spoke with Huck yesterday," Jakob says. "I explained to him that it made much more sense to back Hermann Kinsky's only son rather than his idiot nephew. And, of course, I've promised all the Roaches walk-ons in the film and small gross participation. They'll each get half a point of the distribution deal. We win some prizes at the Sundance Festival, these guys can buy some new suits."

Out of the corner of his eye, Jakob sees the Roaches all smiling at one another.

"Huck is to be my screen face, Felix. Do you approve? I think he'll make a fine alter ego. All the true auteurs need one, you realize. Ford had Wayne. Fellini had Mastroianni. Scorsese had De Niro. Lynch—"

"Jakob," Felix yells, licking frantically at his wound. He's scrambling, dizzy with the reversal. He stammers, "Don't do this, please, think of the film. This climax, beaten to death by the angry mob, it's derivative."

Jakob laughs, pats his cousin's cheek, looks around to the Roaches.

"Didn't I tell you, people? Everyone's a critic."

He turns back to his cousin.

"You're a lowbrow schmuck, Felix. I'm a postmodern artist. I know all the images and I steal from the pool. It's all collage, cuz. Juxtaposition. Besides, if all else fails, the snuff market is making a big comeback these days."

Jakob leans down and kisses Felix softly on the cheek, whispers in his ear, "You know, I was going to play this part myself. But I'm glad I reconsidered. You're so much better in the role."

He straightens and turns to Huck.

"Now remember people, we'll only get one take here. We've got to make it work the first time. He's the anti-hero at the end of the road. I'm going for tight close-ups here, so don't anyone block the face. I need to see the real terror as his fate dawns upon him."

He steps back, frames Felix's head between his hands and whispers, "You look absolutely doomed, Felix. You're such a natural."

Then he claps the hands together, turns to Vera Gottwald, nods and yells, "Annnnd. Action."

TIGHT SHOT -HEAD OF THE DOOMED MAN

as it turns side to side, struggling futilely against the garrote, the eyes beginning to bulge, a gurgling noise beginning to emit from the tortured hole that is the mouth.

MED SHOT -THE TRAIN YARD

as the leader of the angry villagers, the self-appointed AUTEURCUTIONER, pulls a pistol from his pocket and erupts in a horrible laugh that echoes across the landscape.

Several villagers shudder. The Doomed Man begins to convulse but is held on his knees by the hands of the crowd.

TIGHT SHOT -THE HAND OF THE AUTEURCUTIONER -SLOW MOTION

as it lifts the pistol through the smokey night air and brings the barrel to rest against the bulging right eye of the Doomed Man. Intercut the various sound tracks—the diseased lung, the July Sweep sirens, the cries of the little girl lost—all played at half-speed.

TIGHTEST SHOT -EYES OF THE DOOMED MAN - SLOW MOTION

as the auteurcutioner pulls the trigger and a bullet discharges from the pistol barrel and tears into the eyeball, through the cornea, through the anterior chamber, the lens, through the jellylike lake of vitreous humor, tearing through the retina and the sclera, and finally exploding the optic nerve itself. The end of vision. The obliteration of perception.

BLACK SCREEN

NO CREDITS

32

Sylvia walks through the drizzle with this vague, semiconscious understanding that she's heading, eventually, toward the Skin Palace. And she tries not to focus on the fact that the walk holds at least some resemblance to the way she's come to live her life, to the way she perpetually pivots and drifts once she has a glimpse of her general direction. No matter what that direction might be.

For over twenty years, since memories began, since she developed whatever neurons or language skills image-storing capacity necessary for remembrance, she's let events wash over her, take her and turn her. And then in the calm after the wake, she's always accepted her new position. She's continued to move, with a little thought, in whatever direction she ended up facing. As if there was never another choice. As if she's suffered a forgotten virus at one time, maybe in infancy, that destroyed any idea of free will.

She drifted into the movies and took up residence there. She drifted into photography and gave herself away. She drifted into numbness upon the death of her mother and let it take her. She drifted into the banality of the Snapshot Shack and let it cover her. And she drifted into Perry and surrendered without question or thought. Because in each case it was easier than fighting a current. It was easier to ride out forces that she *knew* would be stronger than her own small desires.

Like now, just like now, like this moment, when it's so much easier to accept that it's fated, that she'll go to Hugo Schick, that she'll eventually walk all the way to Herzog's Erotic Palace, to this monument to multiple illusions, this church of light and shadow and manipulation that Hugo has filled with dozens of entwined naked bodies, moaning and writhing for the sake of an imagined masterpiece. She'll stand in the middle of the pretentious, choreographed orgy, totally distant from even the *idea* of all the fabricated connections, of the endless daisy chains of coupling taking place on the floor below her feet. She'll stand alone in the middle of one more crowd, one more gathering of interconnected people, and like a child, like a powerless toddler, without rights or skills, she'll ask Schick why she's there. She'll ask why the events of this week have taken place, what knowledge she's supposed to gain from all that's happened.

She'll go to the Skin Palace, to Hugo Schick, to the filming of *Don Juan Triumphant,* knowing there will be no real answers. Just another turning of the tide. Because movement feels better than stasis. And because she still doesn't know what else to do.

Was her mother supposed to impart some kind of wisdom before she passed on? Was there supposed to be some very old ritual whereby on a given night, a specific event determined by a phase of the moon or a vision or a biblical code, Ma was to wake her, to sit her in the kitchen and brew tea, to bring their faces close together, kiss the forehead with a long and warm touch of mother's lips, bring those lips finally to Sylvia's ear and whisper words of revelation and epiphany? Did Ma's ovaries kill her before that clarifying night could take place and she left Sylvia, one of those occasional freaks, one of the uninitiated, the uninformed who stumble around on rainy nights like this one hoping for some substitute disclosure, for some surrogate imparting of wisdom that will heal her, make her like everyone else, trigger these long-hidden and deeply submerged guidance systems that will once and for all put an end to this perpetual drift?

She finds herself on Coburn Street looking in the window of a camera store called Strand's. She stares down on a blue velvet display of lenses—Hasselblads and Minoltas and Noskowiaks. The lenses are all lined up in perfect rows, black and silver cylinders running from standard, utilitarian pieces to specialty stuff—fish-eyes, ridiculously long telephoto mounts. All this glass bent to alter vision.

A police car pulls past, shines a spotlight on her back. She turns around and waves, imagining what she looks like—hair hanging, sopping, clothes drenched through.

The light gets extinguished and the cops move on and Sylvia turns back to the window. She looks beyond the front display to the interior of the shop. It's lit by a single, dim lamp in the rear and all she can really make out is a glossy sign hanging above the service counter that reads *The Electramatic 35: Calibrate the Moments of Your Life*.

She walks on, finds an open coffee shop called Café Arco. The night manager is a young Spanish guy who's totally involved in a worn paperback with a grotesque cover whose title—*The Monk*—seems oddly familiar. Sylvia orders an espresso, takes a seat and tries not to listen to the argument of a miserable twentysomething couple in an opposite booth. The woman holds her voice at a low mumble, but the man keeps interrupting her monologue, punctuating her long sermon over and over with the same demand—*Just tell me why you won't*.

Someone has left an old children's *Highlight's* magazine on the table. Sylvia opens it to the rear and focuses on the hidden picture puzzle until the doomed romance vacates the place. There's only one other customer, a young man in a dark, rain-rumpled suit, hunched over his coffee at a corner table. He's got his back to her and Sylvia sits and stares at the rear of his head. Every now and then, the guy lifts a hand from his mug and rubs it over his face, as if he's having difficulty staying awake. She hears him struggling to breathe as if he's suffering a terrible chest cold.

Finally, he swallows the last of his coffee, fishes in his jacket pocket, comes out with a handful of change and drops it on the table. Then he pushes his chair back and gets up to leave and their eyes meet.

"It's you," Sylvia says, recognizing the huge ears and the bony face, "from Der Garten. The owner's son."

The young man rears back as if he's been accused of something. His eyes squint at her and then recognition plays across his whole face and he says, "The film woman."

"The film woman," Sylvia agrees. "I'm sorry but I don't remember your name."

"Jakob," he says with an embarrassed tilt of the head. "Jakob Kay."

"I'm Sylvia Krafft."

"Ms. Krafft," he begins to stammer, "I assure you, I honestly did not mean to—"

She waves away his apology.

"It was my fault," she says, "I was having a very bad day. I was misinterpreting everything."

"In any event," he says, the origin of his accent still unknown, "I am sorry if I bothered you."

She nods her acceptance and suddenly wants to keep him here a bit longer. She pushes the opposite chair out with her foot and says, "Would you like to join me?"

He stares at her like he doesn't quite understand, then slowly starts to shake his head *no*.

"I have some business. There is someone waiting—"

"It's a raw night," she says. "And it sounds like you have a pretty awful cold."

"It's nothing really," his eyes moving from Sylvia to the door and then back again.

"I don't know if you've heard," she says. "But they're reopening the Ballard Theatre."

Jakob's hand goes back over his face, comes down to his neck and tugs at his collar. He nods slowly, then slides into the chair. She lifts her coffee toward him, raises her eyebrows. He declines her offer.

"I know the Ballard," he says. "I've been there. A few years ago. I hadn't heard this."

"It's a rumor. I don't know how reliable it is."

"Always the case," Jakob says, "with rumors."

There's an uneasiness they both wish wasn't there, something more attributable to the night than the chemistry. They stare at each other until the level of discomfort extends across the room to the clerk behind the counter, who calls out to them, "We'll be closing up soon."

Jakob tries to clear his throat and manages only a wet-sounding gurgle.

"Well," he says, "I do have someone I must meet."

"I suppose," Sylvia says, "I do too."

Jakob stands up awkwardly, looks out the door to the street, turns up the collar of his suit jacket.

"I wish," he says, bowing his head to her, "we had met under different circumstances."

Sylvia tries for a smile.

"We both like movies," she says. "Maybe we'll bump into each other sometime."

He nods but doesn't say anything, then walks out of the coffee shop and into the rain.

At twenty to midnight Sylvia leaves a five-dollar bill under her cup and walks back outside. She stays off the main drag and moves over cross streets until she comes to Aragon Ave. She rounds the corner onto Watson at a club called Propa Gramma and moves north toward the Skin Palace.

One of Hugo's meatboys is standing a solo watch inside the locked doors of the theatre. As Sylvia approaches, he starts shaking his head and saying, "We're closed tonight."

"I have an appointment," she tries through the glass. "With Mr. Schick."

He stares at her with a blank face until a voice from inside yells, "It's all right, Mr. Franco. Let her through."

The bouncer turns a deadbolt, opens the door and steps aside to let her pass. She enters the lobby and stands for a second pushing her wet hair back on her head until a voice calls from above, "You'll catch cold, my darling."

She looks up to the center of the lobby's balcony and sees Hugo Schick, dressed up in a Nazi SS uniform. He looks down on her, smiles, bows his enormous, bald head forward until she thinks he's going to swan-dive over the railing, then rights himself and begins to brush at his lapels.

"It belonged to my grandfather," he says, indicating the uniform. "You like?"

She tries to push her hair behind her ears and says, "You didn't tell me this was a formal event."

He starts down the right-side stairway.

"Momentous, yes," he says, "but not formal, my dear."

He approaches, takes her hand, squeezes it, lifts it up and, of course, brings his head down slightly and kisses it.

"As you'll soon see, the dress for tonight's gathering is anything but formal."

She pulls her hand free.

"Where'd you get the pictures, Hugo?"

"Has no one ever told you, Sylvia," he says, the almost-patient father figure, "you mustn't, you can*not* rush the more important things in this life?"

"And tormenting me is an important thing for you?"

He looks over her and gives a kind of sad smile, shakes his head slightly.

"One of the achievements of my career," he says, "has been my ability to prolong the moment. You can't imagine how complex a task this can be, Sylvia. Too much prologue and the eye gets bored. Not enough, and there's no time for the anticipation to build. It's an instinctual talent. It's born here," rubbing his stomach.

"Why did you go after Perry? Is it because he works for Boetell?"

"You're so American, my love," he says. "Now let me take your raincoat. We have a long and wonderful night ahead of us."

There's no question he'll have everything played his way. He's the director. Her opinion is to walk away or accept his terms. It's a matter of how badly she wants explanation, how much she needs definitive answers. So she

unzips the slicker, pulls it off and hands it to Schick. It's
not that she has some idea that what Hugo tells her will
change things. It's just that she's so disgusted by ambigu-
ity at this point that she's willing to walk this thing through
to the end. Even if what she hears is exactly what she fears.
Even if the voice of revelation isn't that of her mother, but
an egomaniacal Austrian pornographer.

"Let me have Mr. Franco bring you a robe," Hugo says.

"I'm fine as is, thanks."

"But you're soaking—"

"I'll dry."

He gestured to her camera and says, "I knew you
wouldn't disappoint, Sylvia."

"The night is young, Hugo."

He takes her hand again and starts to lead her up the left-
hand staircase.

"My work, as you know, is my life," he says. "And I
can't help but feel that with the completion of tonight's
filming I'm surrendering to mortality."

"Happens to the best of us," she says.

"There will be other features," ignoring her, "but they're
just cookie-cutter entertainments. They will have their
flourishes. They'll proudly bear the mark of Schick. But
there will never be another epistle from the purest center of
my heart."

"Well, we've each got just so much purity to go around,"
she says.

They come to the top of the stairs, walk past the entrance
to the theatre proper and start up the spiral stairway to the
studios.

"We began *Don Juan Triumphant* seven years ago. We
filmed just one week each year since then. This was my
plan from the start. Our starlet, Miss Pauline, was just
eighteen at the time we began. She lacked much of the as-
sertiveness we've all come to love."

He stops at the landing and looks down at Sylvia, trapping her in the narrow circle of metal. "You don't know where Leni is tonight, do you?"

"Leni didn't show? On your last night of filming?"

He stares at her.

"I believe she may have run off with my assistant director. I finally find someone who knows what he's doing and she seduces him and kidnaps him. She is a plague sent from the angry god of cinema."

"What are you going to do?"

He squints and says, "A Leni Pauline cannot stop the fulfillment of this film. I can shoot around the hole that is Leni Pauline. Her absence is a minor technical difficulty. I've dealt with far worse. Besides, this is Don Juan's night. The scenes all belong to him."

They come to a stop in front of the double wooden doors spray-painted *Henrick Galeen Memorial Studio*. She hears Hugo take a deep breath, sees him square his shoulders. He stares straight ahead and whispers, "Once I go in, I do *not* come out until it is done."

Then, before Sylvia can respond, he straight-arms the doors and they fly open to the full extent of the hinges and inside the studio you can hear all sound sucked away immediately, as if a machine had been turned off.

He stands framed inside the doorway, surveying the landscape. Sylvia lags back, stays in his shadow, follows as he slowly enters this cavernous loft. And his people stare back at him as if he were Hannibal or Napoleon or Cecil B. DeMille, some conquering entity inflated larger than life by vision and ego. Some force that can change the course of the moon.

He comes to a stop a few feet inside the studio, stands quietly, then brings his hands up to chest-level and presses them together as if in prayer, an enormous, mutant, fascist altar boy. And then he begins to bow slightly, over and over, in a running semicircle aimed at his entire congregation.

A wave of applause comes back at him, starting slowly at first, but building to an ovation which Hugo eventually waves down.

"My people," he says to the room in a booming, theatrical voice, "my little family, my fellow dwellers in this madhouse we call art, I welcome you all tonight for the conclusion, after seven years of backbreaking, soul-crushing labor, after hundreds of hours of exposed film, after countless changes of cast crew and scripts, and yes, my friends, my family, after births and deaths and lost loves and betrayals and too many trips to the brink of financial disaster, we come to the final night of our story. Tonight, the myth shall be made whole. The tale completed. My work ended. And the thing itself, the film, birthed into this wretched world. And so," a pause and another small bow, "it ends as it began. With love. With courage. And with passion. I say to you, my people, my children, let us begin this last night in Eden."

No applause now, just a respectful, earnest hush. And then Hugo brings his hands around to his back, locks them together and begins a pre-filming tour of his soundstage. Sylvia catches up next to him and says, "Very impressive. Now, about the photographs you sent me—"

He looks at everything except her.

"Did you like them?" he says, for the first time acknowledging the shots of Perry and Candice. "They're technically crude, but they have a certain bite, don't you think?"

"Just tell me what—" she begins, but he cuts her off.

"I take it you've brought plenty of film?" he says, meaning it's not yet time for their heart-to-heart.

They stroll past a line of tables filled with platters of food and pastries. A young woman dressed in someone's clichéd idea of a French maid's uniform—something out of a thirty-year-old imported farce—is lighting sterno cans underneath silver chafing dishes.

"No, no, Mariette," Hugo barks without looking at the girl. "Nothing is to be served until after three. I don't want the smell of food distracting them from their work."

They come to half a dozen people engrossed in various duties from planting bottles of Möet in crystal serving buckets to slicing open cherrystones to chiseling a fat block of ice into what might turn out to be a rosebush in full bloom.

Apparently satisfied with the preparation of the feast, Hugo marches toward the set and comes to stand behind a classic director's chair with *Schick* inscribed on the back. He grabs a script out of the chair and holds it against his chest.

"I must confess my nervousness at this moment," he says. "So many of the greats have taken their turn with the legend. Gabriel Tellez may have been the first. But they all had a go at it. Byron. Shadwell. Mozart. Espronceda. Molière. Shaw. Even Bergman, The list goes on and on."

"And now," Sylvia says, "we add Schick."

He looks at her, frowns slightly. "You'll discover I've taken quite a few liberties, so to speak, with the myth."

"No guts, no glory."

He nods. "A coarse phraseology, but the truth is the truth. An artist interprets the old myths for the new age, yes? His job is not so much to decode as to re-code."

"Well," she says, "there are only so many stories."

"Exactly," he says. "And style is everything."

She nods but he's not looking at her. He seems to be dazing slightly, staring out at the set, but not quite focusing.

"It's so tragic, Sylvia," he says, "when an artist peaks too soon. I think, so often, of Welles."

She stays quiet.

"I've been working on this film for so long now," he says, "I feel as if the only thing to do upon its completion is expire."

He opens the script and brings his face down close to a

page, then immediately closes it and says, "Do you feel prepared, my child?"

She stares at him until she remembers why she's here— Hugo wants her to photograph his work tonight. Hugo wants a record of the genius in the grip of his art.

She nods, steps back, lifts the Canon, focuses in on him and shoots the first image of the series. She keeps the camera at her eye and says, "When will you answer my questions, Hugo?"

He stares into the viewfinder for a while, then says, "You're quite sure you want all the answers, Sylvia?"

She lowers the Canon. She keeps her voice even. "I'm here, aren't I? I brought my goddamn camera, didn't I?"

"At three o'clock we break for dinner," he says. "You and I can dine. And talk."

She takes a breath, not sure what to do. "You set me up from the start, didn't you, Hugo?"

He looks surprised.

"You came to me, Sylvia," he says. "Don't you recall? You came to the theatre on the day of the riot. You sought me out."

She wants to say something, to voice some contradiction or insult. But nothing comes out. He reaches out, puts his hand on her shoulder and says, "Keep your eyes open, Sylvia. Tonight won't come again."

Then he claps his big hands together and people start scurrying to various stations and jobs. Hugo's got three cameras ready on dollies, two boom mikes, and two simple banks of lights mounted high near the ceiling. It looks like a fairly second-rate production in light of his speech. A step above an amateur video shoot, but not much of a step.

The set resembles an enormous dance hall. At one end of the room four musicians, two men and two women, all with narrow black bow ties secured around their necks, form a naked string quartet seated on cheesy and cold-looking metal folding chairs. Above them, mounted on the brick wall, is a hand-painted sign that reads *Club Sevila*. The rest of the room is outfitted with such a dizzying array of anachronisms that determining what time period Schick is going for is almost impossible. The design strikes Sylvia as the quintessential nightclub from hell. It's sort of a hybrid—the classic New York hotspots of the thirties and forties, places like 21 and the Stork Club, crossed with something vaguely Germanic. It's a location from your queasiest dreams, the perfect locale for Desi Arnaz to bound onto the stage and sing "Babalu" to Hermann Goering and his date.

And the club is populated by a stunning array of freakish, disparate characters in the gaudiest, most mismatched costumes imaginable. There are dozens of actors and actresses arranged at cocktail tables and dressed in loungewear from Mars, lingerie from the nightmares of a disturbed carnival geek. The view through Sylvia's camera looks as if Halloween has spontaneously broken out in some tacky clinic for schizophrenics.

Hugo takes a long, slow look around the set, seems to meet the eye of every performer and technician. Sylvia focuses in on him with the camera, watches him through the lens as a makeup man leans over and dabs a little pancake on his glistening forehead. Hugo pulls down on the hem of his uniform jacket, then nods to a young woman in jeans and a blue work shirt.

The woman calls out, "All right everyone. Quiet on the set. Cameras roll," then steps out in front of one of the cameras and holds up an old fashioned clapboard, says, "*Don Juan Triumphant*. Scene Seventy-two. Take one," smacks the clapper down on the board and jumps back next to Hugo who shouts, top of his lungs, "And action."

The room falls to silence. A beat goes by. Then the naked quartet is cued and, to the sound of screeching violin and cello, Hugo, the Virgil of the porno-tour, pushes out his chin and stork-walks into the center of Club Sevila, clasps his hands in front of him and initiates the movie's finale, the consummate narcissist to the end.

Sylvia focuses in on the director, zooms until his enormous head is squeezed within the box of her vision, until Hugo's mouth is a cavernous vacuum that begins to move.

"This, our final circle of hell, can be a very liberating residence. Don Juan has an eternity to indulge his carnal impulse. You, my sweet voyeur, my audience and my customer, are not nearly so lucky. Waste no more time. Join us in the consummation of a lifetime of yearning. Excise the oppression. Cast off the yoke of inhibition. Let the beast inside ride free and wild tonight," his voice escalates to a roar. "Let this rapture begin."

And all the performers begin to tear each other's clothes off. Hugo starts prompting and directing, matching partners up, instructing, his hands flying, letting loose buttons and zippers and hooks and fasteners of all variety. Costumes are flying in the air as more flesh begins to fill the set, all of it young and toned and unreal.

Suddenly Sylvia's watching an entire stage full of copulating men and women groping and heaving and thrusting and moaning. The actors are acrobatic and wildly imaginative. Hugo, the ringmaster, the carnal dance instructor, stays in his SS uniform throughout the orgy, and once he sees everyone is well-lubed and arranged in a chain of copulation that snakes across the floor from wall to wall, he climbs back to center stage, stands for a moment with his hands clasped behind him, rigid, at full attention, staring down the camera, a prissy general surveying the messy plains of his conquest. Then he pulls two long baton-like sticks from behind his back and holds them out in the air like an orchestra conductor. He extends them downward with a flourish until they touch the closest firepot and burst into flame, become skinny little torches. Hugo turns sideways, bends the trunk of his body backwards, the dome of his skull finally parallel with the stage floor. He lifts one torch to his mouth and inserts it slowly and deeply, pulls it out extinguished. He performs the same feat with the other torch, a bit faster this time, popping the burning stick down into the cavity of his face and withdrawing it seconds later a charred black wick. And then he comes upright, turns forward, and blows out a full lungful of breath that fires a jet of flame into the air above the sexual performers, a tongue of orange fire that seems to roll outward in liquid-ish, spiraling balls. Waves of an inferno from the belly of the Austrian beast.

Sylvia stares at the scene through the camera until she feels a tap on her shoulder. She turns to see the soundman holding a slip of paper up in front of her face. She takes it from his hand and he moves off without a word. She opens the paper and reads

**I'm downstairs
and I can't stay long
—Leni**

33

The theatre is in darkness. Even the aisle lights have been turned off. Sylvia stands in the doorway and tries to spot some movement. She walks down the center aisle until she can turn back and look up into the balcony. But she can't see a thing. She suddenly feels like she's at the bottom of an enormous swimming pool filled with black ink. Finally she lets out a whispered yell.

"Leni?"

There's no answer, but that horrible waltzing Muzak

starts to play at the wrong speed through the faulty sound system. She's too tired to find anything funny in Leni's games tonight.

"Just knock it off," she yells.

The screen fills up with light. Above Sylvia's head, in the shaft of movie-beam, she sees countless particles of dust drifting through the air. She follows the shaft to the screen. She watches black numbers, numbers as big as houses, run onto and off the screen. Then there's a cloudy image that takes a maddeningly long minute to focus. When it does come clear, she's watching something familiar—a young woman, naked and sleek, watching her own beautiful reflection in a huge, oval, gilt-framed mirror. It's that stupid soft-core flick that Perry and she saw at the Cansino Drive-in last week. The Meyer Dodgson film, *The Initiation of Alice*. But this is a lousy print of it. The image is jumping all over the screen and the focus cuts in and out. It looks like a pirated print, maybe even one of those street-cuts they shoot right off the screen with a video camera.

Why the hell does Leni want her to see this?

She slides into an aisle seat. She doesn't really remember this part of the movie. It seems like some kind of overly artsy dream sequence. Alice's reflection is replaced in the mirror by three muscular lovers. She *steps through* the mirror into their waiting arms and a languid, gauzy mingling begins as the heroine gives herself over completely to three pairs of stroking hands and roving mouths.

And then the point of view gets completely confused. It's as if the cameraman lost hold of his equipment. There's a stuttering jump from the lovemaking on the screen and into the darkness and then out of darkness and onto a neon sign that reads

The Cansino Drive-In Theatre
Adult Films Nightly
$10.00/Carload

Whoever stole this movie took it from the same drive-in screen that Perry and Sylvia watched it on. They must have filmed from one of the trees that borders the back end of the car lot.

Her stomach begins to slide into a horrible clench, as if she's willed what she knows is about to come. The camera begins to pan over the rooftops of all the cars in the parking lot. It shoots the roofs of the Chevys and Chryslers and a lot of vans and pickups. Sylvia sees young couples sitting and lying on the hoods and trunks, laughing, drinking beer, smoking cigarettes and joints, eating popcorn and the horrible microwave pizza from the concession stand.

And she knows where the camera is going to move next. She knows it and can't do anything to stop it. So she watches, helpless, frozen as the camera pulls farther back and the drive-in screen becomes that much smaller and the cinematographer finally finds the Skylark convertible with its top rolled back. The shot zooms in slowly.

There's Perry. Naked below the waist, sitting in the backseat, his head lying over the crest of the seat, tilted toward the moon, his eyes closed, his lips pulled into his mouth.

And there's Sylvia. Naked, mounted on top of him, chest to chest, her knees crushing into the seat, riding Perry, holding onto his head. There she is, twenty feet tall, having sex on the big screen of the Skin Palace.

A single set of applause breaks out and she jumps up from the seat and turns to see Leni behind her, staring up at the movie, her mouth smiling and her head shaking.

"You bitch," is all Sylvia can think to say and Leni stops clapping but continues to stare at the screen.

"You're looking like a real star up there, Sylvie."

"Who did it?" Sylvia makes herself ask.

"Who do you think?" Leni says, coming down the aisle. "The Schickster always dogs his enemies—"

"I wasn't his enemy—" Sylvia starts and Leni shakes her off.

"No, but your Perry was." She pauses and adds, "You were just there."

Sylvia looks up in the balcony to the projection booth. "Did you run it? Is anyone else up there?"

Leni puts a hand on her shoulder, lowers her voice. "Forget it, Sylvia. He had a dozen prints made before you two were back in your goddamn apartment."

Out of the corner of her eyes, Sylvia sees her face getting bigger on the screen, a tight shot as she builds toward climax. And here in the theatre, her hand comes up to take a slap at Leni's face, but Leni catches her by the wrist and holds her arm up in the air.

"Sylvia," Leni says, "I'm probably the only friend you've got in this pathetic city right now."

"How do I thank you?"

Leni drops hold of the arm. "If Hugo knew I was down here showing you this he'd go crazy. He'd probably sic some of his muscleboys on me. This is one of his big chips, Sylvia. He needs it for the right moment. He needs to hand it to the media when Boetell and Perry make their move. He needs to humiliate them as soon as they start building steam. Your boyfriend sits down at a press conference to yell about the new crusade against filth, Hugo makes sure all the reporters present have a video-cassette of *this*," pointing to the screen, "waiting on their desks by the time they get back to the *Spy. Anti-smut lawyer stars in porno flick.* Great headline."

"But it's obvious we didn't know this was being filmed."

Leni looks up at the screen. "Maybe. But do you think that will matter?"

"But *I* didn't do anything."

"No," she says, "you didn't. It's a filthy world, Sylvia. The innocent get kicked a lot."

"Why did you show it to me, Leni?"

"Thought I'd give you a little advance warning. So you could decide what to do."

"My options are pretty limited."

"Oh, c'mon, is it that bad?"

Sylvia looks at her and says, "Not for you . . ."

She lets the rest trail off and Leni says, "You're embarrassing me with your gratitude, you know? I've got to get out of here."

Leni steps back, turns and calls out into the rear darkness of the theatre, "Hey, Counselor, you're up," then she pats Sylvia on the shoulder and starts to walk for the exit.

Sylvia looks in the direction of the yell and sees someone getting up out of a seat near the last row underneath the balcony. She knows it's Perry before she even sees his face in the light of the movie. He comes down the aisle awkwardly, hands in pocket, comes next to her and just stands there.

"You think we'll get nominated?" Sylvia says, knowing he won't get the reference.

"I'm so sorry, honey," Perry starts and Sylvia looks at the screen and shakes her head to shut him up.

"The thing is," she says, "we've got such stiff competition. I hear *The Perry and Candice Show* has gotten rave reviews. Four stars. I hear you're even better in that one."

He closes his eyes. If he starts to cry she knows she'll punch him right in the mouth.

"It's funny, Perry," she says, "but I honestly think I can live with it better than you. I can live with the idea of greaseballs from coast to coast renting the video of us-at-the-drive-in. Every night, horny little guys from L.A. and Chicago and Detroit forking over three bucks for a peek at the *real thing*. I think I can accept it better than you can, Perry. 'Cause you're such a vain son of a bitch. And you look like shit up there."

He's breathing heavy. He loosens his tie, trying to figure

out how to play her as if she was one more tough customer at a Walpole & Lewis conference table.

"We've got to get out of here, Sylvia."

"You get out—"

"We can talk at home—"

"We don't have a home, you bastard."

He takes her arm and she rips it away from him, gets ready to punch and kick if she has to.

"Look," he says, getting frantic, "this thing is about to get out of hand, okay? When your friend there called me—"

"Her name's Leni."

"—We were just finishing up the logistics for tonight's march."

"We'll save a seat for Eddie Meade and the good Reverend Boetell," she says and nods her head toward the screen. "God, Perry, look at the way you're clawing my back there. I hadn't noticed what a real savage you were. Does Candice like it on top, too?"

"Sylvia," he says, "They're on their way here right now. All of them. Paige Beatty and WAR, Boetell and the FUD people. They're going to make some headlines tonight."

"And Schick is going to do them all one better tomorrow morning. This is the public's favorite story—self-righteous scumbag hypocrites caught in the sins they've screamed about. They'll probably make a movie of the week—"

"I didn't do anything *wrong*," he yells.

"Outside of betraying me, you mean. Is Candice coming tonight? I know how much she loves a good party."

"I'll get an injunction," he babbles, "I'll impound every film, every photo—"

"You're a goddamn idiot, you know that, Perry," and she genuinely wants to laugh at him. "Hugo doesn't play by your rules. You've already lost. You're a lightweight with bad instincts, Perry. Your first time out in the big leagues and you pick the wrong scapegoat. You were a joke to Hugo. Your credibility is gone. You're an insult to family values.

All the bad ink is going to piss off Walpole & Lewis in a big corporate way. Boetell is just going to have to take his account elsewhere."

"I'm not going to let this happen, Sylvia. I'm—"

"It's already happened, Perry. For Christ's sake."

"We have to go now."

They stare at each other. She watches his Adam's apple bob as he swallows.

"Get out of here, Perry. My movie isn't over yet."

And after a minute, with the sputter from the projection booth the only sound in the theatre, he surprises her by giving up, just turning and walking toward the exit. No need for any slapping or kneeing. No need for a big, cheesy finish.

She watches him disappear through the swinging doors. When she looks back to the screen, the lovers in the back of the Buick have finished up and lie in a pile of flesh and sweat. But the camera stays on them. It's a static, boring shot. An aggravating picture.

There's no motion. No progression.

34

Jakob stands in a doorway across the street from the Hotel St. Vitus. He's not sure what to do with his hands, having given the Seitz to Vera Gottwald for safekeeping. He looks up at his home of the past year, its cold, castle-like facade seeming to lean out over Belvedere Street even more then usual, the angles seeming sharper than normal, the spires somehow appearing taller than before. Even the heads of the gargoyles seem to have grown larger over the course of the past week.

He sits down on the stoop and wonders how his family managed to arrive at this point. He thinks back on the last days in Maisel that now seem like a fading dream, more myth than truth.

He remembers Papa's supper-table talk of emigration seeming to increase. But Jakob wasn't really paying much attention. Not even the attack on Yitzhak Levi-Zangwill could dampen the boy's passions. He was thinking of Felice, dreaming of Felice, fantasizing the lewd story lines about the woman round-the-clock. As she placed a bowl of Cockova' on the table, he gritted his teeth and stared at the curves of her breasts under her bib apron. As she sat by the night's dying fire and finished the last of the mending, he imagined his hand taking in the warmth and smoothness of her thigh, his fingers rolling over the small mole on her left shoulder.

He began to perspire continually. His concentration deteriorated to a single, obsessive longing. His notebook screenplay dissolved into both soft-and hard-core musings about his governess-*cum*-lover. He'd be scribbling a scene intended to culminate in a prolonged gun battle only to find the doomed hero undressing an older mystery woman on a speeding train while the other passengers appeared to sleep. In the night, Jakob would cry out at the climax of a lascivious dream, loud enough to wake Felix. And all the while his anxiety grew in proportion to his lust. Because he couldn't determine where this erotic madness would end. Because he was the fifteen-year-old son of the busiest gangster in central Maisel. Felice was a thirty-year-old washerwoman from the Schiller ghetto. Just the thought of this union had an unreal quality to it, required a fantastic leap of faith to traverse its improbability. Were Jakob watching this affair unfold on the screen of the Kierling, he'd shake his head at the inconsistencies of the script, the logic glitches, the lack of foreshadowing and back-story buildup. But as the passion transpired in the mundane commonality of his real life, he could only go along with it, give in to the most primal and elemental impulses he's ever experienced.

Then came the week the Kierling managed to secure a print of *The Big Sleep*. And the rumor spread among the regulars that the theatre was closing. That Yitzhak Levi-Zangwill, now blind and broken, was selling the cinema and emigrating to Jerusalem.

Felice left another note to arrange a rendezvous in Devetsil Park. She wrote that she'd be wearing the black stockings and the red lipstick the boy loved so much. Jakob was wheezing from anticipation as he ran down Havetta Boulevard. But when he saw Gustav Weltsch pulling a steamer trunk through Loew Square, his lungs began to labor from dread rather than expectation. And when he entered the Park and found their usual bench empty, his heart began to pump as if he'd overdosed on his camphor injections. He sat and waited until nightfall, but Felice never arrived. He waited an hour after sundown, after the horrible, haunting supper bells from St. Wenceslas Abbey had rung. He waited as the first-showing crowd filed out of the Kierling and into the cafés as the second-showing crowd replaced the first. He waited until the cafés had dispatched the last of the drunken, credo-spewing students back to their dormitories.

He tried to pray, but could not, and so instead repeated dialogue from random films, sometimes mouthing entire scenes, reciting all the parts, whispering the scripted words as if they were sacred petitions in some ancient and holy language.

As he spoke, he stared at the second-rate marble Pietà at the rear of the park, the mother cradling the limp body of a martyred son, mourning a loss that will never go away, grieving an absence that can never be relieved.

And when he finally ran out of the movie-prayer, Jakob got up from the lovers' bench and walked across the park to the statue, stepped up to the base of this stone testament to the relentless tragedy of this life, and peered behind the statue where he saw the body of Felice Fabri.

Both of her eyes had been shot out.

The boy let himself fall down on top of her. He pulled her head next to his own, smearing his cheeks with the drying blood. He rolled into a sitting position, lifted Felice into his lap, held the weight of her head in his hands. Her skirt rode up on her thighs and he could see the patterns of contusion where the stockings had been ripped away. His chest began to tremble uncontrollably. He brought his mouth to hers, felt the coldness, brought a hand around and touched the lips, wiping the lipstick where it had smeared.

And then he convulsed, his head snapping backwards in a seizure-like series of twitches, his vision blurring, dissolving, until all he could see were flashes of grey and white, monstrous shadows that seemed to be approaching.

He woke to find himself in his own bed.

Papa was sitting on the edge, wiping the boy's forehead with a washcloth.

"I am not angry," Papa was saying.

Jakob tried to sit up. Gustav Weltsch, on the other side of the bed, pushed him gently back to reclining.

"You had us very worried, my son," Papa said.

"I knew he'd be at the movie house," Felix blurted from across the room.

"Thank goodness the projectionist called us," Gustav said. "This flu is serious business."

"You can't go running to the films when you are sick like this, Jakob," Papa says. "You should know better. Passing out in the cinema. Where is your sense, my boy?"

Papa made a head motion for Gustav and Felix to leave. He waited until the bedroom door closed and then pulled the covers up to Jakob's chin. He brought his head close to the boy's ear and whispered, "You rest now, Jakob. You get some more sleep."

Papa folded the washcloth precisely and placed it on the nightstand. Then he stood and turned out the light. Jakob stared up at the man's bulk, just his father's outline, nothing more that that, barely visible in the darkness.

"Felix has packed all your things for you, like a good cousin," Hermann Kinsky said walking to the door. "You get to sleep now. You need your strength, Jakob. We have a long journey ahead. But you can sleep on the freighter. The sea air will do those lungs a world of good. And when we arrive in America, you will be as fit as the rest of the family.

The chapel is in darkness as Jakob steps through the door. His father's head is in silhouette, outlined only by the dim shine of the street lamp outside the stained-glass window. Hermann is seated in his chair but swiveled away from the altar/desk. It's possible he's fallen asleep, though the son can't hear the heavy, guttural snore that normally signifies Papa at rest. If it were someone besides Hermann, he might believe the man was praying, speaking hopefully to a God who continues to hide his face.

Jakob stands in the doorway for a while, staring at the back of the father's head. And though the boy is tempted to give way to what's now an instinct and begin finding alternative ways to view the room, seeking interesting camera angles, methods of using the faint light to the best advantage, he refrains. He simply stands and breathes and stares at the rear of the head until the silence is broken by Hermann's voice, sounding unusually low and tentative.

"You have your mother's sense of timing, Jakob. She always knew when I needed to speak with her."

Hermann turns his chair around. He's holding a framed photograph in both hands. He continues to stare at the photo as he talks to the boy.

"Where is your cousin?"

Jakob gives the hint of a shrug and says without any sarcasm, "Oh, Papa, am I my cousin's keeper?"

Hermann brings his face forward a bit, tried to get a better look at Jakob, as if he senses for the first time that his son might possibly be more than a tubercular repository of trivial dreams. Then he shakes his head slightly and looks back down at the photo.

"When your mother and I were first married, she would often wait up for me. Like this. Very late into the night. I'd return home to our flat on Budec Road. Six stories up, I'd climb those filthy stairs and wondered if she'd be spying through the crack in the door as I came around the corner. I'd give her my work sack. Maybe a few eggs. Half a loaf of plum bread. Once a bottle of Becherovka and a freshly slaughtered goose. Your mother loved me very much, Jakob."

The son just nods.

The father gestures to the opposite seat. Jakob sits down, unfastens the top button of his shirt and loosens his tie.

"Schick kept you working late."

"He's a very dedicated man," Jakob says.

"You need that in life," Hermann answers, modulating his own voice to an identical volume. "You need to care deeply about what you do and why you do it. You can't rely on luck."

"I don't believe in luck," Jakob says.

"Neither do I," Hermann says. "But what do you believe in, Jakob? Besides the movies."

Jakob ignores the question and says, "Can I see it?" motioning toward the photograph.

Hermann stares across the table and just when Jakob thinks his father is about to say *no*, Papa slides the picture across the altar. Jakob picks it up and looks at his mother's face, still a girl, not much older than Jakob is now, dressed in what must have passed as a wedding gown in those desperate times. Holding a bouquet of some sort to her chest.

And staring out, slightly unfocused but somehow contented, pleased, happy with whatever thoughts had lodged in her mind at that moment twenty years before.

"She was a beautiful woman," the son says.

Hermann shakes his head.

"Beauty is nothing. She was my religion. As close as I will ever come to having one. To worshipping something. To believing in a better moment. I have wondered, if she had lived, if she could have perhaps taught me to see things as she did. Maybe just a bit. If we'd had more time."

"I'm sorry," is all Jakob can think to say.

"Your father is a brutal man," Hermann says. "I want to say that I had to become this way, but perhaps I was born this way."

"It's a brutal world, Papa."

"Is that what the movies tell you?"

"Among other things."

They sit in silence, stare at those parts of each other's face that aren't buried in shadow, until Hermann whispers, "Do you know what it's like to live without any kind of faith, Jakob?"

"I don't think I do, Papa. But faith isn't a static thing. It's a process. It's a methodology. A way to get someplace else. And it comes and goes."

"Sometimes, son, it never comes."

"I think you have to want it. Very badly. You have to look in the right places."

"You've seen so much in eighteen years, Jakob?"

"I've seen a lot of things."

"From the comfort of a velour seat, squinting at a white screen."

"No, Papa. From next to your elbow. With my eyes wide open."

Another bout of silence that Hermann again breaks up by asking, "Where is Felix, Jakob?"

This time, Jakob answers, "I think maybe he's visiting Johnny Yew."

The boy doesn't know what to expect, but after a second, Papa pushes his bulk back in the chair so that his face is lost in darkness. And then Jakob hears what might be a small laugh. A kind of suppressed chuckle. The father gets out of the chair and walks to the window.

"You know you've been a great disappointment to me?"

"I'm sorry about that too, Papa," Jakob says. "But life is full of disappointments. That's one of the things I've seen."

He hears the old man walk back toward him, come to a stop behind his chair.

"And what," Hermann asks, a little breathlessly, "is your greatest disappointment, my son? Did they close your favorite theatre one night? Did your favorite movie leave town?"

"No, Papa," Jakob says, pushing his hands into the pockets of his suitcoat. "Not at all." He waits a moment, lets himself compose Felice's face one last time. "There was a woman. Back in Maisel. She took care of me. She tried to help me. To teach me. She loved me."

A long moment of hesitation until Hermann says, "The fishwife?"

"Her name was Felice, Papa. Don't pretend you don't remember."

"The fishwife from the Schiller ghetto?"

"What happened to Felice, Papa?"

"That woman I hired to clean and cook for us? She was a maid, for God's sake—"

"She was all I had."

"She was twice your age, Jakob," catching his breath, his hands on the back of the chair. "I had to dismiss her. I knew we were leaving for America. I had to let her go."

"What did you do, Papa?" Jakob asks. "Does it matter so much if you tell me now?"

"We were making arrangements to leave. I couldn't bring her with us, son. She was a bad influence on you. I could see what was happening. She infected you with her movie sickness. She had you at that theatre day and night. It wasn't right. I couldn't—"

"You killed Felice, didn't you?"

"She was a victim of the pogroms. Like the others—"

"No," Jakob yells, trembling. "Just say it. Just tell me. Pay me that little respect."

Hermann has sat all night in the chapel trying to find another way, slouched before his desk like a well-tailored Abraham agonizing over his duty, choking on promises and vows and long-held notions of how the world is put together. And knowing that those long, tormented hours could only lead to this moment, when his hand edges up the flap on his jacket pocket and his fingers plunge into the felt and touch the always cold, twice-reinforced metal string of the Schonborn.

"I have told myself there was no other way. I have tried to convince myself that she was a very evil influence on my son, making him soft, filling the head with nonsense. I knew what she meant to you. I told myself I had to free you so you could start new here in the States."

The hand withdraws the piano wire, loops ends around fingers.

"But I do owe you the truth. As my son, I owe you my honesty. And I have to confess, I know, without doubt, that I killed her, in part, as a touch of revenge, Jakob. For what happened at your birth. For how your life was traded for that of my wife."

"Papa," is all the boy can say and no matter how hard he attempts to restrain the muscle, tears well and start to roll from his eyes. Tears for Felice. And for his unknown mother. Maybe tears for Papa. Maybe even some for Felix.

Hermann steps back from the chair, raises his arms and starts to bring the garrote down to his son's neck.

And he finds the barrel mouth of a revolver touching his throat at the Adam's apple.

"Jakob," he says.

Jakob swings out of the seat and around to face the old man. He wipes his eyes with the back of his free arm, and pushes the barrel tighter against the fat, fleshy throat.

"A gun?" Papa's voice going high, his face actually brightening.

"Don't you recognize it? It's kind of a family heirloom."

"You're carrying a gun?" the meaning of the last several seconds still dawning on Hermann.

"Carrying is the easy part, Papa," Jakob says and cocks the firing hammer. "Would you like to see me use it?"

The father's hands come up to shoulder level as his fingers open and the length of the Schonborn drops to the floor.

"So, Felix is really—" the father begins and Jakob interrupts.

"You're going to be shorthanded around here for a while, Papa. Just you and Gustav."

"We'll manage," Hermann says, unable to contain the smile bursting over his face.

"*This* is what you wanted, isn't it?" Jakob says, chin-chucking the old man with the commandment's pistol. "To see if I could do it? If I was capable?"

"You just told me what a brutal world we live in."

Jakob lifts the gun from under the chin to an inch above the nose. He pushes the barrel in, applies pressure until Papa closes his eyes.

Then he uncocks the pistol and lays it down on the altar. His father's chest heaves.

"I'm opening the wall safe on my way out," the boy says. "I'm taking what I think is a fair amount. My birthright, so to speak. Enough to get me started. Tell Weltsch to keep an eye out for my company. It's called *Amerikan Pictures*. We'll be going public one of these days."

"I'm sure you'll make a fortune," Hermann says. "I may want to invest myself."

Jakob shakes his head, gently pushes his father aside and walks back to the door.

"I don't think so," he says, watching the old man sink back into shadow. "But come by sometime. I might put you in a movie."

35

Sylvia walks out of the theatre blinking against the light, moves down the corridor and into Schick's office. She goes to the bar, pours a glass of absinthe and looks at the couch. Resting on the cushions is the framed poster for *Don Juan Triumphant*. It depicts a teenage Leni Pauline, the Leni that existed seven years ago when the filming of the masterpiece first began, a Leni who still looked like a cheerleader-turned-bad and just off the bus, with the smooth ghost of baby fat only recently starting to fade from her face. She's positioned on her knees in some vague period-costume, a sort of low-cut medieval gown that makes her breasts defy gravity. Her eyes don't have any of their current hardness, their reflective calculation, and Sylvia wonders if this is the work of a talented airbrush artist or a true representation of the past.

She moves to Hugo's desk and takes the massive seat, rests her drink in her lap, picks up a fat, bound script from the desk and reads

DON JUAN TRIUMPHANT
(revision 91, pink sheets)

"They have perfected a science of blinks"
—Geoffrey O'Brian

then opens to the last few pages and reads

554 INT/CLUB von SCHICK
    Don Juan and Sylvia begin to rise back through the
mouth of hell, all the while tangled in a passionate embrace. Sylvia becomes reanimated. Sylvia's body is
covered in reflective glitter. The couple begins to
Tango.

    She throws the script back on the desk, swivels the chair
around, puts her feet up on the credenza and looks up at
the rest of the framed posters from Schick's seven self-
proclaimed favorites. And there, in the space where *Don
Juan Triumphant* had been, there's the variant *Madonna
and Child.* Maybe the one she saw in the lobby during her
first visit. Maybe something new.
    She closes her eyes and tries to imagine what the poster
would look like for Perry and her movie.
    Then she opens her eyes and stares at the Madonna's
face. And she knows it's a forgery. It's a talented attempt
to reproduce an original Propp. But it's not a Propp.
Hugo's picture gives nothing up. It's a facade. A veneer.
It's a death mask that says *I'll never tell you a thing.*
Propp's pictures are exactly the opposite. No matter how
cleverly, how purposefully, the photographer tried to hide
her, the woman looks out of the shadows and says *Here's
the only truth I have left to tell you.*
    Sylvia thinks, *But Ma, I'm too tired to understand it.*
    "Isn't she beautiful?"
    If Terrence Propp expected her to jump and dump her
drink in shock, he's disappointed right now.
    Sylvia doesn't even turn around to face him. She just
holds the glass up in a toast position, over her head so it's

visible above the back of the chair. She looks at the portrait of the Madonna and says, "Daddy, you made it to my party after all."

The real surprise is how easily the sarcasm and hostility slide out of her throat.

Propp doesn't respond. Not that she expects him to.

"Let me guess," she says. "There's a tunnel that leads under the Skin Palace."

Still nothing, so she's forced to swivel to the front and finds him looking out the window down at the street.

"Where's the gang?" he says, without turning to her.

"Up in the studios," she says. "They're filming the big finish to Hugo's masterpiece."

"I envy a man," Propp says, "who knows when he's at the height of his career."

"What about a woman?"

"My experience with women," finally looking, "such as it is, says they don't measure themselves that way."

"She nods, takes a sip, says, "You ran off pretty quickly last night."

He tries to smile and misses.

"I remembered," he says, "I'd left something back on the stove."

It should feel like he's making fun of her, but it doesn't.

"Come over here, Sylvia," he says, the voice so resigned, his fingers gently bending down the Levelor blinds.

She goes to the window, takes a seat on the sill. Outside, a crowd is massing in the street. Perry's horrible little alliance. They're lining up in their specific pockets, the Women's Resistance not getting too close to Boetell's army, but both groups mimicking a pseudo-military stance, a little coiled, a lot of hands on hips, a collective and unnatural posture, tense with the silence of their thoughts. They're bent into two wings with Perry and Candice and

Ratzinger between them, opposite the main entrance to the Skin Palace.

Into the mix rolls a large silver van. Painted on the side in a fluorescent-red script trimmed with glitter are the words.

The Reality Studio
"the fastest news-magazine in America"
now syndicated globally

There's a mini dish-antenna mounted on the roof. Three people jump out of the vehicle like a SWAT team, but instead of bearing assault rifles they carry cameras and microphones and ropes of black, rubbery looking cable. Perry waves the team over and goes into an immediate huddle with a tall woman in a blue blazer, gesticulating with his hands, thumping a fist into a palm and nodding with conviction. Ratzinger and Candice look on approvingly.

Reverend Boetell paces before his people in a poplin suit that's too white and light for the New England fall. As he walks he taps his ever present Bible against his right leg and keeps his eyes screwed closed, moving his lips in conspicuously passionate prayer.

Still staring out on the street scene, Sylvia says to Propp, "The other night at the diner, you asked if I'd taken a look at the Aquinas I bought?"

He doesn't say anything but she feels him turn from the window to look at her.

"The answer," she says, "is yes. I looked at the camera. I looked in the film magazine. That's what you wanted, isn't it? That's what you wanted me to do?"

After a long time he says, "What did you find, Sylvia?" his voice so close to cracking, like some pathologist who suddenly can't find his professional distance. Like someone whose last tool for defending himself has irreparably broken.

"I found," she says, "some pictures from a long time ago."

She turns and meets his face. One tear has streamed from the corner of his left eye.

"What am I to you?" she asks, as gently as she can.

"I'm so sorry," he says.

"That's not the right answer."

He nods, has difficulty swallowing. He says, "You make choices in this life. You make choices. Things happen and you can't go back."

"Just say it for me, please. Who is the woman in the photographs?"

She watches his throat quiver. After a while, he says, "Have you ever been out. With the camera. You find a spot. You find your subject. You wait for the moment. You wait for a long period of time. And you find you've waited too long."

"Or," she says, "you haven't waited long enough."

He reaches over, puts his hand just barely on her cheek. His voice goes so low she has to read his lips.

"Can't you forgive me?"

She covers his hand with her own.

She says, "I'm asking for even less than an apology. I'm asking for a single piece of information. I'm asking for the sound of your voice. A few simple words. One confirmation."

He just stares.

And she can't stop herself from taking things one more step, from forcing the progression no matter how badly instinct says what's to come will hurt her.

She says, "Until I know what to forgive you for, how—"

The window above their heads splinters with a loud thud. They both cringe down to the floor and look up to see a fat shard of glass trapped in the blinds. They stay on the floor for maybe a full minute, then Propp gets up first and looks and Sylvia follows, both on their knees, peering gingerly through the gap their fingers poke in the blindslats.

A small pocket of Boetell's holy rollers have come forward, stepped out to the front of the crowd. One of them holds a placard, freshly painted by the looks of the dripping red ink, that reads *Get Out Now.* Sylvia looks for Perry and can't find him anywhere, though she sees Ratzinger and Candice arguing over the hood of Boetell's Chariot of Virtue, Ratzinger banging a fist on the Cadillac, uncharacteristically ruffled.

She spots bricks and rocks clutched in various hands. She doesn't see any police cars or uniforms. She doesn't even see any of Hugo's payrolled muscle.

"Something's wrong," she says.

"I think we'd better heed their advice," Propp says.

Sylvia looks from his face to the variant *Madonna and Child.* She looks back again to his face. She tries to imagine him as a young man holding a camera up to his eye, surrounded by decay, twenty or thirty hours without sleep, possessed by conflicting needs he can't name let alone control, focusing, again and again, on a woman he'll soon abandon.

Sylvia leads the way down the corridor toward the rear exit she used on the day of the riot, but before she can push outside, Propp takes her arm, gestures to an old, wooden door on their left and says, "You were right. Down in the basement, there is a tunnel."

She starts to shake her head *no,* but he turns the knob and pulls the cellar door open and suddenly Fernando, Reverend Boetell's chief gofer, is standing in front of them looking shocked and almost losing his balance on the top stair. He's dressed in a pair of green zip-up workman's coveralls with some kind of logo-patch stitched over his heart and a red baseball cap too tight on his head. And he's carrying a bulky, rusty-metal tool chest.

Before Sylvia can say anything, Fernando ducks his head and rushes between them and out the rear door.

Propp and Sylvia look at each other. Propp pokes his head into the darkness of the cellar stairwell, comes back out into the hall and says, "What the hell was that?"

They follow Fernando's path out into the alleyway next to the Skin Palace and swing up onto the fringes of the crowd, but he's nowhere to be seen. And now there's an awful tension in the air, almost the antithesis of the chaos that was here earlier in the week. There's a feeling of false stillness, this sense of a fraudulent vacuum. There's no changing, no baiting, not a single catcall. There's not even much talk, just a lot of abbreviated mumbles and head-nodding. It's as if a veneer of calm has been painted over everything. There's a palpable absence of randomness, as if something monstrously harsh has been decided and the decree passed on to the mob without the use of language. As if everyone massing outside the Skin Palace shared one angry brain under excessive and building pressure.

Propp and Sylvia move through the bodies to the back rim of the crowd, both looking around for Fernando, trying to get a sense of what's about to happen. Sylvia steadies herself against Propp's shoulder and climbs onto the same mailbox she used to shoot up the riot. Up in front, she spots Boetell whispering into Ratzinger's ear. Ratzinger is staring at his wristwatch, maybe oblivious to the Reverend's babble.

And then the noise comes from the north end of Watson and the attention of the mob pivots to watch the last of Paige Beatty's troops, her elite guard, swing around the corner of Goulden Ave, still chanting their castration march, now even more intense than when Sylvia first heard them outside the Rib Room. She looks back to see Boetell kind of absentmindedly rubbing his hands together like some greasy, fat rodent and the sight makes her nauseated so she looks back to the platoon, to Paige out in the lead, to the constellation of stubborn phallic candles still flickering in the drizzle.

Paige lifts the red bullhorn to her mouth and points it skyward toward the roof of the Skin Palace.

"Mary and Martha," she yells, her voice made mechanical by the horn, her syllables electrically dulled a bit, "drop the sheets now."

There's a collective intake of breath from the crowd and in that second Sylvia sees Ratzinger walking away from the mob, heading for a Mercedes sedan that's parked halfway up on the sidewalk a block past Herzog's. He doesn't look back and he doesn't run. He just disappears into the car, kicks over the engine and drives away.

Sylvia turns her attention back to the roof.

From the front two corners at the top of the Skin Palace, figures can be seen heaving clumps of pillowy white material over the edge of the parapets. The sheets billow out on the night's breeze, resemble for a moment parachutes being unfurled on a current of cold air, then sail downward, almost, but not quite, in synchronized glides. The sheets flap and come to a rest, hanging close to where the sidewalk meets the building's foundation. A pack of women tear out of the crowd and run to the sheet's hems to tie them down, secure them in place against the breeze. They look like a well-trained yacht crew, everyone assured of her particular duties and performing them with the speed and precision of an eternal instinct.

Sylvia thinks for a minute that Paige is making some kind of visual statement, that she's "wrapping" the building, like the artist Christo. That she'll give a detailed exegesis of her complex symbolism to some indulgent *Spy* reporter and tomorrow's paper will translate her meaning for all.

But then Paige speaks through the bullhorn again, saying, "Start the projectors," and from the rooftops of the buildings across the street, Sylvia sees tiny bluish circles ignite and then beams of light, shafts of expanding illumination, fire down on the new wall of sheeting. And Herzog's Erotic Palace is no longer a building but a massive, bizarre canvas, an enormous movie screen simultaneously presenting dozens of moving images. And the images are all of the hard-core S&M variety. And the images are all overlapping, bleeding into one another until the whole projection seems like a horrible hundred-foot hallucination. A violent, nightmare vision from a special section of hell. A raw and confusing dream where elongated women are perpetually manhandled and desecrated and beaten into positions of acrobatic submissiveness.

Paige Beatty is projecting sadistic fantasies onto the face of the Skin Palace itself.

Paige has somehow coordinated an offense that Sylvia already knows, standing here just seconds after its birth, has instantly evolved into legend. The planning must have been backbreaking—amassing such enormous sheets, scrounging up industrial projectors, smuggling projectionists onto the rooftops, and then, finally and most important, willing this craziness, this whole visual stunt, into something so far beyond a stunt. Into a ritual. A ceremony. A blitz of light divorced from sound. Into a larger than life art form and ideology, a cumulative image whose meaning won't let the observer alone for a long time, if ever again.

Whether by chance or analysis, the sheets are completely covered with images. There's no margin, no border of white to show where the movie ends. There must be seven different movies playing from one end of the building to the other. It's like going to a drive-in where rival projectionists are battling for dominance but no one is winning. It's like a drive-in with a multiple personality disorder. And if she keeps watching, Sylvia knows it's going to give her a headache because there's no way to distinguish exactly where one film leaves off and the next one begins. And she thinks maybe this is one of Paige's many points.

Because the movies are being shown on sheets rather than real screens and because of the distance of the projection and the fact that they're outside and there's moon and street lights, the images thrown up on the building look a bit faded. But that doesn't detract from the graphicness of their content. There's a good chance that Paige will end up in jail tonight, not just for storming and seizing someone else's property, but for publicly displaying these films for anyone walking down Watson Street to see.

There are women shackled and being blasted with firehoses. There are women bent over a row of Ping-Ping tables being paddled on their behinds. There are women being pursued through dark woods by men with dogs and rifles. There are women bound to hospital operating tables. There are women being burned at the stake in open fields by men dressed in flowing black robes. There are women on their backs and on their knees. Handcuffed. Manacled. Chained. Tied down with ropes. Tied down with belts.

Sylvia looks to Paige and the banner that her lieutenants are flying high over her head—*Intercourse is Genocide*—then looks back up at these despicable images playing high on the front of the Skin Palace.

And she feels she's missed something. She's not sure what the abominations silently repeating on the enormous sheets have to do with intercourse. As far as she can see, there's no sex taking place on the sheets in her view. Just image after image of brutality.

She looks out over the crowd which seems to be growing. She feels like everyone has more knowledge than she. Like everyone else understands all the central connections of this life, all the primal pictures. Sylvia looks at Paige again and then looks up. On the front-facing screen, ten feet above Paige's head, is the central image, stationary, static, more like a photograph than a movie, but also more horrifying than anything else being projected. This is *the* picture, the one that everyone will carry home with them, the one Sylvia will carry for the balance of her natural life: a naked woman, hanging, crucified on a wooden cross, planted on the top of a stark and desolate hill. There's no one around the woman and when you focus on her image everything else on the sheet/screen dissolves. Her head is hanging down so you can't see her face. Blood is running from her hands and from her feet. Sylvia closes her eyes for a long second then opens them. Pinwheeling all around the crucified woman are the other images from the other movies. But this martyr just stays absolutely still on the cross. And absolutely fixed in Sylvia's brain.

Is this what happens to the Madonna?

"How much longer?" Paige screams into the shivering silence of the crowd. "How much longer will we allow the horror?"

As if on signal, the mob erupts into a scream of rabid, cheering approval and Paige clusters into a three-way hug with her lieutenants. When they release, Paige relights her phallus-candle with a disposable butane, brings up the bullhorn and screams, "Free at last."

A handful of women break out of the assembly and run forward to the steps of the Skin Palace. They're carrying what look like brightly colored plastic rifles. They form a fairly precise line, bring the rifles up and buttress them against their shoulders and fire. Fat streams of water shoot fifty feet into the air and Sylvia realizes they're firing those super squirt guns, the kid's toys that are so popular lately. But when the wind comes and she gets the heavy chemical odor of gasoline or lighter fluid, she knows they're not squirting water. Their liquid barrage is arcing, making it above Paige's head and soaking the screening sheet.

"They'll burn down the goddamn building," Sylvia says to Propp and jumps down from the mailbox.

When the gunners exhaust their spray tanks, Paige turns her back to the crowd, clasps her hands together around her candle, and throws it into the air. It sails, starts to dive and bounces off the middle of the sheet, the central image of the crucified woman. The fabric catches immediately, starts to burn, flames licking upward to begin a run of consumption. And the mob goes crazy with screams and whistles and horn-blowing. The fire increases its strength, gaining on the sheet, feeding faster on the accelerant with every passing second. The images of beating and torture and humiliation start to dissolve upward and outward into a charred black that wastes into smoke. The drizzle is having no effect on the blaze.

Sylvia watches, drunk on the spectacle, shivering. She watches the crucified Madonna begin to blacken and instantly fade. She watches the woman in agony begin to crumble upward and vanish like a magic trick that's performed too fast for understanding, her misery dissolving instantly with each lick of flame. And as Sylvia stares, she goes into one of those helpless moments when sound seems to ebb away, when all that's left is a very narrow field of vision, as if her eyes can no longer pivot in their sockets, as if her pupils were frozen into a singular position that assured her brain she'd take this one image in.

Only this image.

And in that instant of locked-up, intensified vision, she sees the explosion.

TIGHT SHOT -THE EYE OF HUGO SCHICK

as seen framed in the round, black circle that is the perimeter of the lens. He is looking through the Panaflex. He is a maniacal cyclops, insatiable and feeding on just this latest meal of manipulated imagery. But it is to be the last meal for the Doomed Artist, as we pull back to

WIDE SHOT -INT HENRICK GALEEN MEMORIAL STUDIO

where the entire cast of *Don Juan Triumphant* are engaged in an immensely complicated orgy, well on its way to a synchronized and unanimous crescendo as orchestrated by Hugo Schick from his position behind the camera.

TRACKING SHOT -THE MOUNTAINOUS DAISY CHAIN OF WRITHING FLESH

as the camera passes face after glimmering face contorted into masks of imminent, passionate explosion.

MED SHOT -HUGO SCHICK, THE DOOMED ARTIST

as he pulls back from the camera and drops his face into his hands and weeps with the realization of his achievement. CAMERA takes the place of Hugo's eye and looks through his lens to see

WIDE SHOT -INT HENRICK GALEEN MEMORIAL STUDIO

as the walls dissolve, implode, cave inward and are replaced by new and moving walls of fire, waves of rolling blue flame that stretch from collapsing floor to collapsing ceiling, a new world of inferno replacing instantly the prior, physical world. Sound track fills with a chorus of screams, ultimate pleasure succumbing to ultimate pain. The mountain of coupled flesh is consumed by a Technicolor holocaust in special effects display that could only be engineered in hell itself.

FINAL SHOT -THE FACE OF HUGO SCHICK

as the Doomed Artist's eyes sear and melt and fade.

Possibly, Sylvia sees it with a clarity that no one else in this mob can achieve. She sees the first-floor windows blown outward to the street, the shards of glass raining down on the instantly scrambling and screaming crowd, the way the gust of flames roll outward to the street, like the fire was liquid, like it was some transplanted ocean wave of orange and blue, coasting, ball-like, jetting through the portals of the Skin Palace windows. And then the second-floor windows follow suit, shattering in unison as if detonated, tremendously hot air pushing outward over the street, over the bodies colliding with one another, the heat singeing the hair of the closest protesters. The building seems to be belching flames, spitting tongues of fire from every orifice.

And, like a perverse reflex she can no longer control, Sylvia flashes on Tara being burned to the ground in *Gone With the Wind*. On the disastrous skyscraper in *The Towering Inferno*. On John Wayne in *Hellfighters*. Kurt Russell in *Backdraft*. On *Spontaneous Combustion* and *Inferno in Paradise* and *The Flaming Urge* . . .

She sees Paige Beatty down on her knees, bleeding from the side of her head, her back to the Skin Palace, shocked, not comprehending what's happened, looking as if a hand had reached down from the sky and picked her up and pitched her back down to the pavement. Looking as if the Skin Palace itself has struck out at her, responded to her theatrical dissent with retaliation.

She sees people running everywhere, trying to cover their heads with their arms, packs of runners slamming into other packs. People scrambling, falling, trying to get anyplace else. Horrible slapstick.

And then the sound fades back in and Sylvia hears the noise of fireworks, that booming, thunderous, slightly muffled roar of explosion. And she's in Propp's arms and he's trying to steer her away from the noise and light.

She lets her head turn in to his chest, but she keeps her

eyes open. Someone checks into their backs and they go down onto the pavement, Propp on top, and Sylvia tears open the knee of her jeans and the skin underneath, Propp pulls her up by her right hand and they run through a gauntlet of fleeing, screaming individuals, people reduced to fleshy, charging panic by terror and confusion.

And then they're down a side street, still moving, staying close to the storefronts and running away from the Skin Palace until Propp pulls her to a stop and says, "Your leg."

They sit on the curbstone and Sylvia looks down and sees blood has soaked through her jeans. But she doesn't feel any pain yet. Propp gets up on one knee as people run past. He takes out a white handkerchief, slowly pulls back the torn denim, and dabs gingerly at the wound.

He looks up at her and they stare at each other. Sylvia starts to hear sirens in the distance.

"In the cellar," she says, "where we saw Fernando . . ."

Propp nods, holds the cloth flat against her knee.

"He must have been opening the gas lines. Boetell will blame the whole thing on Beatty and her people."

Sylvia jumps back up to standing and the first blast of pain shoots from her knee up to her heart and she screams and starts to fall and Propp catches her in his arms.

"Schick is still inside," she yells and Propp just stares at her.

"And all his people. They're up in the studio. They're up there filming."

She struggles for a minute in his arms and then collapses against him.

He hugs her into himself. He says, "They might have gotten out," into her ear.

Then he says something else, but Sylvia can't hear what it is above her own sobbing and choked breathing. She feels like she's going to pass out and she hangs onto Propp's neck and the water pours through her eyes until everything she sees is obscured, refracted, almost glittering.

And she looks over Propp's shoulder as he pats her back, rubs his hand against her back in circles, the way you'd attempt to calm an infant who's trying to wake from a nightmare. The way you would try to comfort your child. Your baby. This small creature convulsing with fear and confusion and the absolute horror of the unknown.

Sylvia lays her head against his shoulder and stares out across the street. The sirens are closer and louder now. She scans the storefronts through tears. She doesn't even try to focus.

But she can still see the sign where everything began:

Jack Derry's Camera Exchange.

So she closes her eyes and holds on to this stranger.

36

They go back underneath the Canal Zone, under the safe cover of concrete and asphalt and red-brick arcs. They end up sitting at the counter of St. Benedict's Diner, killing a bottle of something called MD 20/20, neither of them saying anything, not looking at each other, just working on the sweet wine, pulling it down their throats with a lazy persistence, as if this was the only job left in the world.

The last thing Sylvia remembers is wondering, if she sold everything she owns—the Aquinas and the other cameras and all the darkroom equipment—would she have enough cash for a down payment on the Ballard Theatre?

She could take the place over from the Loftus Brothers, re-open it as The Pink Cage and show an endless succesion of women's prison movies. *Caged Women. Caged Fury. Caged Heat.* Maybe even *Born Innocent.*

And then sometime later, Sylvia ends up asleep, lying sideways in one of the booths, her knees pulled up to her stomach, crouched in, fetal, as if once again she was back on her mother's zombie-couch, living in Rita Hayworth's black-and-white world, sinking into a kind of timeless dreamscape where all five senses are perpetually numbed.

When she wakes, her head is pounding and her knee is inflamed and burning and Propp is gone. There's a note written directly onto the Formica tabletop in red marker.

Gompers Station
The Madonna's Chamber
Midnight.

She sits for a second in the booth and stares at the words. She's so tired of messages. She's so tired of decoding and translating symbols and images. *This means this. This does not mean something else.* She licks the heel of her hand and feels how gritty it is. Like sandpaper. Like the tongue of a cat. She rubs at the tabletop, but instead of wiping the words away, she simply smears them into a red mess, the letters still readable but bleeding into jagged angles and runny lines.

She leaves the diner and walks the railroad tunnels away from Gompers. After maybe an hour, she locates a rickety stairway that leads up into some anonymous Canal Zone basement, finds an exit and emerges into a freight alley off Rudolphe Road.

At the mouth of the alley, Mojo Bettman, the legless newspaper vendor, is perched on his fat skateboard with his back to her. She walks past him, then turns to see he's selling the latest edition of the *Spy.*

Spread out on the sidewalk in front of Bettman, fanned like enormous playing cards, Sylvia sees copy after copy of the same photo of Paige Beatty being hauled into a police car, trying to resist, her hands shackled behind her, a riot-helmeted cop forcing her headfirst into the rear of his cruiser.

Bettman rocks slightly on his stumps, holds a folded paper out toward her, says, *"Fanatics Bomb Local Porn Hall,"* in this old-fashioned, newsboy chant.

She stares at him, then moves down Rudolphe.

Back at the apartment, she finds the kitchen door wide open and the gruff and sloppy noise of drunken men seeping out at her. She walks to the edge of the living room, stands hidden behind the doorjamb and looks around the corner. She sees a frat party that's degenerated and turned the room into a grungy pigsty. She sees Mrs. Acker passed out on the couch, a cat asleep and wrapped around her throat like a thick, woolly scarf. She sees Eddie Meade and Garland Boetell sitting on the floor, side by side, their backs propped against the couch, both of them wildly disheveled and pathetically soused, each with a bottle of Scotch in one hand and listlessly fighting with their other hand for control of the television remote. Sylvia turns her head so she can see the screen. She expects to find pictures of Herzog's in flames. Instead, she sees Perry and herself at the Cansino Drive-in, frozen in mid-copulation by the pause button.

"Hey, Perry-*boy*," Meade barks, sounding a little like the Reverend, "Don't you worry now. I'll get you a real job downtown . . ." and his words degenerate into a rolling, phlegmy cough.

Sylvia finds Perry on the floor, head under the coffee table, unconscious.

She goes into the bedroom. There isn't much she wants

to keep. She gets a duffel from the closet and crams it with jeans and sweaters and she leaves without any notice.

Down in the darkroom, she unclips the seven prints from the dryline, shuffles them into an ordered pile, sits on the step stool, holds them in her lap. She puts her thumb on the lower right corner of the pile, holds the stack tightly with her left hand at the left margin. Then she riffles the prints. As if she can animate the photographs. As if the Madonna will get up off her perch, walk forward until she's a full-faced close-up, and tell Sylvia what to do.

She finds a manila envelope under a pile on the work table, puts the prints inside and seals it, then puts the envelope inside the duffel and pulls the zipper closed, She turns off the darkroom light and starts to move out of the cellar, stops and walks to the Peg-Board where the electrical wiring for the house is mounted. She locates the main circuit breaker for the whole of the building and throws it to *off.*

Sylvia spends the rest of the day and night moving from theatre to theatre until she's seen every movie currently in release. Over and over, in the brilliance of Technicolor and Panavision, she sees men and women come together and break apart, as if this was as inviolable a fact of nature as photosynthesis or the survival of the fittest. In between, a lot of guns go off and cars chase each other and inevitably crash.

She drinks so much cola and uses so many movie-house rest rooms that by the time she watches her final credits scroll up toward the ceiling, she thinks she's come close to damaging her bladder.

And by midnight, she's back at Gompers Station.

She finds her way into what she's now naturally, instinctively, thinking of as *The Madonna's Chamber.* On the marble column stump, a figure is posed with something in its arm and her breath goes shallow and her heart belts against the inside of her chest.

But then the figure turns and some light plays down on the face and she sees that it's just Propp and what he's cradling is only his Diane Arbus rucksack. He stands and comes to her, his arm fishing inside his bag as he walks.

"I've got something for you," he says. He pulls out a stack of snapshots and hands them to her.

"Like an old spy movie," Sylvia says. "Two people meeting in the shadows."

"In a train station, no less."

"Exchanging information."

"You've watched," he says, "too many Peter Lorre movies."

"No question," she says, then takes her manila envelope from the duffel and hands it to him. "I've watched too many movies altogether."

He doesn't say anything. He doesn't even look at the envelope, just crams the package into his bag, He takes her arm and points to the remains of the main stairway that are now just a slanted incline of rubble.

"Did you see the news?" he asks.

She shakes her head *no*.

"They found what was left of Schick and his company—"

"I really don't want to hear it—"

"A lot of conflicting reports, but the main take is that the woman—"

"Paige."

"Yes, Paige, she'll likely be charged."

"She didn't do it . . ." Sylvia starts to say and lets it go.

Propp nods as they reach the top of the stairs and start to walk across the open lot toward the freight yard.

"Still," he says, "it'll make a great film."

They walk the rest of the way in silence until they come to the tracks where a string of freight cars, all the color of deep rust, sits for the engine to pull out. Every other car bears the faded words Elias Freight on its loading doors. The last car has its doors rolled up, but Sylvia can't see anything inside.

"What are they hauling?" she asks.

He gives a small laugh and just stares at her.

"Where are they headed?" she tries.

"South, I think. Or maybe west."

They stand and listen to the diesel powering up until Sylvia makes herself say, "Why after all these years? You were just a dead milkman to me. I didn't even have a face for you."

He looks at her as if she's talking another language, but he doesn't say a word.

"Didn't you love her?" is all she can manage.

He shifts his stance, stares at the freight car, finally says, "If you mean the woman in the pictures—"

"You know who I mean."

"Yes, I love her."

"Then why?"

His eyes start to blink. Sylvia can see him pulling in on his lips. And she still can't make it easy on him.

"My whole life came apart this week," she says. "You're leaving now. Can't you just tell me why you did this to me?"

"I didn't do it," he says. "I swear to you Sylvia—"

"Just confirm it or deny it," she says. "Are you my father"

When Propp hugs her, crushes her against himself, kisses her forehead for a long minute, she can feel the shake of his crying. She can feel his tears against her forehead.

He breaks off and moves for the car as the train starts to roll. He jogs along the next to the tracks for a second as he heaves his bag up and into the boxcar. Then he picks up speed, chooses his moment, and throws his body inside, the last leap that will take him out of Quinsigamond forever. Sylvia watches the train roll out for a few minutes, slip down the rails like film rolling into a projector. Twenty-four frames a second.

She turns away and looks at the small stack of photos in her hand. They're shots of her from the other night. The shots of her as the Madonna. Sylvia in the remnants of the Berkshires nightgown. Perched on the marble base, looking up into the balcony. Half a dozen shots of Sylvia as an icon. Sylvia as a myth-figure.

Except for the last picture. It's clearly not part of the set. It's an old, faded image. A portrait shot. Full-face this time. No shadows. Nothing obscured. It's a photo of her mother as a young woman. Looking out at the photographer with a shy smile, leaning over a wooden crib, wearing a housecoat. And lifting an infant, delicately, perfectly, into the air.

After leaving her duffel at St. Benedict's Diner, she comes back up onto the street and starts to walk. She avoids the Canal Zone, makes a loop around its perimeter and enters Bangkok Park from the other direction.

She walks down Goulden Ave until she comes to the intersection of Granada, picks a corner and takes a position sitting on the curb. She waits an hour. Then another. No one bothers with her. Now and then she pulls the camera from the cover of her jacket and takes aim at something easy. A neon sign that flickers the words *Brasilia Beef.* A young Hispanic kid stumbling out of the Granada Cantina, steadying himself against a light post. A bicycle that glides past under the direction of an individual whose face is totally hidden by a hooded sweatshirt.

When a pack of bodies turns the corner onto Granada, she expects to be overtaken by one of the Park gangs, until she notices that the individual in the center of the group is carrying a movie camera up on his shoulder. It's that young kid—Jakob Cain—the boy she met at Der Garten and the coffee shop. He's surrounded by a circle of thugish-look-

ing bodyguards, all of them dressed in Schickian khaki safari jackets with epaulets and waist belts. As they pass,
silent, all the eyes wide, the boy nods to Sylvia and aims
his movie camera in her direction. Then they continue
down the street. Sylvia lifts her Aquinas and focuses in at
the stitching on the back of one of the jackets—

Amerikan Pictures Presents
Little Girl Lost
coming soon to a theatre near you

She aims and she focuses, but she doesn't shoot any pictures.

Sometime just before dawn, when the street is momen-
tarily deserted and the last breeze of the night blows the
lighter trash down the length of Goulden like filthy rag-
weed, she spots a beat-up old pickup rounding the corner
and rolling toward her. It's an old Ford covered with huge
blotches of paint primer and bearing an out-of-state license
plate. Sylvia stands up and the driver's window comes
down a crack. She sees a woman behind the wheel who has
gone too long substituting coffee for sleep. The driver's
eyes are blinking and her head gives a sharp twitch just before she speaks.

She says, "Is there a motor lodge around here?"

Sylvia stares at her. The woman is wearing a pink nylon
smock and a white plastic nametag, about the size of a
stick of gum, that reads *Gretta*. Sylvia looks at the foot
well on the passenger side. It's loaded with empty brown-
stained paper cups and a half-folded road map.

"You're on the wrong side of the city."

Gretta looks out at the street and says, "Is there a gas station near here?"

"Take your next left," Sylvia says. "In a couple of miles
you'll hit an all-night place."

Gretta nods and Sylvia waits for a thank you, but the

truck just rolls away slowly and swings onto Goulden. Sylvia brings the camera up and follows her movement. In the rear bed of the pickup, wedged between piles of ragged luggage, her face hanging over the tailgate and looking out on everything she's passing, is a young girl. Maybe ten or twelve years old. Her hair is pulled back into some kind of loose braid and her bottom lip has a tired pout to it. She's holding something in her hands. Her eyes are wide and there's a good chance she's staring at the photographer.

Sylvia twists the lens a bit, barely nudging the girl's face into sharper focus, gingerly pushing for just that much more clarity.

And then she opens the shutter.

The title of the movie is The Rosy Hours of Mazenderan. *It's a foreign film, dubbed carelessly into a hilarious English. The actors and actresses move their mouths for long moments after the noise of their dialogue has finished. The images on the screen are unusually faint, as if a bulb had burned out and no one had bothered to replace it.*

The woman, at one time an actress of some renown in certain circles, sits behind the wheel of her Citröen and tries not to make judgments about the performances she's viewing. She tells herself it would be unfair given the quality of the print she's seeing and the fact that she's viewing the movie outdoors, on a shabby drive-in screen.

Instead of forming a critical opinion, she lets the images roll out before her, get processed by her optic nerves without any accompanying valuation or assessment. She knows there are people who would tell her she's deceiving herself, that this is an impossible feat. She has nothing but contempt for these people.

The former actress is being fed popcorn by her companion, a classic drifter possessed of a nervous demeanor. The drifter is reclining with his head in the woman's lap, a bucket of popcorn propped on his stomach and his long legs hanging over the car door.

The drifter was hitchhiking when he met the woman. He was leaving the city with no specific destination in mind. He looked disheveled and distracted, the kind of man you might cast as a serial killer in a horror movie. He was tall and round-shouldered with a crown of clown-like red hair and doughy skin. He looked as if he'd only recently ended a hunger strike.

He got in the Citröen on route 64 and the woman asked him for gas money. The drifter explained that he had no money at the present time, but that he was owed a final paycheck from the management of the Cansino Drive-In Theatre, where he had been employed for the past week as a projectionist. He had even been allowed to live in the small projection booth. The woman agreed to drive the man to the theatre.

The drifter said he had been a salesman for a time, but he would not elaborate on what he sold. The woman said nothing of her former profession.

When the paycheck was retrieved, the drifter signed it over to the woman, scribbling only Jack on the rear endorsement line because he could no longer remember any more of his name.

In fact, he can no longer remember very much about himself beyond random flashes, dull images of what seem to be chronically fading memories: darkrooms, red lights, pieces of glass bent into odd shapes and sizes.

The woman accepted the paycheck and, as it was dusk, suggested they stay for the first feature of the evening. The drifter fetched a tub of popcorn.

The woman glanced into the rearview mirror of the Citröen, pulled her lips in, puckered them out.

And now the screen is alive with shadows and motion. Bodies float across the expanse of white matte. The woman, for some reason even she can't fathom, trembles in her seat.

The drifter stares up through the windshield at the night sky, all this distant light, and says, "What's wrong? It's only a movie."

Dissolve

roll credits

The author is indebted to the following works and wishes to express his gratitude to the authors:

Raw Talent, by Jerry Butler; *The Haunted Screen,* by Lotte H. Eisner; *The Official 50th Anniversary Pictorial History of The Wizard of Oz,* by John Fricke, Jay Scarfone, & William Stillman; *The Devil Thumbs a Ride,* by Barry Gifford; *From Reverence to Rape,* by Molly Haskell; *Film Noir, The Dark Side of the Screen,* by Forester Hirsch; *Signatures of the Visible,* by Frederic Jameson; *The Liveliest Art,* by Arthur Knight; *Worcester's Best,* edited by Elliott B. Knowlton; *Women in Film,* by Annette Kuhn with Susannah Radstone; *Great American Movie Theatres,* by David Naylor; *The Nightmare of Reason,* by Ernst Pawel; *Cut: The Unseen Cinema,* by Baxter Phillips; *Preminger,* by Otto Preminger; *The Films of Rita Hayworth,* by Gene Ringgold; *Film Noir,* edited by Alain Silver and Elizabeth Ward; *Movie Palaces,* by Ave Pildas & Lucinda Smith; *Porn,* by Robert Stoller, M.D.; *Hard Core,* by Linda Williams; *Video Hound's Golden Movie Retriever;* and especially, *The Phantom Empire,* by Geoffrey O'Brian (from whom I have borrowed the term *media overfarming*).

The descriptions of the Chapter House and the Virgin and Child sculpture are taken from explicating plaques at the Worcester Art Museum.